THE
FAVOUR

Alan Reynolds

Fisher King Publishing

THE FAVOUR

Published by
Fisher King Publishing
www.fisherkingpublishing.co.uk

Print ISBN 978-1-916776-43-2
Epub ISBN 978-1-916776-44-9

Also by Alan Reynolds

'A favour becomes a debt if there is an expectation of its return.'

Alan Reynolds

Chapter One

Friday, December 31st, 1999, millennium eve.

Carole Worrall was at the dining-table in her dressing gown, staring into a mirror, carefully applying her make-up ready for the evening's celebrations. She was in a good mood, humming to herself as she went about her routine. The curtains were drawn on this drab winter's evening, but the electric fire, with its faux logs glowing in the hearth, was providing plenty of heat. The two-bedroomed apartment felt cosy.

As a fully qualified beautician, recently appointed head of cosmetics at one of the major departmental stores in Newcastle, appearance was everything. Her recently coiffured, shoulder-length, dark hair shined in the luminescence emanating from the three wall-lights which provided the illumination for the room.

Her husband, Brian, known by everyone as Bigsy, due to his six-foot-two frame and uncompromising personality, was reading the newspaper on the sofa in his favourite tracksuit. He scratched his stomach through the nylon/polyester material as the trouser waistband cut into his skin. The TV was on in the background showing the six o'clock news.

Millennium eve, and there was a great deal of excitement on Heathcote Estate, the Gateshead concrete sprawl, which housed the two, twenty-story, tower blocks and about five-hundred surrounding pebble-dashed houses, typical of the 1960's austerity building projects. Bigsy and Carole had lived in the apartment on the fourteenth floor of Heathcote Tower for over three years.

"Have you seen this in the paper, pet, about this millennium bug…? Says here the world's going to end at midnight tonight. Some people are even stockpiling bog-roll; can you believe that?!" said Bigsy, raising his eyes from the evening newspaper and glancing in

Carole's direction.

"It's ok, pet; I've got plenty in," replied Carole, turning from her mirror momentarily.

"I think it's a load of bollocks meself, mind. I mean what's the worst that can happen if the computers stop working at midnight?"

"You mean apart from all the heatin' going off and all the cash machines not working."

"Aye, apart from that?" replied Bigsy, still looking over his newspaper.

"Could be a problem if you were flying in a plane somewhere."

"Just as well we're only going to the club then."

He paused and went back to his paper before continuing. "Glad we don't live in Ponteland... I wouldn't want to be under the flightpath tonight."

"Fat chance of that, the houses 'round there cost a fortune."

"Aye, serves 'em right if one does come down then."

Carole switched on the hair-dryer again drowning out any conversation for a couple of minutes.

"Who's looking after the shop tonight?" asked Carole eventually, satisfied that her hair was just so.

"Young Rikki's on till nine. I'll call in on the way to the club and lock up. Won't be much trade after that, any road."

Nearly three months earlier, Bigsy had become the proprietor of the video store in the precinct. It was a place he knew well having done the odd shift there on and off for almost two years, a small untaxed supplement to his normal dole money. The original Greek owner had died suddenly in early October and his widow wanted a quick sale so she could return to Cyprus to be with her family.

"What time is the taxi booked for?" asked Carole.

"About nine, I said we'll be ready after I've locked up the shop," replied Bigsy.

Just then Bigsy's mobile phone rang.

"Hiya Wazza, bonny lad," said Bigsy. "You ok...? Good, I was just telling our Carole we should be at the club around nine-thirty. Not much point in getting there any earlier, it'll be full of kids running about... Aye, will do. See you later."

Bigsy turned to Carol. "That was Wazza, said we'll see him at the club around nine-thirty."

"Aye, that's champion. Gives us plenty of time."

The event was advertised as a gala evening at Seaton Working Men's Club, to celebrate the new millennium. It gave Stan Hardacre, the club secretary, the opportunity to push up the prices. New Year's Eve was always special, however, and a top local disco was booked. Tickets had sold out weeks ago, even at the exorbitant price of five pounds, a two-pound increase on normal entrance fees.

"Have you got the tickets, Bigsy?" asked Carole.

"Aye pet, I've put 'em in my jacket pocket."

At just before nine o'clock, Bigsy was dressed in a pair of smart trousers, shirt, and sports jacket. His dark hair hung down to his collar, but tidier than usual. He left the fourteenth floor via the lift, which was working, for once. There was the familiar smell of urine and disinfectant which made the trip only marginally more attractive than using the stairs. Bigsy tried to hold his breath for the duration.

He left the tower block and crossed the road to the precinct, the small shopping parade in the shadow of the two high-rises. As he walked towards his video shop, he looked proudly at the brightly coloured signage, 'Hollywood Nights', which shone like a beacon in the gloomy evening. An appropriate, if incongruous, name he had given the store after he had assumed proprietorship. It certainly had more of a ring than 'Heathcote Video Store', the previous name.

A row of three retail establishments served the precinct. As well as Bigsy's video shop, there was the general store, owned and run by Mr. Ali and his son Jamal, and an off-license which, with its graffiti-scrawled metal grills, resembled more a prison. It was the place where kids would hang out most evenings, riding around aimlessly on their push-bikes. Litter was scattered around the frontage, the only waste bin overflowing. Empty cartons, discarded soft drink cans, and plastic bottles were being tossed around in the breeze. The whole area looked unkempt.

Bigsy entered the video store. Inside, it was bright and welcoming, with spotlights highlighting stills from the latest blockbusters.

Rikki Rankin was just cashing up. He was the son and stepson of the late 'knob-head' Trev Rankin and his 'poxy missus' Pauline, drug addicts that had both died from a heroin overdose back in the summer. Having supplied the drug, Bigsy had felt some responsibility towards Rikki and decided to take the lad under his wing. The new attention had been the making of young Rikki, who, prior to Bigsy's intervention, was already heading down the road of petty crime.

"Hiya Rikki, bonny lad, how's it been?" asked Bigsy.

"Hiya Bigsy, man, aye, not bad… It's been quiet like you thought."

Bigsy took the cash from Rikki, put it in a bag, and then they left the shop together. Bigsy remembered to turn out the lights and set the burglar alarm; a condition required by the insurance company. One of the many outgoings Bigsy had to begrudgingly finance as a new business owner.

"What you up to tonight?" asked Bigsy, as he made his way back towards the tower block.

"Nottin' much, meeting up with Stevie and maybe watch a film at his place." Stevie Leonard was Rikki's best buddy.

"Well, you be careful tonight; there's going to be a lot of weird stuff going on later."

"You're not talking about all that bug stuff that's been on the telly, are you?"

"Aye, you just be careful is all I'm saying," said Bigsy and they said their farewells.

Carole, wearing a fashionably short, fake-fur coat over a little black dress, hair and make-up immaculate as ever, was waiting at the entrance to the tower block trying to keep warm.

"Just pop the cash up to the flat, pet, won't be long," said Bigsy as he approached.

"Hurry up pet, it's brass monkeys oot heya," replied Carole in her strong Geordie accent. She started hopping from one foot to the other to keep the circulation going, then blowing into her hands.

Bigsy returned after a few minutes to find Carole in the waiting taxi. The short journey to the Club took less than ten minutes, and the couple arrived in style; not many members could afford a taxi.

The pair walked up to the entrance and joined the small queue waiting to get in. The sound of disco music could be heard from the bar area at the end of the corridor. Stan Hardacre was manning a table in the lobby, dressed in an overcoat, ensuring no-one got in without paying.

Bigsy handed Stan his tickets and, after exchanging convivial greetings with him, Bigsy and Carole walked along the corridor past the notice boards advertising future events, darts leagues, and so on. At the end of the passageway, they reached the large members' lounge where all events were held.

The place was heaving, with kids running around creating mayhem. Disco music was blaring out from two enormous speakers at the side of the small stage. Chairs and tables were stationed cafe-style around the even smaller dance area of parquet flooring cut out of the sticky carpet. A thick smoky fug hung in the air, fuelled by umpteen cigarettes, making it difficult to see from one side of the room to the other.

"I don't know why I bothered to give up smoking, pet. You could get cancer from just one night in here." Bigsy shouted loudly to be heard above the racket.

Carole had been nagging Bigsy for years to give up smoking, and the crunch came when she told him it could affect his 'performance', according to an article she'd read in the paper. That, and the fact that she didn't particularly enjoy kissing an ashtray. So, after copious nicotine patches and a great deal of willpower, Bigsy had kicked the habit. That's not to say he didn't fancy a smoke now and again; tonight was a case in point.

Bigsy went to get the drinks while Carole joined her aunt Alison at the table that Stan had reserved for them. There was a queue of about twenty people at the bar jostling for positions waiting to be served. He caught his reflection in the mirror at the back of the counter and drew his hand through his dark swept-back hair; it was a habit and made no difference to his grooming. Enjoying almost celebrity status as someone who had made a success of his life, he was greeted warmly by numerous friends and other acquaintants.

Alice, the seventy-year-old resident barmaid, was on duty with Wazza's Mum, Hazel, and a small bevy of other temporary female staff, hired to cope with the crowd. In an effort to make the occasion special, Stan had ordered special uniforms for the barmaids consisting of very short black skirts and white tee shirts emblazoned with 'Happy Millennium' across the chest. At least that's what they should have said. Unfortunately, the supplier, who had agreed to print them at a special price, had misspelt the word 'Millennium', and they all read 'Millennium'. Alice had been excused the requirement to wear the outfits. "Too bloody cold," she had told Stan.

Bigsy surveyed the scene as he waited his turn, the girls trying desperately to maintain some decorum behind the bar as they bent down to get mixers from the lower shelves. No wonder the bar was doing a roaring trade. Stan was on for a good take tonight.

His turn came, and Bigsy gave Alice two fifty-pound notes. "Put that behind the bar for us Alice, pet, and have one yourself."

"Ta Bigsy, pet," said Alice.

Making his way to the table with his 'broon' - Newcastle Brown, the local drink of choice, and a bottle of red wine for the girls, Bigsy noticed the array of decorations festooned around the room giving a very celebratory feel to the club. In daylight, it looked way past its best. The dance floor was packed with youngsters and parents as Abba bellowed from the back of the room with the D.J. in a hazy spotlight working his record decks behind.

At the opposite end of the room from the stage there were a couple of cubicles like those in American diners with brown plastic, leather-look, bench seats around the sides. Despite their rather distressed appearance, they were much sought after and Bigsy had paid Stan a premium to reserve one of these for his guests. The table was slightly sheltered from the worst of the din, which at least enabled them to have the semblance of a conversation.

Once the drinks had been distributed, Davie Slater, known by Bigsy as 'Slate', came over to the group to extend his greetings. Slate, as well as being a talented footballer and part of the Sunday league football team, had a reputation as a comedian and was never short of a joke. Tonight, was to be no exception.

"Hiya Bigsy, Carole." He nodded a greeting to Alison.

"Slate, bonny lad, what're having?" asked Bigsy, shouting to make himself heard.

"Cheers Bigsy, a broon will be fine, ta," replied Slate.

"Well, if you can get to the bar, ask Alice to put one on my tab, I'm not fighting my way back up there for a while," said Bigsy.

"That's ok, ta very much. Hey, have you heard the one...?"

A big groan heralded the pending arrival of one of Slate's jokes. He ignored the remarks and ploughed on.

"A bloke goes to the doctors and says, 'doctor I keep thinking I'm Tom Jones'." A pause for the punchline... "'It's not unusual,' says the doctor."

At which point Slate curls up with laughter. His small audience at the table chuckled politely.

"Slate, you'll have to do better than that, I've heard it," said Bigsy, taking the wind out of the young man's sails, but, not to be outdone, he continued with more excruciating stories until Bigsy excused himself and went to the gents.

The men's facilities were also packed and Bigsy had to wait for a vacant stall. The floor was awash with overspill and beginning to smell; he was glad to leave. Recovering his breath, he walked along the corridor towards the members' lounge when he noticed his best buddies, Wazza and Chirpie, waiting in the small queue at Stan's ticket-table. They had just walked from the flats. Bigsy went over and greeted them warmly. He was surprised to see Chirpie's wife, Joy, was with him; she rarely went out.

Joy was a huge woman; various guesses had been made at her exact weight, but twenty stone was the starting point for most estimates. She was dressed in what looked like a tent and had arrived on her own by taxi ten minutes earlier. Unfortunately, Chirpie had the tickets, and she had to wait in the lobby for him to arrive; Stan wouldn't let her in without one.

Bigsy greeted her warmly. "Joy, pet, haven't seen you for ages."

"Wasn't staying in tonight, you never know what's going to happen if what they say in the papers is right," replied Joy. "What if the fookin' leccy goes off? Can you imagine, no telly?"

"I don't think you've got anything to worry about," said Bigsy, reassuringly, and he led the group to his table.

"Hi Chirpie, and… Joy? Lovely to see ya, pet," said Carole, with just a hint of a surprise inflexion in her voice. They made room for the new arrivals on the bench seat.

Just then Alison's son, James, known by everyone as Polly, arrived with a young female companion. He made the introductions. "This is Veronica," he said to the group, and they sat down, Veronica next to Carole. With Joy taking up at least two people's places; the table seating had now outgrown its occupants and space was very tight.

Carole was intrigued. It had been four months since Katya had returned to Kosovo and she had not seen Polly with a girl since.

Being close to his mother, Carole knew that their split had hit him hard.

Katya, as well as a near neighbour on the fourteenth floor, had become a close friend of Carole. She had been even closer to Polly, and they had enjoyed a very intense and physical relationship for a couple of months in the summer.

Katya had fled the country with her young son, Melos, the previous March, and was eventually evacuated to the UK, and re-settled in Heathcote Tower together with another refugee, Edi. She was placed in an apartment just along the corridor from Bigsy and Carole and was quickly taken under their wing.

She had met Polly on the local recreation ground whilst taking Melos for some fresh air. Polly had a passion for kites and was always there testing out his latest creation. She was immediately attracted to him. Polly was a student at the local Art College and a talented photographer. At nineteen he was almost six years younger than Katya, but his boyish charm and boundless enthusiasm was exactly what she had needed following her tragic experiences in her homeland.

Katya's husband, Ibi, had been fighting with the Kosovan Liberation Army, and she had received a message that he had been captured by Serb militia and, she believed, killed. Katya made the decision to flee her homeland, but her escape from Kosovo was traumatic. She had endured more sorrow in her twenty-five years than most would see in a lifetime.

"What do you do, Veronica, pet?" asked Carole.

"I'm studying art and media studies at the University with Polly," replied Veronica in an accent that Carole would describe as 'posh'.

"You're not from round here," proffered Carole.

"No, I'm from a small village in Cambridgeshire," replied the student.

"What brings you to our neck of the woods?" asked Carole, grilling Veronica for as much information as she could.

"My sister's here at Newcastle Uni studying to be an architect. It made sense for us to get a place together," replied Veronica.

"What are you having, pet?" interrupted Bigsy, almost yelling to make himself heard from across the table. The noise levels had increased.

"A bottle of lager will be fine, thank you."

'What about you, Polly lad?"

"Just a broon, ta Bigsy," replied Polly, and everyone moved up further to allow Bigsy space to get to the bar. The crush now becoming exceedingly uncomfortable.

As the evening moved towards the turn of the century, Carole noticed how distracted Polly was, his mind clearly somewhere else. She knew exactly where. With Veronica having excused herself for a visit to the ladies, Carole moved closer to Polly.

"Penny for 'em."

Polly jumped, as if awakened from a dream.

"Eh... sorry Carole, pet, I was miles away."

"Aye, I could see that alright, and no prizes for guessing where."

"Aye, you're right. I try not to think about her, but tonight I just wished she was here. I do miss her so much."

"Aye, I know you do, Polly, pet, but you <u>will</u> get over it, just takes time."

Carole put a motherly arm around her cousin by way of comfort.

"Young Veronica seems a canny lass."

"Aye, she is, and we get on well enough. It's just..."

Polly was interrupted in mid flow with Veronica's return to the table.

"Have you seen how they have spelt 'Millennium' on the tee shirts?" said Veronica; to which there was only limited interest.

"How about a dance Polly? I could do with some exercise," asked Veronica, seeing there was no room to sit down. Polly got up and made his way to the packed dance floor and Veronica followed.

Carole moved closer to her aunt.

"Polly doesn't seem his usual self these days," said Carole.

"No," replied Alison, with a look of concern. "He's not been the same since Katya went back. He was really fond of her you know. He's stopped making his kites, and I've not seen any new photos for ages. I don't know how he's getting on at college; he never says anything to me. He's always brooding about. I was hoping he might perk up now he seems to be with Veronica."

"Aye, I noticed that. You can only let time take its course."

Bigsy returned with a round of drinks and perched himself on the end of the seat next to Wazza. Carole was still engrossed in conversation with Alison.

"Hey Wazza, are you going be ok for the match on Sunday, bonny lad?" asked Bigsy.

"Aye, if I'm sober by then… Ankle's ok now, just a sprain," he added.

As the clock ran down, even Bigsy became contemplative, which was unusual for him. He was not prone to ruminating.

Everything had changed for him when the refugees arrived. It had coincided with his flirting with the drug trade, a chance to earn some money, but there had been five killings during the brief time he had been involved. Everton Sheedie, the local dealer, and his associate Layton, the Rankins, and Hughie Bonner, the under-cover policeman who had come close to exposing the ring, had all died.

Hughie Bonner's murder particularly lay heavily on his conscience. Although it had been carried out, presumably, by Everton and probably Layton, by informing the dealers that he had uncovered the policeman's identity, Bigsy's actions had directly resulted in his death. The pictures on the television and in the newspaper of his grieving widow and the two boys had disturbed Bigsy and caused many sleepless nights.

Then there was the favour.

Edona Bukosi, known as Edi, was the second Kosovan refugee to be housed in the tower block. To earn extra money for her daughter,

11

Arjeta, she had turned to prostitution. Unfortunately, her activities had been discovered by one of the local women, Pauline Rankin, wife of 'Knob-head Trev', and stepmother of Rikki. As pay-back, Pauline and some of her friends caught Edi and threw her from the roof of the building, killing her instantly.

Bigsy had been told of Pauline's involvement by Rikki, and with the lack of any interest by the police, prompted him to mete justice. The Rankins were both heroin addicts and he needed to get hold of some uncut heroin to deal with them. The drug had been readily supplied by Errol Sheedie, Everton's brother.

Bigsy was afraid that one day this favour may be called in.

"Are you getting another round in before Big Ben?" asked Carole, shaking Bigsy from his reminiscences.

"Eh... oh, sorry pet, miles away, what did you say?"

"You're as bad as our Polly. He's been mythering an' all. What is it about New Year's Eve? You're supposed to be enjoying yourself," admonished Carole. "I said, are you getting a round in? Big Ben'll be on in a minute." Her voiced had raised a couple of notches to ensure Bigsy had not misheard the message.

"Aye, pet, just on my way. What's everyone having?"

Bigsy made a note of the order, then proceeded to the bar with Wazza and Chirpie in tow to help with the glasses.

The occupants of the table spread out, taking up the vacant space.

The bar was heaving, and it took several minutes for Bigsy to get to the front to be served. He placed his order, and, with their drinks replenished, returned to the table, where the occupants were in good spirits.

With two minutes to midnight, the club was at fever pitch with the excitement of the new millennium approaching.

The D.J. plugged a lead into a radio which was tuned into the BBC. The club went quiet as the first chimes of Big Ben heralded the year 2000.

Bong... bong...

Bigsy, Wazza, and Chirpie stood up and closed their eyes, screwed their faces up and put their fingers in their ears, as if waiting for a big explosion, a rehearsed little wheeze. Everyone around the table fell about laughing.

Boooong

"Happy new year everyone!" cried the D.J. and the whole club started singing 'Auld Lang Syne'.

Just then there was a large bang from outside the club and some worried looks were visible among the crowd. Bigsy went outside to see what all the fuss was.

"It was some kids setting off fireworks. Don't think we'll be seeing Armageddon tonight," he reported, as he returned to the table.

Everybody was hugging each other and wishing happy New Year and raising their glasses, toasting the new era.

"I shan't be unhappy to see the back of 1999, that's for sure," said Bigsy to Wazza.

Carole was in earshot.

"What do you mean pet? You've got your own business and doing well. I've got a feeling that it's just the beginning. I think we should think about moving this year. I bet if things carry on like this we could afford a small place in Jesmond or even Cramlington." She had no idea of her husband's concerns.

"Aye, pet, maybe we can," Bigsy replied, with no real enthusiasm.

"You know your trouble, Bigsy Worrall? You've got no ambition." Carole planted a big kiss on Bigsy's forehead.

"Funny how New Year's Eve makes you maudlin. I was thinking about me Da earlier. I wish he was here," said Bigsy.

"I know you do, pet," said Carole, and squeezed Bigsy's hand.

Polly and Veronica joined them at the table from the dance floor.

"We're headin' off now. Taxis'll be hard to come by later on and we've got to get across town," said Polly.

"Are you ok for cash?" asked Alison, as a concerned mother.

"Aye Ma, thanks. Don't fret, I'll be fine," replied Polly.

They said their goodbyes and headed for the exit.

Several others had also decided to head home having seen in the momentous occasion, realising the world wasn't going to come to an end. The dance floor was now more accessible.

"How about a dance, Bigsy?" asked Carole.

Normally the chances of getting Bigsy onto the dance floor were about as remote as teaching a fish to ride a bike. His co-ordination skills would make a walrus look graceful, but tonight was different. He would try for Carole. So, to the strains of Stevie Wonder, they took to the floor.

"*I just call to say I love you,*" sang Bigsy to the chorus in Carole's ear, catching the romantic charge of the evening.

"Give over pet, you'll start a riot with that noise," said Carole, destroying a special moment. Bigsy's lack of Karaoke skills was renowned at the club.

After the record had finished, Stan grabbed the microphone and announced that the advertised spectacular firework display would start in the car park. Those that remained made their way to the windows for a closer look. A few hardy souls went outside; it was a frosty night.

Stan, naturally, had taken charge as firework-lighter and, sure enough, a couple of rockets whooshed their way skywards. The children who were still there were enthralled as the burst of colour cascaded to the ground.

"Not much of a bang," observed Chirpie, who was now in the car park alongside Bigsy and Carole. Joy didn't fancy standing for any length of time.

"Not much of a show either," commented Bigsy, after about five minutes when the fireworks had been exhausted.

"What d'you expect for a fiver?" said Stan to a disappointed couple and their five children who had stayed specially to see the fireworks.

As they made their way back inside, Bigsy felt a vibration in his pocket. His mobile phone was ringing.

"You carry on, pet, there's a phone call, I'll just take this. Probably Ma wishing us a happy New Year," said Bigsy.

'Number withheld,' said the display.

Bigsy pressed the button with the green telephone and before he could speak came a voice from the past.

"Is dat you, Bigsy, mon?"

A familiar, deep resonant West Indian timbre echoed into Bigsy's ear. The blood drained from his face, his finger burying deep into his other ear to ward off extraneous noise. His hand holding the phone started to shake.

"Errol, bonny lad, happy New Year. To what do I owe this pleasure at this time of the morning?"

The voice continued. "Happy New Year to you, Bigsy, mon, I tought you would still be about. I wanted to let you know we are coming up North tomorrow, dat's today, now, I reckon, and wanted to drop in to see you. I have a proposition I want you to give serious consideration to."

"Aye, bonny lad, what time do you want to meet us, like?" replied Bigsy, trying to hide his panic. "Four o'clock...? Y y yeah, that'll be fine." Bigsy managed to stammer. "At the working men's club where we met last time... D'you recall how to get here, like...? Well, you give us a ring if you get lost... Aye, you too," and Bigsy rang off.

Suddenly the last four Newcastle Browns were starting to rebel, and he threw up against the back fence of the car park.

Chapter Two

Bigsy made his way back inside, disturbed by the phone call.

"Are you ok Bigsy, lad? You look like you've seen a ghost," commented Wazza, as he approached the table.

"Aye, just parted company with a few broons that's all."

"You lightweight, Bigsy," said Wazza, to the amusement of the rest of the party.

Carole was more concerned though.

"You don't look right, pet. You're not coming down with anything are you?"

"No, I'll be fine, pet, just something disagreed with us, that's all." Bigsy sat down contemplating Errol's call.

Out of Carole's hearing, Bigsy spoke to Wazza and Chirpie who had seen Bigsy take the call.

"That was Errol Sheedie, wants a meet tomorrow afternoon."

"What's he doing phoning you up at this time of night?" asked Wazza.

"Says he's got a proposition for us," replied Bigsy.

"Bloody funny time to be calling though," commented Chirpie. "Must be important."

"Aye, I was thinking that meself," said Bigsy.

"Did he say what it was about?" asked Wazza.

"No, just said he was coming up here tomorrow and wanted a meet," said Bigsy.

"When?" asked Chirpie, recognising his buddy's concern.

"Four o'clock, here, at the club."

"Well, I'll be with you if you need some company," said Wazza.

"Aye, me an'all," added Chirpie.

"Ta lads, I'll take you up on that. It'll be good to have you about."

Bigsy had not said anything to Wazza and Chirpie about the heroin purchase that had resulted in the death of Trevor and Pauline

Rankin, but they had met Errol on his last visit to the Northeast. The West Indian had come up from Brixton to claim his brother's money from the final drugs run Bigsy had made prior to Everton's murder. Bigsy had been hiding the cash in the central heating vent of his flat.

He'd politely declined Errol's offer of continued work, despite the opportunity of making good money; it had caused him too much grief. The thought of Carole finding out frightened him more than any contra-temps the police. After all, he was now a legitimate video shop owner and had no desire to return to the dangers of drug running.

But he owed Errol, and there was no getting away from that indebtedness. It wasn't a question of money; honour was at stake, and no amount of money would cover that. He was left with no option but to see Errol and hear him out. The thought, however, worried him.

Around two a.m. the D.J. played the final record, and what was left of the partygoers started to disperse.

Outside the club, a taxi was waiting to take Bigsy and Carole home. Wazza, Chirpie, Joy and Alison were hovering around the club entrance.

"How are you gettin' back?" said Bigsy.

"Walking," said Wazza.

"Don't be daft, bonny lad, you don't want to be wandering around here this time of night. Jump in there's plenty of room... What about your Mam, Wazza?" said Bigsy.

"She's alright, ta Bigsy, she'll get a lift back from Stan when they've done the glasses."

So, the six of them squeezed into the black cab. Joy was sat in the middle and was taking up at least two seats. Once again space was at a premium.

Bigsy was still feeling low when he and Carole got back to the flat, a combination of several broons and Errol's phone call.

"You sit down and make yourself comfortable, I'll make us a

brew."

Carole disappeared into the kitchen, while Bigsy sat down on the sofa with his head in his hands. Carole returned after a few minutes with two mugs of steaming coffee.

"Here you are, pet, you drink this; it'll perk you up."

He raised his head; his eyes were red. "Ta pet, I'll be fine."

"I can think of something to take your mind off things," said Carole and kissed his forehead.

Saturday 1st January 2000.

Despite Carole's best efforts the previous evening, Bigsy had not slept well, his mind racing at the possibilities, another drug run, a trip to Columbia to negotiate with the Cartel, a hit on an unscrupulous rival? All the permutations were running through his mind and causing a great deal of anxiety. Why now, just when his life was turning for the better and the chance of getting away from Heathcote? A hypothetical question he couldn't answer.

At eight o'clock, he took a mug of tea to Carole. She was in a deep slumber.

"What time is it?" asked a half-awake Carole, her hair dishevelled and make-up absent.

"Just after eight," he replied.

"Eh, no, eight o'clock! That's the middle of the night. I wasn't thinking of getting out of bed before eleven."

"That's ok; I'll put a film on or something. I won't disturb you, pet."

"What's up Bigsy? You've not been right since you took that call last night. Who was it?" Carole asked, sipping her tea, trying to focus.

"Just some business, nottin' to fret about," replied Bigsy. Carole let it drop.

"You go back to sleep; I'll wake you up at eleven. I think I'll pop out for some fresh air."

Bigsy went back to the lounge.

The flat was comfortable enough for two people and Carole had made sure it was tastefully set out with little clutter. The leather sofa was new and dominated the room or would have done if it wasn't for Bigsy's entertainment centre, a large television, video, satellite, sound system with big speakers and his pride and joy, a DVD player. There was a cabinet in the corner which looked like a chest of drawers but contained two or three hundred videos, including several from his under-the-counter stock for those special nights with Carole. A small dining table with two chairs was in the opposite corner. The kitchen was kitted out with the latest appliances, dishwasher, washing machine/drier, fridge freezer and a large modern oven. Carole continually complained it was too small, but it served its purpose.

Bigsy slipped on his tracksuit and a pair of trainers, then left the flat and took the stairs down fourteen floors to ground level to get some exercise.

It was a cold, misty morning on the estate with the smell of fireworks lingering in the air, adding a gloomy feel to the start of the new millennium. He noticed the soggy carcass of a spent rocket lying in the gutter having delivered its joy to watching children the previous night. It seemed to sum up everything.

He looked up at the grey sky as he crossed the service road to the precinct. He thought about calling into the video shop and sorting out the returns from the previous night, but, instead, dropped in on Mr. Ali's. The general store had been open since seven o'clock, despite it being New Year's Day. Bigsy exchanged greetings with his business neighbour and mooched about the aisles not looking for anything in particular.

"No papers today, Mr. Ali?" asked Bigsy, forgetting the bank holiday restrictions.

"Not today Bigsy, back to normal tomorrow," replied the

storekeeper. "Are you opening today, Bigsy?"

"Aye, I've asked young Rikki to open up at two o'clock." Bigsy walked out having purchased a packet of extra strong mints, and decided to make his way to the recreation ground to clear his head. He was still mulling over his pending meeting with Errol.

He made for the underpass which went under the dual carriageway, the main link that went from the town centre to the motorway. As he walked along the dingy tunnel in almost total darkness, his feet sloshed through puddles and crunched on the broken glass from the smashed lighting. They had long since been put out of action by yobs.

His mind suddenly went back six months earlier, when he had arranged to meet knob-head Trev. He could picture Trev staggering up the footpath towards him in the murk of the underpass, clearly off his head, and Bigsy handing him the two packets of uncut heroin that would ensure his death and that of his 'poxy missus'. He paused before walking on and thought again. Now was not the time for remorse; he had done what he had to do. It was justice, Heathcote style.

He walked on through the small industrial estate and onto the short tarmac pathway which led onto the playing fields of the recreation ground, or 'rec' as it was more commonly known. He took out his handkerchief and wiped away the damp from one of the benches that surrounded the football pitches and sat down. It was eerily deserted this time of the morning.

It was chill, the mist gradually giving way to thick clouds which rolled in with a stiff wind from the Northwest. Bigsy started to recall some of the many goals he had scored on this ground. The goalposts stood naked without their nettings, dotted around the area like some modern sculptures. There were six pitches marked out, and on Sundays most would be in use. The penalty areas around the goals were churned up and became a quagmire after a rain shower, not the most conducive ingredient for attractive football; but it didn't matter; this was home.

Bigsy was trying to shake himself from his introspection, when he was suddenly aware of someone walking towards him. He was slim with unruly sandy-coloured hair and carrying a large kite.

"Hiya Polly, kidder, what you are doing out this time of day? I thought students didn't get up till dark."

"Hiya Bigsy, didn't expect to see you here either after last night's festivities."

"Aye, just wanted to clear my head, like."

He stood up from the bench; the back of his tracksuit bottoms were wet from the dew on the seat.

"I was going to try one of my kites out. Haven't done much lately," said Polly.

"Aye, our Carole said she'd not seen you about with your kites for a while."

"No, seems I lost my interest."

"You're still missing our Katya, I reckon," observed Bigsy.

"Aye," replied Polly, and the two of them enjoyed a few minutes debating life.

"What you need to do, bonny lad, is sort yourself out and get back out there."

This was the extent of Bigsy's counselling skills, but Polly felt better for having a man to confide in. There had been no shortage of advice from his mother and Carole. It had also been cathartic for Bigsy to think about someone else's problems.

Eventually, Bigsy made his way back to the flat, refreshed by his walk and meeting with Polly. As he reached the tower block, he looked back towards the field and could see a kite flying high over the rec.

Carole was already up when Bigsy returned to the flat, reading a magazine on the sofa and tucking into a bowl of cereals. She looked up as he entered the room.

"Hiya, pet," she said, as he walked towards the kitchen.

"I'll just make us a coffee."

"You ok, Bigsy? I've been worried about you," she shouted. "You were tossing about all night, and I've not seen you out this time of day after a do at the club unless you're playing footy."

"Aye pet, don't you fret. I'm fine, honest."

A few minutes later, he returned to the lounge with two mugs.

"Guess what... I saw our Polly on the rec." He handed Carole her drink.

"What was Polly doing there this time of day? Seems early for a student."

"Aye, that's what I said. Taking one of his kites out... Look you can see him from here."

Carole got up and went to the window where she could see the distant figure.

"That's a good sign," observed Carole.

Around midday Bigsy phoned Stan at the club.

"Stan? Bigsy here... Aye, great night, ta... What about you...? Four-thirty...? You must be knackered, man... Stan, I need to ask a favour. What time are you closing the club this afternoon...? Three o'clock...? Champion, can I use the committee room about four? Aye, I've got a supplier coming up from the smoke, and I need a bit of privacy, like... No, sorry, can't, the shop'll be open then... Thanks Stan, that's great. Any chance you can do us a few sarnies an' all...? I don't know, a mixture I suppose, enough for five. I'll square up with you tonight, if that's ok... Ta Stan, you're a star. What...? You'll leave the back door open? Oh, aye, ok, I'll be back in about seven. Aye, see you then."

Bigsy rang off and phoned young Rikki who was out at his mate Stevie Leonard's house.

"Rikki, kidder, are you ok opening up this afternoon and doing the shift for us...? Aye, till ten. I'll pay you time and a half seeing how it's bank holiday... Aye, I'll pop round later about six to make

sure you're ok... Champion, I'll drop the keys off with Mr. Ali."
Bigsy rang off.

Bigsy shouted to Carole in the bedroom. "Just popping to the shop. Do you want anything, pet?"

"Aye, you can get us a bottle of milk."

Bigsy went down to the shop, gave the keys of the video store to Mr. Ali, and collected the milk.

As the time moved closer to the meet, Bigsy was getting more and more anxious, and it was having a purgative effect requiring several visits to the bathroom. It did not go unnoticed by Carole.

"You been eating dodgy kebabs again, pet?"

"No, must be those broons from last night."

"But you threw up most've them in the club car park, as I recall. Are you sure you're ok?"

"Aye, I'm fine, but I'm going to give the shop a miss tonight; I've asked Rikki's to cover for us."

Bigsy paused, then continued.

"I'm popping out to see Stan about half-three with Wazza and Chirpie. I shouldn't be long... Then I might get me head down for an hour or so."

"What're you going 'round there for?" enquired Carole.

"Just some business, that's all."

Carole let it drop. She knew better than to dig too deeply; some things were best left alone.

At three-thirty, Bigsy took his jacket from the coat-peg by the front door and pecked Carole on the cheek.

"Shan't be long, pet," he called, and made his way to the ground floor, the lift again surprisingly available. The Millennium bug obviously hadn't bitten the elevator.

He waited outside the flats in the gathering gloom of a winter's early evening, the streetlights illuminating the tower blocks in an eerie glow as they rose majestically from the ground. Bigsy noticed some windows were lit up, others were not, indicating who was in and who was out. This time of day on a Bank Holiday most were watching, or more likely sleeping in front of, the television.

After a few minutes he heard the distinctive sound of Wazza's stereo blaring down the road. After a few seconds, his souped-up Escort came into view.

"Turn that fookin' noise down. You'll wake the fookin' dead," shouted Bigsy, to be heard over the cacophony. "Jeezus, it's enough to do your head in."

Wazza complied, recognising Bigsy was not in the best of moods. Chirpie, who was sitting in the passenger seat, got out and folded the front seat down and climbed into the back among the speakers, his six-foot frame struggling to adapt to the confined space.

The sound system was Wazza's pride and joy and the pièce de résistance of several customisations that Wazza had undertaken on the car. "Nought to sixty, eventually," was Chirpie's comments on the vehicle.

Bigsy couldn't be too choosy however, as he was still only halfway through a three-year ban for drink-driving and, even after he had completed his sentence, with the prohibitive cost of insurance, he was doubtful if he would be able to afford to drive again. It was fortunate that Carole had her own car, a rather tired-looking VW Golf, which could get to the supermarket for groceries or to the Metro Centre for a shopping expedition. Luckily, in Wazza, he had a buddy who seemed only too ready to act as chauffeur, subject to a contribution towards petrol.

They arrived at the car park at the back of the club around ten-to-four, and the three of them sat in the Escort waiting for their visitors to arrive. They made a formidable band of brothers, having been friends since school. Their friendship was unbreakable; they would always look out for each other. Today was a case in point. The only other car in the car park was Stan's new Volvo.

At precisely four o'clock, the black 5 series BMW, which last adorned the car park some six months earlier, glided slowly towards them from the main road; its springs coping effortlessly with the undulations and potholes of the cinder and gravel surface. Bigsy felt the need for the toilet again but managed to stave off any unwanted accidents.

"Pleased to see the punctuality hasn't slipped," said Chirpie, breaking the tension. It had been a standing joke that the 'Rastas' were always on time.

Bigsy and his two buddies emerged rather less than gracefully from the Escort. Chirpie, nearly hanging himself on the seat belt, popped out from the back, and promptly sprawled in a heap on the gravel.

Errol on the other hand exited stylishly from the passenger seat of the Beamer. The driver also got out but stayed just behind his boss.

Errol was as imposing as Bigsy remembered. He was about the same height and build, but that was where any similarities ended. With his clothes and bearing, Errol had a style that was far-removed from Bigsy's world. He reminded Bigsy of Morgan Freeman.

Errol preferred a neat haircut unlike the dreadlocks worn by his late brother, Everton, and was wrapped in a very expensive looking Afghan coat to ward of the cold in these less-than-temperate climes. His gold jewellery rattled on his wrist as he made his way to Bigsy. He offered his knuckle for a touch, the greeting of choice among the 'brothers'. Bigsy reciprocated to a huge roar of laughter from Errol who then proceeded to embrace Bigsy in a man-hug. It was not a familiar greeting in the Northeast and felt odd, but Bigsy responded accordingly.

"Bigsy, my mon, it's so good to see you," said the West Indian warmly, in a gravelly voice, redolent of Barry White.

"Aye, you too, Errol, bonny lad," replied Bigsy, hoping the lie wouldn't show.

Errol laughed loud again. "I love dat 'bonny lad' ting. It's so cool, Bigsy, mon."

Bigsy was trying to attune his ear to the broad Jamaican accent.

"I've got us a room in the club, like, where we won't be disturbed. It's brass monkeys out here."

"Dat's cool Bigsy, mon, we'll follow you."

Bigsy, with Errol beside him, strode towards the back entrance of the club, with Wazza, Chirpie, and Errol's associate following.

The back door was strengthened to deter burglars and Bigsy needed all his strength to pull it open. They were immediately hit by the stench of last night's party. The heady smell of beer and cigarettes would linger for days. The function room was unusually silent and in darkness as they walked past, but Bigsy noticed that a significant clean-up operation had taken place, leaving the room comparatively tidy.

"Through here," said Bigsy, turning right down the corridor of the entrance lobby. A door at the end, next to the main entrance said, 'Committee Room, Private'.

It was in darkness and Bigsy searched for the light switch. He found it beside the door frame and the room was soon bathed in the harsh light of a hundred-watt bulb. It was comfortable enough, with a television perched on a make-shift shelf just below the ceiling and a couple of armchairs facing it. There were honours boards depicting past Presidents of the club, dating back to the 1960's, around the walls. In the middle, surrounded by eight chairs, a large table. The sandwiches that Bigsy had ordered were in the middle of the table, with two bowls of crisps covered with Clingfilm, and a large flask containing what looked like coffee next to them. Cutlery and mugs were on a separate table.

There was a note from Stan placed strategically on the top of the sandwiches which Bigsy picked up and read. *'Bigsy, here's the sarnies you ordered, and I've thrown in a few crisps and a flask of coffee. If you want any beer or anything from the bar help yourself and let me know what you've had so I can add it to the bill. See you later, Stan.'* Bigsy was impressed.

"Well dis is really hospitable, Bigsy mon," said Errol.

"Ta Errol, I thought you would be wanting some scran having driven all that way, like," said Bigsy.

Errol was having trouble with the translation.

"Dat's really kind of you, mon. Shall we get down to business?" He spoke in a tone that suggested compliance.

Bigsy took the covering off the sandwiches which had started to curl up at the corners and handed them to Errol and his companion. Errol politely declined. "I have a special diet I have to stick to from my personal trainer."

Luckily, the rest of them had no such inhibitions and tucked in like a plague of locusts. Wazza picked up one of the mugs and blew into it to shift any dust, and poured some coffee. He handed the drink to Errol but, again, he politely declined.

"Dat's really kind of you to go to all dis trouble. I said to Denzel we would be made very welcome up here," said Errol. "Oh, I forgot my manners... Bigsy, dis is Denzel Gibbons... Layton's bruddah."

Bigsy could see the resemblance now. Layton was Everton Sheedie's courier who delivered the drugs to Bigsy and collected the money the following day after the drops.

"Hiya Denzel, bonny lad."

Bigsy offered his knuckles for a touch. "I was sorry to hear of Layton's passing. He was a canny lad alright. I read about it in the papers, very sad. I'm sure he's been greatly missed."

"Tanks Bigsy mon. Layton often mentioned you, too," replied Denzel, in a similar accent to his boss.

Wazza and Chirpie nodded their acknowledgment, as Bigsy introduced them to the pair.

Pleasantries over, it was time to get down to business.

Errol took off his overcoat and made himself comfortable.

"Dis is de issue I need your help wid Bigsy, mon," announced

Errol.

He paused as if composing himself, which added an unintended air of drama to the already tense atmosphere. He continued gravely, looking at Bigsy then his two companions in turn.

"You will realise dat I can't let Everton's murder go unpunished. It is a question of honour."

Bigsy felt a shiver run down his spine, thinking for a split second that he was being implicated in some way.

Errol continued in his West Indian drawl. "You may know dat Denzel here was also dere dat night when Everton and Layton were shot. Took one in de shoulder himself and nearly died."

Bigsy nodded to Denzel in acknowledgement; Errol paused, and then continued.

"I can tell you as much as we know… De evening he and Layton were killed, Everton got a call from a contact from way back called Lionel in a club dere on de Waterfront... Scalleys, I tink de name is. Everton did a little business from time-to-time wid him for old time's sake. But Lionel said he wanted a special consignment which de normal suppliers couldn't deliver; it was a bigger order than what Everton would normally do."

"It was Scalleys we delivered to," confirmed Bigsy.

"Yes, dat's de one, dat's de drop," said Errol.

"So, this contact, Lionel, called Everton to fill the gap, like…? Seems fair enough."

"Yes, we tought it was. Everton was very careful about going north of de river. He knew it could cause trouble, but later, he was called by a man with a foreign voice, Eastern European, Everton said… maybe Russian, Polish, dat kind of ting. After he got de call, Everton phoned me and said dat de man wanted to talk to him about some business to supply some of de clubs on de Waterfront. Everton knew dey were finding it difficult to meet de demand and dey were worried about losing customers, dis is why Lionel had called Everton earlier. De man told Everton he wanted to talk about sharing resources. As you know, it's a big area, many clubs and pubs and someting we had been trying to break into."

"Yeah, I remember," said Bigsy. "Everton told us to be careful, like, but he said it was cool."

"As I said, we tought it was. You made de drop dat night and Everton got de call just after."

"So, you think Everton was set up by the drop we made? They thought you were trying to muscle in, like?" said Bigsy.

"Dat's what we tink," replied Errol. "It makes sense."

"So, d'you know who's in the frame?" asked Bigsy.

"Dat is de probalem; we don't. We have been making some serious enquiries with all our contacts. Denzel has been keeping de supply chain ticking over de south side, but no-one's saying notting. I've even put out a contract, ten thousand pounds to anyone who can get us a name or, better still, take out de low life dat done it. I need my revenge, and I sure am going to get it. Dis is where you come in, Bigsy. I know you don't want to be involved wid de supply ting anymore and I gave you my word on dat and I will keep it."

Bigsy exhaled.

"De favour I need from you is to do some digging around for me for a while. I want you to visit de clubs and make some discreet enquiries. Find out what you can about who is supplying de north of de river. Who is dis Russian, Polish or whatever? You will report to me by phone every week." Errol paused, waiting for a reaction. "Now I don't expect you to do dis for nottin'. I will pay you five-hundred pounds a week plus expenses. Just let me know how much dey are, and Denzel will cover it for me. If you can find de scum who killed my bruddah you can have de ten grand dat is on the contract. Do we have a deal?"

Errol said it in a tone that made it difficult to say no.

"I will need to use Wazza and Chirpie here as well, they are my right hand," said Bigsy.

"Dat's up to you; I don't care, but you will need to be discreet;

you know what I'm saying. It could be very dangerous. Dese people are bad dudes and dey will kill you if they find out. Your security must be total, or you will end up dead like Everton and Layton," said Errol solemnly.

Bigsy looked to Wazza and Chirpie for some reassurance.

"The way I see it is this," said Chirpie, making an unusual intervention. He rarely contributed whilst in company. "We did alright by Everton, and I think the people that took him out deserve to be held to account, like."

Errol was having trouble with the dialect but got the idea.

"Well said, Chirpie, mon," said Errol, and gave him a big grin.

"What about the bizzies?" enquired Bigsy.

Errol was lost.

"The police…? Won't they have summat to say if you go 'round topping off Ruskies on their patch?" asked Bigsy.

"De police don't have a clue. Dey have been so-called 'investigating' de murders for six months and have no idea. I do have a contact in de constabulary who slips me de odd snippet now and again. Dey know dey can't catch dese guys on deir own and I tink dey would be more dan happy for us to do de job for dem."

"Now that's an interesting thought," said Bigsy and he paused for a moment. "Have they got anyone on the inside, do you know? They did have that Hughie Bonner bloke, the cop that died."

"I don't know for certain, but I don't tink so." There was a reflective pause. "Dat was unfortunate, I told Everton dat he went too far dere… killing a policeman was bad. A verbal warning or a broken leg would have probably done de trick. I said we don't want to kick up a hornet's nest, and it did cause a lot of grief here, and on de other side of de river as well, from what I heard. Raids going off all over de place. But dey never found nottin' to link it wid Everton, dat I am aware of. I tink dey have given up on dat investigation as well."

Bigsy was trying to take it all in. On the one hand he was not trafficking drugs or negotiating deals with cartel barons from Columbia, but on the other, he may be taking on the Russian Mafia, and their reputation was something to behold. Still, it could be worse, but at this moment, he had difficulty in thinking of anything that was.

Bigsy took his time as if giving the proposition due consideration. He knew in practice he had little choice in the matter.

"Aye, Errol, bonny lad, we'll do what we can to help. We'll make some enquiries, but we'll need a few introductions, like. The contacts will have changed since we did our last drop."

"No probalem… Dat's great news Bigsy, mon," he said with a beaming smile, his teeth seemingly lighting up the dismal room. "I will get Denzel here to give you his number. It will be good for you to meet up and exchange information. He can tell you more what happened dat night," he said looking his younger associate.

That did little to reassure Bigsy.

"Did he not tell the bizzies, sorry, police?" queried Bigsy, referring to Denzel but directing the question at Errol.

Errol looked at Denzel, who was keeping his council, and answered for him. "No, he told dem he didn't see who it was. But he had a good look at de guy with de gun and reckons he can recognise him again. We want to take care of dis ourselves. We don't want anyone going to prison wid a life sentence. Dis was murder and de punishment where we come from is death. 'An eye for an eye', as dey say."

"Fair doos," said Bigsy, and his thoughts momentarily went back to the Rankins and his own retribution. He could readily identify with Errol's sentiments.

Bigsy looked at the plate on the table, the sandwiches were all gone.

"Would you like a brew or something stronger for the journey before you go?" asked Bigsy, recognising the conversation was drawing to a close.

"Dat's very kind of you Bigsy, mon. You certainly live up to your reputation of being hospitable people up here."

Errol reached in his pocket and Bigsy jumped inexplicably, half expecting to see a gun. Instead, it was an envelope. He handed it to Bigsy.

"Dis is for you. It is your first week's wages up-front, as a token of goodwill. I will expect to hear someting from you on Friday."

Errol got up, followed by Denzel, and Bigsy led them back to the car park.

"Nice place," observed Errol, who was looking back at the club. "Nottin' like dis in Brixton, a pity."

Bigsy watched as Denzel took the wheel of the BMW, then sashayed out of the car park into the passing traffic, turning left towards the A1 and the long journey home.

"Shite," said Wazza as he unlocked the Escort. "What'll we do now?"

"I have no idea, bonny lad," said Bigsy, as he climbed into the passenger seat with Chirpie trying to find the seatbelt in the back.

Chapter Three

Millennium eve, Lapugovac, Kosovo.

Katya Gjikolli was also in reflective mood this night. She was curled up in front of the log fire, her shoulder length blonde hair tied back, head resting on her knees, watching the dying embers in the grate as they changed colours, red, orange, yellow. The knitted shawl given to her by her mother, was around her shoulders helping to ward off the cold. Looking deep into the burning logs she could make out canyons almost like a moonscape as they gradually turned to ashes.

The electricity had long been cut by the local generating company, barely six hours a day was the rationing now in these challenging times, as the country tried to rebuild itself following 'the ugly years'. Candles lit the small living room, casting ghostly shadows on the wall. Her son's 'lobster pot', filled with his favourite toys, was in the corner. She remembered the excitement of the Metro Centre and her feeling of wonderment as she walked around the baby-store where she bought it. She'd never seen anything like it. She thought of Carole and her generosity, not just in financial terms, but in her spirit; taking in a total stranger and making her feel wanted and loved.

Then there was Polly.

She thought of him every day; in fact, he was never far from her thoughts. She didn't know why or how, but he had unlocked something in her that had been repressed, imprisoned like a toy clown on a spring. He had provided the key that had released it from its shackles. There was no turning back; she had experienced a passion and intensity of love she had never thought possible. The genie was out of the bottle, never to return.

She remembered the phone call... 'that' phone call.

She was making coffee for Clara Davenport, the Community

Liaison Officer, in the small kitchen in her flat in Heathcote Tower. They had become good friends, and Katya had asked her to call to discuss applying for UK residence which she was entitled to do as a Kosovan asylum seeker.

In her brief time as a refugee, Katya had impressed everyone with her language abilities and the kindness and support she had shown to her fellow Kosovans. She had also excelled as a teacher, a profession she had taken up following university. She had worked in the small primary school in her home village, but, like many others, had been forced to flee the pogrom. Having settled well in the UK, she was offered a part-time post at the local pre-school centre at the other end of the estate, and had made an immediate impression. She was liked and respected by everyone, particularly the children. Clara was in no doubt that her credentials would make her an ideal candidate for permanent residence.

She also wanted to discuss adopting Arjeta, Edi Bukosi's three-year-old daughter. Following Edi's tragic death, Katya had been looking after Arjeta and very quickly became a surrogate mother. Arjeta had been almost smothered with affection by Edi and it had left a huge void after she had died. Arjeta was an intense child, but showed a lot of affection for Katya's son, Melos, and looked after him like a baby brother. The thought of her ending up in a Kosovan orphanage was beyond comprehension, and Katya felt some responsibility towards Arjeta, partly blaming herself for Edi's unfortunate demise.

Then came the call that had changed everything. Katya was in the kitchen making coffee.

"Katya, it's a man with a strong foreign accent... He says his name is Ibi," called Clara from the lounge.

Katya dropped the mug she was holding, and it crashed to the ground, smashing into pieces, spraying the kitchen floor with hot coffee.

Clara handed the phone to Katya. "It's ok, I'll clear this up."

"Ibi?" It was all she could say, in a faltering voice.

The voice responded in Albanian. Katya had to retune her mind to her native language.

"Katya...? I am calling from the Refugee Council... in Pristina. They gave me your number... You are in England, yes?"

"Yes..." said Katya, dumbstruck. "How, how are you?"

"Ok, I am alive...I have been in prison... They let me go two weeks ago... I have been staying at your mother's."

"Mami...? How is she?"

"She is well. She let me stay with her so I can recover my strength. How are you, in England?"

"I am well...So is Melos... your son." There was a pause.

"Yes, your mother said I had a son... I did not know."

"No... he is well."

"That is good... So, when will you return...? Soon, I hope... I have been to the cottage to see if it is still there and good to live in. I want to make it perfect for your homecoming."

Katya couldn't take it in, her world had been turned upside down.

"I do not know; I will need to find out what is happening."

"Ok, you find out and let me know. I will phone again in one week at this time."

He rang off before Katya could say anything, and she nearly collapsed.

She was shaking when Clara came into the room with a refreshed mug of coffee.

"I've cleaned up the mess," said Clara. "Goodness, child, you've gone as white as a sheet. Was that your husband, on the phone?"

"Yes, I thought he was dead... Thank you,"

It was all Katya could manage as Clara handed her the drink. Then she sobbed bitterly.

Clara put a consoling arm around her. "What are you going to do?"

"I really don't know Clara; I really don't know."

She took a sip of coffee contemplating the implications of the call.

"I'll stay for a while if you like," offered Clara.

"That's very kind," replied Katya. "But I think I need some time on my own."

Clara left and Katya went to the window and looked across towards the recreation ground. She could see Polly flying one of his kites and was overwhelmed by sadness.

This should have been an over-joyous occasion; her husband had been miraculously resurrected from the dead, but it didn't feel like that at all. She had moved on, significantly. It had been a bolt out of the blue, all her plans and ambitions had suddenly come crashing down. Her future was in ruins.

Then there was Polly.

She couldn't leave him now, how could she? She had never experienced such love. Going back to Kosovo filled her with dread; there were too many painful memories. She would have no job; her school was derelict, and there were reports of shortages following the bitter conflict; what sort of life was that?

She belonged here now, surely.

Then there was Melos and Arjeta to consider. What about their future? Would they not be safer and enjoy a better life in England? No, she must stay.

But at the back of her mind something nagged at her; she knew she had to return. It was her responsibility to be with her husband, her duty even, and with her upbringing, she had been conditioned to comply. Perhaps it was meant to be.

As she sat gazing into the fire, she recalled the conversation with Polly. She sighed deeply at the recollection. He had begged her to stay, pleaded with her. Life would be meaningless without her. Katya told him she felt the same but, like it or not, her duty lay elsewhere. She had no choice; she would have to go back to Kosovo and the chances were that they would never see each other again.

The pain for both of them was incredible.

Carole was amazing. Katya had called 'round later that afternoon and told her what had happened. Carole just listened, as Katya poured out her feelings. Afterwards, they both cried, but Carole didn't judge and didn't put any pressure on her. She just said that Katya had to follow her conscience, and everything would take care of itself.

Over the next few weeks, Katya made all the arrangements to return to Kosovo. Clara handled all the necessary paperwork and liaised with Jenny Wheatley from the Refugee Council to ensure everything went smoothly. Katya was granted a temporary custody order over Arjeta; all the authorities were more than happy to agree. The orphanages would be at breaking point as the refugees returned. She was given a small amount of money, a resettlement grant of two hundred and fifty pounds.

Katya worked her notice at the pre-school club and many tears were shed on the last day by the staff and children. Katya was heartbroken having to say goodbye, she had grown fond of all the children, even the 'rascals' as she called them.

Bigsy had offered to pay for a leaving do, disco and all, he had said, but Katya declined. It was going to be hard enough and she wanted no fuss.

Katya smiled to herself at the memory.

By August 1999, nearly all the Kosovan refugees living in Britain had chosen to stay for the winter, despite the end of the conflict. In fact, fewer than four hundred had registered to go back to their homeland under the official resettlement programme. Most were concerned about the continued instability in Kosovo. There were horror stories from early returners who found their houses had been destroyed and were left with nowhere to live. Then there were the reports of land mines; it was still an extremely dangerous environment.

Katya's departure date was arranged for Tuesday 24th August. A special charter would fly from Leeds/Bradford airport where they had arrived just under four months earlier. How things had changed in such a brief time. Katya would join another hundred and twenty or so other refugees who had decided to go back. Flights to Kosovo, up until this point, landed in Skopje, Macedonia, which required an additional eight-hour coach trip. The airport in Pristina had been reserved for military aircraft only. Katya's flight, however, had been given special permission to fly direct into the capital, a four-hour journey.

She continued to receive phone calls from Ibi each week at the same time from the Refugee Council offices. He told her he had arranged to pick up her and the children from the airport. A friend had agreed to get him through security; civilians were not allowed to enter the airport. He confirmed that the cottage had not been destroyed, and he was making it a home for them.

She tried to gauge her feelings towards her husband after each phone call, but all she could feel was emptiness. It was like talking to a stranger. There was no warmth, no tenderness that two lovers would feel after a time apart, contemplating the reunion. Love didn't come into it; her only love lay elsewhere.

Carole agreed to take Katya and the children to the airport in Leeds, a two-hundred-mile round trip. Katya was grateful for the offer; it would be a difficult enough journey without the added complications of public transport. The flight was due to depart at three-thirty in the afternoon; coincidently the same time the refugees had landed in the UK at the end of April. They would leave Heathcote early to ensure they arrived at the airport in good time.

Packing was very difficult. Such was the generosity of Carole and the local people; Katya had acquired a good wardrobe of clothes for her and the children. The 'lobsterpot' had presented a problem but, fortunately, it came apart, and with some coaxing, she was able to fit it in her suitcase together with the recliner, another essential part of Melos' kit. Carole had also presented Katya with a large case of make-up and cosmetic accessories as a parting gift, but that would have to stay behind.

Edi had also amassed a big collection of things for Arjeta, and she wanted to take as much as she could, but it was impossible to carry all their belongings. Katya had boxed up what they couldn't take, including the make-up and cosmetics. Carole had agreed to send it on once Katya had established a base.

On the evening of 23rd, Katya went along to Bigsy and Carole's, taking the children with her. Polly's mum Alison would normally have agreed to babysit but being protective of her son, the relationship with Katya had become strained. Polly was inconsolable.

The evening was a sad occasion full of reminiscences; the Metro Centre trips, the night at the Working Men's club; the many stories from the pre-school club and so on. With an early start ahead of her, Katya left around nine-thirty to make her final preparations. Arjeta and Melos were both asleep and Carole helped Katya carry them back to her flat.

Katya had written a letter to Polly which she gave to Carole to give to him.

It read:

'My darling Polly, I don't know how I have lived these last few weeks I have missed you so much and I think about you all the time. I am so sorry for all the pain I have caused you. I never wanted our love ever to end and nor will it. I have to go home, you know that, it is my duty, but I do so with a very heavy heart. I hope you find love again; I know I shall not. Not like ours, not ever. I will think of you

always.
All my love
Katya xx

At the airport, there were dozens of other refugees waiting for the plane returning to Kosovo, looking bewildered and afraid. There was no media interest, unlike on their arrival; the conflict had long since been consigned to history. Carole helped Katya with the bags, while Arjeta looked after Melos who was back in his old buggy. Carole hugged Katya and they said their farewells.

"You make sure you keep in touch, Katya, pet. You've got my phone number, and you know the address," she shouted as Katya and the children went through the door into the departure lounge.

As she drove away, Carole was wiping away the tears.

After the regulation queues and delays at the airport, the group eventually boarded the plane. It was unusually quiet, no-one seemed to want to speak, everyone anxious about what they would find on their return. Burnt out homes, limited supplies, the trauma of atrocities, and the new worry of land mines, would be just some of the challenges that lay ahead. They would have to start again and build a new country.

The plane landed at around eight-thirty p.m. local time, and it was starting to get dark. Katya had Melos in her arms with her sling bag over her shoulder, Arjeta was toddling beside her quite bemused at all the commotion. For the first time she asked Katya in Albanian if they were going to see *'mami'*. Arjeta had not mentioned her mother for a while and it disturbed Katya that she should mention her now.

There was a long wait for their baggage at the carousel, and it was almost ten o'clock by the time they had cleared customs and immigration. Everyone was checked thoroughly.

Katya felt anxious as she eventually made her way out of the airport arrivals exit. Arjeta was pushing Melos, safely strapped in his buggy. As she got outside, she noticed it was much warmer than when she had left the UK, humid even. She looked around. There were military vehicles everywhere, some NATO, but mostly tagged 'KFOR', the new peacekeeping force. She had managed to get a trolley which was piled high with bags and luggage. The airport had been fairly relaxed about the weight allowance as the aircraft wasn't completely full.

Katya waited at the drop-off zone in front of the main building and then she heard a familiar voice.

"*Katya, alo Katya*," and Katya looked at the man speaking and made no connection.

"*Është më, Ibi.'*"

"Ibi?"

Katya couldn't believe her eyes. Ibi had aged about twenty years, he was gaunt, his clothes didn't fit him, and he was walking with a serious limp. His hair was receding and unkempt, there was a scar over his right eye, his face was speckled with red spots, and he looked as if he hadn't shaved for some time. He was just twenty-eight years old.

With two children in tow, there wasn't much time for pleasantries, and Katya just leant over and kissed him on both cheeks. They continued speaking in Albanian.

"You look different, where is your scarf... And jeans! Where did you get those?" He scowled in disapproval.

He looked again before Katya could speak. "You are wearing too much make-up; you look like a '*prostitutë*'. You will have to wash that off when we get home."

Katya ignored the remark. "This is your son, Ibi; this is Melos," she replied. Ibi took hold of his son and held him tightly. Melos screamed.

"And who is this one?" asked Ibi, pointing to Arjeta.

"I told you on the phone, I have taken custody of her. She is

Edi's daughter."

"Ah yes the one who jumped off the roof."

"She didn't jump; she was thrown off."

"They told me at the Refugee Council that she jumped. I asked them about her when you told me you were bringing home another mouth to feed."

Despite not hearing Albanian for a couple of months, Arjeta clearly understood what was said and immediately started crying.

Things were not going well. Katya just wanted to get back to the UK, back to Polly.

"I have borrowed a truck from one of my friends. It is over there." He pointed to a rusting heap which could hardly comply with that definition.

They made their way to the car park, Katya pushing the trolley and Ibi carrying Melos who was still crying. As they got closer, Katya could see the tyres were bald.

"Is this ok, Ibi? It looks dangerous."

"Nonsense, I am a mechanic; I fixed it. It is ok."

They proceeded to put Katya's bags and luggage on the open trailer before squeezing into the cramped cab.

"What is the cottage like?" asked Katya.

"It is ok; I have cleaned it up."

"So, it wasn't set on fire then?"

"No, but the next house it is just a ruin. I don't know why ours was spared."

"What about Major Kraniqi... Qazim?" asked Katya.

"What about Qazim?" responded Ibi, as he drove along the road away from the airport.

"He was dead in our cottage when I came back to collect my things, before I left."

"Well, he's not there now. I heard the Serbs had picked him up; they said they had shot him in a gun battle. The Serb papers made a thing about it. I was told this by another prisoner... What was he doing in our house?"

"I don't know. Probably looking for shelter, but he was dead when I saw him. He'd broken in through the back door."

"But why did he come to our cottage?"

Ibi's questioning was becoming more aggressive, and it seemed like an interrogation.

"I told you, he came before, the day after you were captured to deliver your message."

"And you made him feel at home... welcome, did you?"

"What do you mean by that?" asked Katya not liking the implications of the question.

"Nothing," said Ibi.

Arjeta started to cry, hearing raised voices. Katya comforted her.

The truck bounced up and down on the pot-holed road as it made its way through the darkened countryside, throwing up clouds of dust. It had clearly not rained for some time. Katya stared out of the window trying to trace the journey, but she could not make out any landmarks; streetlights were not available in Kosovo.

The trip was long, and it took almost two hours to complete the twenty miles. The remainder of the journey was completed in silence. Melos had thankfully gone back to sleep. Arjeta was just looking confused and sat sucking her thumb staring into road ahead. This was not the homecoming Katya had envisaged.

Katya was still staring in the fire, tears welling in her eyes as she recounted her story in her mind, trying to make sense of the last four months.

The truck lumbered on down the narrow lanes and approached the village. As they turned a corner, Katya saw her old school illuminated momentarily in the headlights. It was now in ruins. Katya caught her breath in horror; so many good memories came flooding back. The children, she suddenly thought. What had happened to the children?

It was gone midnight when she recognised the brow of the hill where previously she had stooped low to check the cottage almost five months earlier. Then she saw the three cottages and couldn't believe her eyes. The cottages on either side were just burned-out shells, as Ibi had described. Their cottage was intact but there were bullet holes across the front wall.

"Why was ours spared?"

There was no reply from Ibi. He stopped the truck outside the front door where the garden used to be. It was overgrown apart from two tyre tracks. Ibi got out and took Melos from Katya. The boy had now woken up and was screaming. Katya got down and lifted Arjeta from the cab. She was fast asleep.

Ibi unlocked the front door and Katya shivered, despite the clammy, sticky night. She went inside and immediately recognised the decor and layout, but it wasn't home, not as she knew it. The room was lit by two hurricane lamps that Ibi had acquired, bathing the room in a dim, ethereal light.

The dining table was still there, and she could still make out the stains of blood engrained in the veneer. The fear came back.

"Oh my god," she exclaimed, but out of Ibi's earshot. He had returned to the truck to fetch the baggage.

Katya was carrying both children. Arjeta, half asleep, asked where she was. She spoke in Albanian.

"Home darling, home," replied Katya.

"Mami; mami," Arjeta cried.

Katya hugged her. "No darling."

There was a small sofa facing the fireplace which at this time of year was not lit. The air was heavy and hot, and the room had a strange musty smell. Katya lay Melos down on the sofa with Arjeta and both were now sleeping again.

Katya went through the ground floor into the kitchen. The

backdoor to the garden where she had made her earlier escape had been fixed and seemed secure. The cooker looked ancient compared to the one in her flat, and different to the one she remembered cooking on. There was no washing machine; the fridge was empty, and had been turned off. With only three hours of electricity a day, it was pointless storing perishable food. There was some bread in the larder which appeared reasonably fresh and a few tins of food, but not enough to live on for any length of time.

Ibi returned with Katya's case and bags.

"Been shopping I see," nodding to the various carrier bags.

Katya didn't respond. She walked past Ibi without a word and went upstairs. A mattress had been put on the floor of the spare bedroom, presumably for Arjeta, but it had not been cleaned. There was dust everywhere. Katya would sort that out in the morning. The main bedroom still had the double bed and Melos' cot against the wall. It looked as if nothing had been touched; it was exactly as she had left it back in March.

She had another flashback of Serb soldiers jumping from their lorry; she shivered again.

The small bathroom would need a good clean, but she would see to that; her priority would be to get some supplies and the children settled.

She went downstairs and picked up Arjeta from the sofa. She noticed Ibi had gone to the small bureau and taken out a large bottle of vodka and was swigging from it in gulps. Katya watched in horror.

She took Arjeta upstairs and laid her down on the mattress then went to the cupboard where she kept her bedlinen. Luckily, they hadn't been looted by the Serbs. She took out a sheet and pillow. They were damp and mildewed but would have to do for tonight. She would air them outside tomorrow.

She made Arjeta comfortable, then settled Melos down in his cot and he was now in a deep slumber. She dreaded the next move.

She went back downstairs and collected her suitcase and took it up to the bedroom. As she started to unpack, she heard Ibi struggling up the stairs having consumed nearly half a bottle of Vodka. She jumped as he appeared at the door and started rummaging around her clothes in her luggage.

"What's all this? You've been whoring in England while I was rotting in a Serb prison."

Katya was not putting up with this.

"Go away Ibi, you're drunk. We'll talk about this in the morning."

"I want to know what you have been doing while I was giving my life for Kosovo."

His voice was raised, his eyes wide with anger.

"I was having your baby!" Katya snapped back.

This was a different Katya, not the meek schoolteacher that Ibi had remembered.

Ibi made a lunge for her but fell against the bedside table, hitting his head on the corner, then passed out.

Katya left him there and put her suitcase in the spare room. She would finish in the morning. She went downstairs and curled up on the sofa, leaving the hurricane lamps turned on; there were too many ghosts. She could hear strange noises, not the familiar sound of the rumble of traffic that ran past Heathcote Tower, but different sounds; trees rustling in the wind, which brought back memories of her escape through the forest.

Sleep was elusive.

Then, just as she had managed to drift off, the cottage was shaken by a clap of thunder. It was about three-thirty; it woke Katya with a start. She sat up on the sofa; her eyes were wide with fright. She was momentarily disorientated, as flashes of lightning lit the room. It was terrifying, reviving memories of gunfire from an earlier time.

She looked around the room, the hurricane lamps had burned out. She lay back down on the settee and instinctively curled up in a ball, foetal-like, as if it would provide some form of protection. She could hear the rain pounding on the windowpanes and the barren earth outside. The room lit up like daylight as flashes of lightening raced across the sky, quickly followed by further shuddering reports. The children were thankfully undisturbed, exhausted by their ordeal of the previous day. She had no desire to go upstairs again unless absolutely necessary.

After twenty minutes the storm abated, and she managed to drift back to sleep. She was restless, the couch not really conducive for a good night's slumber. Old nightmares returned, rough soldiers, grimy hands violating her. Then she could hear Melos crying.

She went upstairs and picked her son from his cot. She could see Ibi lay on the bed with a large weal across his forehead. He was dead to the world. Katya just wished he was dead.

She took Melos downstairs and found some jars of baby food in one of her carrier bags. With no hot water, it would be a cold serving. She could hear Arjeta calling and Katya went back upstairs to fetch her, leaving Melos in his recliner. She made a sandwich for herself and Arjeta from the meagre offerings from the larder, some bread and cheese, and started to think what she should do.

It was obvious Ibi was a changed person; his actions the previous night had frightened her. Ibi had never shown any malice towards her before; they had always enjoyed a good and close relationship. She knew he had a temper, but his anger was always aimed at the Serb regime and the war.

Then there was the drinking. He had never shown any inclination towards alcohol before.

Suddenly she heard a noise from upstairs. The bed creaking followed by heavy, laboured footsteps pounding on the bedroom floor, the sound reverberating around the living room. It could have been the old giant from Jack and the Beanstalk. Down the stairs, getting closer and closer, Katya lifted Melos into her arms and stood in front of Arjeta as a protecting mother would.

Ibi staggered into the living room, his shirt dishevelled and creased, undone to his waist. Katya noticed his trousers were worn and stained. Without any acknowledgement, Ibi sat on one of the chairs at the dining table with his head in his hands and let out a groan. Katya put Melos down and went to him.

"Let me look at your head."

She checked his wounds. His eyes stared at her, not a good stare, but blank of emotion. His breath smelt stale with a strong trace of alcohol.

There was a large bruise and congealed blood on his forehead; two days' stubble flecked his chin. He looked terrible.

"Wait here."

She went to the kitchen and ran some water into a bowl, then returned with some salt and a towel, and proceeded to clean him up.

"Ouch!" he cried, and grabbed her arm with some force.

"Let go; let me clean this."

As Katya dabbed the wound she noticed other, older scars on his head and around his face.

"Is there any coffee?" said Ibi.

"There's no hot water," replied Katya.

"The stove works; it uses bottled gas. I put in a new bottle yesterday. It should last a few days if we are careful," replied Ibi, his speech still slurred.

Katya returned to the kitchen, turned on one of the gas taps, and struck a match. The burner ignited in a strong, blue-coloured flame. She filled up the kettle and placed it over the heat.

She looked out of the kitchen window for the first time, and saw the open field that she had raced across to escape from the Serbs on her last visit to the cottage. Beyond that, the forest; she shivered again. Memories, terrifying memories, came flooding back.

She found a jar of coffee and some powdered milk in the larder. There were four mugs on the shelf, and she took two down and poured in the boiling water. Katya returned to the lounge. Ibi was still at the table, his head in his hands. Katya put one of the mugs in front of him. Melos was in his recliner being entertained by Arjeta.

Ibi picked up his mug, and Katya suddenly noticed his right hand.

"Your fingers, what have you done to your fingers?"

The nails were completely missing, and the digits were spread at strange angles.

"Oh that."

Ibi put down the mug and stared at his hand.

"The Serbs," he said falteringly. "They took out my fingernails one by one. They tried to get me to tell them where the headquarters were, what was our strength, when we would attack, but I told them nothing. Then they put my hand on a bench and hit my fingers with a hammer. I blacked out. It went on for three days. They did other things..."

Ibi paused for a moment and took another gulp of coffee.   H e continued.

"They put me in a cell for weeks on my own, just a bucket for company, very little food. Then I was moved to another prison with other KLA comrades, some I recognised, barely. They had suffered as I had. They were mostly Muslims, and they taught me to pray and that helped. I owe Allah a great deal."

Katya gasped in horror. Perhaps this would account for his behaviour, but not excuse it.

She spoke in a soft voice. "Go clean yourself up, Ibi; it will make you feel better."

Ibi looked at Katya, his eyes still not completely focused; he made no reply. He finished his coffee, then struggled from his chair and made his way unsteadily back upstairs. She heard him running water in the bathroom.

Making the most of his absence, Katya went into the kitchen and emptied the rest of the hot water from the kettle into the sink. She took off her tee shirt and jeans, and started washing herself using the soap that was beside the sink. Making sure Ibi was still upstairs she removed her bra and pants and finished her wash down. She would hope to have a shower later if the electricity was on.

She finished her bathing, dried off, and quickly dressed before returning to the lounge just as Ibi came down the stairs. He looked more presentable, but Katya still couldn't believe it was the same man she said goodbye to almost two years ago.

Ibi had joined the KLA in December 1997, and Melos had been conceived the night before he left. Katya had only received the occasional scribbled notes from him, and it was Qazim Kraniqi, Ibi's commander, who had trekked overland from a skirmish with Serb militia twenty miles away to tell him of Ibi's capture. He described how he had watched as Ibi was dragged out of a cottage he had been defending by many Serb soldiers, seemingly unconscious or, more likely, dead. This was in December 1998. Katya fled Kosovo the following March when it became too dangerous to stay, and made the dramatic escape which led to her eventual evacuation to England.

"We will need some supplies, and I really want to visit my mother today. Can we use the truck?"

Katya had written to her mother from England via the Refugee Council, and told her of the pending return to Kosovo. She had received no acknowledgement but assumed the message had got through. There were no phones.

"I will drive you after I've had something to eat," replied Ibi.

Katya wasn't sure if he was in any state to drive, but there was little traffic about, only KFOR patrols. Most of the locals were farmers and, with petrol limited, would be using horse and cart or the occasional tractor.

Katya found some eggs in the larder and made Ibi toast to go with it. She collected a few things together that she would need and placed them on the seat of the truck; the trailer was soaking wet from last night's deluge. The storm, however, had done nothing to ease the humidity.

Securing Arjeta in the front, Katya got in and sat next to her. Then Ibi handed Melos to her and Katya held him on her lap, trying to keep him occupied. Katya told Arjeta that they were going to see her mother.

"*Mami!*" Arjeta exclaimed.

"No, Arjeta, my '*Mami*'." Arjeta started crying.

Ibi locked the door of the cottage. He got in the truck and started up the rusting ancient Scania, then headed south, down the narrow road to Lapusnic.

Chapter Four

The ten-mile journey to Lapusnic took well over half an hour, the truck making heavy weather of the undulating roads which were mercifully quiet. Despite his obvious hangover, Ibi managed to get them to Maria Vitija's cottage without incident. There had been little conversation en route; Katya couldn't think of anything to say, and Ibi seemed to be in a mind of his own. As they pulled up in front of the house, Ibi took something from his pocket.

"Put this on," he demanded and handed Katya a scarf.

She tied back her blonde hair and pinned the scarf in place.

"You are not wearing make-up, that is good," continued Ibi.

It had not been a statement. Katya hadn't had time to put on make-up and would not normally wear it for a visit to her mother's.

"And tomorrow, no jeans, just skirt. You are in Kosovo now, not whoring in England."

The statement shocked Katya, but now was not the time to pursue it.

The storm clouds had disappeared, and cottage looked beautiful in the late summer sun. The white-washed exterior gleamed. Flowers everywhere, giant Hollyhocks stood guard over the small gate that led a crazy-paved pathway to the front door, and a neatly trimmed hedge surrounded the garden. It could have been a picture on a travel brochure advertising the joys of Kosovo, if only.

Maria had heard the sound of the truck and came running out. She was in her fifties, widowed now, but looked well; her hair also tied below a scarf. She still retained her posture and figure which had been inherited by her daughter.

Katya got out of the truck, and Maria ran up the path to greet her. She hugged Katya with a warm embrace. Unable to contain the joy of seeing her daughter again, tears flowed down her face. Ibi was holding Melos.

She looked at Melos, then spoke in Albanian. "My sweet thing, how you have grown."

She took him from Ibi and hugged him to her. Melos stared at his grandmother and smiled.

"And this must be Arjeta." She lifted her up and cuddled her.

Maria was overwhelmed with joy at having her family reunited again.

"Come in, come in, don't stand outside." She led them into the cottage carrying Melos, Arjeta pushing the empty buggy.

The cottage was older than Katya's, and still had a range in the living room where all the cooking was done. There were black beams running along the ceiling; hooks embedded in them where, as a child, Katya could remember her father hanging hams to mature. Despite the summer heat, the fire in the range was lit and giving off heat; there was a kettle and saucepan boiling water on top.

Katya looked around the room; it was just as she remembered it. A dining table was pushed against the wall with three chairs around it; a small bureau and sofa completed the furnishings.

It was late morning, and Katya felt good to be with her mother again, back in the house where she had been brought up.

"I didn't know if you would come today or not. I thought you might be tired from your journey," said Maria.

"I am, but I had to come to see you as soon as I could. I have missed you so much."

"You must tell me all about your time in England. I have made some cakes, and I will make you some dinner later,"

After a few minutes, Maria returned with some coffee and the home-made scones she had prepared. Katya helped herself and gave one to Arjeta. Melos was in his recliner and Arjeta started to feed him with small pieces.

She looked at Ibi. He had only eaten a small mouthful and had said nothing by way of greeting to Maria. There seemed to be an atmosphere between them.

He finished his coffee and stood up. "I have some business to do while I am here. I will be back by three o'clock to take you home."

Ibi turned and left the cottage without any 'farewells' or 'thanks'. Katya heard the truck start up and drive away.

"What was all that about?" asked Katya.

"I don't know... Ibi is a troubled soul. It was very difficult when he stayed here. He turned up out of the blue just after he was released from prison, in a terrible state. I told him he could stay and recover. He'd been back to your cottage and found you weren't there, so he came here looking for you. I told him you were in England, and I gave him your telephone number. He said that he'd called you, but after that, his behaviour changed, and got really bad. He was drunk almost every night. He would leave here after dinner and go into the village and visit the local bars. He would be vile and abusive when he returned, saying all kinds of things. Wanted to know why I hadn't fought the Serbs like he had done. He thought you would be 'whoring' in England. Kept using that word, horrible, horrible things. He was here three or four weeks but in the end, I couldn't stand anymore and told him to leave. He went back to your cottage. and I haven't seen him since till this morning. That was over a month ago."

"But that's terrible... I had no idea."

"There was nothing I could do to contact you and explain."

Katya looked down at the floor in thought.

"But I do have some better news," continued her mother, brightening her expression. "You remember Afrim, the farmer who took you back to the cottage that morning?"

"Yes, of course, nice man," replied Katya.

"Well..." she paused for the right words. "He is now living here." Her expression was one of joy.

Katya thought for the right words. "What, as man and wife, you mean?"

"Yes, that is probably as you would say it," replied Maria, rather hesitantly, not knowing what her daughter's reaction would be.

"But that is wonderful news. I am so pleased for you. It is not right that you live here on your own. Where is he?"

"He has gone to his farm to get some things. We knew you would be coming today or tomorrow, and I told him you and Ibi would need fresh supplies. He will be back shortly."

"Oh, I am so pleased for you.' Katya got up and gave her mother another hug.

"Now come on you must tell me all about your news. You look so different... and so well."

"Thank you, I am well." Her expression disguised her true feelings.

They talked for a long time, Katya telling her mother all about her time in England, her flat, her shopping excursions, Carole, her teaching job, and of course, Edi. She hadn't mentioned Polly.

"She looks a dear little thing," said Maria looking at Arjeta. "I can see why you want to keep her."

Katya had bought a colouring book and some crayons, and Arjeta was now seated at the table drawing.

"She loves drawing, spends hours colouring," said Katya.

After an hour of catch-up, they could hear the sound of a tractor pulling up outside. Katya recognised it straightaway and more painful memories flashed through her mind.

"That will be Afrim," said Maria, and went to open the door.

Afrim appeared with an array of produce - potatoes, beans, spinach, parsnips, eggs, even some bread and fresh milk.

"Hello, Katya," said the man, as he entered the cottage carrying the produce in a large cardboard box. He handed it to Maria who put it in the corner by the front door.

"Hello, Afrim." Katya went to the man and hugged him.

"I am so happy to hear your news. I told *mami* that she needed a good man to look after her."

Afrim smiled. "Thank you, Katya, but I think I owe you an apology."

"An apology? Whatever for?"

"That day when I took you back to your cottage on the tractor, I should have had more courage and taken you to your door and seen you were safe, instead of making you walk the last miles. It has worried me since."

Katya thought back at the problems that might have solved, but it was too late to change things now.

"That's ok, we managed."

They sat down and the questions continued.

"How did you get to England?" asked Afrim.

He and Maria listened as Katya described her rescue by the NATO patrol and her journey to Macedonia. She left out the 'incident' in the forest.

Katya wanted to know more about Afrim. She had met him before when she stayed at her mother's cottage for the few weeks just after she had learned of Ibi's capture, but at that time, he was only an occasional visitor.

"I still have the farm; it's not far, my son manages it now," said Afrim.

"How many children do you have?" enquired Katya.

"Just my son; he was too young to fight and luckily the Serbs did not trouble us."

"And Mami tells me you lost your wife."

"Yes, over ten years ago… cancer." He looked down for a moment.

"I'm sorry," said Katya.

"Thank you, it is long ago now. Your mother and I, we became close over the last few months, and she asked me to move in." Maria held his hand and squeezed it affectionately.

He looked at her. "I am very fond of your mother; I want to look after her."

"And I thought I was looking after you," interrupted Maria and started laughing,

"Yes that's true," said Afrim.

The body language was obvious.

"Well, I am so happy for you," replied Katya, holding her mother's hand.

The time flew by, catching up on all the gossip. Maria had made them lunch and the three of them sat down as a family and ate together for the first time in a long while. The children were spoiled by Maria with treats and, importantly, attention, and Arjeta particularly seemed very happy to be in surroundings that were more familiar to her. Melos kept trying to crawl across the floor a further indication he was growing up.

Just after three o'clock, the sound of Ibi's Scania reverberated outside, almost shaking the cottage. He didn't come in, just stayed in the truck with the engine running. The family left the cottage and walked up the path to the waiting truck. Afrim helped load the provisions on the back. Katya got in and Maria passed her the children, Arjeta, next to Katya with Melos on her lap. His buggy was on the floor. There were no seat belts.

Ibi pressed the accelerator, expelling a cloud of fumes from the exhaust, and the truck pulled away. Straightaway, Katya detected a strong smell of drink in the cab. The lorry began swerving across the road from one side to the other.

"Ibi you have been drinking," said Katya. Ibi turned to her, his eyes glazed in a stupor. "You fool, you will kill us all. Stop the truck, I will get Afrim to drive us back."

"Don't bother, I don't want you to come back… whore, bitch."

He slammed the brakes, almost sending them into the windscreen. Melos started to cry.

They had only gone a hundred yards or so. Katya opened the door and lifted out Arjeta, then leaned in and got Melos and his buggy. She slammed the door of the truck. Ibi drove off at full throttle, throwing up clouds of dust as the back wheels hit the grass verge.

The small group headed back to Maria's cottage, with Arjeta again pushing the buggy. Melos was still crying.

After a few minutes, they were back on the front doorstep of the cottage and Katya knocked.

Maria looked in surprise. "What are you doing back? What's happened?"

Katya explained the events.

"You can stay here; we have the room. That man is dangerous, whatever anyone says. I don't trust him; his head has been turned. He is a monster."

Maria got them all settled, and Afrim made some coffee.

"I will have to go back soon. All my clothes and the children's things are there," said Katya.

"Don't worry, Afrim will drive you back tomorrow and you can collect what you need. He will make sure you are safe, won't you dear?" Maria looked at Afrim.

"Of course," Afrim replied.

"Thank you, that is very kind," said Katya.

"It's the least we can do, I am just sorry that your homecoming wasn't more welcoming."

Katya looked down; she felt a deep sadness, and just wished she were back with Polly.

The next day Katya woke up in her old bed, the one she slept in as a child. It had a familiarity about it, the same smells and feel. She had slept better that night, despite all the traumas since they had returned. They had made a makeshift bedding for Melos, a mattress on the floor surrounded by cardboard boxes. Arjeta had got in with Katya, which was not ideal, but they managed. Her mother and Afrim were in the main bedroom. It seemed strange to Katya, but she was pleased her mother had found someone to make her happy.

She washed Melos and Arjeta and made her way downstairs. She sniffed the air as she got to the living room.

"What's that smell? It's wonderful."

Maria had made them all a cooked breakfast with bacon, eggs, bread and tomatoes, a relative feast. With the restrictions on the electricity supply, it was necessary to cook using the range on a regular basis, despite having a modern cooker.

The cottage renovations included a shower, and Katya had been able to make use of the facilities during the on-time when the electricity was available. Yesterday, it was six p.m. until nine p.m.

"When would you like to go to your house?" asked Afrim after they had finished breakfast.

"Whenever you are ready."

"The tractor's outside, but I'll go back to the farm and collect the car. It will be more comfortable," replied Afrim.

He was gone about half an hour when there was the sound of a vehicle pulling up outside the cottage, a five-year-old Toyota Corolla.

Maria offered to look after the children.

So, with Afrim driving, they made their way back to Lapugovac. Katya had dispensed with her scarf and that <u>was</u> a statement.

The journey took about twenty minutes, the Toyota eating up the miles comfortably. They arrived at the cottage, but it looked deserted. There was no truck outside. Katya found her keys and let herself in, Afrim following close behind with a cardboard box.

Katya went through the downstairs and collected Melos' toys and things, including his lobster pot, then went upstairs. She gasped in horror as she saw her suitcase upside down on the bed with all her clothes scattered across the bedroom, torn to shreds. Afrim appeared at the door.

"My God, why has he done this?" he said, looking at the remnants of Katya's clothes.

She went to the bathroom and all her makeup had been poured

down the toilet. Empty bottles were scattered across the floor. The words, '*putanë*!' (bitch), '*whore*,' were scrawled on the mirror in red lipstick. Katya started sobbing.

Afrim saw the message and put a consoling arm around her

"Come on Katya, let's get you home; you don't deserve this."

He looked at the devastation. "*Bastard!*" he muttered under his breath.

There was not much to put in the box, but a couple of pairs of shoes were salvaged, and some underwear Ibi had not found that Katya had put at the back of the drawer in the bedside table. Afrim dismantled Melos' cot and carried the pieces to the car, then manoeuvred them behind the front seats.

After a final check, they returned to the Toyota. Katya locked up and put the box of belongings in the boot.

"I wonder where he is," said Katya.

"You are well off without that one," said Afrim.

Katya was glad to be away from the cottage; the memories were too raw.

They arrived back at Maria's cottage, and Afrim told her what had happened.

"I can't believe it. Why would he do that?" asked Maria.

"Exactly what I said," replied Afrim.

Maria disappeared into the kitchen and came back a few minutes later with coffees for them. Melos was asleep and Arjeta was drawing at the table, quite contentedly.

"I will need to go into Pristina, to get some new things and get some money," said Katya, having recovered her composure. "Is there a bus at all?"

Maria looked at Katya incredulously.

"Buses...!? There're no buses I'm afraid."

"No, they can't get the fuel," said Afrim. "But I have a better idea... I need to get back to the farm, it's a busy time for us with the harvest, but you used to drive didn't you?"

"Yes," replied Katya. "But not for a long time. Ibi showed me."

"That's ok, then you can borrow mine. I shan't need it for a while with all the work on. There's a petrol station on the main Pristina Road which has fuel. You can fill it up there."

"What about insurance?" asked Katya.

"I wouldn't worry about that; they don't bother. Nobody will pay up anyway with what's going on. They will just say that any damage is due to an act of war," replied Afrim.

"Well, if you don't mind, thank you."

"I'll need you to take me back to the farm; I can use the tractor when I've finished," said Afrim. "I can show you the car controls on the way."

"And I will look after the children," said Maria. "I will enjoy spending some time with my grandson and my new granddaughter."

Just after lunch, Katya got in the driver's seat of the Toyota and started the engine; it sprang into life immediately. She worked out the gear shift and, with Afrim supervising, nervously pulled away.

After dropping off Afrim, it took over an hour to get to the capital. The journey was a real eye-opener for Katya. She could see first-hand the damage that the war had inflicted on her country. The road surface was pitted with holes from regular use by military vehicles which slowed down the Toyota to a walking pace at times. There was very little 'normal' traffic, just the odd tractor and horse and cart. The villages she passed showed all the evidence of the ravages of war. Devastated and burned-out shells of buildings were everywhere. Ruined houses, ruined lives, Katya sighed in desperation at the destruction and the work that lay ahead in rebuilding any sort of society.

Pristina too had changed since Katya had last visited. The landscape resembled a war zone, although most of the buildings were intact. Pristina had suffered one bombing incident towards the end of the war when an American air-raid targeted the Post Office, the Telephone system, and the Serb Military headquarters. There were civilian casualties.

Jeeps and trucks were everywhere, mostly KFOR, but some still bearing the NATO logo. She suddenly had a flash back to the NATO lorry that had come to her rescue when her life was hanging by a thread. She headed to the commercial district and found a parking spot next to a deserted shop. The area was like a wasteland, dereliction everywhere. Katya locked the car and headed into the centre. Many buildings bore the scars of conflict.

There were more people about as she reached the city centre and she looked around for her first port of call, a bank. She had the two hundred and fifty pounds which she would need to change into Deutschmarks, still the main currency in Kosovo. Most places would accept dollars but at a poor exchange rate. She went inside the first bank she came to. It was busy and she had to wait for over fifteen minutes before she reached the front of the queue. She placed the sterling notes on the counter and the teller checked it twice, then rattled off the latest exchange rate and their commission. She counted out the equivalent Deutschemarks which would keep Katya going for a while. She would need more money soon though.

Outside the bank, she turned left and started to head towards the local market. She needed to buy some clothes to replace the ones Ibi had destroyed. As she walked, she noticed something else was different. Being a predominantly Muslim country, before the war, Western-style clothing was not very common. The traditional attire was headscarves and long dresses or skirts reflecting the Albanian influence. Now, it seemed, many women were dressed in casual clothes. Most of these would probably be foreigners working for the various aid agencies. Some older men were wearing the Qeleshe, the traditional white hat, but otherwise, it was predominantly jeans and tee shirts. It was an interesting observation and made Katya more determined not to fall back into the 'old' ways. Things were different now; she was different now.

She turned a corner and came to a big square which was full of parked military trucks. She took in the scene; it was not how she remembered it, and then she noticed a queue of people waiting outside one of the buildings. Out of curiosity, she walked in that direction. As she got closer, she could see it was the local headquarters of the Refugee Council. There was a sign in English and Albanian. This was where Ibi had made his phone calls. She bypassed the queue and went inside; she had no idea why, just curiosity.

It was mayhem. Lines and lines of people queuing at a row of desks manned by assistants, all dispensing advice, listening to stories of hardship and giving solace to the occasional grieving relative. She looked at the sorry sight. The men seemed to have the same pallid complexion and gaunt features that Ibi had. There was so much grief and suffering, people shouting and crying, looks of despair. Katya found it hard to take in.

Suddenly she heard a voice call out behind her. It made her jump.

"Katya...? Katya Gjikolli...is that you?" An English voice.

Katya turned around and saw a familiar face. He was wearing military fatigues.

"Captain Drury?!" said Katya, recognising her former boss from the refugee camp in Macedonia.

"I don't believe it. What are you doing here?" asked the captain in his familiar military English. "I almost didn't recognise you. You look so different from the camp, amazing."

"*Faleminderit*... Er... thank you," replied Katya, retuning her language to English. "I have returned to Kosovo some days ago... I am here in Pristina to change some money."

"It is so good to see you... Look, have you got a minute?"

"Yes of course," replied Katya, still trying to take in her reacquaintance

She followed him along a corridor and into one of the offices.

The desk was strewn with paper, maps, pens, files, folders and there was even evidence of half-eaten sandwiches. The shelves and cabinets were littered with paperwork of every description. Katya remembered the captain's office at the camp; nothing had changed.

"I can't believe you are here; I think you must have been sent from heaven! Are you looking for a job?"

"Well... y y yes," stammered Katya.

"That's good... I don't mind telling you, you were the best assistant I ever had. Things were not the same after you left. Look, I desperately need someone to co-ordinate things. I'm in danger of sinking beneath this mound of paper, not to mention the bureaucracy." He scanned the office. "As you can see... When can you start?"

The captain seemed to have aged in the intervening months, Katya noticed. Although only in his early forties, his hair was showing flecks of grey at the sides. He still had the energy that she remembered, and he paced about, speaking quickly, as if trying to capture as much time as he could. He was showing the signs of a stressed man. Katya was trying to keep up.

She thought quickly. "Well, anytime... Tomorrow if you like... Although I will have to sort out a few things. My mother is looking after the children... I am staying with her."

"Excellent, excellent," said the captain, not really taking in the answer. He paused for a second as if recollecting his thoughts before continuing his barrage. "I still can't believe you're here." There was a sense the relief in his voice. "And you can start tomorrow...? That's superb... You have no idea... Look, I'll need to sort out the admin... No, on second thoughts, you can do that, tomorrow."

He began to laugh. Katya remembered his manner and capacity for work from the camp. There was no doubt that without his energy and infectious enthusiasm for getting things done, it could have been a complete disaster. She, on the other hand, was a steadying influence and kept him grounded when it looked like they would be overwhelmed. They had made a good team, and Katya would always be grateful to him for his support, particularly arranging her evacuation.

She smiled and felt a tinge of excitement at the prospect of the work ahead, a chance to be useful again.

Captain Drury changed tack as if martialling his thoughts. "Now then, ah yes, listen, I'll need to keep in touch with you; there are always flaps on."

Katya could not translate. The captain's eye contact was lost as he rummaged through a couple of drawers. "Where are they? Where are they?" he muttered under his breath.

"'Flaps?' What is 'flaps'?" asked Katya, totally confused.

He looked at her for a moment, not really concentrating on her response, and then refocused and looked at her. "Oh… yes, sorry, er, panic stations, that sort of thing."

Katya made the translation.

"Now, where have they gone?"

He was still rummaging, and then suddenly found what he was looking for in the bowels of the cabinet.

"Ah, here they are."

He picked up a box of brand-new mobile phones which were still uncommon in Kosovo. A network had only recently been established, but limited to Pristina and the surrounding towns. He handed one to Katya.

"You will need one of these. I'll get Andy to set it up for you."

"Who's Andy?" asked Katya.

"Andy Fleming... comms."

"What is comms?"

"Sorry, communications. Don't worry it'll be fine. I can't believe my luck, you turning up. You are the answer to my prayers," said the captain, smiling broadly.

"Can you get here by ten hundred hours tomorrow?"

"Ten o'clock… tomorrow morning?"

"Yes, sorry… Or earlier," added the captain.

"I will try," said Katya. "What about money?"

"Yes, of course, we will pay you... I'll let you have details tomorrow. Look, I'm sorry, I'm really in a hurry; here's my number… Er, ring me if you have any problems." The captain handed her a slip of paper with a number written on it.

"Follow me. I'll take you to see Andy."

The captain got up and strode down a corridor to another office which had the word 'COMMUNICATIONS' stencilled on it. Katya had trouble keeping pace. He opened the door and a geeky-looking lad in his twenties was sat behind a desk deeply engrossed in the back end of a computer in bits on the worktop.

Andy looked up from his work. He seemed annoyed at being disturbed, but brightened up when he spotted Katya.

"Ah, Andy, this is Katya. She's going to be working with us, can you sort this out for her?"

The captain gave him the phone, then looked at Katya. "Right, I must go. See you tomorrow, thank you, thank you."

He turned and disappeared back down the corridor.

Andy carefully put down his soldering iron and started unpacking the phone. Katya had his undivided attention. He spoke in English and started going through the various settings, then put in a new SIM card. Katya was trying to keep up. He completed his instruction and handed Katya the phone.

"There won't be much of a signal once you get out of Pristina, but it will be useful around town. Unfortunately, you won't be able to use it internationally just yet; we don't have the network, but there is unlimited credit, so you won't have to worry about topping up… This is your number." He wrote it down on a piece of paper and handed it to Katya; she was trying to translate everything. "This is the box; it's got the charger and instructions inside. Any problems, just give me a shout."

It was like being hit by a whirlwind. Her mind was all over the place.

"Thank you very much. It will be fine, I am sure," said Katya.

She was familiar with working a mobile phone from her time in England. Polly had even tought her to text. She suddenly thought of him again as she looked at the phone and wondered what he would be doing. She quickly shook off her retrospection and walked back down the corridor, passed the queues; they seemed relentless.

She left the building, hardly able to take in the last few minutes. It was only by chance that she had decided to go inside the Refugee Council building. On such events, the fates of lives lie.

Before she headed for the car, she needed a clothes shop. She didn't have a lot to spend; her money from the grant would have to last her until she received her pay from her new job. She managed to find a shop off the main square, not what she was used to at the Metro Centre, but she was able to purchase a new skirt, probably shorter than Ibi would like, and a couple of tops. She had her jeans which she would wear when not at work. She would never wear a scarf again she vowed.

She found the car and made her way back to Lapusnic. Just as she was approaching the village, she noticed the garage that Afrim had mentioned, and stopped for petrol. It was a very basic affair with a small service bay and just one single pump. The proprietor approached her as she vacated the car and proceeded to fill the tank.

She paid with the Deutschmarks she had changed from the bank; she couldn't belie the price.

"Due to the shortages," said the proprietor when she queried the cost.

A few minutes later, she arrived back at her mother's cottage, her mind still buzzing from the recent course of events; she couldn't wait to tell them her news. She was greeted by Maria, as she walked through the door; Afrim was still at the farm. She outlined what had happened.

"This is a big commitment… But I will be helping refugees returning from all over the world. It is absolute chaos in there; you should see it." Katya was unable to contain her excitement.

Maria hugged her daughter.

"That is really good news. It will give you some independence, and the money will be useful. I will look after the children of course."

"Thank you, I didn't think you would mind. I will be able to pay you once I get my money sorted out."

"Don't be silly, these are my grandchildren; I don't want any money. It will give me a chance to be with them. We have a lot of time to catch up."

Just then, the familiar sound of the Lanz Bulldog tractor was heard outside. It juddered to a halt. Afrim had arrived with more produce. The earlier batch was still on the back of Ibi's truck.

Katya regaled her news again to Afrim.

"Well, why don't you keep the car for the time being. Like I said, I won't be needing it for a while, not with the harvest going on."

In her excitement, she had not considered transportation and was grateful for the gesture.

"Thank you… That is so good of you."

Chapter Five

Millennium Eve, Katya continued staring in the embers, now just a glow in the grate, and the temperature in the cottage was dropping. She pulled the shawl around her shoulders tighter, partly to retain warmth, partly as comfort. She wondered what the new year would bring her. She continued her reflections.

During the autumn months, she worked at the Refugee Council Offices for Captain Drury, Bruce, as she was allowed to call him. Most days it was chaotic, but she had retained her talent for organisation and to get things done. The captain worked her hard, which she relished. Katya quickly gained an excellent reputation and was widely respected at the Refugee Council. Her language skills were particularly in demand as she was frequently required to call the UK, Australia, or the US with refugees' queries.

Afrim continued to let her borrow the car, and life at her mother's cottage settled into a pattern that suited everyone. Maria was thrilled to have her family around her and put on a wonderful party in September to celebrate Melos' first birthday. Even Arjeta was beginning to feel at home. Maria would frequently take the children for walks or Afrim would take them to the farm on his tractor.

Financially, Captain Drury was as good as his word. Katya's salary was almost double what she was earning as a teacher at the school in Lapugovac. She gave her mother a proportion each month for keep, despite her protests. Unbeknown to Katya, Maria had opened a bank account for the children and was paying Katya's rent into it.

In the country, security continued to be a major issue; it was still a dangerous place. Politically, there was a great deal of confusion.

There was a regime of sorts, the main authority being held under a transitional UN administration and a NATO-led peacekeeping force, the KFOR. However, there were many reports of reprisals by renegade gangs of former KLA fighters against the Serbian minority who had remained, mostly in the north of Kosovo close to the Serbian border. The authorities could do little about it due to lack of manpower and resources.

Katya reflected on some of the harrowing stories she had heard during her work; one man stood out. She was at one of the desks when he approached her from the queue. He resembled a ghost and reminded Katya of the newsreel pictures of Auschwitz survivors. He'd come to enquire if there had been any news of his son who had been taken prisoner in April by Serbian police; he had heard nothing since. It was a common enquiry.

Then he told Katya his own story. He had been on a lorry fleeing the town of Podujevo in northern Kosovo near to the Serbian border. A police squad stopped the column and separated all the men and ushered them into a large barn. They were then ordered onto two buses through a gauntlet of Serbian police who beat them with wooden clubs. The men were taken to basement cells in the main police station in Pristina, forced to give up all their money, wedding rings, watches, belts, and any other valuables, beaten again and questioned. The rooms where they were interrogated and beaten had blood on the walls, he said, as guards held men by the neck and forced their heads into the concrete. One day, a Serbian guard came into the cell and put his pistol into a prisoner's mouth and pulled the trigger, but no bullet was in the chamber. At this point, the man said, many of the men in the cells were begging to be shot.

This was a familiar tale, but no more palatable to be heard. Katya just hoped that the guilty people would be eventually held to account at this barbaric treatment.

There was another occasion when Katya was handing out small boxes donated by relief agencies to a group of about fifty men who had arrived in Pristina two days earlier after a month in a Serb prison. One tall, painfully skinny man, probably in his early thirties, kept going through the same motions over and over again, opening up the box which contained a children's notebook, a pen, a fresh set of grey trousers, a pair of socks, a belt, and a striped polo shirt, all still in their plastic wrappings. After touching the items, he closed the box, got up and walked around, agitated. After a few minutes, he opened the box again and repeated each step. This happened several times and Katya and a couple of other volunteers who were helping were devastated to see the pitiful sight.

Katya's main activity was trying to help reunite families and supporting the team in Pristina coordinating activities on the ground, fielding numerous questions, and providing help with travel arrangements. She loved the work and felt she was making a real difference.

One day in October, Katya had another surprise. She had taken her lunch break as normal in a local cafe and was reading some papers on a table by the window. As she drunk her coffee a voice called out from another table.

"Katya...? Is that you?' An English voice.

Katya turned to acknowledge the enquiry and recognised the person immediately.

"Anna?"

It was the Norwegian Special Forces doctor who had treated her at the reception centre at Pec, where Katya had been taken after she had been rescued by the NATO patrol.

"What are you doing here...? I don't believe it," said Katya, and she went over to join her.

Doctor Henricksson got up and greeted Katya with a warm embrace.

"Katya, it is so good to see you again. I wasn't sure if it was you; you look so different. You were in a bad way when I first met you."

"That seems a long time ago now," replied Katya.

"But what are you doing in Pristina?"

For half an hour, there was a non-stop catch-up. Katya described her experiences, her evacuation to the UK and eventual repatriation. She told Anna about her new job and her work with the refugees. Anna recounted her adventures accompanying the NATO forces around Kosovo and her eventual posting to Pristina. She was now engaged with supporting the relief effort, treating returning former prisoners of war. Too soon, Katya had to get back but there would be many subsequent meetings and a growing friendship.

As Katya continued her reminiscences, she smiled and wondered what Anna was doing on Millennium eve.

At the end of November, two events happened that were to take Katya's life in yet another direction.

It was a Wednesday and Katya had been called into Captain Drury's office. He was at his desk reading a memo, surrounded by mountains of paper. He looked up from his reading.

"How would you like to go back to England?"

Katya was momentarily speechless, unable to process the question.

"What... England? What do you mean...? To do what?"

"Well, looks like they've hit something of a snag over there... Seems many refugees don't want to return to Kosovo."

"It is no surprise; I can understand," she commented.

"Yes... as you know, they've been told they don't have to go back if they feel unsafe or unhappy, so of course, they're not signing up to the repatriation programme... not in the numbers the U.K. government was hoping for, anyway. So, they're trying a different approach." He looked at the memo again. "I have the details here. It's called, 'Explore and Prepare'."

Katya listened attentively.

"It's a new programme, and I quote... 'which will allow heads of families to return to Kosovo and assess living conditions while the rest of the family remain in Britain'."

He put the note down and looked at Katya.

"Do you remember Jenny Wheatley in Newcastle, the Refugee Council Coordinator?"

"Yes, of course," replied Katya. "We got on very well."

"Yes, I've spoken to her; she said that... Well, there's a major reorganisation going on in the UK, and she's taking up the position of national coordinator in London, that leaves a vacancy for her old job in Newcastle. I've recommended you."

Katya looked at him in disbelief.

"I didn't want to say anything until I'd got confirmation from H.Q."

Before Katya could respond, he continued. "You'll be responsible for liaising with refugees in the North of England, managing the repatriation programme or helping with the asylum process, depending on their circumstances. You'll be reporting directly to Miss Wheatley in London. Your language skills will be invaluable; there're still a lot of frightened people there. I'll see to all your necessary visas and documentation. We will of course cover all travel costs and give you a rent allowance towards accommodation, as well as your normal pay... Any questions?"

He spoke quickly, as he was inclined to do, and Katya had to really concentrate to make the translation. She was lost for words.

"When would I start?"

"Not until the New Year... mid-January, probably."

"And how long will it be for?"

"Initially, it will be for six months, but it could be longer. I'll get you a one-year visa just in case."

"What about the children?"

"I wouldn't think that will be an issue; I'm sure the centre will be able to make arrangements for you. They're desperate to have someone with your experience on board."

"I will need to speak to my family, but, yes, I would love to," said Katya. She was now visibly shaking.

That evening, driving back to the cottage, she couldn't wait to tell her mother her news.

Maria of course couldn't share Katya's joy; it would mean losing her daughter and grandchildren again, but didn't let it show, and congratulated Katya on her good fortune.

"When would you have to go?" asked Maria.

"In January probably, so we do have some time to spend together."

"Where will you live?" asked Maria.

"I don't know, somewhere in Newcastle I expect," said Katya. "That's where I will be based."

Afrim was sat on the settee, listening to the conversation. He stood up and went to Katya.

"I am pleased for you. I think it is something you need to do. It is obvious you want to return to England by the way you talk about your time there... and don't worry about your mother; I will take very good care of her."

Katya felt less apprehensive about leaving her mother now she had Afrim. At least, this time, she wouldn't be leaving her on her own.

They had their evening meal continuing to discuss Katya's pending departure.

Katya wondered about Ibi. They'd had no contact with him since he left in the drunken stupor in August, much to everyone's relief, and to some surprise. Katya wanted nothing more to do with him. Any sympathy she may have had, disappeared that night.

At around nine, Katya had settled the children down and was chatting to Afrim while her mother made a drink, when there was a familiar sound outside; the hissing of airbrakes, the grinding of heavy tyres on gravel and the awful sound of the V8 diesel engine.

It went quiet as it was turned off.

Afrim and Maria looked at each other. Katya stared at the two of them anxiously.

"Ibi?" said Katya.

There was a heavy knock on the door, impatient, demanding.

"Come out Katya, I know you are in there. I want to talk to you."

There was further frantic knocking.

"Come out bitch, whore."

Katya got up.

"No, I'll go," said Afrim, and he got up and opened the door.

Ibi charged in, knocking Afrim to the floor.

"There you are, bitch, whore, you're coming home with me," slurred Ibi, trying to stand upright.

Then Katya noticed a gun in his hand and gasped in horror. She thought quickly.

"It's alright Ibi, I will come with you. You don't need a gun. I am pleased you have called. I was telling mami I needed to see you, to see if you were ok. Where have you been? We have been concerned about you."

"What do you care? How many men are you sleeping with at the Refugee Centre? I know you work there; I have seen you in your short skirt. How much do they pay you? *Prostitutë*," shouted Ibi.

"I work there, Ibi, trying to help people like us, trying to help put lives back together again, making a difference."

She was keeping calm trying to engage him. Afrim was groaning trying to get up from the floor. Ibi kicked him in the ribs, and he fell back down.

"No, Ibi, leave him alone. I will come with you. It will be ok, don't worry. Think about Melos. He misses his daddy."

"He's not mine; he looks nothing like me," retorted Ibi, holding onto the door frame to keep his balance.

"Yes, he is, Ibi, there's no-one else; it's all in your head. The Serbs did this to you, can't you see?"

Ibi went quiet, contemplating the last statement.

"It's alright, Ibi; I will come with you. There is no need to get angry, or hurt anyone, let's go now you can tell me about it in the truck. I will just get my coat; it's in the kitchen."

Katya went to the kitchen and snatched her coat from behind the door. Ibi was just stood with his gun, waving it around in his hand. His speech was becoming more incoherent.

"You, get in the lorry," Ibi ordered.

Katya put on her coat and opened to the door. Ibi grabbed her wrist tightly. She was starting to panic, worried that he might do.

"Come on Ibi, let's go home, please," said Katya, speaking slowly in a very passive voice.

Ibi started to respond. Katya recognised she needed to remain calm and complicit. It was clear Ibi needed psychological help, but for the moment they were all in danger. Any resistance could lead to all manner of irrational behaviour, and with Ibi holding a loaded gun, she couldn't take any chances.

Ibi snarled as he slammed the cottage door shut behind them, and dragged Katya by the wrist up the garden path to the waiting lorry. Katya got in the passenger side of the cab followed by Ibi in the driver's seat. He started the engine. The V8 roared into life, echoing around the front of the cottage.

"You won't be sorry Ibi; I will be good for you," said Katya, trying to get him to focus on the drive. She was shaking, petrified at what he might do.

The engine growled, responding to the pressure on the accelerator, and Ibi released the huge handbrake lever, depressed the clutch, and headed down the road in the direction of Lapugovac. He gradually picked up speed, and Katya talked to him, reassuringly.

"Why haven't you been round to see me, Ibi…? I have missed you… We have all been worried."

"What do you care, bitch, whore, *prostitutë*?"

"I just want to understand, tell me what I can do to make it better."

"You can't do anything; the Serbs took <u>that</u> away."

"What do you mean?"

Ibi continued, "The Serbs didn't just mess with my hands, you know." He paused. "Oh no, that's not all they did, not by half. Do you know what they did, do you? Do you really want to know?"

Ibi was becoming agitated again.

"It's alright Ibi, just tell me if you want to, everything will be alright." Katya spoke softly in controlled tones.

Ibi started sobbing, his driving becoming more erratic.

"They poured boiling water over me when I wouldn't tell them what they wanted, first my back then... my... '*gjenitale*'. It's not a pretty sight down there."

Katya gasped at this.

"But why didn't you say something; we can sort it out. I can get you some help, proper help."

"Help! No-one can help; what can they do, eh? I thought I could handle it; I thought it would be ok, but when I saw you at the airport, I knew. I knew something was different."

"Ibi it's me, Katya, your wife, I thought you were dead. I would never have betrayed you; you know that."

Too late, she realised what she had said.

He thought for a moment taking in this information, processing the words, assessing the nuances.

"So, you have been with someone. You bitch... WHORE!"

Katya unwittingly had stirred up a hornet's nest as Ibi's anger rose again.

"No, Ibi, no." Katya tried to undo the damage, but it was too late.

Ibi turned and looked her, his eyes filled with hate. His driving was out of control. He was careering all over the road, driving much too fast. He still had his gun in his hand.

Katya was on full alert, her reflexes sharp; then a thought hit her. There was a steep uphill gradient about halfway to the cottage which would slow the truck, but there was an even steeper slope down the other side. There was a sharp left-hand bend at the bottom of the incline where the road crossed a river. In his present state, Ibi could never control the vehicle, and, with the weight of the lorry, it could be travelling around sixty or seventy miles-an-hour by the time they reached the corner. She would have to get out before then. Her right hand felt the door handle; she didn't think it was locked.

Ibi was talking to himself, cursing incoherently. Katya was trying to stay calm.

A few minutes later, they were starting the ascent and the lorry's speed reduced sharply as it struggled against the incline. Ibi crunched down the gears.

"Bitch, whore, bitch, whore," he kept repeating, over and over again; his eyes wide, but not focussing.

As they approached the summit, the truck was travelling at no more than a brisk walking pace, Katya could see the verge on her side had disappeared, as another road merged from the right. The Scania made a ninety-degree left turn and started to descend the steep gradient.

Now!

Katya released the catch, and the door flung wide open by the force of the turn. Katya jumped out and rolled away. The door slammed back shut as gravity propelled it in the opposite direction. Ibi, distracted by her exit, was thrown to the floor of the cab by the momentum of the turn. He was disorientated and confused; his foot unable to control the pedals. As he tried to right himself, hampered by his drunken state, the truck was veering first one way then another, hitting the verge on each side. Like a stampeding animal, the speed increased, forty, fifty, sixty, sixty-five. Ibi struggled to regain control. At the bottom of the incline, it reached the turn to cross the river, but the Scania was driving itself and made no allowance.

It smashed into the parapet and exploded into flames.

Katya got up off the ground, none the worse for her tumble, just a few grazes, and could only watch in horror at the conflagration at the bottom of the hill, some two-hundred metres away, as the burning truck lit up the skyline.

She heard a car approaching behind her. The head lights flashed; it was Afrim. He wound down the window and shouted.

"Are you alright, Katya? Are you alright?"

Katya ran to the car. "Yes, Afrim, I am ok,"

"What about you?"

"Yes, yes, I'm fine. Quick, jump in and we will see if we can do anything."

They reached the truck which was now well alight, and Katya could only watch with sadness as the flames shot skywards. There was a shape of a man in the driver's seat but not moving, being consumed by flames. There was nothing they could do. Katya turned away sobbing.

Katya controlled herself and reached for her mobile phone, but there was no signal. A few minutes later, a KFOR patrol arrived at the scene to investigate. It had been in the vicinity and had seen the fire. They called the emergency services from a walkie-talkie, but it was an hour before a fire-crew eventually arrived. The truck had already burnt itself out.

The lieutenant in charge of the patrol wanted to know what had happened. Katya told them that the truck belonged to her husband, and they were following him home in case it broke down. Her husband was worried about the brakes, she said. This was the story she and Afrim had agreed while they waited for help to arrive.

Katya managed to speak to Captain Drury from the patrol jeep and told him of the accident. Despite the heavy workloads, he told Katya to take a few days off to take care of all the arrangements.

There was no formal inquest into Ibi's demise; cause of death was confirmed as 'accident', but the truth was, Ibi had been another casualty of the war.

Ibi had no family, his parents had both died while he was at university, and his elder brother had been killed in the fighting. The funeral was therefore very low key, just the family, and Captain Drury which Katya had appreciated. Katya's mother looked after the children in the church and, apart from the odd baby-noise, they were well-behaved.

Katya felt sadness of course, but not a deep sorrow as one would normally expect when losing a loved one. Ibi was not the same person she had left two years earlier. That's the Ibi she wanted to remember, and she had already grieved for him.

Katya introduced the Captain to Maria and Afrim, and he made a fuss of the children,

He bent down to speak to Arjeta. "I don't know what I am going to do when your mummy leaves me." Katya translated for Maria and Afrim, and they smiled.

"The same goes for us," said Maria, and Katya translated for the captain.

Following the funeral, the family descended on the cottage in Lapugovac and proceeded to clean it up. Afrim's son had also volunteered to help. It was quiet on the farm, just preparation for the winter snows, which would come at any time.

Maria was shocked when she saw the state of the cottage. Katya had always kept it tidy, but Ibi had violated the place. The house was damp and dirty, the walls had been daubed in graffiti as if squatters had lived there. Only now were they really beginning to understand the extent of Ibi's mental state. They would never know what had happened to him during the time he had gone missing. It took a few days but gradually, with a concerted effort, the place became habitable again.

Later, Katya, Maria, Afrim, and the children were back at Maria's cottage, seated in the living room enjoying a relaxing cup of tea. Maria had a question. "What do you intend to do about the house?"

Katya and Ibi had bought the cottage from Ibi's inheritance after his father had died and it would belong to her once the paperwork had been completed.

She took a sip of her drink. "I don't know. I will try to sell it, or perhaps I might just rent it out while I'm away; there are always people looking for places to live, but right now I need to move back."

"Move back...? But why?" said Maria. "You don't need to do that, surely...? There are so many bad memories here... and what about the children; it will be more disruption for them?"

"Yes, that is true, but I can't leave it empty, someone will move in."

This was a real issue; with such a shortage of housing in Kosovo following the devastation, any property left empty would be quickly utilised by squatters.

"No, it is right that we move back here; it will give you your life back life back as well. You have had little privacy since we moved in."

"We don't mind about that, do we Afrim?" said Maria. Afrim agreed.

"No, of course not."

"Well, if you're certain, then," said Maria. "But I hope you will let me look after the children while you are at work."

"Yes of course," said Katya, and hugged her mother.

The following weekend, the second week of December 1999, the family moved back to Katya's cottage with the help of Afrim and his ancient tractor. Katya had a different feeling this time; it was as if the evil spirits of the past had been exorcised.

That evening with the children asleep, Katya sat down and started writing a letter. She had resisted the temptation to phone, even though she had access to international calls; it had been too painful.

She started:

'*My dear Carole*

I am so sorry I haven't written before but things have been very difficult here. There is so much chaos we have no postal service in Kosovo, so I haven't been able to send a letter. I am asking a friend to post this when they go back to England for Christmas, so I hope you receive it ok. I have been staying at my mother's cottage with her. I have some news I wanted to tell you. I have been working for the Refugee Council here in Pristina for three months and they are sending me back to England in January for six months. I will be working in Newcastle looking after the Kosovan refugees in the North of England. I miss you so much and can't wait to see you again. I hope you and Bigsy are well. I will ring you when I arrive. I have so much to tell you. Please say hello to Polly.'

Much love

Katya

The letter would be posted in England just before Christmas.

For the next few weeks, Katya continued her work with the Refugee Council. Afrim was happy for Katya to continue to use his car until she left for England, so each morning she made the journey to her mother's cottage to drop off the children.

Katya knew it wouldn't take long to rent the cottage; there were no shortage of takers, but by chance she happened to mention it to her friend, Anna, at one of their regular lunch-time get-togethers. Anna jumped at the opportunity; she was looking to rent somewhere away from the United Nations barracks where she was stationed. It was an ideal solution. A visit the following weekend sealed the deal, and Anna would take over the tenancy as soon as Katya left Kosovo.

Millennium eve, Katya finished her ruminations. She picked up a poker and jabbed at the final dying embers; ash fell into the grill below the grate. It was getting cold now, but it wasn't worth wasting another log. She looked at her watch and counted down to herself.

Midnight

Happy New Year; the start of a new millennium and with it came hope and excitement at what may lie ahead. She made her way upstairs and looked at Melos in his cot and Arjeta who was in the spare bedroom both sleeping peacefully. Outside it had started to snow again. A new chapter was soon to begin.

Chapter Six

Heathcote Tower, Gateshead, Monday 3rd January 2000.

It was a Bank Holiday, but with the sales in full swing, Carole was working. Her department would be manic, but at least the journey into town would be quieter than normal.

Bigsy had slept in, and was reading Friday's paper looking at the television page as he ate his breakfast. He had worked Sunday afternoon and evening in the video shop having given young Rikki the time off for covering the previous day. Trade had been quite brisk.

His mind however had been on other things. Errol's private-eye role had caused him a great deal of consternation. He had hoped his days of involvement in the local drugs trade, however indirectly, were behind him; an episode in his past not necessarily bathed in glory. Even yesterday's Sunday league football game had not gone well, his usual focus missing. Heathcote Rovers had lost 2 – 0 in a game they were expected to win.

Bigsy was ruminating, hardly concentrating on the tabloid pages he was scouring. He knew he was committed to the mission; his indebtedness to Errol had ensured that. The consequences of turning down such a request were unthinkable. The problem that Bigsy was wrestling with was where to start. Errol was paying good money and would be expecting a quick return.

Then there was Carole. He had not dared mention his latest extra-curricular enterprise to her, too many questions would be asked, and he hadn't thought of any suitable excuses yet. He would have to sort out something soon; she'd already commented on his anxious demeanour. This was an equal priority. To accomplish Errol's task, he would have to do some leg work which would require some club visits, and they did not tend to get going until at least midnight, certainly at weekends. Carole would probably notice any regular stop-outs. He needed the toilet again.

Bigsy winced at the memory of his last escapade. The first drug drops for Everton in May had resulted in him being consigned to the spare room when he'd returned home late. Then Wazza was stopped by the police while carrying a consignment of merchandise, and finally they nearly ended up being caught by an undercover policeman whom Everton, Bigsy had subsequently learned, had murdered. It didn't get much worse.

At least he had made a start. Errol had suggested a meet with Denzel, to get some local intel; Bigsy was starting to use the appropriate jargon. They had arranged to meet that afternoon at two o'clock at Bigsy's video store which would be quiet at that time of day. Wazza and Chirpie had also agreed to be there. Bigsy had already arranged to cut them in on the deal in return for their support, splitting the cash three ways.

He was fidgeting and could do with a cigarette.

It was turned ten, and he rang Wazza on his mobile, just for a catch-up.

"Hiya bonny lad, you still ok for the meet with Denzel…? Champion. Look, I've been trying to think how we're going to get a lead on the guys who killed Everton... No, I've got no idea, man. Can you think of anything…? No, me neither… Can you give it some thought, like, and can you ask Chirpie if he's got any ideas an' all…? Aye, will do, see you later."

Not much inspiration came from his buddy, but while he was speaking he suddenly had an idea that might just satisfy Carole, which would be a major hurdle crossed if it worked. He would give it a try tonight.

At a quarter-to-two, Bigsy made his way to the ground floor. He regretted taking the lift; someone had used it as a toilet again and the pungent smell of urine was almost overpowering. Glad to be in the fresh air, Bigsy crossed the service road in front of the flats and into the precinct to his shop. It was a cloudy afternoon and bitterly cold, the temperature having struggled to get above freezing all day.

Bigsy entered the store, reset the burglar alarm, and put the lights on. The room was quickly bathed in florescent lighting. There were a few single spotlights, highlighting displays featuring the week's new blockbusters and best sellers, using flyers from the video companies.

He had converted the old kitchen into an office. It also held his 'under-the-counter' stock, the much-in-demand adult videos which Bigsy had been supplying before he had taken ownership of the store. It was a sideline that had proved very lucrative.

It was a small room and, with the four shelves of videos taking up much of the space, it was cramped, but there was enough room for a small table with a couple of chairs. There was also a refrigerator against the wall next to the fire exit where Bigsy kept the milk, coffee and biscuits. On the other side, the sink and drainer which had a kettle, and four mugs turned upside down waiting to be used again.

After a couple of minutes, Rikki turned up; it was his turn to take the shift, and came into the office.

"Hiya Bigsy, how's it going?"

"Rikki, bonny lad, champion man, champion," replied Bigsy. "I'm having a meeting in here today, so I shan't want any interruptions, like. If anyone wants any specials this afternoon, tell 'em to come back tonight, you got that?"

"Aye Bigsy, will do."

Rikki made himself comfortable behind the counter waiting for the clientele.

A couple of minutes later, Wazza and Chirpie came into the shop together and joined Bigsy in the back room. They exchanged greetings, then started bemoaning the loss in the football match the previous day.

"I don't know what was wrong with you yesterday, Bigsy lad,

you couldn't hit a barn door. You could've had a hat trick if you had your shootin' boots on," commented Chirpie.

"Aye, Chirpie lad, you're not wrong there. Mind, I did have a few things to think about, like."

At two o'clock, Rikki knocked and put his head round the door.

"There's a fookin' big Rasta in the shop, says he's got an appointment," said Rikki in hushed tones, which was just as well as he would not have seen his next birthday if Denzel had heard.

Bigsy got up and went into the shop.

"Denzel, bonny lad, good to see you. Come on through to the back; we won't be disturbed."

Bigsy led Denzel into the office. At Bigsy's request, Rikki brought a couple more chairs in from the shop and, with a squeeze, managed to get them around the table. Comfort would be a luxury.

Bigsy made the introductions. "You met the lads on Saturday, you remember, Wazza and Chirpie." The pair acknowledged Denzel with a nod of the head. There was no flamboyant greeting charade.

Denzel wore dreadlocks, but not as long as Everton used to. He was tall, and strongly resembled his brother Layton, with slightly leaner features, almost certainly younger.

Bigsy had got to like Layton in the brief time they had done business together, and it was clear the respect had been mutual.

Bigsy put the kettle on.

"Coffee, lads?"

"Ta Bigsy, two sugars," said Chirpie.

"Same for me," said Wazza.

Denzel declined and took out a small bottle of mineral water from his long, expensive-looking overcoat.

After the catering arrangements had been satisfied, Bigsy started the conversation.

"Thanks for coming over Denzel, appreciate it. I've been thinking a lot since the meet with Errol, and I thought you could give us some background, like, give us somewheres to start."

Denzel took the top off his bottle of water and took a sip. He spoke in the same West Indian, Geordie brogue that Layton had used.

"Where would you like me to start?"

"Well, you could tell us what happened when you were hit, like," replied Bigsy.

The three of them listened as Denzel went through the course of events that had led to the demise of Everton and Layton and seriously injured him.

"I tink Everton was getting greedy. He was doing alright with de money from trade south of de river. It had been cool for a long time, but he was wanting to get some of de action from de new clubs on de riverfront. It was where de serious money was being made."

Denzel paused and sipped at his water.

"As you know, Everton got a call from Lionel at Scalleys to see if we could supply some merchandise. Lionel said de usual supplier couldn't deliver and it was Friday which, as you know, is a busy night."

"When was that?" asked Bigsy.

"I don't know, earlier, late afternoon sometime. It was lucky Everton had plenty in stock. He tought dis could be our chance, you know, to expand our operation." Denzel sipped his water. "We tought we was doing dem a favour which could pay dividends later. You know, help in future negotiations. Everton knew Lionel, not well, but he was a contact from way back, and he had Everton's phone number, so he was not too worried. Dis was de one on your route. I tink you made de drop dat night on de Waterfront, dat right?"

"Aye, about nine-ish, summat like that, as I recall," replied Bigsy. Wazza and Chirpie nodded in agreement.

"Yeah, anyway, it would be about de same time, I guess, or maybe a few minutes later, Everton got a call from dis man Errol mentioned, wouldn't give a name, but Everton said he had a foreign voice."

"Aye, I remember, Errol saying that," said Bigsy. "What did he say?"

"De man said he wanted to discuss business with Everton and to meet him at Mr. Gee's, dat's de big club in town, at eleven o'clock. We tought dey must have been pleased wid our service and wanted to give us more orders."

"How did they get Everton's number, like? He told us only a few people had it."

"We don't know; we tink it must have been Lionel; it's de only way. It would make sense."

"Do you think Lionel was going freelance, like?" said Bigsy.

"We don't know, it's a possibility, but I don't tink so. More likely, dey was using Lionel to get to us. All we know is Lionel called Everton for a favour. As I said, he just he told us dat dere supplier had let dem down. Unfortunately, we can't find him to find out."

"What do you mean?"

"Lionel's disappeared. No-one's seen him since dat night."

"That's handy... So, what happened next?" asked Bigsy.

"Everton and Layton were at de lock-up when I arrived with de money from my drops," said Denzel.

"I didn't know you were carrying for 'em an' all," said Bigsy.

"Best you didn't, for everyone. Security was good," replied Denzel. "Everton said about de meeting at Mr Gees and asked me if I wanted to go along, so we left de lock-up just after ten and went off to de club. We got dere about half-ten or dereabouts. Everton knew the doorman, Sol, he used to work in a club in South Shields Everton used to supply. So, we got in ok and sat at de bar waiting. We had been dere over an hour and we tought someone was playing us around. Then one of de barmen came over and asked if one of us was called 'Everton'. Everton said yes, and de barman said he had a message for him. Everton asks de barman who was de message from, but he said he didn't know but sounded foreign."

"Foreign? The same one who had phoned before?' asked Bigsy.

"Must be, but Everton didn't speak to him dis time."

"So, what was the message?"

"He said to meet him outside de side door in ten minutes."

"Didn't you think this strange, like?" asked Bigsy.

"Not at de time, we tought he was just being cautious, which was a good ting," replied Denzel, and he took another swig of water. He looked down and stared at the table.

"Dat's when it all went off. De barman let us out de side door fire-exit which led to de alley. Dey was waiting for us, two of dem. One, I didn't see clearly, he was just stood at de top of the alley, a look out, I tink, but de other who shot Everton and Layton was a big guy, rough… evil looking, shaved head. He had a tattoo here," Denzel pointed to the back of his head just above the neckline. "Den he turned round and pointed de gun at me. I don't remember anyting after dat till I woke up in de hospital surrounded by police."

"What did you tell them?" asked Bigsy.

"Nottin' very much; it was a week before I could speak. I was in a really bad way; I lost a lot of blood, but dey was talking about gang wars and stuff, and I said I didn't know what dey was on about. Told dem we was just enjoying a night out."

"Did they ask what you were doing in the alley?" asked Bigsy.

"Dey mentioned it, but I said we just were waiting for someone and dat was it. Dey asked a lot about drugs, but I told 'em I didn't know nottin' about dat. In fact, dey was not as bad as I tought dey would be. I tought dey would give me a going over but dey didn't."

Denzel took another sip of water. "They did ask if I knew someone called 'Hughie Bonner'."

Bigsy's blood ran cold at the name.

"Why did they ask that. Did they say?" asked Bigsy.

"Don't know, I didn't know de name," replied Denzel.

Bigsy breathed a sigh of relief, Everton had obviously kept the matter of the undercover policeman to himself, but the mention of

Hughie Bonner's name had disturbed him, and his stomach was churning big time.

Quickly changing the subject, Bigsy continued. "What about this man with the foreign accent; have you been able to find out who he could be?"

"No, Everton said he tought the accent was Russian or something like. Dat's what he said in de car when we was going to de club. But dis is de probalem, Bigsy, we can't go around asking too many questions. De police will be keeping an eye on me, and if I go to de clubs I tend to stand out if you know what I mean. Dere ain't too many bruddahs around here."

"You have a point there, bonny lad. But Errol said you had taken over Everton's work. The bizzies will be on to you in no time."

Denzel looked at Bigsy with a serious expression. "You make a good point Bigsy, mon. But after I got out of de hospital, I disappeared for a while till tings cooled down. Errol sent up another bruddah to carry on de trade. I don't get involved no more wid de carrying."

Bigsy was starting to question the decision to hold the meeting at the video shop. With hindsight, too close to home, but it was too late now.

"Is there anything else?" asked Bigsy. "Anything at all?"

"Errol told me to tell you everyting I could, and I have told you about all I can, but I can give you a couple of contacts in de clubs which might help."

"Ta bonny lad, anything you have will be good," said Bigsy.

They discussed arrangements for future communication, and Denzel gave Bigsy a mobile phone number which Errol had set up specifically for this purpose. There was no trace-back, Bigsy was assured.

Denzel handed Bigsy a piece of paper with the two names of his contacts written down. "One is Everton's contact, Sol, who still works on de door at Mr. Gees most nights; he's a bruddah. The other's a honkie I did some business with some time ago. Use to work de decks at Scalleys where you made de drop for Everton. I don't know if he is still dere or not."

"And what about this Lionel bloke, the one at Scalleys? He was on the door when we made the drop... big guy. You said he's disappeared."

"Oh, yes, we seriously want to speak to dat mon if you find him, Bigsy. He was de mon dat called-in de one-off order, but like I said, he disappeared after de hit. Nobody knows where he is. We asked around."

"Well, I would certainly recognise him if I met him again, like. What about the bar guy at Mr. Gees?" continued Bigsy.

"We made some enquiries about him as well, but he left dere before I got out of de hospital, no-one's seen him since."

"Bit of a coincidence," observed Bigsy.

"Dat is true, dere are a few people gone missing just now."

After a few more minutes, Denzel left, and Wazza and Chirpie joined Bigsy in deep discussion.

"What're you going do, Bigsy, lad?" asked Wazza.

"I don't know, but I think a visit to Scalleys is going be a good starting point, see if we can see who's doing deals. See if we can get a lead on this Lionel bloke," replied Bigsy.

"What's this about the boat on the Waterfront, I don't know of any?" asked Wazza.

"What d'you mean?" asked Bigsy.

"The guy on the deck?" said Wazza.

"No, you big wazzock, 'works the decks'... a D.J.!" replied Bigsy with a laugh.

"Why didn't he say so, save a lot of confusion?" responded Wazza indignantly.

"Well, the sooner we start, the better, as far as I'm concerned," said Chirpie.

"Ok, shall we say tomorrow night, nine o'clock? It may be

quiet on a Tuesday, mind," said Bigsy and they agreed to meet the following day with Wazza offering to provide the wheels.

"Now comes the tricky bit," said Bigsy.

He was not looking forward to his pending discussions with Carole. Wazza and Chirpie both laughed.

It was late afternoon when the three left the video store together. With the schools on holiday, it was still quiet, but there were several cars parked up in the marked-up bays. Their owners in Mr. Ali's or the off-license, or maybe paying a visit to someone in the tower blocks. The lads didn't take any notice of the silver Renault in one of the parking bays. Nor would they have seen the Leica zoom lens pointing in their direction, or heard the urgent click-click-clicking of the camera's motor drive.

The three buddies headed for the flats as the driver of the Renault picked up his walkie-talkie.

"Orange 2 to control, over."

"Come in, Orange 2."

"Followed target to a video store on Heathcote, been in there for over an hour, which is some serious browsing in my book. Didn't come out with anything that I could see, so presumably was a meet, over."

"Any ideas who? Over."

"No, but three white males just left the store. Didn't recognise them but we have some pictures. Maybe just a coincidence, but you never know. Probably local, they've just gone into one of the towers. Over."

"Control to Orange 2, log the details and come in we'll take a look. Out"

The silver Renault moved slowly out of the parking bay, through the precinct and headed down the Brompton Road.

Six-thirty p.m. Bigsy was in the kitchen making a cup of tea when the key turned in the lock and Carole let herself in.

"Hiya pet, that was good timing, just making a brew," said Bigsy. "Had a good day?"

"It was manic, absolute manic. We were on the go all day, my feet are killing me."

She walked into the kitchen, gave Bigsy a peck on the cheek and retrieved a mug of reviving tea.

"Put your feet up, pet, no rush with dinner," said Bigsy.

"What's brought this on? You're usually famished," replied Carole.

Bigsy had to think quickly, he was worried he might have played his hand too early and raised Carole's suspicions. She knew him very well, particularly when he was trying to get around her.

"Nottin', pet, I had a sandwich s'afternoon, that's all, so I'll be alright for a few minutes, like."

She took her drink into the lounge and sat down. She took a long reviving sip.

"Ahhh, that's better."

She looked at Bigsy who was back on the sofa, watching the television.

"Taking the day off tomorrow. Thought I might go to the Metro Centre and have a look at the sales," said Carole.

"Aye, why not? Get your own back," replied Bigsy with a nervous chuckle.

Carole was employed on a five-day week basis, but was regularly required to work bank holidays and Saturdays, the store's busiest times. She was allowed to take days off in lieu to compensate.

Bigsy put his hand in his pocket and pulled out a couple of twenty-pound notes. Since his financial status had improved, he took to carrying a 'wad' as a token of his new-found wealth, and to impress others.

"Thanks pet, what's this for?" asked Carole, looking at the money suspiciously.

"Thought you could buy yourself something special, like, in the sales."

"What're you after?" teased Carole.

"What...? Nottin', nottin' at all," replied Bigsy too quickly. "Thought it would help with the shops, like," he added, trying to head off the possibility of any other explanation. Now was not an appropriate time to raise the pass-out issue.

Carole went to change and after a few minutes came back wearing her slob-out gear, a pair of jeans and a loose, long sleeve sweatshirt.

Half an hour later, the television was on in the background as they sat down to eat their evening meal, a microwaved cottage pie, frozen peas, followed by apple crumble with custard.

"This is champion, pet," said Bigsy, tucking in trying to time his run.

He made the play.

"You remember I had that business on in May which earned us a few bob, like?"

He put a fork load of mash potato in his mouth.

"Aye, I remember. Caused you a lot a grief as I recall," replied Carole, which was not the response Bigsy was looking for, but continued. He finished the potato and refilled his fork.

"Aye, but it was worth it, I couldn't have bought the shop if it hadn't been for that. A good investment as it turned out." He replenished his mouth with a pile of peas.

"What about it?" pressed Carole.

"Well, this afternoon I got a phone call from this bloke, the one I worked for before... out of the blue, like, wanting to know if I was up for doing some security work for him, just temporary, mind, while his regular guy's off. In hospital apparently, a hernia or summat," he added quickly, trying to finish his mouthful.

"What d'you mean, security work?"

"Just working a couple of nights a week at some club he owns, with Wazza and Chirpie, like. You know, making sure there's no bother and nobody's dipping their fingers in the till and that."

The cottage pie was fast disappearing from his plate.

It seemed plausible to Bigsy, but Carole was definitely not buying it, not yet. There was going to be more interrogation before she would be satisfied.

"What do you want to do that for? You're making good money at the shop."

"Aye, but this is extra, like," he said, chewing the final mouthful. "And there's a big bonus at the end, if it all goes well." Dinner was now consumed.

"What sort a bonus?"

"We're talking serious money, pet… between the three of us, like."

He was not being drawn on the exact bounty, now that would cause a serious problem. He put his knife and fork together indicating his main course was finished.

"And who's going to look after the shop while you're off clubbing the night away?"

"I'll sort that out, no problem. Rikki's mate Stevie's always looking for work."

Bigsy was hoping he had covered all his bases. He picked up his spoon and started on the crumble.

"When are you starting this little jaunt of yours then?"

"Tomorrow night, if that's alright. I said I would have to square it with the missus, like," replied Bigsy, trying to manoeuvre a hot piece of apple that was burning his tongue. He waived his hand frantically across his mouth trying to fan it cooler.

"Huh, and when have I had any say in anything? You always do what you want," replied Carole indignantly.

"No, no, pet, that's not true. I always consider you; you know that," said Bigsy, having swallowed the offending morsel. This wasn't altogether correct, but Carole was beginning to waiver.

Either that or she was getting tired of the fight. She had made her feelings known. It would be under sufferance.

"Look, there's some extra cash for the Metro Centre," said Bigsy and took another fifty pounds from his wad and gave it to her. "Call it 'on account'." He swallowed another spoonful of crumble.

"On account of what, Bigsy? That I'm sackless," replied Carole, using the local word for 'stupid'.

"No, don't be daft, pet. I couldn't do it without you, you know that."

That alerted Carole again, and she was still not totally convinced. The signs were not right.

"Look, I got some money up front and, if you're going to the Metro Centre tomorrow, you might as well have it now."

Carole weighed everything up. She had made her point, but, in his defence, Bigsy had come up with the goods in the past and was making a serious go of the video store.

"Aye, ok, but don't you be getting yourself in any bother. There's all sorts about late at night. I've been reading in the papers, drugs and all kinds going on."

"Thanks, pet, and don't you fret, I'll be fine," said Bigsy, as he finished the rest of his pudding.

"I'll see to the washing up. You put your feet up you must be knackered after the day you've had."

Carole's instincts were still on red alert, and she knew he was up to something; his behaviour pattern had shown a distinct change, but she was beat and had lost the energy to start another debate. She was grateful for the respite from the day.

After Bigsy had washed up, he returned to the lounge with a glass of red wine for Carole, another bad sign.

"Thanks pet," she said and let it pass.

Tyneside Police H.Q,, Newcastle Central Police Station; Six p.m.

It was a hectic evening in one of the major incident rooms. The team investigating the killing of Detective Craig Mackenzie had reduced in number since it had started in June, but there remained fifteen officers working on the case and the associated local drug scene. The perpetrators were still at large, and there was a determination to catch those responsible.

Despite the inclement winter temperatures outside, the central heating made the room oppressive. Worse still, there was a thick layer of smoke hanging in the air, adding to the general fug.

Detective Superintendent Adams was giving an update for the benefit of a couple of new officers and also to give the team a chance to refocus. Adams was a career policeman with over thirty years' service, well-respected by his fellow officers. Tall and slim, with a smoker's pallor, his sports jacket looked well-worn and in need of a press, his tie knot not snug in the neck. He spoke with a southern accent.

He was standing at the front of the room with his team, also stood, giving full attention. Behind him was an incident board which gave an overview of the investigation. It was covered in pictures and flow diagrams. At the top was a photograph of D.S. Craig Mackenzie, aka, Hughie Bonner. Adams picked up a cigarette and took a long drag before addressing his team. There was some fresh information.

"For those of you new to the case, our colleague, D.S. Mackenzie was working undercover and the night he died, he'd been pursuing a lead at Scalleys Nightclub on the Waterfront. According to his liaison officer, he was sure that there was a significant amount of drugs being traded there. The last message from him said that he was due to meet a potential supplier, but didn't say where. We are, though, pretty sure that man was Everton Sheedie." He pointed to a photograph at the side of the board.

He continued. "According to contacts, Sheedie was running the drug trade south of the river, however, he was himself murdered a couple of weeks later coming out of Mr. Gees club in Commercial

Road in what appears to have been a turf-war hit. Also killed was an associate, Layton Gibbons. Gibbons' brother, Denzel, was seriously injured in that hit, and spent some time in hospital. He was interviewed at the time, but, unfortunately, was unable to give us any meaningful leads. After he left hospital, he dropped off the radar, but he resurfaced last November. We've been keeping tabs on him since, but he seems fairly quiet, no obvious indications that he's dealing."

He paused tracking the journey along the flow chart.

"However, this afternoon, we followed Gibbons to a video shop on Heathcote Estate. He was there for over an hour, and we believed met with these three men."

Adams produced three grainy pictures from the earlier shoot and placed them on the board.

"This one is Brian Worrell. Nothing major on file, three 'D.I.C.s' (drunk in charge), and had a pull for suspected distribution of porn videos. No charges were made, lack of evidence."

He pointed to the second picture.

"This one is Colin Longton, did some community service for driving a stolen vehicle a few years back."

"And finally," pointing to the third picture. "We have Danny Walker. Nothing much on him either, but he was questioned about the videos alongside Worrell."

He continued his briefing. "Nothing obvious here and it maybe unconnected, Worrell runs the local video store, but that's about all we know, certainly nothing to suggest any connection with drugs at this stage."

"Perhaps he's shifting porn again. Is it worth a search?" asked one of the watching officers. It had been a while since they had any decent videos to browse at Police HQ.

"Possibly, but for now let's just keep an eye on them, see if anything turns up," replied Adams.

The team were dismissed and filed back into the adjoining office, where they had their individual desks, leaving Adams staring at the incident board.

Chapter Seven

Tuesday 4th January 2000

Carole and Bigsy had had a lie-in, and it was gone nine o'clock before Carole got up to make some tea. She was returning to the bedroom in her pink pyjamas with two mugs in her hands when she noticed some letters on the door mat. She was going to ignore them; the gas bill was due, but on top of the bills, circulars, and a belated Christmas card, there was a smaller, rather dog-eared envelop with writing she did not recognise.

Out of curiosity, she put down the mugs on the living room table and went to pick it up. Post-marked 'London', she opened it up and squealed in delight as she read it. Leaving the mugs on the table she rushed into the bedroom and shouted to Bigsy who was in a deep slumber.

"It's from our Katya. We've got a letter from Katya," she exclaimed excitedly.

She read it out to Bigsy and re-read it to herself. Bigsy was still half asleep.

"What's that, pet… from Katya?"

"Aye, pet."

She returned to the lounge to retrieve the mugs still holding Katya's letter. Back in the bedroom she handed Bigsy a steaming mug of tea and started to read it again.

"I canna believe it; she's coming back to Newcastle, it says here. Katya's coming back here. How good is that!?"

"Coming back?" asked Bigsy, trying to steady the mug in his hands.

"That's what she says. I must tell our Polly, he'll want to know about this," said Carole, getting back into bed still clutching the precious letter.

Bigsy started drinking his tea.

"Where's she going to live?" asked Bigsy.

"She doesn't say but it would be really brilliant if she could move back around here."

"Can't see that happening. Flats are like gold-dust; they stick all the waifs and strays in Heathcote as soon as they can these days."

"Aye, but her old flat's vacant again after them radgies moved out after Christmas. I'll speak to the council and see what's happening."

"Why don't you give that Clara a ring, you know, the one from Community Liaison? She may know something."

Bigsy put his head under the pillow trying to get back to sleep.

"Aye, good idea, pet, I'll ring straight after breakfast, bit early yet."

Carole went back into the living room, excited about the news; she had to speak to someone. She picked up the phone and dialled.

"Allison? It's Carole, is our Polly about? What d'you mean he's still in bed, it's the middle of the day? Can you wake him up, pet? I've got some news he'll definitely wanna hear."

There was a wait and eventually a comatose Polly answered.

"Auntie Carole?" he said, still half asleep.

"Polly, I've got some news... Katya's coming back! Isn't that amazin'?"

Polly was awake now, registering the information.

"What, how? When?"

"This month sometime, she's going be working in Newcastle... I don't know... Why don't you pop up, you can read the letter? She's asking after yas."

Ten minutes later, Polly had made the two floors from twelve and was knocking on the door.

Carole opened it. "Come on in, Polly, pet, would you like a brew?"

She looked at him. He still looked half-asleep, his track suit was creased, and his hair dishevelled. He was wearing flip-flops despite the cold.

"Aye, that would be champion, ta."

Carole handed him the letter and went to the kitchen.

When she came back, Polly was still pouring over the letter.

"Wow, this is something I wasn't expecting."

"I wouldn't be getting your hopes up too high, pet, you don't know what's been happening. I was watchin' a documentary last week, and it's still bad out there."

"Aye, I saw it an' all. I still can't get her out my head, Auntie Carole,"

"I know that, pet. What about that Veronica, she seemed a canny lass?"

"Aye, she was, but she went back home after New Year's Eve, and I don't think we'll be getting back together. It wasn't working out."

"Sorry to hear that, pet."

Polly finished his tea and got up to go.

"I'll let you know as soon as I hear anything," said Carole, and Polly left with mixed emotions.

After breakfast, Carole scoured the Yellow Pages, looking for a phone number for the Community Liaison Department and, after some digging, managed to find it. She dialled.

"Hello, Community Liaison, Clara Davenport."

"Thank goodness for that! Clara, pet, it's Carole Worrell, Katya's friend from Heathcote. You remember?"

"Carole? Of course I do. How are you? Good to hear from you, and I think I might know what you're ringing about."

"Katya's coming back. I've had a letter from her today!"

Carole was still unable to hide her excitement.

"I know. You won't believe this, but I've had a letter today from Jenny Wheatley, you remember Jenny, from the Refuge Council? She says that Katya will be arriving on Wednesday 12th and starting work the following Monday. She's asked me to help find her somewhere to live."

"That's why I've called, pet... Her old flat's empty. They put a family of radgies in it after she left, but they've gone. A right load of delinquents they were an' all, glad to see the back of 'em. She would want to get back here, I know that."

"Well, I know James Stead, I spend half my time speaking to the council housing department, he's the head there. I'll give him a call, see what I can do. I may be able to pull a few strings."

Carole gave Clara her mobile phone number and promised to keep in touch.

After a shower and tidy up, Carole walked to the garages and retrieved her car, then headed the old VW towards the Metro Centre, retail heaven. It would be heaving, as the schools were still off, but with Bigsy's cash in her handbag, she was happy. Bigsy was still in bed when she left.

Today was going to be a long day for Bigsy Worrell. With the pass-out from Carole now duly stamped, he was mulling over his plan of action. Actually, he didn't have a plan of action, just a few random thoughts.

He got up just before midday and made a call.

"Hiya, Wazza, bonny lad, how're you doing?"

"Knackered," came the response.

"Aye, yeah me an'all. Look, I've been thinking about tonight; I think we should see if we can track down that D.J. fella at Scalleys that Denzel mentioned and make his acquaintance. The D.J.'s are the guys in the know. They see everything that goes on, they do. He may know something about that Lionel bloke on the door an' all."

"Aye, makes sense," Wazza agreed.

"What time'll you be ready?"

"Dunno, nine, nine-thirty," said Wazza. "No good going too early, there'll be no-one there."

"Aye, true enough. Ok, if we leave here about nine-thirty that should be about right."

"Aye, I'll be ready then."

"Yeah, ok, see you later, bonny lad," and Bigsy hung up.

Bigsy opened the video shop at two o'clock, as usual; he had some paperwork to do. He wasn't expecting to see Carole from her shopping trip until late afternoon. He also needed to speak to Rikki about Stevie Leonard and whether he would be up for some work. He hadn't noticed the silver Renault which was again parked in the adjacent parking bay.

He went through his usual routine and unlocked the returns cupboard which the members used to post their videos back when the store was closed. They would need to be checked and put back in their rightful place on the shelves behind the counter. He took out close on sixty videos and put them in a cardboard box ready for logging in and filing; it had been another busy night.

Rikki walked in and joined Bigsy who was putting the float in the till.

"Hiya Bigsy, how're you doin'?"

"Aye, bonny lad, I'm ok," replied Bigsy. He continued chatting to Rikki while he was finishing sorting out the till.

"I wanted a word with you about young Stevie. D'you think he'd be interested in doing some shifts, like. I've got some business on, and I may be out a couple of times a week and I don't want to leave you on your own."

"Aye, he'll be well up for that. I'll give him a call and get him down here," said Rikki excitedly.

"Aye, you do that, I'll be in the back. Can you log in and file these for us?" Bigsy handed Rikki the box of returned videos.

About half an hour later, Stevie Leonard turned up and Bigsy conducted his first job interview in the back room; that is, he told Stevie what his hours would be, the rate of pay - cash in hand of course, and what Bigsy expected, "no fookin' messing about."

Another hurdle crossed.

"Orange 2 to control, over," came the static-fuzzed voice to the control room at the police HQ.

"Control, over,"

"Target one in video store now for two hours, nothing happening here. Suggest return tonight, over."

"Ok with that, Orange 2, come on in," and the silver Renault eased out of the parking bay and disappeared into the early evening gloom.

The atmosphere in the lift hadn't improved as Bigsy descended the fourteen floors. It was not always possible to hold your breath for the couple of minutes it took to reach the ground, especially as three other people had joined the downward journey en-route. Bigsy acknowledged them as neighbours but didn't know them to speak to. Such was the life in the tower blocks; for the most part everyone kept themselves to themselves.

It was nine-thirty, and Bigsy made his way to the entrance of the flats; the fog had got thicker, he noticed, as he stepped outside into the chill winter air.

He had called in at the video shop earlier and Rikki and Stevie seemed to be coping alright, in fact Rikki was really enjoying his role as supervisor. He would lock up.

Carole returned about five o'clock from her visit to the Metro Centre and was in a good mood. The letter from Katya and the shopping spree had really lifted her spirits. Bigsy was ruing the fact that he had chosen tonight to go out. The thoughts of what might have been on offer crossed his mind.

The sound of Wazza's stereo system once again preceded the Escort's appearance from the garages behind the precinct. Wazza pulled up alongside Bigsy and Chirpie got out of the front and moved into the back.

"Wazza, turn that fookin' noise off," said Bigsy.

"Sorry, forgot," said Wazza, as Bigsy got in and put his seat belt on. Chirpie was in the back to avoid having to swop over.

"So, it's the Waterfront then?" confirmed Wazza.

"Aye," said Bigsy. "See if we can find that D.J."

"What's his name?" asked Chirpie.

"Good question," said Bigsy.

He rummaged in his pocket and pulled out the crumpled piece of paper that Denzil had given him. Bigsy was staring at the scribbled writing in the random light of passing street illumination. "I canna read this. Looks like 'Daryl something'. We'll have to wait till we get there."

"What're you going to say to him, if he's there?" Chirpie had a knack of asking penetrating questions.

"I've got no idea, bonny lad. I'll have to give that some thought," replied Bigsy.

The innocuous looking Vauxhall Cavalier kept a discreet distance.

"Orange 4 to control... over."

"Control, over."

"Following Ford Escort, registration P435 TXV, containing three males, including target one, crossing Tyne Bridge heading north, over."

"Received Orange 4, out."

Wazza found a parking space in one of the side streets which led down to the river. The regeneration of the Waterfront in Newcastle was still in its infancy and much of the area resembled a building site, but a few bars and a nightclub, Scalleys, were open and attracting some good business, particularly at weekends. On a bleak Tuesday night in early January, it was eerily quiet; the bars looked relatively empty as the three walked past.

They found Scalleys. It was almost as Bigsy had remembered it, but some refurbishment had taken place. The front of the building hadn't changed but had been painted and smartened up. He paused for a moment, looking at the façade, and reflected on everything that had happened since they last visited there in June, the evening of the drug drop that had led to the shooting of Everton and Layton.

"It looks dead," said Chirpie.

"Aye, you're not wrong there, bonny lad," replied Bigsy.

They walked to the entrance and, as Denzel had said, there was a different man on the door, looking very smart, and very hard, in a security company uniform. He had a shaved head and was possibly an ex-boxer judging by his far-from-straight nose and shrivelled ears. He obviously worked out judging by his enormous chest and narrow waste.

"Looks like fookin' King Kong," whispered Chirpie to Bigsy as they approached the door.

Bigsy noticed the badge on his jacket breast-pocket, the words, 'SD Security', beneath that a coat of arms exuding a look of propriety.

The doorman was entertaining himself chatting to a couple of giggly and rather drunk clubbers. He gave no more than a cursory glance to the three as they passed through the door to the entrance lobby. The ticket office was basically a man with a table and a tray of cash. Another, equally hard-looking, security guard hovered close by to ensure there was no problems or arguments about the entrance fee. Loud disco music was emanating from an adjacent room.

"Three please, bonny lad," said Bigsy.

"Fifteen pounds mate," said the cashier in an accent that wasn't local.

Bigsy made a mental note to add that to his expenses for the week.

The drugs drop in the summer was concluded around the back of the club in the service area, so this was new to them.

They made their way through a set of double doors in the direction of the 'fookin' racket' as Bigsy had described it. The club was virtually in darkness, illuminated by a revolving silver ball, highlighted by a spotlight, which sent star-like images around the room. It was about a quarter full, and the central dance area sparsely populated. Six or seven girls were dancing around a pile of handbags on the parquet floor. Layers of cigarette smoke hung in the air like mist on a mountain.

As clubs go, it was reasonably presented. The dancefloor was surrounded by metal balustrades which separated the seating area from the serious clubbers who wanted to dance the night away. The seats looked fairly new, and the tables reflected the glare of flashing coloured lighting reverberating to the beat of the music. The sound system was crisp coming from four speakers hanging from custom-made holders suspended from the ceiling. There was a good balance of tone between treble and bass according to Wazza. He was the expert on loud music. At the back, there was an area reserved for eating, with pristine white tablecloths and appropriate place settings with candles in small glass holders in the middle of each table. A couple sat at one of them engrossed in conversation and a bottle of house red. The lighting was much lower here and in the corners of the club allowing for more intimate moments.

The three made their way to the bar. Again, as with the rest of the club, it reflected the benefit of investment, a hard-wooden surface about twenty-feet long with padded faux-leather front topped by strip lighting. It was much brighter here.

"Three broons, pet," said Bigsy to the young waitress.

She was wearing a tight short skirt and a revealing top. Not the apparel for wearing around town, but not out of place in these surroundings.

"Fifteen pounds," said the waitress in a disinterested manner.

"Fookin' hell," said Bigsy and almost choked.

He was forced to stifle a complaint; his new persona as private investigator required him to be a cool dude, and therefore money was no object... plus, Errol was picking up the tab. It would be another addition to his growing expenses inventory. Bigsy handed over a twenty-pound note.

She counted out his change. "No fivers, sorry."

Bigsy handed back a pound coin to the barmaid. "Is Daryl on tonight?"

"What, the D.J.?'

"Aye," said Bigsy.

"Aye, he's on now?"

Bigsy looked across at the D.J.'s set up and saw a guy in shadow, head down synching his next track.

"That him?"

"Yeah," she replied, and went to serve the next customer.

The three of them made their way to the corner out of direct line of the speakers; at least they could have some semblance of a discussion.

"What're you going to do now?" asked Chirpie.

"Just a recky. I think we'll just have a look round and see what's going on," replied Bigsy, stroking his chin, thoughtfully. "Maybe see if we can get a lead on our old friend the doorman."

"You're getting to sound like a fookin' bizzie, Bigsy, lad," commented Chirpie. Bigsy looked indignant but ignored the remark.

"Orange 4 to control... over."

"Control, over."

"Target one entered Scalleys nightclub on the Waterfront with two white males, await instructions, over."

"Wait and observe, over."

"Will do... Orange 4 out."

After about an hour, the club was starting to get busier and there was a queue at the bar. As he waited to be served with the next round Bigsy noticed that the D.J. was not at the desk; a much younger person was changing the records. Bigsy scanned the club and saw the regular D.J. heading for the gents.

"Hey Chirpie, can you get the drinks in for us? I'm going to grab word with the D.J."

Bigsy gave Chirpie a twenty-pound note and went off in the direction of the toilets.

They had a cover story. Bigsy had originally concocted the idea that they were ex-army buddies and were looking for an old buddy who worked as a bouncer or something at one of the clubs, thought it was Scalleys.

Chirpie wasn't that keen. "Do we look like fookin' ex-army?"

"Aye, you have a good point there," replied Bigsy. "Can you think of anything?"

Wazza suggested that Lionel owed them money and they wanted repayment. They would pay a percentage of the debt to someone who gave them the lead.

"I think that idea has more legs," said Chirpie, and so plan B it was.

Bigsy waited outside the toilet for the appearance of the D.J. The door swung open.

A man in his early thirties appeared, pretty looking with immaculate grooming and stylish clothes.

"Hiya bonny lad, you Daryl?" said Bigsy.

"Who wants to know?" said the D.J.

"Denzel Gibbons said to speak to you, thought you may be able to help us, like, on a little matter. The names Bigsy, Bigsy Worrell."

The D.J. looked at Bigsy with some suspicion, then looked around to check no-one was about.

"Yeah, I know Denzel. How is he? Haven't spoke to him in ages. Good bloke, Denzel. Used to get me some great tracks... What do you want? It'll have to be quick; I'm due back on in a couple of minutes?" said the D.J.

"I'm looking for a bloke who used to be on the door here about six months ago, big guy, Lionel his name... Lionel Johnson?"

The D.J. looked puzzled. "Ah Jonno, you mean. Strange you should be asking about him. Two dudes came in last week wanting to know where he was. I didn't speak to them; it was my night off. Gemma behind the bar told me."

"What the one falling out the bra?"

"Yeah," said Daryl and chuckled.

"What do you want with him?"

"Ah, he owes some money to a mutual friend, and he wants it back," said Bigsy.

"Yeah, that's what they wanted."

Daryl paused and looked around anxiously to make sure there was still no-one about. He continued in hushed tones, continually looking over his shoulder.

"Look, nobody knows where he is. He left here some time ago not long after I started, beginning of June time. Didn't speak to him much, just said 'hi' on my way in. Sometimes catch him on a fag break round the back. There was a rumour he was doing drugs. One night someone else was on the door. Don't know what happened, the boss didn't say."

"Who is your boss? Would it be worth asking him, like?"

"Nah, doesn't work here now. Look, I've said too much already. I'm only speaking to you because Denzel's a mate." He pushed past Bigsy. "Got to get back."

He stopped for a second and looked behind him anxiously. "Look, you could ask Gemma, see if she knows anything."

"Oh, ok, ta, bonny lad, I'll do that."

Daryl turned and went back into the club. Bigsy decided to use the facilities as he was there; he was deep in thought. He eventually returned to his seat; the noise appeared to have gone up several decibels, and relayed the content of his conversation with Daryl to

Wazza and Chirpie.

"What're you going do now?" asked Wazza.

"Going to see if I can speak to the young lassie behind the bar, see if she knows anything," replied Bigsy.

"What the one fallin' out her frock?" asked Chirpie.

"Aye," replied Bigsy.

Bigsy watched the bar waiting for an opportunity to question the buxom Gemma. It was now approaching one a.m., and the club was in full swing.

"I'm getting too old for this," said Bigsy, as he surveyed the gyrating dancers and ogling males standing with their bottles of Broon hanging onto the balustrades.

Then Bigsy noticed Gemma leave the bar and head off in the direction of the toilets. Bigsy turned to his buddies.

"Now's me chance, be back in a mo." He got up and followed her.

Bigsy felt self-conscious standing outside the ladies, and had to move a couple of times as other clubbers approached the female domain.

Ten minutes went by before Gemma made her exit.

Bigsy trying to look cool, as though it was an accidental encounter, made his move.

"Hiya pet, you Gemma?" before should reply, Bigsy continued, "Daryl said you may be able to help us, like."

"Who are you?" replied the girl.

"I'm Bigsy, just need some information, like. There's cash in it for yas." He pulled a twenty-pound note from his wallet.

She eyed the money and looked again at Bigsy, studying his face, looking for any sign of threat. She saw none. She took the note.

"Aye, not here though. Come through the back," and Bigsy followed her through a 'staff only' door into an empty restroom. Gemma walked quickly and pushed open an 'emergency exit' at the end of the room. They were at the back of the club, the same place where Bigsy had done the deal with the doorman some six months earlier. The drop in temperature was noticeable.

It was cold, and the fog still hung in the air. A couple of other bar staff and waitresses were chatting and smoking close to the doorway. Gemma ignored them and led Bigsy into a corner of the alley out of earshot.

"Not allowed to smoke on duty," she said, noticing Bigsy eying the smokers.

Bigsy gave her the spiel. "It's like this, Gemma, a friend of mine's owed some money by Lionel Johnson, used to work here on the door. Not surprisingly, he wants it back, like, and I get some commission if I find him. Can you help us out, pet? I'll make it worth your while."

Bigsy spoke quickly, partly nerves, partly not allowing her to interrupt and divert his train of thought. He also did not want to appear threatening which would almost certainly mean she would clam up.

"Why should I talk to you?" Bigsy pulled out another twenty.

"They'll be some more if I can find him. What do you say? Will you help us?"

"What d'you want know?" she said in a strong local accent, putting the note in her purse.

She took out a pack of cigarettes and lit one. Bigsy inhaled as she puffed the smoke into the cold air. He could murder one right now.

"When did you last see him?"

"Not for ages. He left last year. June sometime, I think. It was just before I went to Ibiza. One night he just didn't turn up. I remember because the boss went mental; he had to go on the door."

"Was that the old boss? Daryl mentioned him."

"Yeah, there've got new people now. There's a manager who deals with everything, Asif's his name, Iranian I think, s'what I heard."

"Daryl also said some other guys were asking about him."

"Aye, that's right, a couple of blokes were in asking about him a few weeks ago. Daryl thought they might be bizzies."

"Did they speak to yas?"

She was starting to shiver, goosebumps appeared on her neck and shoulders. She was rubbing her upper arms to keep warm.

"Aye, but I just said I didn't know anything, which was right. You don't talk to bizzies 'round here. There are some right scary blokes about on security. Wouldn't want to be messing with them, that's for sure."

Just then 'King Kong' from the door came around the corner and into the alley. He looked across at Gemma and Bigsy.

"Shite," said Gemma, and she grabbed Bigsy's head and started giving him a passionate kiss.

The doorman walked away.

"What was that all about?" said Bigsy, trying to compose himself.

"They call him 'the monster'. He'll do us over if he knows I've been talking to yas. Look, I have to go," and she ran back through the side door and disappeared inside the club.

Bigsy followed and made his way back to his buddies.

"Did you get anywhere?" asked Wazza.

"Aye, more'n I was expecting."

Bigsy related the details of Gemma's information, and the interlude caused by the appearance of King Kong. "Tongues and all," he added, with a grin.

"One for the road, lads, and then we'll call it a night, what do you say?" said Bigsy.

Wazza had been on orange juice since the first round and was not enamoured with the thought of another one. He still had a half-full glass.

"Nah ta, I don't think my constitution would stand another."

"Aye, go on," said Chirpie, and Bigsy made his way to the bar.

It was quieter now, almost one-thirty, with people making their way home. Bigsy was the only customer waiting and ordered a couple of broons. Gemma was back serving and got him the drinks.

"Ta Gemma, for the info, like," said Bigsy quietly and passed her a scrap of paper.

"Look, this is my mobile number. If you get any bother, or think of anything else, call me, right?"

"Aye, ok."

She slipped the note into the waistband of her skirt and covered it up with her top.

"Keep the change," said Bigsy as he took the drinks.

Bigsy went back to his table with the round making a mental note of the evening's bar tab.

The three were finishing off their drinks when Bigsy noticed four men come in the club. Three of them were wearing the same uniform as the doorman; the other was darker skinned, possibly Middle Eastern.

"Don't look now, but these guys look tasty," said Bigsy.

Immediately Wazza and Chirpie looked around.

"I said don't look!" exclaimed Bigsy.

"They're not here to talk about the weather," said Chirpie.

"No, that's for sure," replied Wazza.

"I think we just may have our first lead," said Bigsy, and they watched the gang deep in conversation.

Just before two o'clock, Wazza spoke, stifling a yawn, "I don't know about you, but I'm for my bed. Are you coming, Inspector Clouseau?"

"Aye, I think we've done enough investigating for one night," replied Bigsy, and the three of them made their way out the club. Bigsy noticed there was no-one on the door as they left.

The cold air hit them as they walked back toward the Escort.

"Orange 4 to control... over."

"Control, over."

"Target and associates have left the club and heading towards Heathcote. I think that's it for tonight, over."

"Affirmative Orange 4, go get some sleep... out," and the Cavalier disappeared unnoticed into the night towards the Western By-pass.

Chapter Eight

Wednesday 5th January 2000.

Bigsy was sound asleep when Carole brought him a cup of tea at seven-thirty.

"What time did you get in, pet? I never heard you."

Bigsy, awakened from a deep slumber, moaned. "Urgh, don't ask. Must've been about two-thirty, pet," and he put his pillow over his head.

"And how many nights are you going to be doing this for? You'll be knackered."

Carole put his drink down on the bedside table next to him.

"Not on again until Friday; I'll be ok."

"Aye, well I'm off now, see you tonight, if you're not asleep."

Bigsy made some noise in response which didn't sound human. Carole left him to it and went off to work.

The next time Bigsy woke. it was gone ten-thirty, and his earlier tea was stone cold with a dark skin floating on the top. He got up and made more tea and put some bread under the grill for his breakfast.

After he had eaten he took out his mobile phone and made a call.

"Denzel, bonny lad, Bigsy... Aye, ok, you...? Champion... Look, I've got some news. Me and the lads went to Scalleys last night and got some info which may be useful. The doorman. Jonno, went missing in June about the same time Everton and Layton got shot. Didn't turn up for work the next night and no-one's seen him since. Maybe nottin', but it seems something of a coincidence, if you ask me. The other thing is, the guy on the door, real hard-core he was, was wearing a jacket with the name 'SD Security' on it... No, never heard of 'em, but three more blokes came in late, wearing the same jackets. They were in a meet with an Arab-looking guy. Aye, as I said late, about two o'clock, I guess... No, I don't know. Could have been a bloke called Asif. I was speaking to one of the barmaids, and she said she thought the manager of the club was Iranian or something. You may want to check him out an' all."

Bigsy paused before continuing.

"While you're on, Errol said you're going to pick up me exes, just checking like, because it was a bit pricey at the club. Thought I'd mention it. Ta Denzel, bonny lad, that's champion." Bigsy rang off.

Back at Police HQ, Detective Superintendent Adams was assessing the latest developments. Again. he was in the meeting room containing the incident board, seated casually on a desk. His team were gathered round. The door had been left open to allow some fresh air into the room.

"We've been watching Brian Worrell for a couple of days, nothing significant to report, but he did visit Scalleys nightclub on the Waterfront last night with Longton and Walker."

D.S. Frasier, an important member of the team who had been with the investigation from the start, offered his perspective. "Could be just a night out with the lads,"

"Yes, true," agreed Adams. "But they don't seem like seasoned clubbers to me, and Tuesday night's not the liveliest night in town. So, what were they doing there? Did they meet anyone?" He looked at the group. "What's the latest on Scalleys?"

Another team member, D.S. Tunney, answered. "Well, according to his notes, we know that Craig was interested in Scalleys; he paid a couple of visits there just before he was killed. He'd made contact with one of the doormen, a guy called Lionel Johnson and made a couple of small deals through him. He was hoping he could lead him to the main players. We made some enquiries early on in the investigation, but it seems he'd disappeared before we could get to him. Rumour is, he's done a runner. None of our contacts have any info on him."

"What's Worrell's interest in Scalleys? Any thoughts?" asked Adams.

"Could be just a coincidence, guv," said Frasier.

"Yes, but it's a big one. Have we got anyone inside?"

"Not yet, guv," replied Frasier.

"Let's get someone in there; see if anything turns up," said Adams.

Before opening the shop, Bigsy paid a visit to his mother, Mar Worrell. Bigsy would drop in to see her two or three times a week. Mar and her late husband, Joe, were a devoted couple, and Mar was finding it difficult without her partner. Bigsy was concerned that she was giving up and, although only in her late sixties, seemed to be looking much older recently.

The silver Renault followed the bus to the Bensham Estate which was not easy as it stopped every hundred yards to let on or drop off passengers.

"Orange 2 to control, over."

"Control to Orange 2, come in."

"Target has entered a bungalow, 14 Freeland Road, on Bensham Estate, over."

"Those are old people's bungalows, can't see that being a drop... will advise. Control out."

A few minutes later the Renault had a call.

"Control to Orange 2, over."

"Orange 2; come in control."

"Be advised, property is sheltered accommodation rented to a Mrs Flora Worrell, over."

"Looks like he's paid his mum a visit, sweet... control; Orange 2, out."

Bigsy opened up the video shop at two o'clock as usual, and, later that afternoon, Rikki and Stevie turned up to do their shift.

The store was quiet and the three were in the back kitchen drinking a brew when Rikki turned to Bigsy.

"Have you seen that car parked up outside? There's a couple of blokes inside. I noticed it there yesterday an'all, not local. I reckon it's the bizzies on a stake out, like on the telly. I was watching 'The Bill' the other night; it was just like that."

Before he could finish the sentence, Bigsy spurted out the tea he had just taken in.

"Shite!" he exclaimed under his breath, but louder than he intended which alerted Rikki.

"Are you sure?" said Bigsy.

"Aye, take a look for yourself. It's still there, the silver Renault."

Bigsy put down his mug on the kitchen drainer and went out the back door to the yard which acted as a service area behind the shops. It was large enough to take the vans and small trucks which frequently delivered produce to Mr. Ali's and the off license. Bigsy had just one delivery a week from his video supplier and it tended to stop out the front for the couple of minutes it took to offload.

To the right of Bigsy's back door were three large industrial dumpsters piled high with rubbish from the retail outlets. A ten-feet high, white-painted wooden fence with razor wire trailing across the top surrounded the yard which was accessed by a large gate used for deliveries. It was shut.

Bigsy peered through a gap in the wooden slats and could just see the silver Renault parked in the precinct car park as Rikki had described. He squinted trying to make out the occupants. One was reading the paper; the other was drinking coffee from what looked like a flask. He had something round his shoulder which Bigsy couldn't identify at first but then realised it was a shoulder strap for a camera.

Bigsy quickly went back inside.

"What do you think?" asked Rikki. "You don't think they're

after your mucky videos, do you?"

"I don't know, but better be on the safe side, eh? Quick, you and Stevie get 'round to Mr. Ali's and see if they've got anything to put 'em in."

Bigsy let the lads out the back door and waited for them to return. A few minutes later they came back with two large cardboard boxes that once contained packets of washing-powder.

Back in the viewing area/kitchen, Bigsy had started to remove the adult videos from the shelves. It would make a hole in his cash-flow for a while, but it had to be done.

"Right lads, give us a hand get those videos into those boxes, and be careful there's a lot of dosh tied up in these."

The lads passed the hundred or so adult videos to Bigsy one by one and he carefully filed them in alphabetical order and closed the lids.

"What're you going to do with them?" asked Rikki.

"I don't know, but the quicker we can get them out of here the better."

Bigsy pondered the dilemma. He couldn't store them at the flat, Carole would go mental and what if they searched the flat? He shuddered at the thought. The question was academic, in any case; there was no way they could get the boxes past the car without being spotted; it would look obvious.

He had an idea.

"Rikki, pop 'round to Mr. Ali's again and ask him if we can keep a couple of boxes with him for a couple of days while we have a change round. If he's ok with that, get him to open his back door for us; it'll be easier."

Rikki walked next door, trying not to arouse any interest from the watching policemen.

Bigsy waited anxiously by the back door, and after a couple of minutes, Rikki came through from the shop nonchalantly carrying a bottle of milk.

"Aye, no problem, Jamal's gonna open the back door when he's finished serving," said Rikki, and casually put the milk in the fridge.

They sealed the boxes with gaffer tape. "We don't want to shock the neighbours," said Bigsy.

After five minutes, there was a knock on the back door. It was Jamal, and Rikki and Stevie helped carry the two boxes into Mr. Ali's storeroom. They were heavy, and the lads had to make two journeys.

Bigsy breathed a sigh of relief, but he knew that it was not the only issue in which the police might be interested. He sat in the kitchen finishing his coffee, which was now cold, thinking. He picked up his mobile and called Wazza and told him of the events.

"What're you going to do, bonny lad?" said Wazza.

"I'm going to be careful, very, very careful. I think I'm going to bore them into giving up."

"But you've done nottin' wrong, Bigsy."

"I know that, but do they? I think I'd better let Denzel know. They'll be on to him an' all... Yeah, see you later."

Bigsy rang off and made a call to Denzel.

"Denzel, bonny lad, we may have a problem. It looks like the bizzies could be on to us. There's an unmarked cop car outside the shop; two blokes, one of them's got a camera and everything. What do you want us to do?"

There was a pause.

"Hmm. Dat's bad. I tink we need to be cool, Bigsy mon, be on de safe side. Are you ok to carry on with de investigation? You will need to be discreet; you know what I'm saying?

"Aye, I can do that. Do you still want to meet up on Friday, like?"

"Yes, we can meet at de Working Men's Club again, but make it later around nine-thirty, roads'll be quiet."

"Aye, bonny lad; that makes sense."

"Tanks for letting us know. I will see to tings dis end."

So, for the next couple of days, Bigsy went about his own boring life as a video-shop proprietor. Life for the watching detectives was turning very tedious indeed, and by Thursday evening, the observers were getting restless.

"Orange 2 to control, over."

"Control to Orange 2, come in."

"Ten p.m. Target locking up video shop and entering the flats. That's about it for the night. Nothing else to report. Await instructions, over."

"Break off for tonight. We'll give it one more day and then look at the options. Control out."

"Roger that." The call was logged, and the silver Renault exited the parking lot once more.

Friday evening Carole returned from work with more news. She opened the door, loaded with shopping and made her way to the kitchen where Bigsy was pouring two mugs of tea.

She pecked him on the cheek and, before he could say anything, revealed the details of her news.

"You'll never guess what, I got a phone call this morning from that Clara, and she's managed to get Katya into her old flat. How good is that?" she said animatedly. "I've taken tomorrow off and Clara's bringing me the keys so we can clean it up for her."

"That's champion, pet," said Bigsy, far from sharing Carole's excitement. He was in his own, rather distant, world.

"Are you ok, pet? You seem quiet," said Carole, as she started making the evening meal.

The microwave started.

"Aye, pet, sorry I was thinking about the shop."

"No problems are there, pet? I thought you were doing well."

"Oh... er, no, no, it's ok. Just thinking about stocking up more of them new DVD's that's all."

"I think that's where it's going, meself. We were talking about it at work. They're all buying 'em now."

"Aye, pet, aye," said Bigsy, still not really concentrating.

The discussion was interrupted by a phone call on Bigsy's mobile. He didn't recognise the number being displayed.

"Hello," said Bigsy.

After a pause, a voice came on which he didn't recognise immediately, but clearly in a state of some anguish.

"Is that Bigsy?" The voice trailed off for a moment as though distracted or interrupted.

Bigsy took the opportunity to move out of the kitchen and out of Carole's earshot.

"Aye," replied Bigsy.

"It's Gemma from Scalleys," her voice was barely a whisper, and Bigsy had to concentrate hard to hear. "Two of them security blokes just been 'round wanting to know what I was doing talking to you the other night. Threatened to break my legs if I went blaggin' my mouth off."

"Fookin' hell, pet, what did you tell 'em?"

"Nottin', I just said you were a bloke I fancied, and we'd come out the back for a chat, like." Gemma's voice was shaking.

"Did they hurt you at all?" asked Bigsy.

"No, they slapped me about, and then they left me alone?" she said, clearly distressed.

"When was this?" said Bigsy.

"About half an hour ago. I just turned up for work. I was in the kitchen, and they just came in and pinned me to the wall, like. I don't know what to do. I'm scared, Bigsy, really scared."

"Security guys, you say. What did they look like, these blokes?"

"Scary, real hard cases, shaved heads and everything. Not seen 'em before, not Scalleys, but they were wearing the same uniform as 'the monster'. I reckon it was him that said summat. He saw us in the alleyway, you remember?"

"Aye, how could I forget," said Bigsy. He paused for a moment to think. "They were wearing the same jackets, you said; what, the 'SD Security'?"

"Aye."

"Where are you now?"

"I've locked meself in the nettie."

"Listen, Gemma pet, you can't stay in the bog all night. If they've left you alone, you'll be alright; just keep your head down. You've done nottin' wrong, and they must've believed your story. Probably just trying to put the frighteners on you."

"Aye, well they've certainly succeeded on that account."

After further reassurances, Gemma gradually calmed down.

"Look, pet, just keep your head down, you'll be ok. Call us again if you get anymore bother."

He rang off. The call troubled Bigsy, but it got him thinking. 'SD Security', the name kept cropping up. Were they involved in some way? It was a hell of a coincidence, but in what way and how? Bigsy hadn't worked it out yet. Then he had a brainwave which he would discuss with Chirpie later.

He heard Carole's voice from the kitchen. "Your tea's ready, pet."

They were on the sofa eating their evening meal from a tray in front of the TV. Carole continued talking excitedly about Katya's pending return, but with Bigsy concerned at the recent course of events, he was not really concentrating on the discussion.

"And Clara's calling 'round at ten o'clock tomorrow morning to help me clean up the place. Are you listening, Bigsy? I thought you'd be more interested, pet."

"What? Sorry, pet, just some business that's all. I'm fine."

Carole let it pass and got up to do the washing up.

"Are you still off clubbing again tonight?" shouted Carole from the kitchen.

"Aye, be off about half-nine," shouted Bigsy.

"I can't say I'll be waiting up for yas."

Bigsy went into the kitchen to continue the discussion.

"That's ok pet, it'll be late, but I'll be picking up some money, so I should be able to contribute to Katya's welcome party."

"Aye, that'll be champion pet. You just mind what you're doing, that's all."

At just after nine o'clock, Bigsy said goodbye to Carole and made his way to the ground floor; there was still no improvement in the lift aroma problem. Bigsy had arranged a little diversion to enable him to escape the eyes of the watching constabulary.

As he came out the lift, Rikki was waiting on his bike and, seeing Bigsy, pedalled straight towards the Renault. At the last minute he turned the handlebars, and the force of the turn threw him onto the bonnet. As part of the ruse, he had padded his elbows and knees with newspaper and was wearing his crash-helmet to mitigate any personal damage.

With Rikki theatrically rolling on the floor the officers jumped out of the car.

"Are you ok?" said the first officer. The second started to examine the Renault's paintwork.

"Aye, I think so," he said holding his ankle. "My brakes just went."

Rikki got up gingerly and checked himself over.

Seeing there was no damage to the vehicle and Rikki was none the worse, the officers returned to their observation duties.

Meanwhile, Bigsy had left the tower block unseen. He made a swift right turn onto the walkway around the side of the flats and down through the tunnel under the expressway. On the other side of the subway was the road to the industrial park, and Wazza was waiting in the Escort. Bigsy got in; Chirpie was in his accustomed position in the back. The music was turned off.

"Well, that worked ok; they never saw a thing. I'll have to see young Rikki gets a pay rise," said Bigsy as he got in the car.

"Right, off to the club then. Let's hope Denzel doesn't get spotted, either," said Wazza.

They arrived at the working men's club just before nine-thirty and parked in the corner of the cinder plot, away from prying eyes. The club's outside lighting did not illuminate all of the area and it was pitch dark on the edges. It was a bitterly cold evening and there were just three other cars in the car park.

Just then, an anonymous-looking white van entered from the main road.

"This looks like him," said Bigsy.

Wazza flashed the lights of the Escort. Denzel parked up and walked towards Wazza's Escort.

Bigsy got out, followed by his two buddies. Denzel looked very different.

"Hiya Denzel," said Bigsy. "What've you done with the hair, bonny lad? I hardly recognise you." They met and touched knuckles.

"I decided to change de style."

"Aye, you've done that alright. You've picked a good time to shave your head; it's brass monkeys out here."

Denzel's dreadlocks had been completely shorn, leaving a short, frizzy haircut.

"I hope you weren't followed, bonny lad."

Denzel took out a cap from his pocket and put it on.

"No, Bigsy, I was very careful."

"You comin' in for a drink?" asked Bigsy.

"No tanks, Bigsy, mon. Need to get back."

"Ok, no problem, bonny lad. What have you got for us?" asked Bigsy.

Denzel took an envelope out of his pocket and handed it to Bigsy.

"Dis is de money from Errol. He asked me to say he was pleased with what you've done. Dere's enough to cover de expenses."

"Ta, Denzel." Bigsy pocketed the envelope. "Can you thank

Errol for us an' all."

"Yeah, sure ting," Denzel continued. "Dere's someting else you should know. We've been making some enquiries about dese SD Securities people. It's run by a dude called Sonny Daniels. Used to be a boxer way back. He's a serious player wid some nasty associates, most've done time. Remember Sol Miller I told you about, de doorman at Mr Gees?"

Bigsy nodded, taking in every word. "Aye."

Chirpie and Wazza were just stood alongside him. Denzel looked at the three.

"Well, he works for dem now. He used to work for another firm, but he tells me dey were taken over by SD Security. Sol couldn't say too much, dey watch dem all de time with cameras and all sorts, very dangerous dudes. Word is dey are trying to get all de clubs to use SD people on de doors so dey can control de traffic dat way."

"Drugs you mean?" enquired Bigsy. He looked at Wazza and Chirpie and raised his eyebrows.

"Yeah... We tink it's possible dese guys maybe involved in de killing of Layton and Everton. It makes sense and dey certainly have de track record, but we need more information before we can go for dem, Errol wants to be certain."

"Aye, I can see that. Will this Sol guy be willing to speak to us, like?"

"Yeah, I can set dat up. I'll call him and let him know. Anyway, I hope dat helps with de investigation." He looked at his watch. "Look, I need to go. I'll be in touch."

Denzel said his goodbyes and made his way back to the van, then drove off into the night-time traffic.

Bigsy opened the envelope and took out some twenties and handed Wazza and Chirpie their cut.

"Ta Bigsy, bonny lad," said Chirpie, pocketing his cash.

"What're you going to do, Bigsy?" asked Wazza.

"I do have something in mind, but it may be dangerous."

Bigsy revealed his brainwave.

"Look, as I see it we're not going to get much asking around, someone's going to end up dead. They've already paid young Gemma a visit. I think we should try to get someone on the books." He looked at Chirpie. "How d'you fancy coming off the dole, bonny lad?"

Chirpie was taken aback. He swept his lank black hair back with his hand.

"Not sure about that, man," he replied, anxiously.

"Well, I can't do it, I'm too well-known" said Bigsy. "And Wazza," he looked at his mate. "Well, let's just say he doesn't have your presence."

At six-feet-three and sixteen stone, Chirpie was more than a match for most in a fight, as he had proved on more than one occasion. He also had a criminal record, minor compared with some of the SD staff, but nevertheless an additional and valuable credential. Chirpie could see the logic.

"Aye, I can see it makes sense. But how're you going to get us in, like? They don't tend to advertise in the Evening Chronical," said Chirpie, trying to hide his lack of enthusiasm.

"I thought we could pay a call on this Sol bloke Denzel mentioned, at Mr. Gee's. He's a mate of his and he may be amenable to putting in a word, like."

"Aye, that might work. Aye, ok, Bigsy lad," said Chirpie.

He had been put into a corner but had no intention of letting down his buddies.

"Come on, let's go and see if we can get Chirpie a job," said Bigsy, as they climbed back in the car.

"And keep an eye out for any bizzies, you two," added Bigsy.

Wazza headed the Escort to town and Mr. Gees.

Having parked in the nearby multi-story, the three buddies made their way to the club on foot. Mr. Gees was in the commercial centre of Newcastle and, as with many of the licensed properties in the locality, was formerly a bank. In common with much of the architecture, it was an ochre/stone structure with Doric columns at the front. It was an impressive-looking building.

There was an alleyway at the side where deliveries were made and bands and D.J.s could drop off their gear. It was also where Everton and Layton had been murdered.

"It's just round the corner." said Bigsy, as they approached. "Stay here a sec, I just want to check out the lie of the land."

From a vantage point across the street, the three could see the two bouncers on the front door. One was white with a shaved head like the one at Scalleys, the other of West Indian origin.

"That must be him," said Wazza, pointing at the coloured man.

Wazza and Chirpie held back as Bigsy walked across the road. It was just turned ten o'clock on a Friday night and busy; the queue stretched around the corner of the building for maybe fifty yards.

Bigsy ignored the waiting clubbers and made his way straight to Sol, to much complaint from the line of eager customers. With his back half-turned to avoid any camera detection he approached the doorman.

"Are you Sol, bonny lad? It's Bigsy Worrell. Denzel said you may be able to help us, like."

The man turned to one side to make sure he was out of earshot of his door-buddy. "Yeah, I spoke to him a few minutes ago. He said to expect you."

"D'you have a break soon? I could do with a quiet word if you could spare us a few minutes."

He looked at the queue. "Aye, yeah ok, it may be a while, though." He checked again. "Look, there's a coffee shop called 'PQs' just around the corner, you'll see it. I'll be there once we've cleared this lot, ok?"

The man's accent was more Geordie than the broad Caribbean tones of Denzel and Errol.

"Aye, ok, see you there," said Bigsy.

Bigsy rejoined his buddies. "He'll meet us in a few minutes. He said to wait for him in a coffee shop down there." Bigsy pointed to the road.

PQ's was one of the new trendy European coffee-shops which doubled as a wine bar. It was less than a hundred yards away and doing a brisk trade as they entered. Bigsy looked around. The flooring was stark wooden boards, and the chairs and tables matched the minimalistic look. There was a blackboard with 'Today's Special' of Pumpkin and Pistachio Risotto chalked on it. It was not an establishment Bigsy was likely to frequent in normal times.

Bigsy looked at the cost. "Fookin' hell, have you seen how much the food is in heya?"

Chirpie nodded. "Aye, it's a different world, bonny lad."

There were only a couple of spare places out of the fifty or so covers. Italian Rock music blared from an expensive looking sound system which, although loud, was surprisingly not that intrusive. Bigsy ordered three beers from the 'barista' while the other two made for a vacant table in the corner. As Chirpie pulled a chair out to sit down it made a scraping sound on the bare floor. Wazza winced.

Chirpie picked up the menu on the table.

"Fookin' hell, don't think much of this?" said Wazza studying the selection of fare. "They've got no burgers... What's Gnocchi for fook's sake?"

"No idea," said Chirpie.

Bigsy returned with the drinks. "No broons, lads, I'm afraid, some Italian piss; five quid a throw an' all."

There were no glasses, and the lads drank from the bottle.

"Here's to Errol," said Bigsy. "He's paying." And the three clinked their bottles together.

"Hey Bigsy, what's Gnocchi?" said Wazza.

"It's Italian for 'potato'," replied Bigsy.

"How do you know that?" said Chirpie.

"Carole bought some once. It was on special offer... tastes shite."

It was nearer twenty-five minutes before the large West Indian entered the wine bar. It was clear Sol looked after himself, his SD jacket hardly disguising his physique. Six feet tall, the obligatory shaved head and a diamond studded earring. He approached the three and sat at the vacant seat next to Bigsy.

Bigsy made the introductions which Sol acknowledged.

"I haven't got long lads; I only get ten minutes. What can I do for you?" He spoke in a deep Caribbean/Geordie dialect.

"Look, I know that we're asking a lot, but d'you think you could get our man here a job," said Bigsy, pointing at Chirpie.

Sol looked at Chirpie eyeing up and down.

"Well, you appear to have all the right physical attributes, but Sonny is very particular about who he takes on. Places a lot of store on trust and loyalty."

"Aye, well that's where you come in, Sol, bonny lad. Do you think you could get him an introduction, give him a reference, like?"

"I don't know if that will help or not. Sonny has his own network and it's not easy to get in. Everything's done by recommendation. If Sonny likes you; you get to wear the jacket."

"Aye, we were hoping you could recommend Chirpie, here," said Bigsy. "There'll be some recognition from Denzel... and Errol of course."

Errol's name certainly registered and Sol's demeanour changed.

"It's a big thing you ask because if he," pointing to Chirpie, "screws up, as the referee, I will be in the frame as well. How do I know if I can trust you?"

"You can speak to Denzel. He'll back us up," said Bigsy.

Sol sat thinking for a moment. "Well, I'll see what I can do, but I can't promise nottin'. Look I've got to go, give us your number, and if I see Sonny, I'll put in a word."

"Ta, that's champion, man. One more thing before you go, where does he hang out, this Sonny bloke?" said Bigsy.

"Yeah, he's got a gym on Argyle Street, most of the guys work out there. You get free membership if you are on the payroll, one of the perks of the job. I'll be there tomorrow."

Bigsy gave Sol a business card.

The West Indian read the card. "Hollywood Nights Video Store, Heathcote Precinct; Proprietor, Brian Worrell."

"This you, Bigsy, mon?" asked Sol.

"Aye, that's my shop, you can get us there, or on the mobile number, any time."

Sol got up and said his goodbyes and left the wine bar.

"Well fellas, I don't think we can do much more here. I think we can give ourselves an early night; what d'you say?" said Bigsy.

"Aye, I'm not unhappy about that," replied Chirpie, gloomily. He was clearly still less than enamoured at his prospective career path.

"Aye, let's be off," agreed Wazza, totally ignoring Chirpie's demeanour, and they made their way back to the car.

"I'll just give our Carole a ring," said Bigsy, punching the number into the mobile.

"Hi Carole pet, just letting you know I'm heading back. We've finished the business early tonight. Aye; see you in about half an hour."

Bigsy checked his watch; it was turned eleven and the streets around the clubs were heaving.

"Have you seen all this. It's busier than Saturday morning on Eldon Square."

Wazza headed back to the flats and dropped Bigsy off on the industrial park where he had picked him up earlier. Bigsy made his way towards the tower blocks via the subway which was in total darkness. He crunched his way through the smashed glass which littered the walkway. "Fookin' yobs," he said to no-one in particular, as he walked towards the streetlights on the other side.

As he got to the precinct, he noticed the silver Renault had gone; all the parking bays were empty.

He got back to the flat having endured the lift once more. As he opened the door, he called to Carole. "Only me, pet. I'm gonna have to speak to someone about those lifts; they're honking."

Carole was seated on the sofa with a glass of wine in her hand, wearing a housecoat; the television was on. She made no eye contact.

"Just watching the end of this film, pet; I wasn't expecting yas back just yet."

"Aye, we finished early, like."

"Aye? Well, let us finish this and you can tell us all about it."

Bigsy headed to the bedroom.

Chapter Nine

Back in Kosovo there was much to do.

Katya was going through a mixture of emotions at the thought of returning to England; some apprehensiveness in not knowing what to expect, and, of course, excitement at the possibility of reuniting with her old friends. Her new job had more responsibility, which would be a challenge. There was a small support staff, but a lot of the time she would be working on her own. Then there were the memories, many memories, mostly, but not all, good.

Captain Drury, as he had promised, had dealt with the necessary paperwork. The visas for her and the children would have been an issue had she not been working for the Refugee Council. The UK Government were not keen to allow returners once asylum seekers had been repatriated. Arjeta's situation also provided a problem in that Katya had been given temporary custody but had not yet formally adopted her; as a result, Arjeta was considered a Kosovan orphan. Again, this had been resolved, and Katya was given Arjeta's passport as 'legal guardian'.

At the cottage, Katya had to pack carefully as there was no opportunity to send anything out of the country; there was still no postal system. The friend at the Refugee Council who had posted Carole's letter in London had offered to take some additional belongings on her next visit, but that would not be until the end of February. Katya considered the offer; it was a possible fall-back if all else failed.

As the days counted down, she started to hand over her work in Pristina to one of her colleagues and the excitement mounted. Then, on the Friday before she was due to leave for England, she received an unexpected phone call. It was from Jenny Wheatley in Newcastle.

Communication with the UK was still extremely difficult. There was no international mobile phone network and only a limited domestic service, but the Refugee Council was operating cross borders on their own network.

Jenny had called to give Katya an update and clarify what she would be doing in her new role. Then she had some news. "I've been in touch with Clara Davenport; you remember her?"

"Yes, of course, we were good friends... She helped me and poor Edi a lot... how is she?"

"She's fine," replied Jenny and continued. "It appears your old flat in Heathcote is available if you want it."

Katya was overjoyed. "Really...! I can't believe it. Yes, that would be wonderful."

"What about the children... while I am working?" asked Katya.

"No problem, we've got a small crèche facility downstairs, here. A couple of the staff bring their children, so it won't be an issue. I'll make sure there are places for you. Just to mention, you'll be on a special charter-flight with some refugees and some diplomatic and Refugee Council Staff. You'll be going to London Heathrow, because of the flight restrictions in Kosovo. We'll get you and the children on a connecting flight to Newcastle Airport which should save a lot of time. You'll be well-looked after and won't have the long delays you had the last time. I'll fax through the times on Monday."

"Thank you so much, that is so kind. There is one thing. Can you let Clara know when I will be arriving in England for me, and ask her to tell my friend Carole, if she has time?"

"Yes, I can do that. I'll ring her later," said Jenny.

It was starting to all come together. Katya couldn't believe it; everything was happening so quickly, but she couldn't wait to be with Carole and Bigsy again.

Then there was Polly.

Katya was not sure what to think or how to play it. She wished she could speak to him in some way and tell him how she felt. She had never stopped loving him and missed him so much.

The following Monday, Jenny's fax duly arrived. Katya would be leaving Pristina airport at eight-thirty, Wednesday morning, and would arrive in the UK at ten-thirty, local time, allowing for the two-hour time difference. There was a connecting flight to Newcastle at quarter-to-one, which would get them in around two o'clock. Jenny authorised a taxi from the airport if necessary.

That evening, Katya called at her mother's cottage in Lapusnic to pick up the children as usual, and Maria had made her a wonderful meal which they enjoyed together as a family. Although it was unsaid, they all recognised that it would be the last time they would see each other for some time. Katya noticed how content her mother looked with Afrim and was happy for them. Things were certainly different from the last time she left Kosovo. Afrim had offered to take Katya to the airport which would mean an early start. They would need to get to the airport by six-thirty.

The final day in Pristina for Katya was a strange affair, a mixture of sadness at leaving a lot of friends and excitement at what lay ahead. At the Refugee Council, the queues at the enquiries desks still snaked back through the main entrance door; nothing had changed in that respect. It would be some while before that would improve, but Katya felt she had made a difference in the time she had been working there.

Captain Drury had arranged a small leaving party, and said some very kind words thanking Katya for her hard work and wishing her well in her new role with the Refugee Council in the UK. There was a presentation of some wine glasses which had been carefully packed so Katya would be able to take them with her. Captain Drury jokingly said he would sort out any excess baggage issues. Later, Katya cleared her desk and took her bits and pieces in a carrier bag to the car having made a tearful goodbye.

Katya collected the children and Afrim and Maria drove with them back to the cottage in Lapugovac. Afrim would pick them up the following morning at five-thirty. There was another sad farewell as Katya said goodbye to her mother. This time she did not feel the same anxiety as she had done the previous March, but it was still a huge wrench after the recent events. As they were leaving, Katya gave her mother one or two bits and pieces that she wouldn't be able to carry on the journey to keep for her. She wanted to leave the cottage tidy for Anna.

Later that evening, Anna called to pick up the keys to the cottage. She had brought with her a bottle of wine to toast the occasion and once the children were in bed the two of them spent an hour or so talking about their hopes and dreams for the future.

After saying goodbye to Anna, Katya put another log on the fire to keep the room warm. Mid-January in Kosovo was cold, and snow lay on the ground, although the consensus was it hadn't been as bad a winter as in previous years. The transport system, such as it was, was working reasonably well and the electricity supply had also improved. The availability had almost doubled since Katya first arrived back in September.

Katya finished packing and put the cases by the front door ready for the early morning start. She would put the final things they would need for the journey in her hand-luggage. She stared again at the fireplace as the logs burned, reflecting on the turn of events of recent months. She had got over Ibi's tragic death; he was in a better place now. What lay ahead was in the lap of the gods, but, when she thought about her return to England and the possibility of meeting up with Polly, she had butterflies in her stomach. She poked at the embers to ensure they would not fall into the hearth and then carried the hurricane light upstairs.

Afrim turned up five-thirty and Katya was waiting with the children. Arjeta was awake and also excited at going on a long journey. Melos was asleep in his buggy. Afrim helped Katya load the car and they set off for the airport, with Arjeta in the back and

Melos asleep on Katya's lap.

The journey to the airport took almost an hour, the snow having returned overnight and, although the roads were open, driving was treacherous. Afrim pulled up outside the airport perimeter where there was a barrier manned by two armed sentries. Katya had been given a special pass allowing them access to the airport service road which was still restricted to military personnel. It was busy even at this early hour with KFOR transport vehicles and armoured cars everywhere. With a glance at the pass, the barrier was raised, and they made their way to the terminal building and the departures gate.

They said their farewells, and Katya hugged Afrim. "Look after *Mami*, for me."

"Of course I will," said Afrim.

With the luggage and carrier bags safely loaded on an airport trolley, Katya watched as the Toyota pulled away and the family headed to the Departures concourse with Arjeta pushing Melos in his buggy. She felt a mixture of emotions.

Pristina airport was run-down and showed evidence of neglect and abuse from the conflict. Katya made her way to the check-in desk and was surprised to see it quiet among the general hubbub in the building. Flights were still infrequent, but there were lines of frustrated people waiting at other desks with many of the few scheduled flights cancelled due to weather problems elsewhere in Europe. Luckily, Pristina was open, and, after no more than ten minutes, Katya was checked onto the special Refugee Council charter. In the departure lounge, Melos had woken up and Katya fed him his early breakfast from a jar.

The departure lounge was again packed, with limited space and no facilities to get food or drink, apart from a small kiosk which was constantly besieged by queuing people. Melos was starting to grizzle at having to sit on Katya's lap. He kept struggling to get to the floor.

"Can I take Melos for a walk?" said Arjeta, speaking in Albanian.

"Yes, but be careful," replied Katya.

Katya was grateful for Arjeta's offer; it would give her some respite. His buggy was now in the hold of the plane. Arjeta held Melos' hand and toddled up the rows of seats and back again. Melos seemed to take everything in as fellow passengers made a fuss of him.

Katya breathed a sigh of relief when the flight was eventually called with a take-off time of nine-fifteen. The rest of the boarding procedure was uneventful, and Katya took her seat on the Boeing 737. It was by no means full, and Katya could have three seats together. She looked around at her fellow passengers. They were a mixture of businesspeople and returning refugees, mostly men, as Jenny had described. There were several people in military uniform.

After four hours, the plane started its descent to Heathrow and landed in a grey and dull morning. With the two-hour time difference, it was now eleven o'clock, local time, which meant less time to wait at Heathrow.

The arrivals area at Heathrow was a totally new experience. It looked as though the whole world was there with nationalities from every part of the globe. Katya stopped to take it all in. There must have been several thousand people milling about; it was mind-blowing. Tannoys constantly chirped flight updates in English and French. Katya looked at the electronic departures board, names of places that she had only seen in atlases. She scanned the long list of destinations until she found what she was looking for; '12.45 Newcastle Flight BA 4078 gate number 56', and made her way to the flight transfer desk. Her baggage would be transferred direct to the Newcastle flight. Without his buggy, Katya was carrying Melos in her left arm with Arjeta holding her right, her hand luggage wrapped round her shoulder in her sling bag.

Following check-in, the family made their way to the departure gate. It took almost another fifteen minutes to reach. The flight had been called by the time Katya arrived. Around the desk there was an adjacent seating area with about twenty people reading or doing crosswords waiting for the flight. One or two businessmen were working on laptops which fascinated Katya. The computers she used at the centre in Kosovo were basic. She found a seat and settled the children, waiting for the flight to be called. After a few minutes, she was chatting with an older woman who was also travelling back to Newcastle. The woman agreed to look after the children while Katya answered the call of nature and bought a takeaway cup of coffee.

Within a few minutes, the flight boarded, and Katya found her seat. Arjeta wanted to sit by the window; Melos was on Katya's lap. A tall, well-built man sat on the vacant aisle seat. He was probably in his late thirties/early forties, white, but not English, with shaven head and rough features; he was very smartly dressed in a two-piece suit and coordinated tie.

Katya politely said "hello"; the man acknowledged and took out a newspaper from his briefcase and started to read. Half an hour into the flight, coffee and sandwiches were served, and the man stowed his paper back in his expensive-looking briefcase perched on his lap. He had declined food but ordered a small bottle of mineral water.

It was time to give Melos his lunch, and Katya needed to get to her bag in the overhead compartment. Excusing herself, she moved past the man and noticed a faded tattoo across the back of his head. She returned to her seat, apologising to the man for disturbing him again.

"No problem," he replied, in a guttural Eastern European tone.

Katya finished feeding Melos, and then Arjeta decided she needed to go to the toilet, which meant disturbing the man again. He was gracious in his understanding. On her return, Katya thanked the man.

"No problem," he replied again, but made little eye-contact.

Katya decided not to pursue conversation further, but as a former language student, the accent fascinated her; possibly Russian.

After a few minutes, the captain announced that the plane would be making its final descent and Katya's excitement grew at the thought of returning to her flat. The aircraft landed only ten minutes late and, as soon as the seat-belt sign was switched off, the man beside her got up, nodded to Katya and made his way to the exit with his briefcase. Katya decided to wait until the cabin had emptied before trying to negotiate the children off the plane. One of the air hostesses helped her with the hand-luggage.

After leaving the plane, Katya and the children followed the rest of the passengers to the arrival hall and passport control. Katya was kept waiting while the visas and other documents were examined by a surly officer. Then it was onto the baggage carousel to collect their luggage and Melos's buggy. The airport was much smaller than Heathrow but bigger than Pristina, and, after a few minutes, they were passing through customs and leaving the main terminal.

As she left the airport, Katya took a deep breath. It was warmer than Kosovo but damp and rather dreary with grey clouds scurrying across the rain-laden sky. Fortunately, the family had wrapped up well against the winter chill.

Katya was pushing the heavy trolley with their luggage with Arjeta taking up buggy duty again under close supervision. As Katya looked for the taxi rank, she noticed the man who had sat next to her on the plane getting into the back of a large limousine. She watched out of curiosity, as it pulled away towards the airport exit.

Just then, a familiar voice cut through the cacophony of the crowd in front of the terminal building.

"Katya! Katya!" It was more of a high-pitched shriek.

Katya turned around, and Carole was running towards her arms outstretched. Before she could move, Katya was engulfed in a huge hug almost sweeping her off her feet.

"Carole?!" said Katya just as excitedly. "I wasn't sure whether you would be here. I was going to get a taxi."

They hugged for what seemed a long time, reflecting the emotion of the moment.

"I've missed you so much, pet," said Carole.

"I've missed you too," responded Katya.

Katya was so pleased to hear the Geordie twang again, but had to adjust her senses to understand Carole's excited questioning; "How are you? What was your flight like?" They broke off their embrace and Carole looked at Arjeta and Melos.

"Look at you two," she said, addressing the children. "They've both grown up since I last saw them. They look well, and so do you Katya, pet. Come on, I've got the car in the car park. Let me push your cases; you must be knackered after coming all this way. What time did you start this morning?" she added, without drawing breath, and continued before Katya could answer. "Never mind, pet, I'll have us a nice brew in no time."

It was so good to be with Carole again, just as Katya had remembered her.

They made their way to the car park with Carole pushing the luggage trolley and Katya pushing the buggy with Arjeta holding onto her free arm. Carole put her ticket in the pay station.

"I hope you have not been waiting very long," said Katya.

"No, I've been following the arrival times on Teletext, like, so as soon as I knew when you were landing, I jumped in the car." Katya lost the translation but smiled anyway.

They loaded the car and Katya put Arjeta in the back seat. She had Melos on her lap in the front.

"It's not too far, about half an hour," said Carole.

They moved out of the airport car park and took the Newcastle Road.

"Lovely houses here," observed Katya. "Look at that one," she pointed to an art-deco mansion with a long drive and big iron gates. Even though it was the middle of winter, the grounds looked immaculate.

"Aye, this is Ponteland, very posh area. You need a lot of cash to live 'round here," replied Carole. Katya understood.

"So, you must tell me all your news; there's so much to catch up on," continued Carole.

"Yes. How is Bigsy?" enquired Katya.

"He's fine, he owns the video shop now, so he's not under my feet all the time."

"And Polly?" asked Katya, almost dreading the answer.

Carole turned her head and glanced at Katya for a second before replying.

"Our Polly's been a mess since you left, I don't mind telling you, but he's ok, at the University now. I don't see much of him."

Carole didn't mention her recent conversation with Polly at this point.

"What about you and your hubby?" enquired Carole.

Katya turned to Carole. "He's dead." There was a pause. "He was killed in November, in an accident in a truck."

"I'm so sorry, pet, I had no idea," replied Carole, glancing again at Katya.

"It has not been possible to contact you; it is, how you say? Chaos. There is no telephone, no letters."

It was quiet for a couple of minutes while Carole digested the information.

"So, Clara says you've got a job with the Refugee people in Newcastle," she said, changing the subject.

"Yes, I start next Monday," said Katya. "I have been working with them in Pristina."

"What will you be doing?" asked Carole.

"Helping refugees get home and trying to help them with any problems, like Jenny did for me and Edi when we were here."

After a few more minutes of catch up, the towers-blocks of Heathcote came into view and Katya felt strange, not the excitement of earlier, more a sense of realism and the challenges that lay ahead. There was a touch of nervousness.

The car pulled up outside the flats. Katya got up and looked at the high-rise. Arjeta got out and suddenly, from nowhere, shouted, "*mami, mami*". Katya picked her up and gave her a hug but didn't know what to say.

Carole unloaded the suitcases from the boot and Katya put Melos in the buggy. Arjeta was given the job of pushing Melos and they made their way to the lifts.

There was so much familiarity for Katya. It was almost as though she had never been away. The same aroma of disinfectant and urine caught her nose as they made their way to the fourteenth floor. Carole led them to her flat and found the keys in her handbag. She opened the door, and the small group went in.

Katya noticed how clean everything looked. It smelt fresh and there was a bunch of flowers in a vase on the dining table. "They're from Clara," said Carole.

"That is so kind of her."

She stood motionless for a moment and scanned the apartment in disbelief.

"It's almost as I left it."

"Aye, I think the council decided to leave the furniture for the next tenants. They certainly didn't move anything out after you'd left," said Carole, and walked towards the kitchen. "I'll just put the kettle on. I bet you're gagging."

Katya went to the sofa and stroked the side as if it was a favourite cat and started to daydream.

Whilst Carole was making the tea, Katya continued to look around the flat, amazed how little had changed. The television, dining table, chairs were all the same. She went into the two bedrooms and saw the beds, dressing tables, wardrobes and the bathroom. Although there was some evidence of wear and tear, it was like some cryogenic experiment, frozen in time, waiting for her to return.

In the kitchen, Carole opened the fridge and took out a bottle of champagne that had been chilling. She went to the door and waived it to Katya who was in the lounge still taking in her surroundings. "I thought we could open this later, from me and Bigsy."

"That would be wonderful, thank you so much," replied Katya, momentarily shaken from her reminiscences.

Carole walked in with two mugs of reviving tea and handed one to Katya. Arjeta was already running around the flat pushing Melos in his buggy, seemingly glad to be home.

"We've got you some bits and pieces in, which should last you a day or so," said Carole, sipping her drink. "The rest of the cleaning stuff's in the cabinet under the sink and there's some milk, bread, butter, teabags, coffee, cornflakes, just a few things to get you started."

"That is very kind of you, Carole. I've really missed you."

Katya went to Carole and gave her a hug, almost spilling her tea. Katya remembered fondly how generous the local people were.

After drinking her tea, Carole made her excuses and left Katya to settle in, promising to return around eight to open the champagne.

"Yes, that will be nice. I can get the children to bed and put my things away."

Carole left, and Katya looked around the flat again. Almost instinctively she went to the window and looked across to the rec hoping to see if Polly was flying his kite. The playing fields were empty. It was already starting to get dark, and the rain that had threatened earlier was now coming down.

Katya took the cases into the bedroom and started to unpack. Her main priority was to get Melos' recliner and lobsterpot out and constructed, then she could leave him while she sorted out the rest of the flat. The bed had not been made but there were pillows, blankets and sheets in the airing cupboard. Arjeta was looking after Melos in his buggy and giggled with excitement when Katya explained she would have her old bedroom again.

After an hour or so, Katya had finished unpacking and had fed the children. After the long day she would be putting them to bed early; it would give her the chance to freshen up before Carole returned.

Katya had showered and changed and was wearing a 'sloppy' jumper and pair of jeans. She was feeling much more relaxed now, and was sorting out the kitchen when Carole knocked on the door just after eight. Katya had got two of her new wine glasses from the presentation box, which had thankfully made the journey unscathed, and greeted Carole with the bottle of bubbly from the fridge.

"I hope you can open this," said Katya.

"No problem," said Carole, and expertly grasped the top and gently unscrewed the cork until there was a slight 'pop'. Quickly she poured the foaming drink into the waiting glasses. They moved to the sofa and were soon in animated conversation sipping on their champagne.

As the alcohol started to take effect, Katya provided more detail about her experiences during her time in Kosovo.

"It was terrible, if I am honest, so much sadness."

"What about your hubby?"

Katya looked down. "The war had changed him; he had been tortured by the Serbs, and was a different man. He had started drinking and became… er." She thought for the right word. "Abusive; I could not stay with him. I spent most of the time with my mother with the children. Then he had his accident; it was very sad, but maybe it was for the best."

Katya looked down again.

"What about our Polly?"

"I have never stopped thinking about him. He is always in my heart."

After an hour, and half of the champagne, Carole made her farewells, recognising Katya would be tired from her journey. Katya returned the unfinished bottle to the fridge and was washing the glasses when there was a knock on the door.

She opened the door and recognised the figure standing in the doorway immediately.

"Polly?!" was all she could say.

Chapter Ten

Polly stood there exactly as Katya remembered, a tall, skinny, good-looking student, with unruly fair hair and a wicked smile. He was wearing a tracksuit top, jeans and trainers.

"Hiya, Katya, pet," he said nervously.

Katya stood holding the door almost unable to move, her legs unsteady. There was a long pause with both looking at each other. It was Katya that broke the ice.

"Come in, Polly, come in."

She ushered him inside. Polly sat on the sofa while Katya disappeared to the kitchen. The butterflies had returned. She came back into the room carrying two glasses and the half empty bottle of champagne. Without saying a word, she handed him a glass and started to pour.

"No broons, I'm afraid," said Katya, which raised a nervous smile on Polly's face.

"You remembered?" said Polly, tapping his feet.

"Of course. How could I forget?"

Katya sat down next to him, and for a few moments there was an awkward silence as they sipped their drinks; her emotions were all over the place. Although she had always hoped, she just hadn't prepared herself for this moment. She breathed deeply trying to compose herself knowing she would have to make the first move; she recognised Polly had no idea where he stood. She put her glass down and met his eyes.

"I can't believe you are here," she whispered.

All the pent-up frustrations of the last seven months were surfacing. She grasped his hands; she just wanted to hold him.

"Oh Polly, oh Polly," she repeated, hoping the right words would come to her. "I have never stopped thinking about you. My life has not been the same without you."

He looked down, avoiding her gaze.

"What about your hubby?" he said, sharply.

She looked down. "He's dead, Polly. He was killed, three months ago."

He looked up, engaging her eyes.

"I'm so sorry, pet; I had no idea."

"There was no way I could tell you; it was impossible. Everything is in a mess in Kosovo, no letters, phones. I could not contact you, I wanted to. Every day I thought of you."

She paused and looked down at her drink.

"Also, I didn't know if you would still want to hear from me after what had happened. I could understand if you didn't want to see me again."

She picked up her glass again which was almost empty and took another sip, more silence. Then she continued.

"But there was another problem, a bigger problem. I could not leave Kosovo. There are no visas. I couldn't just get on a plane; I was trapped. So, I just concentrated on looking after the children and my work. I thought I would have to build a new life in Kosovo. I had given up ever seeing you again. Then, one day, they asked me if I wanted to go back to England. I was so shocked. I couldn't believe it, and all I could think of was how I could get back to you."

Katya paused and sipped her drink again, sad at the recollection. More silence as she thought about what to say next. Polly was quiet and staring deep into his glass taking in Katya's words.

"There is something else you should know. My husband was a different man, not the same person I had known; the war had turned him into a monster. We lived with my mother after the first night. He was drunk and called me all sorts of names; it was terrible," she paused again and looked down. "It was not all his fault; I had changed too. I had no feelings for him. I too was not the same person. I should never have gone back, I knew that from the first day, but it was my duty. You understand that, Polly, don't you?"

"Aye." Polly looked at her then turned his gaze to the floor, it was his turn to respond.

"I was thinking about you all the time, wondering what you were doing. I kept thinking of you with him. I was going crazy, man."

"I thought you would have found a new girlfriend."

"I did for a while, but it wasn't the same. I couldn't stop comparing her with you."

More awkward silence as Katya thought about this information. She finished her drink and looked at the remaining dregs of the champagne in their respective glasses.

"That's all there is, I'm afraid. I can us make a coffee if you like."

"It's not coffee I want," said Polly, moving to her and holding her hand.

Their eyes met again, and Polly leaned forward tentatively unsure of the response. She reacted straight away and followed his lead until their lips met, a slow sensuous kiss.

Their love making was urgent but assured, both knowing each other's needs. Later, as they lay on the sofa in each other's arms totally satiated, they both contemplated what had happened. Katya spoke first. She sighed deeply.

"I have dreamed so much of this moment. I can't believe it. I thought I had lost you forever."

"I didn't think I would see you again, either," replied Polly.

"Do you want to stay?" asked Katya, "I don't want to let you go."

"Aye, I'd like that," said Polly.

"It's not very tidy. There are still things to put away."

"I don't care as long as we're together."

They got up and made their way to the bathroom, any tiredness Katya was feeling was overwhelmed by the intensity of the moment. They retired to the bedroom where Melos was fast asleep in his cot.

"Young Melos has grown," whispered Polly, "I can't wait to see him up and about."

"But not just yet," said Katya, looking into Polly's eyes.

They slept soundly in each other's arms until they were awakened by Melos, grizzling for his breakfast. It was seven-thirty. Katya got out of bed and put on her jumper and a pair of briefs; then lifted Melos from his cot and took him to the living room.

"I'll make us some tea," said Katya.

Hearing Katya getting up, Arjeta also got out of her bed in the small adjoining bedroom and followed her. Polly got dressed and joined the family.

"Polly!" said Arjeta.

"Hello, Arjeta," said Polly, and lifted her up high into the air, causing her fits of giggles. "I can't believe she still remembers me."

Katya returned from the kitchen with two mugs of tea. "She remembers a lot of things. She still asks for Edi you know."

Katya sat down next to Polly on the sofa. They both looked at Arjeta as she was playing with Melos who was now back in his recliner.

Katya was intrigued by something and asked the question. "What made you turn up at my door last night?"

"Do you wish I hadn't?" teased Polly, sipping his tea.

"Of course not, I wanted to see you. It was just, well, sooner than I had imagined. I didn't know what you felt about me. I did leave you. I thought you might hate me."

"No, no, I could never hate you, pet, you know that. No, it was our Carol; she phoned me after she had brought you back from the airport. She said that you were talking, like, and she thought you would want to see me. She didn't say anything about your hubby though. She said that she was calling 'round to see you but would make sure she was gone by nine o'clock. I said I should pop up and say 'hello'. I wasn't sure whether to; I nearly didn't."

"So, she's to blame!" said, Katya, and leaned over and kissed Polly.

She continued in a more serious tone. "There are a lot of things I need to tell you. What it was like, how I got back. There is so much to say, but it will wait. We have plenty of time and I have a lot to do."

Taking this as his cue Polly got up.

"Aye, you're right, pet, me Mam doesn't know where I am, I just said I was popping out to see someone."

"She'll be worried. Why didn't you say? You could have phoned her."

"I got distracted, like."

"Ha, yes, that's true. How is she, your mother?"

"She's fine."

"Will you tell her you have been with me?"

"Aye, when the time's right. She knows you were coming back, Carole told her."

"Would you like to come back tonight?"

"Aye, if that's ok. If you're not too busy. That that would be amazin'," replied Polly. "I don't start back to college till next week."

"After eight o'clock would be best, I will have the children in bed by then, and you can tell me how you are getting on at University."

Polly kissed Katya and said goodbye to Arjeta and mad a fuss of Melos in his recliner. He smiled at the attention. "See you later, pet."

Polly left, leaving Katya reflecting on the latest course of events. She wrestled with her feelings, contentment and joy at the reunion she had dreamed of, but never thought for one minute would happen. She also thought of Ibi, not the monster Ibi, but the Ibi she had married and felt sadness for him.

She shook herself from the brooding and got the children fed and dressed then showered and started to tidy up.

Around ten o'clock there was a knock on the door. A large bubbly lady stood there, wearing a bright floral dress, and comfortable shoes, reflecting her native Trinidad. It was Clara.

"Hiya, Katya, girl."

"Clara, how lovely to see you; come in."

Arjeta was with Melos in the living room.

"Arjeta... and Melos! My, how you have grown," said Clara, as she followed Katya inside.

Katya gave Clara a hug.

"Please, sit down, would you like a coffee?"

"Yes, please."

"I won't be a minute."

Clara took off her coat and made herself comfortable.

"Thank you so much for everything you have done for me and for the flowers; they were so nice. I can't believe you were able to get me my flat again; that was such a surprise," said Katya from the kitchen as she made the drinks.

"It's ok, I was able to pull a few strings, I know the housing department manager. I said you would be an important addition to the community."

"That is very kind, thank you," said Katya, bringing in two mugs of coffee.

"No problem, I am just so pleased to have you back."

Katya had got used to speaking English again, and they sat chatting for a few minutes. Clara's boundless energy and enthusiasm had not diminished. Katya described the journey and how things were in Kosovo, the transport and communication problems, and the frustration of not being able to contact anyone outside the country. She told Clara of Ibi's accident, but not all the details. Clara listened intently and offered her condolences.

She then brought Katya up to date with some local news. She explained there were twelve other Kosovan families now settled in Newcastle. Two were in Wesley House, the adjoining tower block.

"You must let me have their address; I will call to see them."

"Jenny Wheatley will have them."

"Yes, of course, I will ask her."

Clara took another sip of her coffee.

"It will be so good to have you here, someone who really understands their situation and speaks the language."

Katya nodded remembering how isolated she felt in those early days.

After another five minutes chat, Clara looked at her watch. "Is that the time? I need to go.".

She quickly finished her coffee and stood up. "Oh, I nearly forgot, Jenny asked me to tell you she will call around either today or tomorrow to sort out one or two things."

Katya thanked Clara's and, with the promise of an early return, saw her out.

Later, Katya got the children ready and headed out; she needed some supplies. Without transport, she would have to shop locally, and made her way to Mr. Ali's. She had withdrawn all the money from her Kosovan Bank account and changed it into sterling, just over eight hundred pounds, but Katya would not get paid for at least another month, so it would need to last a long time. She put fifty pounds in her purse and kept the rest in an envelope in the drawer of the bedside cabinet.

Getting out the lift, she looked up at the skies. It was a cold morning, almost midday, grey with rain around which made everything look so dreary. It seemed ages since she had seen the sun. As she was going through the entrance door, a familiar face appeared heading towards the lifts.

"Alison?" said Katya.

Alison looked at her without too much warmth.

"Hello Katya, our Polly said you were back. I hope you're not going to break his heart again."

"Oh Alison, please don't say that. I would never hurt Polly, I love him."

"Aye, that's what you said before you buggered off back to Kosovo, back to your hubby. He was devastated you know, our Polly."

"I know and I can't undo what is done, but I really love him, Alison, I really do."

"Aye, well we'll have to see, won't we?" Alison turned and walked on towards the lift.

The meeting had troubled Katya. It had not gone the way she had hoped.

The precinct was quiet, the local children had gone back to school after the Christmas break. She looked at the three shops and it seemed little had changed apart from the new sign on the video store, 'Hollywood Nights'. It had added colour to the precinct.

At the supermarket, Mr. Ali made a fuss of Katya and the two children. The shop was quiet, and Jamal was serving the only other customer.

"Carole said you were coming back to Heathcote. It is so good to see you again," said the shopkeeper. "You were missed a great deal at the school you know."

Katya thanked him for his kindness then went down the aisles collecting her needs. She had a long list of things and Arjeta helped Katya put them in the basket. Katya made the decision to start speaking English to Arjeta in the hope she would soon pick up the language again. After a few minutes it became clear that Katya would need another basket, and she returned to the till.

"Jamal will help you with your list and carry it up for you," said Mr. Ali.

Jamal was duly summoned, and helped Katya collect all the groceries, suggesting alternatives and pointing out special offers, resulting in more shopping in her bags than she had anticipated. She did not have much change from her fifty pounds. As he was checking out her purchases at the till, Mr. Ali was curious at the two bottles of Newcastle Browns along with the bottles of red wine.

"Entertaining I see," he commented.

Katya just smiled.

The family made their way back to the flat with Jamal following with a large cardboard box full of provisions. Katya carried the remainder in a carrier bag with Arjeta back on buggy duty.

The kitchen cupboards and fridge looked better now they were stocked up, and, after lunch, Katya put the children down for a sleep. She had bought a newspaper and was reading it when there was another knock on the door.

"Jenny, how lovely to see you, come in; Clara said to expect you. She called round earlier. It's so nice seeing familiar faces again."

They went inside and Katya gave Jenny a hug.

"It's good to see you, too, Katya; we are so pleased you could join us. It will be so useful to have someone with your experience onboard."

Katya went to make yet more coffee, but this time only one cup. She would have a glass of water.

Pleasantries over, Jenny, as professional as ever, was quickly down to business, explaining the office set-up and how to get there.

"There's a parking spot for you."

"But I haven't got a car," said Katya.

"Oh yes, I forgot to mention; you'll be entitled to a car. There'll be some travelling involved, Leeds, Sheffield, possibly Manchester, from time to time. In fact, you'll be having mine; it's only eighteen-months old. I'm changing cars when I move down to London. My new one is being delivered on Monday, so we can do the swap then. You do drive, don't you?"

"Yes, but not in England," said Katya.

Jenny could see Katya's anxiety and reassured her. "Don't worry, we'll sort out all the paperwork and insurance, and I'll be able to do the first few visits with you. I don't leave until the 28th, so we'll have plenty of time to get you settled."

They continued the discussion for over an hour, Jenny giving Katya some updates on cases, particularly the troublesome ones. Katya was trying to take it all in.

Inside, she was beginning to doubt her abilities, but Jenny had no such qualms and reassured Katya. "Don't worry, after a couple of weeks, you'll be fine."

The discussion was curtailed when the noise of crying came from the bedroom. Melos had woken up and Arjeta wandered into the living room and informed Katya.

"Melos është i zgjuar," said Arjeta

"Oh, Melos is awake," translated Katya.

Katya excused herself and went to the bedroom. She returned with Melos.

"What lovely children," said Jenny. She paused. "I was sorry to hear about your husband."

"Thank you," said Katya, and looked down. "They were difficult times."

There was a pause, then Jenny put her cup on the coffee table and got up. "See you Monday... If you need anything, anything at all, just give me a call."

"Yes, there is something; I don't know if my phone still works here. I haven't used it since I left Kosovo. It was the one they gave me in Pristina."

"Oh yes, no problem, don't worry, I'll get you fixed up with a new one on Monday." Jenny made a mental note.

Jenny departed, leaving Katya with a lot to think about. The job she was being asked to do was important, and a lot of time and money had been invested in her. Expectations would be high, and right now it seemed daunting.

Katya spent the rest of the afternoon thinking about these new demands whilst she went about cleaning and getting the flat to her liking. There was more unpacking to do. She still couldn't believe how so little had changed. There were scuff marks on the kitchen lino and some of the kitchen appliances had been well-used, particularly the microwave, judging by the warn-looking on/off switch.

She made some pasta for tea, which was a change from the food she had been eating over recent weeks. She turned on the television to watch the news while she fed the children. There had been no television whilst she had been in Kosovo, and was out of date with world events. The main headline was the continued search for a sunken trawler. She watched with sadness at what the families of the missing fishermen were going through.

She was reading a story to Arjeta when there was yet another knock on the door. It was Carole holding a large cardboard box.

"Hiya, Katya, pet, recognise this?"

"Of course, come in."

Carole carried the box into the living room and put it on the sofa. Arjeta was intrigued,

"*Çfarë është kjo,*" she said.

Katya translated for Carol. "She wants to know what it is."

"Let's open it and see, shall we?" said Carole.

Katya went to the kitchen to a get a knife, then opened the cardboard box, watched closely by Arjeta. It was full of the clothes and bits and pieces that they had been unable to take with them to Kosovo, much of it was Arjeta's that Edi had bought her.

"I hope she will still be able to get into these," said Katya, holding up some of the clothes.

"If she can't, you can take them to the Pre-school. They're always needing stuff," said Carole.

Arjeta excitedly rummaged through the contents and found some long-forgotten toys.

"*Sy! Sy!*", "look! look!" she cried, as she found one of her favourite dolls.

"Have you got time for a drink, I have some red wine," said Katya, closing the box. Arjeta had retrieved the doll and was showing it to Melos in his lobster pot.

"Always got time for some vino," said Carole, and Katya went to the kitchen and opened a bottle of the red and returned with two glasses.

"How's your day been, pet?" asked Carole.

Katya recounted the day and the visitors.

"Have you seen anything of our Polly?" Carole's said, matter-of-factly.

Katya paused and took a sip of wine; she was not sure how to answer the question.

"He called last night, just after you left."

"And!?" said Carole, her eyes wide in expectation.

"Yes, everything is fine," said Katya with a broad smile.

"Oh, that's champion," said Carole, and hugged Katya, nearly spilling her wine. "I'm so happy for yas. I said to Bigsy you and our Polly were made for each other. I can tell these things."

"I should thank you, too. Polly told me you had spoken to him."

"Just trying to help things along."

Katya returned the smile and topped up Carole's glass which was almost empty. Her expression changed.

"I did also see Alison today as I was going to the shops. She didn't seem so pleased to see me; in fact, she seemed almost angry."

"Don't you fret, Katya, pet; she's just protecting our Polly. They've always been close them two, ever since her hubby buggered off. She wouldn't let him out till he was sixteen. She'll come 'round; you'll see."

Katya remained to be convinced. "I hope."

Carole left around seven, and Katya finished putting the children to bed, leaving enough time to shower and change before Polly returned. The central heating was warm and made the flat cosy, a far cry from her cottage in Lapugovac. It meant she could wear a blouse and a pair of casual trousers. Her jeans were in the wash.

Around eight-fifteen, there was a knock on the door and Katya could feel the excitement as she went to answer it.

"Polly… come in."

They kissed warmly.

"I had difficulty keeping my head together today, pet, I don't mind telling you," he said, as he made his way into the living room. "I've been trying to finish off a project for Uni, but it's been hard to concentrate. I still can't believe you're here, pet. I have to keep pinching myself to see I'm not dreaming."

He followed Katya into the kitchen. He wrapped his arms around her waist while she tried to sort out the drinks. Katya giggled like a sixteen-year-old.

"Look, I remembered," she said, passing him an unopened bottle of Newcastle Brown. She poured herself a glass of red wine.

"Champion," he replied, and hit the top of the bottle on the side of the worktop to open it. Katya remembered the first time he did that. The chip on the worktop was still visible.

"I will get a..." She paused for the right words. "A thing to open the bottle, tomorrow."

"How's your day been, pet?" enquired Polly, as they returned the living room

"Very busy." Katya told Polly about the visitors and her impending job.

"I'm getting a car," she said excitedly. "But it will be difficult driving here; it is so different. There was very little, er, traffic in Kosovo, apart from jeeps, trucks and tractors."

"That's ok, I can show you 'round. You'll soon get used to it."

Polly was becoming distracted. "I'm sorry, pet, I'm finding it difficult to concentrate here."

Katya realised the effect her attire was having on him. She smiled broadly.

"We'll have to do something about that won't we?"

She started to undo the buttons on her blouse, and moved towards him.

They made love on the living room floor, reaching the same

heights of pleasure as the previous night's encounter.

They hugged each other for a long time afterwards, each engrossed in their own thoughts.

Katya spoke softly. "There are things I need to tell you."

And as they lay together, she recounted her life during their time apart including Ibi's fatal crash.

"I'm glad you told me, pet, I can't begin to understand what you went through. It must have been hell."

After more revelations, Katya put on her shirt and pants and went to the kitchen to make them both a coffee.

"I saw your mother today, did she tell you?" said Katya, as she came into the living room carrying two mugs.

"Aye, she did mention it."

"She didn't seem very pleased to see me."

"You don't want to take any notice of me Mam; she's always going on about stuff. She'll be ok."

Katya let it drop and changed the subject.

"When do you go back to college?"

"Monday, I've finished all my assignments."

"That's good. Would you like to come into town with me tomorrow, if you have time? I need to have a bank here, and I want to see the office where I am working. You can show me round."

Katya handed him his drink.

"Aye, pet, I've got nottin' planned. I'd love to."

The following day Polly, Katya and the two children caught the local 'Hoppa' to the Interchange in Gateshead and another bus to Newcastle city centre. It was like a real family. Arjeta seemed pleased to have Polly around, and he made a point of talking to her, not that she understood a great deal, but the connection was important. Katya hoped that there would be some stability in her troubled life at last. At one stage, Polly lifted Melos onto his shoulders giving him a bird's eye view of the surroundings. Then he had to do the same for Arjeta.

They walked through the Eldon Square shopping area, which was packed with shoppers. Katya had not visited it before. It was different to the Metro Centre, more spread out, but she was amazed at the different shops. She made a couple of purchases, a bottle opener and a pair of scissors, before the family stopped off for a burger lunch. They found the Refugee Council Offices not far from the Civic Centre and the University where Polly was studying. Katya was happier having seen the office and felt there wouldn't be a problem getting there, although she had yet to experience rush-hour in Newcastle!

Polly took Katya to the same bank that he used in case they needed any references. They went in and completed the formalities. It would take a few days until she got her debit card, she was informed. Katya had always paid in cash; there was no equivalent banking set up in Kosovo, and Polly explained how it would work.

They eventually made their way back on the bus, Katya feeling more content than she had ever done. Suddenly a better future looked possible.

Chapter Eleven

Friday morning, while Polly and Katya were playing happy families, more serious events were taking place elsewhere in Newcastle.

At Tyneside Police H.Q., Detective Superintendent Adams was having his weekly case assessment meeting. Each lead officer involved with the investigation was providing an update of their activities during the week and any progress.

D.S. Frasier went first.

"Nothing much to report on Worrell, or Gibbons for that matter; we've been keeping tabs on them for almost two weeks now and apart from Worrell's visit to Scalleys nightclub on..." He referred to his notebook. "Tuesday 3rd, he's been at home or in the video shop. He did visit a bungalow on Bensham which turned out to be his mother's. Gibbons, much the same, no social activity to talk about. Been in his terrace in Jesmond most of the time, couple of trips to the One-Stop store and that's it. Not sure if it's worth continuing twenty-four-hour static obs, recommend we log and keep them on radar."

"Yes... I agree. I'd love to know why they met up, though," said Adams.

"Could be about videos, Worrell did have that pull for distributing porn," said Frasier.

"No, it has to be drugs. Can't see Gibbons being linked to dodgy videos somehow, but I don't think we have much choice for now. We'll keep them on the board as a possible link and see what happens," said Adams.

DS Tunney followed with his report.

"We've had obs on Scalleys nightclub since Worrell's visit, and this maybe more interesting. I've had a couple of plain clothes in there asking around, making enquiries. Nobody's saying much, but one of the barmaids we tried talking to, a..." He referred to his notes. "Gemma Calder, has been reported missing by her mother, didn't turn up for work the following night, and nobody's seen her since..." Tunney went back to his notes and continued. "We did manage to speak with the resident D.J. there, a Daryl... Anderson, but drew a blank, didn't know anything, or if he did, he wasn't saying. However, we've also been keeping an eye on the security team at the club. There're some real head-cases knocking around, ex-cons mostly. They're provided by a company called 'SD Securities', which is run by a former boxer Sonny Daniels, whom some of you may have heard of from his fighting days. Quite a celebrity at the time, apparently."

"What do we know about him?" asked Adams.

Tunney referred to his notes again and continued. "Interesting character, a Scouser and one-time great hope for British boxing, won silver medal in the 1976 Olympics. Turned professional but was injured in his third fight and had to retire. Moved to Newcastle in the early nineties and established a successful business empire, night clubs, casinos that sort of thing. He contributes to many charities, and has also set up a boxing academy aimed at getting kids off the street. High profile on the social circuit, always see him at prestigious dos, on the face of it, the veritable pillar of society. Lives in a large house just outside Ponteland." He looked up from his notes and smiled. "Knows the Chief Constable, I understand." There was a chuckle among the group. "D.C. Harris has been digging up some background on the company."

"Harris?" said Adams.

"Yes sir." D.C. Wendy Harris, a twenty-five-year-old, high-flying graduate officer, was stood by a laptop. She clicked the mouse, and a PowerPoint slideshow opened on a custom-built screen set into the wall. The room went quiet as she briefed the team. She was assertive in her delivery.

"Interesting set up. There are several companies involved. I've put this together so you can see the connections more clearly. The whole group is owned and controlled by this company 'North End Casinos Ltd'… this is the parent company."

The name 'North End Casinos Ltd' appeared in large letters on the screen.

She continued. "Directors are Sonny Daniels, and an Abdul Aziz, who has dual Saudi and U.K. nationality. We don't know anything about him, no record. Lives in London according to Companies House. The company's turnover last year was over eight million pounds."

One or two officers whistled though their teeth when they heard the figures.

"According to the latest accounts, net profit was just over three. Sonny paid himself a dividend of one point two million and received a salary of two-hundred and fifty k. What you might call a nice little earner."

She paused and took a sip from a bottle of water.

"North End Casinos own two big gaming joints, one in North Shields, Eldorado; the other in town, Klondike."

The names appeared on the screen.

"North End also owns this company." The name 'SD Securities Ltd' flashed up with an arrow pointing to the holding company.

"SD Securities Ltd, as the name suggests, is a private security firm, and provides security for many of the clubs in town. In fact, with one or two exceptions, they now have a monopoly. There are rumours that the takeover of a rival company, 'Faithguard Ltd', was far from harmonious. According to sources, some 'encouragement'…" She made a sign with the first two fingers of both hands indicating the apostrophes. "Shall we say, was exerted to get them to sell up to Sonny."

She paused for another drink.

"As D.S. Tunney has said, they employ ex-cons and various ne'er-do-wells."

There were some quizzical looks from her colleagues at this phraseology.

"Do you mean 'scumbags'?" shouted one of the junior officers, to much raucous laughter.

"Alright people, settle down," admonished the Superintendent. "Carry on Harris."

Undaunted, she continued. "As I was saying, they have some real head-cases on the books, although I doubt if we would find an inventory of personnel. According to the company files, they employ less than twenty people, so most of the workers are going to be self-employed, cash-in-hand merchants. The list of directors of SD Securities Ltd filed at Companies House, show Daniels, of course, and a Roland Carter, whom we know nothing about. More interesting however, is this man, Sergei Hordiyenko." His name appeared on the screen. "Who according to our sources, runs the security side. He's Ukrainian."

"Do we know anything about this Ukrainian?" asked Adams.

"Not much, sir," replied Harris. "But one of the lads did some digging, and it seems our Sergei is a bad lad, all gossip and speculation of course, but he has a reputation as a man to be 'reckoned with'."

She did the apostrophe gesture again, which was beginning to irritate some of the audience. She continued undeterred.

"According to rumour, he was a hit man for the Russian Mafia back home, and fled to the U.K. He was eventually taken under Daniels' wing. According to our sources, he does most of the enforcement for the business. This is all speculation of course; nobody was talking much. Our usual contacts were remarkably reticent when his name was mentioned. We had to lean quite heavily on a couple of people just to get this much."

"Very good, constable, anything else?" asked Adams.

"Just some more on Sonny's empire. The company also owns three night clubs, Scalleys and Mr. Gees in Newcastle, and Lucifer's in Gateshead. As you know we have been targeting these as having 'special interest'."

She avoided the apostrophe this time.

"D.S. Mackenzie was investigating Scalleys before he was killed, and we had the shootings last June outside Mr. Gees. We know that all three clubs have links with drugs, but we have never been able to bring any convictions. Security there is pretty tight. The other thing that occurs to me, sir, is the potential here for money laundering. It is a significant cash-cow and with the amount of money changing hands daily, it would not take a genius to work out ways of channelling drug-takings through the business."

She stopped again for water.

"There is one final piece of the jigsaw. Daniels also owns 'Sonny's Gym', a small enterprise just off the Haymarket. This is not part of the North End Empire but a private project which he uses to promote his charitable enterprises. He trains local up-and-coming boxers and, as D.S. Tunney mentioned, he also takes young lads off the streets and gives them a chance, and if they're any good, sponsors their training. He enjoys a great deal of media coverage and apparently has important contacts in the council. He's also on several committees."

D.C. Harris concluded the presentation and turned off the laptop. She had another drink from her bottle of water.

"Well done Harris, excellent work," said Adams.

"So, let's recap. We appear to have unearthed a massive operation here. It's complex and sophisticated and we will devote resources to this investigation. Evidence is going to be the stumbling block. As you've seen, Daniels is well connected and if this set up is what we believe, he'll be a shrewd operator. We'll need to watch our own security and that of our contacts. These are dangerous people; I don't want another Craig Mackenzie situation on our hands. We'll be getting three new teams on board in the next few days, and they'll need bringing up to speed... D.S. Tunney can you look after that?"

Tunney acknowledged.

"I want any information and leads channelling through me with daily updates from senior officers. I want people on the ground, and we'll continue moving obs and plain clothes in the clubs. I'll update the Chief Constable… and also suggest that he takes Sonny Daniels off his Christmas card list for the foreseeable future," he said with a grin. There was some sniggering from the officers.

The superintendent concluded the briefing and started allocating duties to his team.

On Heathcote, another investigation was taking shape, albeit on a much smaller scale. Bigsy was up and dressed by nine-thirty and was sat watching day-time television; he wouldn't be opening the video store until two o'clock. A call came through on his mobile; 'number withheld', it said on the screen.

He recognised the Geordie/Caribbean accent. "Sol, bonny lad, good to hear from you. Have you got some news for us?"

"You have…? That's champion, man. When's he want us, like?"

"Three o'clock… at the gym. Aye, I know where it is, off the Haymarket… Aye, we'll see you then."

Bigsy rang off and immediately called Chirpie. It was answered on the third ring.

"Chirpie, bonny lad…. Bigsy. Sol's just been on. It appears our Sonny's looking for a new recruit and you're in with a shout. He wants to see you at three o'clock this afternoon. Are you ok with that? Joy's not dragging you off to the Metro Centre or nottin'?"

"Well, I don't know about any interview, and me CV's a bit light. It's been a while," said Chirpie.

"Nah, you'll be alright, bonny lad," said Bigsy.

"But I've got no idea about being an undercover investigator. Mind, I did watch the Rockford Files on tele a few years back, but that's about it." Chirpie was still uneasy at his proposed vocation.

"You'll be fine. All you've got to do is keep your eyes and ears open and get involved in any scams that are on offer and see where it goes. I'll cover your back if necessary," countered Bigsy.

"Aye, ok, man, I'll give it a go, " said Chirpie, his voice reflecting his reluctance.

"That's champion. I'll give Wazza a ring and get him to drop us off. See you out the front about two-ish, that ok?" He rang off.

Wazza turned up with the Escort just after two o'clock with Chirpie in the back, and parked outside the video shop. Bigsy was waiting in the entrance of the tower block, watchful as he walked towards the car. There was no sign of the silver Renault.

"Canna see any bizzies about," he said as he got in.

"Aye, reckon they've lost interest, like," said Wazza as he pulled away.

"Looks like it, but we'll keep our eyes peeled."

They headed into town.

The Haymarket area is a particularly busy part of Newcastle, and Wazza initially had difficulty finding a parking spot. The two large multi-stories were almost full, but eventually he managed to find a space. It was quarter-to-three by the time they arrived at their destination.

Just around the corner from the gym, there was a rather dingy-looking cafe. They went inside and were hit by a miasma of cigarette smoke and fried food. The fifteen tables looked like old fifties-style, with oil-cloth coverings and steel-framed legs. There were four cheap plastic and metal seats placed around each table. There was one vacant, still piled high with the remnants of a family lunch - half-eaten burgers and chips sodden in vinegar and tomato ketchup, spilt tea, and a plastic glass of orange juice. The ashtray in the middle was overflowing. The rest of the cafe was populated with shoppers with screaming children and short tempers. The background pop music was virtually inaudible above the cacophony of the clientele.

"Fookin' hell, Chirpie," said Bigsy, "I hope your interview

doesn't last too long, bonny lad, we might catch something if we stay in here for any length of time."

Chirpie checked his watch; it was five-to-three. His buddies had claimed the table and were moving some of the food debris onto an empty tray.

"Right… I'll be off," Chirpie said, rather nervously, and left his buddies.

"Good luck, bonnie lad," shouted Bigsy, as Chirpie reached the door. Then he was gone, heading for Sonny's Gym.

Bigsy deposited the old food and ashtray onto a shelf that ran along the wall where other trays were piled up, waiting collection. He made his way to the counter and was confronted by a teenager in charge of serving.

"What you havin'?" said the lad.

There was a board behind the counter displaying today's specials in big letters, all 'with chips'. Various cans of drinks were stacked along the back shelf and an ancient coffeemaker was to the left. The work surface was covered with coffee and tea stains, and other unidentifiable jetsam. A filthy dishcloth lay alongside the till with bits of congealed food stuck to it. Next to the coffeemaker, there was the kitchen. The door was open, and someone with a cigarette in their mouth was stood at a deep fat-fryer, cooking more chips. The smell of grease and cigarettes was overpowering.

Bigsy ordered two cappuccinos and watched the youth operate the coffeemaker with the artistry of a concert pianist.

"One-twenty," said the lad, passing over two chipped mugs of strange-looking liquid.

Bigsy gave him one pound thirty. "Keep the change, bonny lad. Remind us not to use this as a waiting room again; it's honking, man," said Bigsy, as he placed one of the mugs in front of Wazza and sat down. "And that lad serving has about as much charisma as a pimple."

"Aye, you're not wrong there," said Wazza.

Meanwhile, as his buddies waited for him in the cafe from hell, Chirpie made his way to the gym. It was over the top of a small parade of shops, just a block or so away. The entrance door was painted in a fading creamy-white colour with the words, 'Sonny's Gym', stencilled in black copper-plate writing. The paint was flaking and in need of a make-over; it was open. A brick was placed against it to prevent it springing shut.

A flight of steep, unlit stairs rose in front of him. After the comparative brightness of the street, Chirpie squinted, adjusting his eyes, as he made his way upwards, he counted fifteen steps, to a small landing facing another door with the name, '*Sonny's Gym - Members only*'. There was a security pad with five rows of numbers attached to the wall to the left of the door; below that a bellpush. He pressed the button.

The door opened and a muscleman appeared; he seemed like a new species. "Yeah?" he mumbled.

"I'm Colin Longton, Chirpie. I've got an appointment with Sonny."

The shaved head turned around, shouted something and then opened the door. Sol Miller arrived and took over from the 'Neanderthal'. He welcomed Chirpie.

"I'll take you through," said Sol. "Sonny's in the office."

Chirpie followed Sol through another set of doors into what was quite an unexpected sight. It was a fully-equipped leisure facility; as good as you would see anywhere. It was bright and airy, and made Chirpie blink until he became accustomed to the light again. He could see the latest running treadmills, static rowing machines, cross-trainers, in fact every conceivable type of exercise equipment required to exert the correct torture on the keenest of keep-fit enthusiast.

There was an impressive weights area, with dumbbells of every description. Several hunks were being put through their paces by fit-looking young men with 'personal trainer' emblazoned on their tracksuits. It was a large area with several televisions showing sporting channels hanging from the ceiling to help relieve the monotony of gym training.

As they walked towards the back of the gym, Chirpie could see a full-sized boxing ring in a separate room, with two youths wearing headguards slugging it out. A coach was on hand giving them encouragement. For a mid-Friday afternoon, it was surprisingly busy, and Chirpie noticed the absence of any women; it was a totally male domain, nothing to distract the serious bodybuilder. The room was full of testosterone and beefcake, honing their bodies to perceived perfection.

Chirpie was led into an office, not large by any means. There were two metal four-drawer filing cabinets against the back wall under a small sky-light window which had strong security bars attached. In front of the cabinets was a desk and along the wall to the right, a row of coat hangers, holding around twenty or thirty brand new 'SD Security' jackets of assorted sizes labelled from forty-inch chest to fifty-four inch. A notice above the clothes rail said, 'If the jacket don't fit; you don't get in'.

Two men were seated behind the desk on rather old, leather executive chairs, the sort with wheels. The darker man, wearing expensive gold-rimmed spectacles, had his head down and was reading a piece of paper he was holding in his hand.

Chirpie remembered him from his boxing days, when he was box-office. Of mixed race and a product of the back streets of Liverpool, Daniels was swarthy-looking, lean and fit. His close-cropped hair was balding at the back and receding into a widow's peak, but there was still a definite edge about him.

As he looked up, the lenses of his glasses appeared to darken, which did nothing to relax Chirpie. He had not been offered a seat.

The boxer eyed up his man as if he would a sparring partner, looking for signs of weakness, scrutinising. He spoke in a strong 'Scouse' accent. There was no small talk.

"So, Colin, why do they call you Chirpie?" Which sounded like 'chair-pee'.

"Cos I'm a miserable bastard, apparently," replied Chirpie.

The man laughed loudly. His colleague, taking Sonny's lead, followed suit.

"I like that, I like that, we need more laughter. I'm always saying that aren't I, Sergei?"

Daniels looked at the white, hard-looking man to his left who nodded, but didn't appear to understand the question.

"You know who I am, Chirpie?"

"Aye, you're Sonny Daniels. I saw you box at the City Hall in seventy-six."

Sonny looked at Chirpie and smiled. "Seventy-six? You must have been about five."

"Seven actually. My Da was a big fight fan and took me along to get me acquainted, like," replied Chirpie, hoping his nerves didn't show.

"Why do you want to work for me, Chirpie?"

"Well, I need a job, I think I can handle it, and I hear you were looking," replied Chirpie, seemingly unfazed by the question.

"Sol Miller has recommended you, erm, how do you know him?" asked Sonny.

Chirpie wasn't prepared for this one. He had no time to think and said the first thing that came into his head.

"We go back a while. I knew him when he had hair," said Chirpie, which again made Sonny laugh, and he did not pursue the question, much to Chirpie's relief. His quick and amusing answers were warming Sonny to him.

"He says I can trust you, erm, is he right?" asked Sonny, with a serious face.

"Aye," said Chirpie.

"Let me say this once. We don't have disciplinary procedures like other places do. There are no written warnings, no annual assessments. There is no such thing as poor work and no second chances. You screw up and we'll break your legs or worse. Is that clear?"

There was no doubting the clarity of the message and Chirpie's nervousness was increasing. His right leg was starting to twitch, a certain give-away.

"Aye," said Chirpie, trying to keep his composure.

"Good, well that's settled then. You look like you can handle yourself, so no problems there. These are the terms and conditions. Listen up... You won't be getting a contract of employment. You get paid ten pounds an hour and fifteen pounds after midnight and at weekends, cash in hand. You give a chit with your hours worked to the club manager at the end of your shift and he, erm, will pay you. We don't deduct any tax or National Insurance that's your problem and, erm, if there's any issue in that direction, we don't know you, is that clear?"

"Aye," said Chirpie.

All through the questioning, the hard-looking man didn't say a word, but his stare was unnerving Chirpie.

"Right then, let's get you fixed up with a jacket." Sonny got up and walked to the rack of clothes. "You'll be working at Mr. Gees to start with, then Sol can show you the ropes. You'll be on a month's trial and, erm, if we like you and you keep your nose clean, you'll be kept on until we don't need you anymore. Oh, forgot to mention, erm, there's no pension scheme either."

He looked at Sergei and chuckled at his own attempted humour.

"Let me see." Sonny eyed Chirpie up and down. "You're a big lad, size forty-eight I reckon," and he pulled a jacked off the peg. "Try this on."

Chirpie got up and put the jacket on.

"That's looks good. Erm, how does it feel?" asked Sonny, smoothing the creases, taking the same care as a bespoke tailor.

"Aye, it's fine," replied Chirpie.

"I place a great store on smartness. I have a reputation to maintain and while you're wearing this jacket you're representing me and should be proud to do so." Sonny spoke as though he was delivering a morale boosting speech to the troops. "I expect you to keep the jacket smart and cleaned and, erm, if you lose or damage it, a replacement will cost you a hundred quid which is deducted from your wages. Clear?"

"Aye," said Chirpie, not knowing what else to say.

"You start tomorrow night, seven o'clock, finish, erm, at midnight. Turn up at the club and report to Sol in your jacket. Any questions?"

"No, it's all clear," replied Chirpie.

Sonny got up, went around the desk and shook his hand.

"Welcome to the club, Chirpie. My lads seem to enjoy themselves. I pay well and there are a few perks. Do you like my gym?"

Before Chirpie could answer, Sonny continued. "As an employee you get a free membership. I like to see my boys keeping fit. I hope I shall see you here, Chirpie."

"Aye," said Chirpie.

As he was about to leave Sonny spoke to him. "Just one more thing, you might want to cut your hair. I prefer to have my boys with short hair, like Sergei here."

This concerned Chirpie, looking at the man's shaved head. He had worn his hair long since the eighties, and Joy liked him that way.

Chirpie looked at the two men and, as the silent one stood up and turned around to extract himself from his chair, Chirpie noticed a strange tattoo on the back of his head, just above his shirt collar.

The man picked up Chirpie's jacket and passed it to Sonny who zipped it up in a suit-holder with the name 'SD Securities' printed on it. Chirpie nodded to his inquisitor and looked at Sergei without any expression. There was no handshake. He put the jacket under his arm and headed for the exit. As he made his way back through the gym, he exhaled.

Sol saw him leave the office and broke off from his weights to meet him at the door.

"How did it go, big man?" asked Sol.

"Aye, fine, start tomorrow. I'll see you at seven at the club. I'm working with you apparently."

"That's good news Chirpie, mon. I'll be able to show you around." Sol turned and escorted Chirpie to the door.

Chirpie made his way back to the greasy-spoon cafe and was greeted by his, somewhat relieved, buddies. Before he could sit down, Bigsy and Wazza got up and were heading out.

"We'll go somewhere else; I can't stand another minute in here," said Bigsy.

As he got through the door he took in a huge gulp of fresh air. A double decker bus went by and he nearly choked on the exhaust fumes.

"Come on, lads, I've had enough of this place for one day," said Bigsy, and they walked back to the car park with Chirpie recounting the experience of his job interview.

Despite his success, Chirpie was less than upbeat about his new occupation.

"He said I need a haircut. I only had one in November. Joy'll think I've got another woman!"

"What're you going to do, Chirpie lad?" asked Wazza.

"I've no idea, man; I'll have to think about it."

It was almost five o'clock before they got back to the precinct. They went inside the video shop and Rikki and Stevie were managing the tea-time rush.

"Everything ok, Rikki lad?" said Bigsy, as he walked past.

"Hi Bigsy, aye, champion," said Rikki, as Bigsy and his buddies made their way to the kitchen. Wazza looked around at the bare shelving.

"Where're your vids, Bigsy?"

"In storage, till the heat dies down, like."

"Pity that, I was going to ask you to fix me up for tomorrow night," replied Wazza.

"I might have one knocking around in the flat I can let you borrow if you're desperate," said Bigsy as he made three coffees.

"Ta Bigsy, that'll be great," said Wazza.

Bigsy completed the coffee-making and put them down on the table.

"Here, get your laughing gear around that. After the cat's piss at that café, it'll taste like nectar from the Gods."

As they were debating their next move, Bigsy's mobile rang. He got up and moved toward the back door where the reception was better. It was another anonymous number. Bigsy punched the green button and listened.

"Aye, this is Bigsy... Daryl...? Aye, bonny lad... yeah, course I remember you. Whatever's up?"

Bigsy listened to the anxious caller. "So, she's not been to work for a couple of days. No, I can see that. No. you get off and keep your head down... Aye, you too."

"Who was that, Bigsy?" asked Wazza. "You look worried."

"Aye, that was Daryl. You remember, the D.J. from Scalleys. Seems like young Gemma, you know, the busty barmaid I had a chat with, well she's not been in work for a couple of days. Nobody's seen her. Her ma's going frantic, as you can imagine. He says some blokes were in talking to her on Monday night and one of the security guys, the one they call 'the monster', clocked 'em, apparently.

Daryl says the guys also had a chat with him an' all, asking questions, like, about drugs and where they could get fixed up. He reckoned they were bizzies. Daryl's doing a runner. Staying with his brother down the smoke. He shifted all his gear after last night's gig."

"How did he get hold of your number?" asked Chirpie.

"That's the strange thing, I gave it to Gemma, and she passes it to Daryl and says if anything happens to her he should phone me."

"Why'd she do that?" asked Chirpie.

"I've no idea, but she must have thought something was up."

"What're you going to do, Bigsy, lad?" asked Wazza.

"Well, we shan't be going anywhere near Scalleys for the foreseeable, that's for sure."

"Is the meet with Denzel still on for tonight?" asked Wazza.

"Aye, said we'd see him at the club at nine o'clock," replied Bigsy. "He may have some ideas."

Nine-thirty, Friday night, Detective Superintendent Adams was at home in his favourite armchair, reading the paper under a standard lamp. After another hectic day there was a calmness in the room, and he was starting to relax. The television was on in the background and the gas fire was exuding a comforting glow as it heated the room.

The phone rang.

"Can you get that, dear?" he said, looking over his newspaper.

His wife was sitting next to the telephone table, knitting. She picked up the handset, listened, then passed it to him.

"D.S. Tunney for you, dear."

"Adams," he said, assertively.

"Right, mark it up, and get forensics down there. When's the tide due in? Ok, that gives us a couple of hours. Can you call in the team and a pathologist? Ok, I'll be there in about half an hour."

He hung up and looked at his wife.

"What is it dear,? You're not going out are you? It's quite late."

"Fraid so, a body's been washed up at Willington Quay. They think it might be the girl we've been looking for. Don't wait up, dear, I might be late."

Superintendent Adams put on his jacket and coat, kissed his wife and left the house. This was going to be a long night.

Chapter Twelve

Earlier, Bigsy had returned to the flat and was in the kitchen making a brew considering his next move. He heard the door open, and Carole came in from work, loaded with shopping.

"Hiya pet," she said, and kissed him on the cheek. "Urghhh, where've you been? You smell like an ashtray in a chippie," she added with a grimace.

"Just in town with Wazza and Chirpie for a coffee. It's ok, I'll get a shower in a minute."

"You better bin them clothes an' all, they're honking. They'll be stinking me washing oot."

"Aye, pet, will do."

He got up and headed in the direction of the bathroom.

Changed, and smelling a lot sweeter, Bigsy returned as Carole was dishing up their evening meal. He turned on the television to watch the news.

Carole brought in Bigsy's meal on a tray, lasagne and peas, with a large portion of instant mash potatoes.

"Ta pet, how's your day been?" asked Bigsy, tucking into his meal with relish.

"Starting to quieten down after the sales."

She sat down alongside Bigsy with her dinner of tuna salad.

"Have you seen anything of our Katya yet?" asked Carole.

"No, nottin'."

"Well, don't say anything, but I think she's back with our Polly. I think it's dead romantic."

"I thought she'd dumped him and buggered off back to her hubby in Kosovo," said Bigsy, with one eye on the television. "I don't think I'd want her after that."

"Aye, but her hubby's dead, and now she's back, there's nottin' stopping 'em."

182

"Well, I think it all seems strange. I thought he was dead already, then he turns up out of the blue, and now he's dead again."

Carole changed the subject. "Thought I'd go to the Metro Centre again on Sunday, see if Katya wants to come. She starts her new job on Monday. I might help her choose some work clothes."

"Aye, pet," clearly not showing much interested.

"Can you give us a few quid, pet?"

"Aye, pet, how much d'ya want?" Bigsy was still engrossed in the television.

"A hundred should cover it,"

"How much!!?"

He had refocused.

"I'll make it worth your while, pet," said Carole with a wink.

"Aye, ok," said Bigsy. "Sunday, you say?"

"Aye, pet."

"Well, I'll be out most've the day. We've got a match in the morning, and the Mags are playing Southampton at four. The Metro Centre'll be heaving."

"Who are you playing?" asked Carole with a mouth full of Tuna.

"Saltwell."

"You're going over to Saltwell? Hmmm, you'll need to be up early."

"No, it's at home."

"You make sure you don't bring your muddy boots in if I'm not about."

"Aye, pet," replied Bigsy, still not really concentrating.

"Are you going out tonight with your security job?"

"Aye, but I won't be late, just a meeting at the club. The security work's gone quiet for the moment."

"Well, I'm not unhappy about that," she said, devouring a lettuce leaf. "Out till all hours, does you no good, you know."

Later, Bigsy met Wazza and Chirpie in the precinct around eight-thirty, and decided to walk to the club; Wazza needed a drink. They arrived twenty-minutes later, and hung around the car park waiting for Denzel. At nine o'clock, an old Mercedes van appeared, not his usual mode of transport. Denzel parked up and joined them by the back entrance wearing a long leather overcoat and cap.

"You coming in for a drink, Denzel, bonny lad? We can use the office where we met up with Errol. It'll be easier to talk, and we won't be disturbed."

Denzel looked around anxiously.

"Aye, ok Bigsy, mon, but I can't stay too long; tings to do."

The four walked around the front and made their entrance. The office was on the left. Bigsy had called Stan earlier and arranged to use the room. They sat down and Bigsy gave Wazza a twenty-pound note.

"Here you go, kidder, can you get the drinks in for us? Three broons and a bottle of mineral water for our man here... right?"

"Yes, tanks, Bigsy, dat's cool." Denzel took off his coat and headgear.

A few minutes later, Wazza arrived with the round, and they got down to business.

"Have you got any news for us?" asked Denzel.

"Aye, you could say that," and Bigsy gave Denzel a full account of the events including the disappearance of the barmaid Gemma, and Chirpie's potential under-cover operation.

"Errol will be very grateful for your efforts," said Denzel, turning to Chirpie.

"There's another thing," Bigsy turned and looked at his buddy. "Chirpie, tell Denzel about the interview... what you told us."

"Aye," said Chirpie. "Well, I went to see this Sonny feller like Bigsy says, and he had this bloke with him; a right evil-looking bastard he was, shaved head, earring, the works."

"That could be any of 'em," interrupted Bigsy. "Tell him about the tattoo."

"Aye, I was just getting around to that. Anyway, when he turned around I noticed a tattoo on the back of his neck. Some sort of animal, like a bear or dragon or something. Only caught a glimpse of it, mind."

Denzel nearly choked on his drink. "Really! That could be it. That's what I saw, de tattoo. What did he look like?"

"Not much more I can say, not someone I'd like to cross. He had these piercing eyes that looked right through you. Sonny called him Sergei," said Chirpie.

"Sergei?" said Denzel.

"Aye, that's what he said," replied Chirpie.

"That sounds like a foreign name," said Wazza.

"The man with the foreign voice," said Bigsy.

"Could be," said Denzel. "And the tattoo. This could be the lead we wanted."

"But if he is your man and he knows you're still alive, won't he be looking for you?" said Bigsy.

"Possibly, but I have been keeping a very low profile. Not many people know I'm back in town, and I look different." He stroked his head with a grin. "I must speak to Errol and let him know." He turned to Chirpie.

"Chirpie, mon, I need as much information on dis man as you can get, but don't put yourself in harm. He is a very dangerous mon."

"Aye, will do," said Chirpie, but not with a great deal of enthusiasm. Only now was he beginning to realise what he had signed up for.

"I'll give Errol a call, and if it turns up he's our man, you'll be in for a nice bonus; I can tell you dat."

"Talking of dosh, bonny lad?" asked Bigsy, looking at Denzel expectantly.

"Of course, Bigsy. I had not forgotten."

Denzel handed Bigsy an envelope which Bigsy put in his jacket pocket.

"Ta, bonny lad, that's champion."

Denzel got up and Bigsy went with him back to the van.

"Dis is good work you guys are doing. It won't be forgotten. I'll see you same time next week, but if you get anyting urgent, be sure to call," said Denzel.

"Aye, will do, Denzel, bonny lad, and give my best to Errol."

They left the clubhouse and walked around the back to the car park.

Bigsy eyed up Denzel's transport. "What happened to your other motor?"

"Taking no chances with de police around. I have four vans, and I am swapping dem about just in case."

"Very wise, bonny lad, very wise."

Denzel got into the van drove off into the night.

Bigsy got back to his buddies and started considering the next move.

"What we need is a strategy," said Bigsy.

"Aye," said Chirpie. "And what's one of them when it's at home? As I see it, I'm the one with my balls in the mangle. I'm the one that's going be working with fookin' King Kong and his merry men, and I'm the one who's supposed to get my head shaved. I mean do I look like a fookin' Buddhist monk?"

Chirpie was not a happy bunny.

"Chirpie, bonny lad, I can see that it looks like you're holding the shite end of the stick, but as I said, you're the only person qualified to do the job, and you're getting a good whack from it."

Bigsy took out the envelope, counted out five twenty-pound notes, and handed it to Chirpie.

"You see," said Bigsy.

"Aye, you're right, Bigsy lad. I'm just concerned, that's all. You didn't see this guy Sergei; I mean, talk about hard-core. I was shiting myself, I don't mind telling you."

"Aye, well, if we can get some more information, maybe Errol and his crowd will come up here and sort him out once and for all," said Bigsy.

"Aye, let's hope so," said Chirpie.

"I know, what if we stick around when you're working, then we can be on hand if you get in any bother? How does that sound?" said Bigsy.

"Aye, that'll be champion, but I'm not getting my haircut for nobody. The missus'll go spare."

"I wouldn't worry too much about that, man. They can't all be fookin' skinheads," said Bigsy.

"I think you'll find they are," replied Chirpie, clearly still unhappy.

After another round Chirpie was feeling better about his new vocation.

"Maybe I'll take the missus to Benidorm. She's always wanted to go abroad."

This elicited wistful looks from his two friends. The thought of Joy in a bikini was frightening and would do irreparable damage to the Spanish tourist industry, Bigsy said to Wazza later.

The three lads walked back to the precinct. Bigsy said his goodbyes and called in on Rikki and Stevie in the video store. It was almost closing time, and Rikki was counting the cash. Bigsy went into the kitchen and called him in. The lad sat down leaving Stevie managing the counter.

"Rikki, bonny lad, I just wanted to say I've been very pleased with what you've been doing over the last few weeks. You've been a big help to us, like. I couldn't have managed things without you."

Bigsy opened his envelope and took out two twenties and a ten. "This is for you; you can call it a bonus if you like. You might want to give young Stevie a cut an' all, but that's up to you. Can you finish up for us? I'll take the cash up with me."

"Aye, Bigsy, no problem, ta very much," replied Rikki, who was quite taken aback by this gesture.

Back in the flat, Carole was watching a film on television.

"You're early, pet. Sit yaself down; I'll get yas a glass a wine."

Carole went to the kitchen and Bigsy took his seat in front of the television and switched over to the sports channel. Boxing was on.

Detective Superintendent Adams reached Willington Quay just after ten o'clock to be greeted with a hive of activity. The scenes-of-crime officer approached the car carrying a pair of thigh-length rubber waders.

"You'll need these, sir," he said, as Adams got out of his car.

The Superintendent opened the boot and took out a spare outer-jumper and put it on. It was a bitterly cold night. He then discarded his shoes and unsteadily negotiated his way into the waders. The officer led the way to the foreshore. A plastic sheeting tent surrounded a spot on the riverbank that was bathed in floodlights. Through the sheeting you could see the silhouettes of people bobbing about doing their work. A flashgun fired off at regular intervals.

In the background the relentless flow of the River Tyne, dark, black, and gradually encroaching, was audible against the low urgent mutterings of those at the crime scene. A deep muddy trench evidenced the meanderings of people shuttling between police vehicles and the site which was now only ten feet or so from the threatening water.

Adams descended the muddy bank, following what was now a well-worn path. His tread squelched as he made his way the twenty feet or so to the bustle of activity.

"How long have we got, officer, before the tide gets here?" asked Adams.

"Not long, sir, less than half an hour," replied the guide.

The Superintendent reached the scene and entered the enclosed area. In the middle was the naked body of a young female, face down in the mud. Her hair was matted, and her back, buttocks and legs were covered with specs of silt and bits of river debris. There appeared to be marks on her body.

"We haven't got long; can someone bring me up to speed?" asked Adams.

Detective Sergeant Tunney spoke. "Female, late twenties, early thirties. Member of the public taking her dog for a walk spotted her from the footpath. She's giving us a statement now."

"Anything on the body that might help identification... tattoos, scars?"

"No, nothing, sir, but forensics say she's been in the water two or three days. Too early for cause of death," said Tunney.

"Ok, let's get her out of here as quickly as we can and close up the site. There won't be anything else around, the river will have taken it."

"Yes, guv," said Tunney, and the team started getting their gear together.

Adams paused for a moment and looked at the body, with sadness.

As he made the steep climb through the clawing mud to the bank he spoke to Tunney who had caught up with him. "Have we got any photographs of that missing barmaid from the nightclub?"

"Aye, I think so, back in the office."

"Let's go back there; I want to have a look."

"You think it could be her, guv?"

"Right age, it's possible."

The two officers looked back and watched as the body was carried on a stretcher towards a waiting ambulance. Other officers were dismantling the lighting and packing away the plastic sheeting. The tide was almost at their feet.

It took half an hour to reach Police headquarters in the City Centre. Adams and Tunney made their way to the operations room.

"Who else is in?" asked Adams.

"D.C. Harris is with the forensic team. She's on her way in, plus the night shift," said Tunney.

"Ok, let's get those pictures of the barmaid," said Adams.

Tunney opened a drawer and rummaged through several folders. He found one with the word 'Scalleys' written on it in felt tipped pen.

"Here you go, sir." Tunney passed the file to Adams.

Opening the file, four photographs dropped out onto the floor. Adams bent down and picked them up and lined them up on the desk.

"What do you think, inspector?"

Tunney looked at them closely. They were at least two years old and not good quality.

"Difficult to say, could be, but I wouldn't like to stake my pension on it."

They were deep in conversation when D.C. Harris entered the room.

"A possible match, sir," said Harris.

"Difficult to say. These photos are not conclusive," said Adams.

"But this one is," said the officer and produced a plastic evidence bag with a security badge inside. "I called in at Scalleys on the way over. Asif, the manager, was very cooperative. Gave me Gemma's security pass. She'd left it behind the bar. They had new ones done about a month ago, so this is as up to date as we're going to get, I think."

"Why did she do that, I wonder?"

"What's that, sir?" asked Harris.

"Leave her pass behind the bar; you would have thought she would have carried it with her."

"Unless of course she was taken from the club," suggested Harris.

"Yes, that would make sense," said Adams.

He thought for a moment, then took the bag from the officer.

"Well done, Harris. Let's see what we've got," and Adams put on a pair of rubber gloves and slowly removed the pass from the bag.

"Well, it's not a hundred-per-cent but pretty close. Yes, I agree with you; I think this is Gemma Calder. Let's put her name up on the board," said Adams.

Adams put the pass back in the bag.

"Can you get this down to forensics we may find some fingerprints, you never know. As soon as we've had confirmation on identity, we'll need to tell the family and get someone in to do a formal ID."

He looked at the pictures that were still displayed on the desk.

He turned to the officer. "Press conference, midday tomorrow. Should catch the evening edition, can you set it up, Harris?"

"Yes guv," replied Harris.

"When can we expect forensics to have time and cause of death, did they say?"

"Should have something first thing," replied Tunney.

The following morning, Adams and the team were back in the incident room by eight o'clock. A lot of activity had taken place during the intervening hours. Adams was scouring the preliminary pathologist's report. A full post-mortem was being carried out within the next half an hour.

Adams addressed the assembled team.

"We still can't confirm identity a hundred percent, but we're pretty sure the body found on the foreshore at Willington Quay last night is that of the missing barmaid, Gemma Calder. Once we've got confirmation, I want a team down to Scalleys interviewing all the staff as soon as you can. Start with the manager, see if you can shake him up. I have a bad feeling about this place."

"There won't be anyone there for a while," said D.S. Fraser. "It doesn't open till seven. Staff usually arrive about six-ish." He scoured his notebook for any useful snippets.

"Ok, start as soon as you can," said Adams. "I've called a press conference for midday; we'll need a positive ID by then."

"We're contacting local dentists to see if we can get hold of Gemma's dental records." replied Harris. "As soon as we've got confirmation, we'll contact the family."

Adams continued his briefing.

"Probable cause of death, asphyxiation. There were ligature marks around her neck suggesting the possibility of a plastic bag, or something like, had been put over her head and fastened tightly. It also appears she may have been tortured before she was killed. The body showed evidence of bruising from a beating with a blunt instrument, possibly a baseball bat, the right size wounds, and there were what seemed to be burn marks across her chest and lower abdomen, possibly from a cigarette. There's also evidence she had been sexually assaulted."

"What about DNA, guv?" asked one of the officers.

"Afraid not, it looks like they used an object of some kind."

The room went very quiet.

Later that morning, Adams received confirmation that the dead girl was Gemma Calder from her dental records. Welfare officers were breaking the news to the family.

There was a media room on the first floor of police headquarters, and at midday, Adams made his way to address the gathered journalists for the hastily arranged press conference, accompanied by D.S. Fraser.

There were probably twenty hacks waiting for the briefing on uncomfortable cinema-style seating. There was a long table at the front with a jug of water and three glasses on top. The room was stuffy, not helped by the numerous cigarettes that had been lit.

Adams entered the room and sat down, immediately pouring himself a glass of water. After the introductions, he outlined the course of events.

"At approximately nine o'clock last night, the body of a young woman was found on the foreshore at Willington Quay. She has since been identified as Gemma Calder who was reported missing by her family on Wednesday evening. Gemma was working as a barmaid at Scalley's nightclub on the Waterfront. I've called this press conference to ask for assistance from the public to help us catch the perpetrator of what was a vicious crime."

He invited questions and was bombarded with requests for more information. He refused to disclose cause of death as they were still waiting the coroner's report. After a few minutes, he got up and left the news conference, leaving journalists with a helpline number, but with more questions than answers.

Saturday in the Worrell household, Carole had gone to work. Bigsy, with the place to himself, was slobbing out. He had had difficulty sleeping with everything going on, and was genuinely concerned about Chirpie and his new role as undercover investigator.

He and Wazza had agreed to be at the club that evening to give some support to their buddy. Chirpie was grateful; it would be some comfort knowing that they would be on hand if there was any bother. Bigsy hadn't told Carole yet.

With the Newcastle football game not until Sunday, he would do the afternoon shift at the video store and catch up on some paperwork. He would also retrieve his special videos from Mr. Ali's now that the heat appeared to be off. He didn't want to lose any more money; customers were complaining and demand on a Saturday night was always high.

He was of course totally unaware of events elsewhere.

That afternoon, Rikki agreed to give Bigsy a hand and between them they managed to drag the two boxes from the stockroom of Mr Ali's store and replenish the shelves in the viewing room/kitchen. The word would go out that the 'alternative selection' was again open for business.

Bigsy headed back to the flat around five o'clock to wait for Carole to return from work and to break the news he would be late back that evening. He didn't think there would be any resistance given the money being donated to the Metro Centre fund, but he was still anxious at the possible reaction.

He picked the evening newspaper off the mat and as he went to the kitchen to put the kettle on he stopped in his tracks. The headline on the front page read:

'Police seek vicious killer of barmaid'.

He read the narrative.

'The body of a young woman found by a woman walking her dog on the foreshore at Willington Quay was identified earlier today as that of Gemma Calder (28) of Brighton Terrace, Grainger Hill. Gemma worked as a barmaid at Scalleys nightclub, a popular Waterfront disco and bar. Detective Superintendent James Adams, heading the investigation, said that it had been a particularly vicious attack and were anxiously seeking anyone with any information. He appealed for any member of the public with information to call on the incident room 0191 735 2232. His thoughts, he said, were with Gemma's family at this difficult time' - Family mourn 'perfect daughter'; See page 2.

Bigsy flicked the next page and scanned the article.

"Jeez no, jeez no," he said, and then called Wazza.

"Wazza, bonny lad, have you seen tonight's Chronical? Well, you better take a look… front page." There was a pause while Wazza retrieved the newspaper.

"Fookin' hell," said Wazza.

"Aye, you're not wrong there," said Bigsy. "A vicious attack… No, I don't know, but we'll have to tell Chirpie. It'll be all over the clubs tonight. Aye, I'll see you in about an hour."

Carole came back from work just after six o'clock, greeted by Bigsy with his coat on.

"Where're you going? I've only just got in,' said Carole, dropping two shopping bags on the floor.

"Sorry, pet, summat urgent's come up. I've got to go out. I've left you some clothes money on the table, should be enough for you and Katya."

"But what about ya dinner? I've got chicken."

"I'll get something, don't fret."

"But, when'll you be back?"

"Don't know but I may be late. I'll try not to disturb you."

Bigsy leaned over and kissed her on the cheek, then headed for the door.

"Bye," he called.

"Bigsy Worrell, you're impossible," she shouted as he closed the door behind him.

Carole saw the money on the table and flicked through the notes, a hundred and twenty pounds. The blow of Bigsy's sudden departure quickly diminished. The flat to herself, control of the remote and no 'Match of The Day', plus some serious clothes money for tomorrow; not such a bad deal after all.

Before she took her coat off, she popped along the corridor to Katya's flat and knocked on the door. Katya answered. "Hello Carole, what a lovely surprise; come in."

She followed Katya into the living room and saw Polly feeding Melos. The boy was up at the table in a new highchair which Polly had bought second-hand from a neighbour that afternoon.

"Well, look at you two playing happy families; I'm so pleased for you both, I really am," said Carole.

"Hello Auntie Carole," said Polly. "You won't say anything to my Mam, will you? She's not come round to the idea yet."

"No pet, course not. Your secret's safe with me, don't you worry," said Carole with a grin. "I've come to see if Katya fancies some retail therapy tomorrow at the Metro Centre, Bigsy's playing football in the morning and off to St James's Park in the afternoon, so I'm not doing anything. We can get some stuff for your work on Monday if you like."

Katya looked at Polly. "Well, I'll be playing football in the morning an' all, so I think you should go, pet."

"That would be wonderful, thank you so much," said Katya.

"I'll come 'round for yas about ten if that's ok," said Carole.

"Yes, that will be fine. I will need to bring the children."

"Aye, pet, no problem."

Bigsy met Wazza and Chirpie in the lobby, and they walked to the garages to pick up Wazza's car.

"Chirpie, you look like summat from the fookin' Godfather," said Bigsy, looking at Chirpie in his sunglasses and smart new 'SD Securities' jacket. "What's with the shades? It's pitch black out here, man?"

"I thought it would make me look the part," said Chirpie, almost tripping up the kerb.

"Close… makes you look a prat," said Bigsy. "And what've you done to your hair? It's all greased back?"

"I thought if I slapped some stuff on it and press it down it would look as if it's short, like," replied Chirpie.

"Well, you can't argue with that," said Bigsy.

They got to the garages and Wazza opened his lock-up and reversed out the Escort. While Wazza pulled down the garage door, Bigsy opened the car and held the front seat forward so Chirpie could get in the back. He sniffed the air.

"What the fook's that smell?" exclaimed Bigsy.

"Oh that? That's probably Joy's hair gel I used," replied Chirpie.

"Smells like a fookin' tart's boudoir. You'll be getting plenty of attention tonight, bonny lad. Just make sure you keep your back against the wall. You know what I'm saying?"

Wazza collapsed with laughter, the banter having relieved some of the attention the trio were feeling.

As they drove off the atmosphere was far from upbeat.

"I saw in the paper about that young lass," said Chirpie. "It doesn't make things any easier, does it?"

"No, it was a bad do that's for sure. I only met her the once, mind, but she was a canny lass," said Bigsy. "Just keep your head down and your ears open, no heroics tonight, just a recky and see what happens. You never know you might get some gossip that gets us off the hook and we can pass it over to Errol."

"Aye, I guess you're right," said Chirpie and they made their way to Mr. Gees and the start of another adventure.

Chapter Thirteen

At six forty-five, Wazza pulled up outside Mr. Gee's and Chirpie unceremoniously extricated his six-foot-three frame from the back of the Escort.

"We'll head off, bonny lad, and see you inside later. It'll be quiet just yet. We'll call back about nine. Don't want to be too conspicuous," said Bigsy.

Chirpie watched anxiously as they drove away. It was not what he was expecting, but it made sense. He walked towards the side entrance of the club as instructed. As he paced down the dark alleyway, he suddenly remembered it was where Everton and Layton were shot.. He checked around to see if there was any evidence, a bullet hole or some blood stains, perhaps. He caught his foot on a raised drainage cover and decided to dispense with the sunglasses; he couldn't see a thing. A high intensity security light was triggered as he approached the door bathing the area in brilliant illumination.

Chirpie pressed the bellpush beside the heavy, metal door and, looking up, he could see a CCTV camera pointing at him. He heard bolts being drawn and a familiar face greeted him.

"Hiya, Chirpie, mon."

It was Sol Miller. Chirpie was relieved to see him.

"Hiya, Sol, bonny lad, how're you doing?"

"Champion, champion. Come in, I'll show you around."

Sol gave Chirpie a guided tour before starting his duties. Mr Gee's didn't open for another half an hour, but it was still a hive of activity. Bar staff were busying themselves checking barrels and pumps and stocking shelves with mixers. Being formerly a bank, the club had a high, ornate-domed ceiling. This produced a different atmosphere to Scalleys, which, by comparison, seemed more manufactured. This place had real character, and you could see why it had become one of the most popular clubs in the city.

The sound system was being tested by the D.J. and the clarity was superb, obviously a very expensive set up; as was the lighting, which gave the club a sympathetic ambience. There was the usual parquet dance floor and tables surrounding it and in alcoves set into the walls, similar to Scalleys.

"Come on," said Sol. "I'll introduce you to a few people."

There was another security guard wearing the ubiquitous jacket who was sitting on a bar stool sipping a mineral water.

"No alcohol on duty," Sol had warned. "That's a sackable offence."

Chirpie considered the word 'sackable'; it was probably literal.

"Chirpie, this is Hashim." Chirpie looked at the man. He would be in his mid-thirties about five feet nine and looked extremely fit. He had dark complexion, gypsy-looking, with very short, spiky, black hair. Chirpie was relieved to see he wasn't the only non-skinhead after all. The man was lean, not muscle-bound as some of the other Neanderthals, but undoubtedly able to handle himself.

Chirpie shook hands with the man.

"From Kosovo, used to be with the KLA, seen a lot of action, didn't you Hashim?" said Sol.

The man nodded without any animation seemingly weighing Chirpie up.

"Doesn't speak much English, came over last July, Sonny took him under his wing as part of his programme to help the refugees. Sonny's done a lot of work and raised a lot of money for the Kosovans," said Sol.

"Pleased to meet you, bonny lad," said Chirpie, prompting an acknowledgement from the Kosovan.

After further introductions, Sol continued with the guided tour of the building. They went along a corridor at the back of the dance floor and through a door at the end marked 'Private'.

"This is the staff room," said Sol.

It was quite large and well-furnished with a few comfortable armchairs, a three-seater sofa and several small low tables. There was a coffee-machine and water-cooler in the corner against a wall. "You can have a ciggie in here if you want, smoking's not allowed on duty," said Sol.

"It's ok, don't smoke," said Chirpie.

Back along the corridor, Sol pointed out two doors on either side. "These are the main toilets." One had a sign, 'Cocks', the other, 'Hens'.

"We have to check these out every half hour; there's often trouble. You need to watch out for drug exchanges. We even get junkies shooting up sometimes."

There was another door on the other side of the dance area with 'Private' appended, accessed by a keypad. Sol went up to it and entered a code. "It's 1-2-3-4," said Sol, with a toothy grin.

It opened onto a corridor and a couple of offices. The first one which was on the left was 'admin' where a smart-looking, very attractive dark-haired woman in a mini-skirt was working on a computer, surrounded by filing cabinets and other office paraphernalia. Further down on the right there was another, marked 'Manager', which was closed but Chirpie could hear voices on the other side. He took it all in.

Sol knocked on the open admin office door. The woman looked up and nodded, then immediately went back to her computer. Sol went in leaving Chirpie in the corridor.

"New guy, just getting a picture for the pass," said Sol. The woman looked up again.

"Ok," she said, and returned to her screen.

There was a Polaroid camera on the desk; Sol took it and went back to the corridor.

"Chirpie, I need to get a picture, for the pass," he explained. Sol lined up Chirpie against the wall opposite the door and took the photograph. The flash made Chirpie's eyes blink. The camera spat out the square single film from the front and Sol watched as the picture emerged. Checking that it was in focus, Sol returned to the office. Chirpie waited outside.

After a moment, Sol reappeared and ushered Chirpie through the security door and back to the dance area.

"You can pick the pass up later; Rashmi will see to it for you."

"The mini skirt?" asked Chirpie.

"Aye, but don't get your hopes up there, strictly out of bounds. She's the deputy manager, goes out with Sergei."

"Sergei?"

"Aye, and he's someone you don't want to be messing with."

Chirpie acknowledged. "Aye, bonny lad, I'd heard that."

"Right, let's rock and roll," said Sol, dramatically.

On the way to the entrance doors, Sol went over the rest of the procedures, where to sign in, the work roster, and the emergency exits. "Make sure nothing, or no-one, is blocking them, health and safety will be all over us otherwise."

He continued his briefing, explaining to Chirpie what he should be on the lookout for.

"The main problem is under-age girls trying to get in, oh, and drink. No-one gets in who is drunk or looks under eighteen. Don't bother with ID; most of the time it's either fake or belongs to their sister. You'll never believe what they do to try to get in."

There was a heavily secured, locked ticket-office to the left of the entrance which looked like it used to house a cash-dispensing machine in the past. Someone was sorting out the float and arranging tickets, ready for the waiting customers.

It was seven-thirty. "Right, opening time," said Sol.

He led Chirpie to the huge wooden front doors. Chirpie could see the ornate carvings on them including what was probably a bank crest, remnants of a by-gone age.

Sol released the bolts and pulled them open. People, mostly young girls, were filed, four deep, down the steps and around the building as far as you could see. Seeing the doors open, the waiting throng pushed forward and Chirpie and Sol had to exert their authority to get the punters in line. The clubbers streamed past the pair. Chirpie wasn't quite sure what was expected but decided just to try to look 'hard'.

It took about half an hour to clear the queue and by eight o'clock it had died to a steady trickle.

"How many's that?" asked Chirpie.

"Less than a thousand, you wait till ten o'clock when it really gets busy," replied Sol with a chuckle.

Everything was running smoothly, when about half-past nine Chirpie experienced his first difficult customer, or more correctly, 'customers'.

Two chubby-looking girls wearing the standard clubbing gear, short skirt and revealing tops walked up the stairs towards Chirpie. Sol was in discussions on the other side of the steps.

He looked at them as they approached; they were barely sixteen. "Where d'you think you're going, ladies?"

"Can you let us in? We're over eighteen. Do you want to see my ID?" said the first girl, opening her blouse to reveal more of her ample chest.

"I don't think so, girls," said Chirpie, politely.

"We'll make it worth your while. Sharon here'll give you a blowjob if you're up for it?" said the second one, pointing to her equally well-endowed friend.

"Sorry girls; now, piss-off," said Chirpie. He had a way with words.

"Fagot!" shouted girl number one and hacked her throat and aimed a spray of spit in Chirpie's direction before staggering away. She grabbed her friend by the arm and heading off into the night with an array of expletives.

Chirpie nimbly dodged the 'gob' which landed harmlessly on the club wall.

Sol had witnessed the event. "You get a different class of punters down here, man," Chirpie shouted.

"Ha, you'll get worse than that before the night's out, you see," replied Sol.

"Thanks for those words of encouragement, bonny lad."

As Sol had said, the queues started to build again around ten o'clock. The club had a maximum capacity, governed by Health and Safety and the fire brigade, and the numbers were tallied at the ticket desk. With around a hundred spaces before the capacity was reached, the clerk would advise the doormen to start the countdown, and then customers were counted in until the 'house-full' notices were displayed. This was a regular occurrence on a Friday and Saturday night, much to the frustration of people who were unable to get in. Some clubbers had travelled long distances to frequent the best clubs and being refused entry often led to confrontations.

This Saturday, despite being only three weeks since the Christmas break, was another busy night and, by ten-thirty, the club was full. Sol collected the 'house full' signs from the ticket office and placed them at the entrance, much to the disappointment, and derision, of the remaining queue.

"Sorry folks, that's it for tonight, I'm afraid," announced Sol.

He and Chirpie stood blocking any attempt of entry. Once the remaining queue had dispersed, Sol closed one of the doors to enable exit for those wishing to leave and made controlling the entrance easier.

"Why don't you take a break Chirpie, fifteen minutes? I'll man the fort. Go across to the staff room and get a brew. Your security pass should be ready if you call by the office."

"Aye, champion, man, I'm knackered, I don't mind telling you."

"A good strong coffee'll perk you up," said Sol, and Chirpie made his way through the second set of double doors and into the club. Chirpie stood in disbelief. Scalleys was big but nothing like this; it was heaving, with around fifteen-hundred people doing what clubbers do; drinking, dancing, and talking, although hearing was a challenge against the background of heavy R & B. The familiar thick fog of cigarette smoke hung in the air.

There was the usual large crowd waiting to be served at the bar which was being attended by at least ten staff, and there were other 'jackets' milling around to whom Chirpie had not been introduced. These would be the late shift, as Sol had described them, eight till three. Chirpie was pleased to be finishing at midnight tonight.

He looked around for his buddies. He'd seen them walk in about nine o'clock, as they had said, but hadn't had chance to say much; he'd been clearing queues. He eventually spotted them sitting on two high bar stools set against one of the columns, consuming broons.

"Hiya, Chirpie, bonny lad, how's it going?" said Bigsy, as he watched his buddy walked towards him.

"Hiya, Bigsy, Wazza; fine. It's been ok, better than I thought it would be." Chirpie was shouting to be heard. "Sol's a canny bloke; he's really looked after me."

"Have you got time for a drink?" asked Bigsy.

"No ta, can't, got to go into the office," replied Chirpie. "I'll be knocking off at midnight, see you then."

"Aye, ok bonny lad, keep your head down, eh?"

There seemed to be a focus about Chirpie that Bigsy hadn't noticed before.

Chirpie said goodbye and headed off towards the door leading to the admin room and entered the code. Approaching the office, Chirpie could see that the girl with the mini skirt was still at the computer. Chirpie knocked on the door and she looked up. She was stunning looking, Asian extraction, slim with long black hair.

"I'm Colin Longton, they said I can collect my security pass, like," said Chirpie, trying not to stare. She got up and went to a tray on an adjoining table where three security passes were waiting for their owners.

"Just a minute."

She flicked through a pile of papers and eventually found

Chirpie's pass. She gave it to him with hardly a glance, then went back to her computer. Chirpie left the admin area, through the secure door and headed for the corridor on the opposite side of the dance floor. He reached the staff room, made himself a strong coffee and sat down on one of the comfortable chairs.

Other members of staff were coming in and out as they had their breaks and went back to their jobs, making little eye-contact with Chirpie, just the occasional nod. He was in his own world, contemplating the evening. After ten minutes, he headed back towards the entrance of the building feeling revived after his caffeine shot.

Skirting the dance floor, he was passing a table when he was aware of an altercation between a man and a young woman. There was a lot of shouting. She was calling him all kinds of names and he was becoming more and more animated. Without warning the man grabbed a bottle off the table by the neck and smashed it on the edge leaving him holding an ugly looking shard of glass about four inches long.

"I'll teach you to go shagging around. No bloke's gonna be looking at you by the time I've finished with you," he screamed, and pushed the bottle into her face... or would have done if a vice-like grip hadn't caught hold of his wrist and stopped it in mid-air.

"If you make one move, you'll be kissing concrete. Do I make myself clear? Now, drop it."

Chirpie spoke with calm authority and the man looked around in complete surprise. He snarled at Chirpie in a rage, but couldn't move his arm from his grip.

"I won't tell you again; now drop it," and the man complied. The girl, now crying and almost frozen with fear, was being looked after by a couple of friends.

Quickly, Chirpie had the man's arm up folded up behind his back almost breaking it. In one quick movement he lifted him from his seat and pinned him to the floor. The man screamed in pain and was shouting obscenities. Other security staff arrived and helped Chirpie lift the man to the floor and frog-march him to the front door.

"You're on CCTV, so don't even think about coming round here again," shouted Chirpie, as the man was deposited down the stone steps of the building and onto the pavement. The man lay there for a moment before getting up, uttering more expletives as he slunk off into the night. Chirpie looked up to the skies. The snow that had been threatening all day, was starting to fall.

As he got inside the entrance lobby, Sol came up to him. "Well done, Chirpie lad, that was real quick thinking. Get yourself inside, Rashmi's put a call in to Sonny; he always likes to be informed when there's any trouble."

Twenty minutes later, Chirpie was back on door duty. It was cold and he and Sol were stood in the doorway out of the descending snow. With the 'house full' signs up there was very little to do apart from dealing with the odd disappointed punters. Suddenly he felt a tap on his shoulder which made him jump. Somewhat startled and on high alert he turned around. It was the beautiful Rashmi. "Sonny would like to see you," she said. For some reason Chirpie was beginning to panic, trying to recount any transgressions.

He followed her back through the club, through the security door, and down the corridor to the manager's office. Sonny was sat behind the desk with Sergei stood at his left shoulder. Chirpie's blood ran cold.

"Sit down Chirpie. Would you like a drink?" said Sonny.

"I'm ok, ta."

Chirpie sat on the chair in front of the desk as ordered. There was a need to visit the toilet, and he was fidgeting involuntarily

"Your first night?" said Sonny, his photochromatic spectacles now enabling some eye-contact, which did little to ease Chirpie's anxiety.

"Aye," replied Chirpie, nervously.

"I heard you handled yourself well, congratulations, and you've got a brain, too." Sonny smiled. "Hmm, I think I made an excellent choice in signing you up. I must thank Sol for the introduction. I'm always on the lookout for new talent."

He reached in his pocket, and Chirpie held his breath momentarily. Sonny took out a wad of cash and peeled off some twenty-pound notes and handed them to Chirpie. "That's an extra bonus, erm, I always reward good work."

Chirpie was trying to interpret Sonny's Liverpool accent; it sounded like 'werk'! He looked at the money and flicked it in his fingers, one hundred pounds.

"Ta very much, just doing my job, like."

"Well, not everybody has your presence of mind, Chirpie," he paused before continuing, "Listen, you may or may not know this, erm, but I have quite a wide range of career opportunities within my organisation..." He looked up at Sergei, then back at Chirpie. "How would you like the chance to earn some real money?"

Sergei appeared to be eyeing Chirpie up, seemingly waiting for a reaction.

"Aye, never say no to some extra readies, like."

"Well, I've got an idea; why don't you come over to the house on Monday? Shall we say eleven o'clock; that's A.M.," he added with a chuckle. "Do you know where I live?"

"I have no idea," replied Chirpie.

"No problem, Rashmi will give you the address. I'll fix you up with a taxi if you like. Call these guys tomorrow; they're part of the organisation. They'll collect you, just tell 'em where you live."

Sonny gave Chirpie a business card headed 'Sonny's Taxis' from a pile in the desk drawer.

"Thanks," said Chirpie, taking the card off Sonny.

"Ok, Chirpie, erm, see you Monday, and thanks. You can sign off and go home now if you like."

It was eleven-thirty, half an hour early.

"Aye, ok, thanks. Monday, eleven, I'll be there."

As he turned to walk away, Sonny called out to him. "Hey Chirpie, the hair, good look... Al Pacino, I like that!" and gave a broad grin.

He called into the admin office. Rashmi was still working on the computer. She asked him to sign a 'chit' which stated the number of hours he had worked. Five, it said. She opened a cash-drawer and counted out fifty-pounds and handed it to him.

"Ta, bonny lass," said Chirpie and put the money in his jacket pocket.

He was on his way out the room, when Sergei appeared from the manager's office and barged past him. Chirpie was at the doorway and turned as Sergei walked over to Rashmi, leaned over her, and made a grab for her breasts. She pushed his hands away and looked around.

Chirpie quickly left the room and could hear raised voices.

He returned to the main club to find his buddies. They were where he had left them, with half-empty bottles of broons looking pretty fed up. Their mood improved as they saw Chirpie coming towards them.

"You finished already, bonny lad?" said Bigsy.

"Aye, let's get out of this place; I've got a bit tell ya," said Chirpie, without stopping. They quickly downed their drinks and followed Chirpie out of the club.

The snow was coming down quite heavily now and the city centre was taking on a Christmas card appearance. As they walked towards the car park, the pavements resembled a white carpet interspersed with the random pattern of footprints.

"We saw you take that bloke out, very impressive, bonny lad. I think you've found your vocation," said Bigsy.

"Don't know about that, spur of the moment. Didn't really think about it."

They reached the car which Wazza had parked in a meter bay on a neighbouring street; it was covered with snow. Wazza cleared the windscreen, got in and started up the engine.

"Hurry up and get that heating on, Wazza, bonny lad. It's fookin' freezing," said Bigsy.

The windscreen quickly misted over, making visibility impossible. Wazza rubbed the glass with the back of his hand to clear an area big enough to see through, then eased the vehicle out of the parking space and into the traffic. Driving was difficult even though the gritting trucks had been out in full force.

Bigsy was anxious to hear the news of Chirpie's adventures.

"You what!? You've got an invite to his house?" exclaimed Bigsy, when Chirpie revealed Sonny's invitation.

"Aye, on Monday. Says there're other career opportunities he wants to discuss, whatever that means."

"Well, that's encouraging. Seems like you made a favourable impression," said Bigsy.

"Aye, seems like it, and another thing, that Sergei bloke was there again an' all. Knocking off the deputy manager by the looks of it. He really is an evil-looking bastard; there's no two ways about it."

It took almost twice as long as usual to get back to home territory and Wazza's lock-up. The journey was spent in quiet contemplation; nobody wanted to say much once they'd heard Chirpie's report. Wazza garaged the car in the lock-up while Bigsy and Chirpie waited for him.

Bigsy broke the silence as they walked back to the flats. "Can't see the game being on tomorrow, lads," he said, looking at the falling snow accumulating on the pavements.

Three sets of footprints trailed behind them. "Aye, we won't see the pitch if this carries on," said Chirpie.

They agreed to plan their next course of action after a night's sleep.

It was twelve-thirty by the time Bigsy put the key in the lock and let himself in quietly. Carole had fallen asleep on the sofa watching the television.

She woke up and looked at Bigsy through half-opened eyes.

"What time is it, pet?" she said sleepily.

"Half-twelve-ish."

"D'ya want a brew? I'll make us one." She got up from the sofa unsteadily and made her way to the kitchen. "Have you had a good night?"

"I'm not sure, pet; I'm not sure," replied Bigsy.

Sunday morning, last night's snow was still lying on the ground. It was eight o'clock, and in the Worrell household, Bigsy was making the tea. While he was waiting for the kettle to boil in the kitchen, he happened to notice his bourgeoning waistline which was seriously hanging over his underwear. A 'muffin top' was developing. He had turned thirty in September and wondered if his best days, certainly in a footballing sense, were behind him. He wandered into the living room and to the window in his boxer shorts, and looked across to the rec. It was white over. The grey of yesterday had been replaced with hazy winter sunlight that reflected from the snow.

His thoughts turned to football. There would be little chance of a game today; you couldn't make out any of the six pitches, but unless they had a call from the referee, the team would still need to turn up ready to play or forfeit the game and face a fine. There would be no such problems this afternoon at St James Park where the beloved Mags were playing Southampton; under-soil heating would see to that. As season ticket holders, Bigsy, Wazza, and Chirpie attended most home games and a four o'clock kick-off would give them a chance for a drink or two before the game in the working men's club.

Bigsy got the call about nine-thirty from Danny Milburn, the club coach, to say that the referee had been in touch and the rec had been declared unplayable, and all the matches were off.

"Thank goodness for that, Danny, bonny lad, I can get back to bed," said Bigsy.

Bigsy had agreed to contact Wazza, Chirpie, and also Polly, who said he was ready to play again.

At ten-thirty, there was a knock on the door. Carole, showered, changed, and dressed in her shopping gear - jeans, sloppy jumper and comfortable shoes, answered.

"Katya, pet, come in," she greeted her friend warmly. Carole suddenly noticed the absence of children.

"Where're the bairns?" asked Carole.

"Polly's looking after them now the football is not playing. He said it would be good for me to have a break."

"Are you going to be alright, pet?" asked Carole.

"Yes, it will be fine. Polly will enjoy looking after the children. He was showing Arjeta how to draw a kite when I left him. It will be good for him as well."

There was clearly a change in the relationship, Carole noticed. It was beginning to show signs of permanency, even though Katya had only been back a few days. It was as though the intervening months had not happened.

Bigsy came in having heard Katya arrive. He was dressed in his match-day attire of Alan Shearer number nine, Newcastle United replica shirt, and tracksuit bottoms. He'd washed and shaved.

"Hiya Katya, bonny lass," said Bigsy and gave Katya a warm hug, "Where're the bairns?"

Katya explained the babysitting arrangements again. "Strange, I never imagined our Polly playing happy families. Mind you, it'll do him good to have some responsibility."

"Aye, that's what I said," added Carole.

She checked her purse to make sure she had her cash. Bigsy produced a twenty-pound note from his pocket and gave it to Katya.

"Put this towards your lunch."

"Thank you Bigsy, that is very kind," and she kissed him again on the cheek.

The girls headed out of the door, leaving Bigsy contemplating his next move on the investigative front.

He phoned Wazza and Chirpie to arrange a con-flab at the club before the match. They would meet in the lobby at one-thirty. Bigsy turned on the television and flicked through the channels.

The shopping trip was as good as Katya had remembered it. Little had changed at the Metro Centre. It was still very busy with a queue of traffic back onto the motorway to get in.

Carole took Katya into some of her favourite shops and bought two smart business suits and co-ordinated tops. Katya remembered how Jenny Wheatley had dressed and wanted to emulate her example.

The two made the most of Bigsy's lunch donation and dined at one of the wine bars which gave them little change from the twenty.

They were sipping their wines when Carole asked a leading question.

"So how long are you stopping here, pet? In England, I mean."

Katya looked deep into her glass before replying.

"The Refugee Council want me to stay for at least six months, that is the agreement, but I have been thinking about this a lot. When I got here I did not know how Polly would be; that was my main worry. He could have had a new girlfriend, or he could have hated me for the way I treated him. I just didn't know. Now though, the thought of leaving him again, well, I just couldn't, not having lost him once. I will tell you something that I haven't told you. Before I found out that Ibi was still alive, I had already spoken to Clara and Jenny Wheatley about staying in the UK under the refugee option, but of course that all changed. My thoughts now are that I will apply for asylum when my time here with the Council has finished. I have not talked to Polly about it, but I know it is what he would want."

Carole looked at her.

"Well, I hope you do stick around, pet. It wasn't the same after you left. Polly was in pieces, and I missed you an' all," she added and held Katya's arm and squeezed it.

"They were difficult times for all of us," said Katya.

Meanwhile, Bigsy and his buddies met at the club as arranged, and, over a couple of broons, discussed the latest turn of events. They were seated by the window, away from anyone's earshot.

"So, Chirpie lad, are you still ok about going to the house tomorrow?" asked Bigsy.

"Aye, I think so. He's paying for a taxi all the way to Ponteland. What about that?"

There was an element of false bravado in his statement. Inside, he was less-than confident.

"Well, don't you go getting into any trouble. Just see what he has to say and get yourself out of there, alright?" counselled Bigsy.

"Aye, that's what I intend to do. I can't say I'm looking forward to it, mind."

The topic was dropped, and the conversation moved onto more immediate concerns, the match with Southampton.

"I think we will annihilate them. I feel it in my waters," said Wazza.

As it happened, Wazza's premonition was almost proved right, not quite an annihilation, but a very good win, none-the-less. Newcastle were totally in control and the Toon Army were celebrating a four-nil score line by half-time.

"Could have had ten," said Wazza excitedly. The team eased off in the second half with only a late goal adding to the scoreline. The majority of crowd of almost thirty-six thousand left the ground contentedly.

"I don't fancy their trip home," said Bigsy, looking at some dejected away supporters making their way forlornly back to their coaches.

When Bigsy got back to the flat around seven, he was faced with a welcome surprise. As well as Carole and Katya, Polly had turned up with the two children. Bigsy made a fuss of them.

After a few minutes catch-up, Katya made their excuses. "I have a very busy day tomorrow," she explained. The party left with Bigsy describing the match in detail to Carole who was feigning interest. She eventually started yawning. "It takes it out of you, this retail therapy."

Bigsy took the hint, turned on the television and started flicking through the channels.

Chapter Fourteen

Monday morning, 17th January.

There were some defining moments on the horizon for Katya and Chirpie.

Matters at Police HQ, however, were not moving forward with as much speed as Superintendent Adams had hoped.

At his morning briefing, he took up his usual position in front of the incident board which was looking increasingly complex. Through the Scalley's connection, Gemma Calder's name had been added to the map and was now part of the wider investigation. It was not just an investigation concerning drugs, extortion, and possible money laundering; there were now at least four unsolved murders.

Adams gave a quick recap for the benefit of the team, using the map.

"If we go back over the last nine months or so, we've got the deaths of Everton Sheedie and Layton Gibbons; our colleague, Craig Mackenzie, and now Gemma Calder."

He pointed to them on the board.

"Then, there's the disappearance of the doorman, Jonno Johnson, which is also a cause of concern, and we now know that Daryl Anderson, the regular Scalley's D.J., has also gone missing."

There were uneasy looks at each other from the team.

"The common denominator is, of course, Sonny Daniels and his organisation, which I don't think is a coincidence, but we need evidence."

He looked gravely at the assembled team.

"Where are we with the interviews at Scalleys? Any further information about Gemma Calder?"

D.S. Tunney responded.

"Nothing to report at all, guv. We've interviewed all the security and bar staff, and the manager. Nobody's saying anything." He consulted his notebook and read from his narrative, "Gemma was a popular girl. She got on well with everyone. Always very punctual… Seems an ideal employee. Certainly nothing to suggest she was involved in anything untoward," said Tunney.

"Any news of her personal possessions, purse, handbag, mobile phone, keys, that sort of thing?" asked Adams.

"No, we interviewed the family, and they've been through all her stuff. No sign of her phone which she always kept with her. Nothing in her locker at the club either, guv. It was empty."

"Doesn't that seem odd?" said Adams. "She leaves her security pass at the club, yet her locker was empty." He paused for reflection. "Let's say she had been abducted when she was leaving work; she wouldn't have had chance to empty her locker. That suggests someone might have emptied it after she was taken." continued Adams.

"That's assuming she used her locker," said Frasier.

"Oh, she <u>did</u>," replied Tunney, firmly. "One of the girls said she kept all her personal stuff in there, make-up, letters, that sort of thing. She even had a photo pinned on the back of the locker door. Everything's gone."

"Anything on CCTV on the night she disappeared?" asked the Superintendent.

"They only keep the tapes for forty-eight hours and re-use them, so they've been wiped. Nothing there either, I'm afraid," said Tunney.

"We've got to go back in there; start leaning on one or two, ask some more questions. Find out who emptied her locker. Watch out particularly for anyone who might be wavering, someone particularly anxious, nervous that sort of thing. What about the missing D.J., Daryl Anderson, he was interviewed wasn't he?"

"Not formally, guv," said Tunney. "Just the plain clothes guys doing some digging just before Gemma Calder disappeared, seemed very evasive, they said. Next night he just took his gear after the gig and never showed up again, just vanished."

"Any friends, relatives who might know where he is?" asked Adams.

"We called at his mother's house, but she didn't seem to be too concerned, which is strange given the publicity around Gemma Calder. You would have thought she would be going frantic," replied Tunney.

"Hmm, I reckon she knows he's safe," said Adams. "Look, pay her another visit, see if you can trace him. If we can get him to talk we may have a lead."

"What about forensics, guv?" asked Frasier.

"Nothing new, I'm afraid. Pathologist's confirmed Gemma Calder's cause of death as asphyxiation. As you know there was signs of torture, no trace of drugs in her system and hadn't been drinking, nothing to provide us with any new leads. We're in danger of grinding to a halt here," said Adams. The frustration was obvious.

"What about Worrell and Denzel Gibbons?" asked Harris.

"They're not a priority, I think we've wasted enough time on them already. We'll concentrate on Daniels and the clubs. There must be someone who knows something. Let's get out there and find them."

"But surely, we should keep them on the board. I mean it <u>was</u> Gibbons' brother that was killed, and he was injured in the same shooting. There must be some connection there. Maybe we should talk to him again. We could lean on Worrall as well, see what he knows," said Harris.

"As I said, let's concentrate on the clubs for the moment."

D.C. Harris folded her arms, clearly unhappy that she had been ignored. There were sniggers from some of the others who were glad to see her put in her place.

Adams picked up his papers and left the room.

There was a buzz in the room, as the rest of the team filed out to continue their investigations.

Back at the tower block, Polly was becoming a permanent fixture, and Katya couldn't be happier. He'd even read a story to Arjeta before she went to sleep, although how much she understood was open to question. He had called into his flat on the twelfth floor on the way back from Bigsy and Carole's the previous evening to collect the clothes he would need for college and also pick up his assignments.

His mother, Alison watched as he gathered his stuff.

"I hope you know what you are doing. How do you know you can trust her? Remember what she did to you the last time."

Polly ignored the comment.

The Refugee Council Offices were less than a quarter of a mile from the University where Polly was studying, so it made perfect sense for them to go in together, particularly the first day when Katya was uncertain of the travel arrangements.

They left at seven forty-five, which gave them plenty of time to reach their respective destinations by nine o'clock. Polly knew the journey by heart, having made the trip countless times. Katya was wearing one of her new outfits and looked very business-like. Polly looked like he always did, the usual student garb of jeans and hoodie top. Arjeta was confused and Katya had to explain what was happening; she was on buggy duties again.

They caught the Hoppa, the local bus, into Gateshead and another from the Interchange. The snow which had fallen on Saturday night had mostly gone but the pavements were covered in a dark slush which made it difficult for pedestrians. Fortunately, the roads were clear thanks to the gritters, and the family arrived at the Civic Centre an hour later, a journey of less than six miles. Katya couldn't help noticing the traffic; it was relentless, and the thought of driving in it filled her with dread.

They got off the bus with Polly helping her with the buggy.

"Good luck pet. I'll see you later," said Polly.

He kissed Katya before walking the short distance to his destination.

Katya was now pushing Melos in the buggy with Arjeta walking close to her as they crossed the busy road at a pedestrian crossing. Luckily, the office was only a couple of minutes away from the bus stop. It was in a smart Georgian terrace with columns either side of the entrance door. There was a dentist surgery on the one side and a firm of solicitors on the other. There was little to distinguish it from the surrounding properties apart from an understated sign on the door that said, 'Refugee Council'. She manoeuvred the buggy up the steps and rang the bell. Jenny Wheatley answered the door and showed Katya inside.

They went through to a reception area where there was a desk. A lady in her mid-thirties, with bleached-white hair and tattoos down her arm, sat behind it,. She was typing into a computer and looked up as the pair entered.

"This is Trudy, we couldn't manage without her," said Jenny with a smile. "This is Katya, the new manager."

"Pleased to meet you," said Katya, while holding onto the buggy with one hand and Arjeta's hand in the other.

"You too," replied Trudy.

Before they could enter into further pleasantries, Jenny ushered Katya. "Come on through, I'll take you down to the children's room where you can drop off the little ones, and then I'll make some coffee and bring you up to speed."

They went through some more doors before descending a few steps into the crèche. The walls were decorated with children's paintings; tiny tables and chairs were dotted around the floor area. Only two other children were present at this time, being supervised by a slim, boyish-looking woman with very short hair and a stud in her nose.

Katya thought she recognised her, but couldn't immediately recall her name.

"Hello, I remember you. You're Mel's partner from the school," said Katya. "Er... Kerry?"

"Close, Kelly, Kelly Meredith."

"Of course, sorry, I couldn't remember your name. How are you? It's so good to see you again," said Katya.

"You too," replied Kelly.

"Have you left the school?"

"Yes," said Kelly. "I've been working here since September, unfortunately there wasn't enough money to keep me on at the pre-school. Mel's practically running it on her own now, what with the cutbacks and everything."

"How is Mel?" asked Katya, "I would love to see her again."

"She's fine. I'm sure we can fix something, I told her you were coming, she would be thrilled to catch up again."

Kelly knew Melos and Arjeta which made life a lot easier and took some weight off Katya's shoulders.

After a few minutes, Jenny led Katya back upstairs.

"It was a surprise Kelly being here; it is so good to see her again," said Katya, as they went through a long corridor and into one of the offices. The name plate 'Jenny Wheatley' was on the door. They entered and, as Katya expected, it was extremely tidy, everything appeared to be in its right place.

"I like to be organised," said Jenny, aware that the room was being scrutinised.

"This is so different after working for Captain Drury," said Katya and smiled.

"Yes, he has a reputation for being disorganised."

They spent the morning going through several files, with Jenny suggesting courses of action and what Katya would need to do in various circumstances.

"You will need to keep an eye on budgets, but otherwise it's fairly straightforward. It will be mostly the 'Explore and Prepare' programme, I think. Trudy and the team do all the arranging, you just have to approve the individual cases."

By eleven o'clock, Katya was feeling a lot more confident.

"Would you like to meet the rest of the team?" asked Jenny, after another break for coffee. "They'll all be in by now."

Jenny led Katya to the staff room where the staff were introduced to her. Suddenly she was all too aware of the responsibility. Managing people would be a new experience.

Jenny took Katya to lunch at one o'clock. The area around the office was packed, a mixture of students from the University and professionals from the various buildings in the vicinity. There was a coffee shop about a hundred yards away where they managed to find a table and continue the briefing.

After lunch, as they walked from the cafe back to the office, Jenny made a suggestion. "I know, we'll pop to the car park, and I can hand over the car. My new one's being delivered around three. I've checked with Trudy and your insurance is ok. You'll be covered under the Refugee Council's policy. Your driver's licence will be ok too, so you shouldn't have any problems with paperwork."

"Thank you," said Katya.

They walked past the office and turned right into a side street, then right again to the back of the terrace, where there was a service road with marked-out parking spaces.

"We have three; one for you, one for the office supervisor, and a visitor's space. They're clearly marked but be careful though, there're clamping firms around so make sure you don't park anywhere else."

"Sorry," said Katya, 'I don't understand, what is 'clamping'?"

"Oh, you'll soon learn about that!" Jenny explained the strict parking regulations and what would happen to the car if there were any indiscretions.

Jenny's car was parked in the 'visitor's' space. Katya looked at it, an eighteen-month-old metallic-blue Ford Fiesta.

"Oh, this is so nice," said Katya, excitedly.

"I've had two child seats fitted at the weekend, so you'll be able to take the kiddies out."

"That is wonderful, thank you," replied Katya.

Jenny showed Katya the controls, then made a suggestion. "I know why don't I take you around the block and you can get used to it."

Katya looked at Jenny with a degree of apprehension.

"Come on, you'll be fine."

Katya sat in the driver's seat, nervously practicing shifting the gear stick and making sure she could find the handbrake.

"It is so strange; everything is the wrong way round."

She started the engine and slowly eased forward out of the car park. She indicated left and merged into the early afternoon traffic. Jenny directed Katya around the inner ring road.

They arrived back at the office after about twenty-minutes. Katya felt better for this brief tour, but it was still a daunting prospect trying to remember all the one-way systems. She hoped Polly would be with her when she left for home later.

They continued chatting as they walked towards Jenny's office.

"Oh, I nearly forgot; I have a new phone for you. It will need charging, but it's all set up. The calls are paid for by the Council as long as you keep them brief. If you want to contact anyone in Kosovo you can use the office phone. Trudy will show you what to do."

A little later, Jenny's car arrived. "Why don't you pop down and see the children while I'm gone, I won't be long."

Katya went down to the crèche; Kelly was pleased to see her. Arjeta ran to her. "*Sy!* Katya, *sy!*" she shouted excitedly, showing Katya the drawing she had done.

"How have you managed with the language?" Katya asked.

"We've been using picture books. I will show you."

Kelly picked up one of the children's books and pointed to a picture of a car.

"Arjeta, what is that?" she said.

"Car," said Arjeta. "Very good, well done."

Arjeta smiled and clapped her hands.

"That is so good, thank you," said Katya. "This will make such a difference to her."

"No problem, I've really enjoyed teaching her."

After a few minutes, Katya went back upstairs to her office and noticed someone had removed the name plate and was fixing a new one. 'Katya Gjikolli, Manager', it said. Katya stood back with a certain pride.

She continued reading through various files, and then came across a thick folder containing a large amount of correspondence.

Jenny came back to the office, gushing about her new car, and, after listening to Jenny for a few moments, Katya picked up the volume of correspondence

"Who is this person?" she asked, pointing to the large file.

"Oh that," she looked at the bulging folder. "That's Sonny Daniels, a very important person. He's raised a great deal of money for the refugees and given work to several of them too. You'll need to make a point of meeting him. He's one of our major benefactors. I'll get Trudy to make an appointment for you to visit him. He's got this amazing house just outside Ponteland. Ten bedrooms, heated indoor swimming pool, gym, stables, the works… and the kitchen, well, it's to die for. Keeps inviting me up for a swim in his pool, but I've been too busy."

"Who is he?" asked Katya.

"Used to be a boxer, I think. He runs a couple of night clubs in town. He's got a gym just off the Haymarket not far from here. He's given free membership to any of the refugees. Even offered me a membership. He's got a lot of contacts."

"Do any of them go?" asked Katya.

"What, to the gym? One or two. There are a couple of Kosovans who work for him as bouncers, they go."

"I don't understand. What are 'bouncers'?"

"Sorry, security guards, doormen. They work at the nightclubs making sure there's no trouble. You'll meet them over the next few days. I'll get Trudy to set up some appointments for you."

By four-thirty, Katya was feeling the pace, and Jenny suggested they adjourn until the morning; there had been a lot to take in.

Having charged her phone, Katya made her first call. Polly was in a nearby cafe with a couple of his college friends and would meet her in five minutes. Katya collected the children from Kelly and left the building. Polly was waiting for her and kissed her warmly then helped her with the buggy.

"How's it been pet? I've been thinking about you."

"Amazing, just amazing," said Katya, already using some of Carole's phrases. "I have so much to tell you, but first I have to show you something, follow me."

Katya took Polly to the car park behind the offices. She aimed her key fob in the direction of the Fiesta which was parked next to Jenny's new Volvo. The hazard lights flashed briefly indicating it was now unlocked.

"Hey, is that your new car, pet? That's champion, I mean..." Polly was momentarily lost for words.

They approached the car, and Katya opened the boot and put in Melos' buggy. Meanwhile Polly negotiated the various straps of the car seats ensuring the children were safely secured. Arjeta was speaking excitedly, and Katya replied in Albanian. She translated for Polly. "She wants to know if this is my new car."

Katya asked her to say the word in English. "Car" said Arjeta, and Polly and Katya clapped. "Well done, well done," said Katya.

Katya started the engine and slowly reversed out of the space. Arjeta was looking around in all directions; she had not travelled in a car seat before. Melos just seemed bemused.

They headed onto the main road. The traffic was very busy, as Polly had said, but with it being slow, this helped Katya as she merely edged the car along a few yards and then stopped. Polly was navigator and, once they had crossed the Tyne Bridge, the traffic eased, and Katya was able to make better progress. The rest of the journey was made without too much fuss, and they cheered as they pulled into the precinct car park.

"What are you going do about getting a garage sorted? It'll get nicked if you leave it here too long." asked Polly.

"What is 'nicked'?" asked Katya.

"Sorry, pet, stolen."

"I rang Clara this afternoon and she is going to see if there are any available, so I hope it will not be for too long. I do have one of these," she said, reaching behind the front seat for the steering wheel lock.

"Well, that's better than nottin'," said Polly, and having secured the vehicle, they made their way up to the flat.

Earlier that day, around ten-thirty, Chirpie was stood outside the tower block waiting for his lift to Sonny's house for his pending meeting, being briefed by Bigsy.

"Now, don't do anything daft, bonny lad, you'll be fine," said Bigsy

But, despite this encouragement, Chirpie was still uneasy about… well, everything really.

"Aye, it's alright for you. You'll be here, sittin' pretty, while I'm schmoozing with the fookin' Russian mafia. Gives me the fookin' creeps, that Sergei, with them piercing eyes and everything. I reckon he understands more English than he lets on, an' all. I mean, he's shagging an English girl, so they must talk about summat."

"What time's yer taxi coming?" asked Bigsy, who was stood alongside his buddy.

"About half-ten."

Bigsy looked at his watch. "Aye? It's that now."

Chirpie was stood fiddling with jacket and patting down his slicked-back hair. It was still cold, but the weather had improved. Most of the snow from the weekend had melted.

Just then, a black Mercedes E Class turned the corner and pulled up in front of them.

"Fookin' hell, bonnie lad, ya don't see many of these roond heya," said Bigsy, admiring the bodywork.

"Aye, that's true enough," replied Chirpie.

The driver got out and opened the back door for Chirpie.

"Be careful, bonnie lad," said Bigsy, as Chirpie got in the back.

Several people in the precinct stopped and stared as the limousine pulled away.

Chirpie sat back in the leather seats and checked himself over for the umpteenth time. His jacket looked fine; it had been kept immaculate in its cover since he last wore it. He combed his hair flat again. He considered Bigsy's advice; it hadn't helped.

It took less than half an hour to reach the entrance to Sonny Daniels' mansion. The grounds, which adjoined the main road, were surrounded by a high stone wall. The Mercedes pulled up in front of two sturdy wrought-iron gates at least ten feet tall. The words 'High Fields' were spelt in ornate metal lettering across the top, one word on each gate and a coat of arms matching the one on the jacket. The driver pressed the intercom button. After a few moments, the gates opened automatically, and the Mercedes purred its way up the long drive and parked outside the entrance of Sonny's house.

There was a large gravel area in front of the building with several cars parked, including a red Ferrari with the number plate 'SD 1', and another limousine, 'SD 10.' Chirpie looked through the car window in amazement.

The driver got out and opened the back door. Chirpie exited rather ungainly and stopped for a moment to take in his surroundings. In front of him was a huge stone-built house, thirties-style, with turrets on each corner. He tried counting the bedrooms but was interrupted by the chauffeur.

"This way sir."

The address unnerved Chirpie even more. The last time he had been called 'sir' was when the police stopped him for driving a stolen car.

The front door opened, and a man in a butler's uniform led Chirpie into a large hallway bedecked with paintings. A wide wooden staircase wound its way up to another level. The first floor, open gallery-style, was visible from the entrance area. There was a corridor running in front of what looked like bedroom doors.

"Please take a seat; Mr Daniels will be with you in a few minutes. Would you like some refreshments, tea, coffee, sir?"

"No ta, bonny lad," said Chirpie, nervously.

After about ten minutes, Chirpie heard a door open along a corridor to the right. Sonny appeared wearing smart casual clothes, his chromatic glasses darkening in the much brighter room.

"Chirpie, erm, how do you like my house?" said Sonny, as he approached.

"Aye, champion," said Chirpie. "You've done it up nice."

"Yes, it is, isn't it? I chose the entire decor myself."

"Very impressive," replied Chirpie.

"Let's go into the billiard room, shall we? I have some other guests you should meet."

Chirpie followed Sonny back down the same corridor. Sonny opened the door and in the middle of the room there was a full-sized snooker table. A rack of cues and rests were lined up against a wall. The low light was hung about three feet from the table illuminating the baize, in pristine condition, no rips or scuffmarks from over-zealous cueing. The rest of the room was in darkness and two people were engrossed in a game. It was Sergei and another gentleman that Chirpie hadn't met before.

"Gentlemen, can I disturb you for a moment? This is Colin, likes to be called Chirpie, don't you Chirpie?" Chirpie acknowledged. "I was telling you about him earlier. He's looking to forward his career in the organisation." The two men stopped their game and acknowledged the visitor.

"Chirpie, this is Sergei who you've met, and this is Mr. Aziz, one of my business associates, from London."

"How d'you do," said Chirpie.

The greeting was acknowledged with cursory nods from the players and the game continued.

"Do you play, Chirpie?" asked Sonny.

"Aye, up the club, like. They've got a couple of tables. Not like these, mind. One of them's got a bit of a roll on it."

"Well, when we've finished our bit of business, you can play the winner; how about that?"

"Aye, go on then," said Chirpie.

After about ten minutes, the game concluded, and the two players joined Sonny and Chirpie in the seating area in an alcove next to a narrow oblong window which looked out across the grounds. Pale winter sunlight bathed the area, obviating the need for artificial light. Two leather settees faced each other with a coffee-table in between. This time, not wishing to appear unsociable, Chirpie did accept an offer of a drink.

Sonny started his pitch. "Chirpie, erm, you indicated you might be amenable to the chance of earning some extra money, right?"

"Aye, always up for more readies," replied Chirpie.

"I need someone to deliver packages to London from time to time. Sergei usually does it but, let's say, he's probably not the right person at the moment, given recent events."

Chirpie noticed a scowl passing from Sonny in Sergei's direction. Sonny saw that Chirpie had seen the look and continued. "Nothing to concern you; let's just say a case of overzealousness... So, erm, I need someone reliable and can handle themselves. You've proved yourself in that corner, plus you can think on your feet, and I like that."

Chirpie was worried and Sonny could see his anxiety.

"Don't worry Chirpie, erm, it's nothing illegal, just a case of being my courier. I can't use Royal Mail, and I don't trust the parcel companies. I can't afford to lose the goods, and I wouldn't be able to get insurance."

The other two guests laughed knowingly.

Sonny continued. "I give you a briefcase, you take the briefcase down to London and come back with another. That's all there is, oh, and I pay you five hundred pounds per trip."

Chirpie had taken a mouth full of coffee and nearly choked.

"What do you think?" asked Sonny.

"Aye, sounds fine to me," said Chirpie. "When do I start?"

"My next consignment will be on Wednesday. One thing... I'll need you to look like, erm, a businessman, no offence. So, I'll get Roland to drop you off at my tailors just up the road from the Gym and get you fixed up with a suit, a couple of shirts and a tie. I need you looking the part. Any questions?"

"Aye, how do I get to London, like? You've not said."

"No, no you're right. We've been using the Heathrow shuttle the last couple of times, but security is very tight at the airports, and I've decided to use the train. Rashmi will get you the tickets. You'll leave on the seven-thirty from Newcastle Central and catch the three o'clock back. When you get to Kings Cross you'll take a taxi to an address I will give you. Leave the briefcase with Mr Aziz, erm, this gentleman here, and he'll give you one to bring back; quite simple. Any more questions?"

"No, I think you covered everything. What about my job at the night club, like?" asked Chirpie.

"Don't worry about that, Chirpie. I'll keep it open for you but, erm, this will take priority."

"Aye, ok."

Sonny paused before continuing. "I needn't remind you, erm, of the consequences for any, how shall I put it? Transgressions. I am paying you well to do a simple job and I have high expectations. You must tell no-one about our arrangement under any circumstances or cause any difficulties for me. The penalties are quite severe as you will know from the recent press coverage; an unfortunate incident which has cost me a lot of money." He looked at Sergei again. "Do I make myself clear?"

"Crystal, bonny lad," said Chirpie.

"Right, that's settled then. Think of Wednesday as a trial run, and, if all goes well then, we'll see what further opportunities I can put your way. Now how about that game of snooker? Chirpie, you will play Sergei."

What Chirpie hadn't mentioned was that, during the recent years of inactivity on the work front, he had become very proficient on the snooker table and was the present club champion. Needless to say, after Sergei had broken-off Chirpie followed with a break of forty-seven much to the amusement of Sonny and the annoyance of Sergei, and won the frame at a canter.

Sergei threw the cue down after the match and stormed off, furiously cursing in his native tongue at being humiliated. Sonny and Aziz laughed, increasing the Ukrainian's ire only further.

Chirpie said farewell to Sonny who gave him some last-minute instructions.

"Roland, here," looking at the chauffeur. "Will drive you to the station on Wednesday and will give you the briefcase, your tickets and details. Here's my mobile number if you have any problems."

He handed Chirpie another business card.

Sonny turned to walk away but turned back. "Oh, erm, nearly forgot, I'm having a party at the house at the weekend, and you are invited. Bring your swimming things. Roland will pick you up if you want to come."

Bigsy was caught off-guard but thought quickly. "Ta, bonny lad, can I ring you on that, not sure what the missus might have planned."

Sonny looked a little nonplussed for a moment at the apparent rebuff, but then smiled and shook hands warmly with Chirpie. "Just let me know; erm, just let me know."

Chirpie was escorted to the waiting limousine by Roland who had been instructed to take him to the tailors and wait before driving Chirpie home. He was following Roland to the parked Mercedes when Sergei suddenly appeared from the side of the house and approached Chirpie with a menacing look on his face, still angry from his snooker defeat. His eyes were wild as if on drugs.

He called out in a strong mid-European accent. "Hey, you, Chirpie, or whatever your stupid name is." Chirpie stopped in mid-stride; the Ukrainian approached him.

"Just because Sonny likes you, don't think I won't be watching. I don't trust you, and it would be my pleasure to tear you in two and feed you to the fishes in the river."

He clenched his fist in Chirpie's face and snarled, animal-like.

Chirpie turned away, trying to look unfazed, and got into the car. As he sat in the back seat, he looked down and noticed his hands were shaking. Roland, the chauffeur, eased the Mercedes down the drive and headed back to Heathcote.

Chapter Fifteen

Roland dropped Chirpie off by at the flats around two o'clock. He'd instructed the driver not to bother to open the door for him. He took his new suit in its smart plastic cover and the carrier-bags with his shirts from the car boot, and, after stopping off at Mr. Ali's to buy a sandwich, called in next door to see Bigsy at the video store.

"Hiya Chirpie, bonny lad, what've you got there? You been shopping?" asked Bigsy, who was pleased to see his buddy safely returned.

"You don't want to know," said Chirpie.

"Aye, I do. Come on through the back; I want to know everything."

Bigsy had just opened up the video shop and, as usual for this time of day, it was quiet; he and Rikki were sorting out some new stock. The new Star Wars film had just been released on video and DVD; Bigsy was expecting a big demand, and he'd ordered several copies of each. Stan had also delivered half a dozen under-the-counter videos for the back-room stock.

He ushered Chirpie through into the kitchen and put the kettle on while Chirpie started to tuck into his tuna and sweet corn bap.

Pleasantries over, Bigsy was keen to get the lowdown on the morning.

"So, go on then," said Bigsy.

"I don't know where to start," said Chirpie. "It was amazing."

Chirpie spent the next hour detailing his experience at Sonny's, from his trip in the Mercedes, his visit to the tailors, and the encounter with Sergei.

"I'm telling yas, he's a right evil bastard that one, and nottin'll change my mind on that score, make no mistake, and I reckon he did for that lass at Scalleys you know," and he mentioned the innuendoes between Sonny and Sergei.

"Aye, you could be right. I need to speak to Denzel and let him know," said Bigsy.

They also discussed the new role of courier.

"Did he tell you what you'll be carrying, like?" asked Bigsy, "D'you think it could be drugs?"

"Nah, don't think so. You wouldn't get much stuff in a briefcase."

"Aye, you're not wrong there. I think you should just get on with it and see what happens. It seems an easy way to earn some readies, that's for sure, and you'll get a trip to the smoke an' all."

"Aye, that's what I thought," replied Chirpie.

"What about the party?"

"I don't know. I'm not keen on getting too close to that Sergei."

"I know that, bonny lad, but it could get us some info, like. I mean you never know who'll turn up."

"Aye, alright I'll give it a go," replied Chirpie, his tone indicating some reservation.

Wednesday morning, six forty-five.

Chirpie opened the door to Joy's bedroom to say goodbye. She blinked her eyes from her slumbers and looked at him twice.

"You look like fookin' James Bond, you do."

Chirpie took the lift to the ground. Luckily, at that time of day, few people who knew him would be about. It was unlikely they would have recognised him in any case. Gone were the shell-suit and trainers. Instead, a very smart Armani two-piece suit with cufflinks and Yves St. Laurent tie. The Ralph Lauren shirt and Gucci loafers completed the ensemble, a real City slicker. It cost Sonny more than Chirpie's wardrobe for a lifetime.

Roland was waiting outside for Chirpie in the Mercedes. Chirpie got in, and Roland handed him the briefcase, a Mezzi chrome with numbered security locks, and the train tickets; then pulled away, heading to the station. Chirpie viewed the First-Class train fare.

"How much!?" he said out loud, and Roland smiled.

It was totally surreal. Chirpie had never been further than Whitley Bay on the train before, and that was on the Metro, which could hardly be called a proper train. He was in a daze and just a little apprehensive as Roland drew up outside Newcastle Central Station.

"Remember you are booked on the three o'clock back, and I will pick you up here when you get in. If you get any problems, you must phone the number Sonny has given you and we will see to it. Everything ok, sir?" asked Roland seeing Chirpie looking somewhat perplexed.

"Aye, I just haven't been on a train for a while, like."

"I understand, sir, but it is quite simple. You just need to get on the London train as we discussed, it will be on platform three, and get off at Kings Cross. Get a taxi to the address on the paper, swop cases and return the same way."

"Aye, I think I can manage that," said Chirpie.

Roland got out of the car and held the door open for Chirpie to exit; one or two people stared.

"Is that the bloke off the telly?" Chirpie heard someone say as he strode, towards the main concourse.

He was beginning to enjoy his new vocation.

The train from Edinburgh pulled in on time and Chirpie found his seat in the First-Class compartment. He watched his fellow passengers get out their laptops and Financial Times. Chirpie hadn't thought about how to amuse himself on the journey, and when the attendant appeared with a free copy of the Daily Telegraph to go with his complementary coffee, he accepted one. It would give him something to read and also go with his image.

As it happened, the journey passed reasonably quickly as he took in the countryside. The briefcase was next him on the adjacent seat; he wondered what was inside. It wasn't heavy and didn't rattle when he shook it, but it was locked on a security code, so any curiosity was stymied. He had the table seat to himself until York when another business-type sat on the seat opposite. They exchanged pleasantries before the new arrival was engrossed in a laptop and paperwork. Chirpie became fascinated by those around him. He was in a totally alien world, but somehow with his new image, he did not appear out of place.

The train arrived at Kings Cross on time, a journey of just under three and a half hours, and Chirpie was amazed at how busy the London terminus was. After some searching, he found the taxi rank and joined a small queue. A brief wait, and his turn came. He got in the back of the cab and gave the driver the address in Southwark. He had difficulty taking it all in as they headed down the Grays Inn Road, down Fleet Street and across Blackfriars Bridge, names that meant something to Chirpie, but had no idea in what context. They turned off Blackfriars Road and into some non-descript side streets, and, after a few minutes, came to the address that was written down on Chirpie's note.

"Can you wait here for us, bonny lad?" The taxi driver asked him to repeat before he understood.

Chirpie raised his eyebrows. "Bloody cockneys," he muttered, out of earshot.

The house was smart, almost out of place from others in the road, some of which looked a little run down. Chirpie went up to the front door and rang the bell. Aziz answered. The switch took place in a matter of seconds. He was ushered into the vestibule, and he handed over the briefcase. Aziz handed Chirpie an identical one which weighed about the same and said goodbye. It was as quick as that.

Chirpie returned to the taxi, and they headed back to Kings Cross.

As they pulled into the rank at the station, Chirpie leaned forward to the open window behind the driver.

"What's the damage, bonny lad?"

"Thirty-two pounds fifty," said the driver.

"How much!? Fookin' hell," exclaimed Chirpie. "No wonder you've all got bloody big houses down heya."

The driver had difficulty in interpreting, and just waited for the money without comment. Chirpie gave the driver thirty-five pounds and waited for the change.

"I'll need a receipt an' all."

He watched the two pound-fifty counted into his hand and accepted the receipt.

There was over an hour to kill before his train was due to leave, so Chirpie passed the time wandering around the huge concourse looking in the shops. He found a sandwich bar which was doing a good trade. While he waited to be served, he could see the price of a sandwich displayed on the wall behind the serving staff. "Fookin' hell," he said to himself. Thankfully, Sonny would be footing the bill, and he kept another receipt for expenses. He also remembered to stock up on a couple of magazines to relieve the boredom of the home trip.

The return to Newcastle was as uneventful as the journey down, and Chirpie was beginning to think he'd won the lottery. A few more trips like this, and Tenerife was looking a possibility, never mind Benidorm.

The train arrived about ten minutes late, at six forty-five, but Roland was at the front entrance in the Mercedes and opened the car door for Chirpie.

"How was your trip, sir?" asked the driver, as he pulled away.

"Aye, champion, bonny lad, no bother, no bother at all." Chirpie spent a few minutes detailing the journey to Roland.

Back at the flats, Chirpie gave Roland the briefcase and in return received an envelope which, out of courtesy, he did not open.

"Can you pass a message on to Sonny for me? Tell him I'll be ok for Saturday, the party, like."

"Splendid sir, Sonny will be very pleased. I can collect you; what shall we say? Seven-thirty. I might even be able to bring the Ferrari."

"You're kidding!" said Chirpie. "Well, you won't be able to stop round here in one of them, bonny lad. They'll have the wheels off before you've got the hand-break on."

Roland smiled. "Don't worry sir, we will be quite safe; Sonny has ways of dealing with vandalism."

"I'm sure he has, bonny lad; I'm sure he has," said Chirpie, as he exited the car without assistance.

"Till Saturday, then," said Roland, and Chirpie watched the Mercedes pull away.

Chirpie made for the video shop and his debrief with Bigsy. As he entered the store, a chorus of wolf whistles greeted him.

"Fookin' hell, Chirpie lad, you look the dog's bollocks and no mistake," said Bigsy. "Where's your Filofax?"

"Very funny, very funny," replied Chirpie. "Make us a brew will yas and I'll fill you in."

They went through into the kitchen where a couple of customers were browsing the adult section.

"Come on lads, piss off, you've been in here twenty minutes," said Bigsy.

The men grabbed two videos and left the kitchen to pay at the desk.

Over a brew, Chirpie detailed his trip to London, although there wasn't a great deal to tell. He did, however, remember the address in London, which he thought might come in useful. Bigsy made a note to pass on to Denzel.

The trip however, had affected Chirpie. In fact, it had been a life-changing experience; chauffeur-driven cars, taxis, first-class travel. "I could get use to this, Bigsy, man."

"Aye, but don't get carried away, bonny lad; this is not real. As soon as you've served your purpose you'll be back here, brassic as usual," counselled Bigsy.

"Aye, you're not wrong there." Chirpie let out a big sigh.

It was Katya's third day in her new role and was on her own for the first time. Jenny had gone down to London for a briefing, and was, coincidentally, on the same train as Chirpie, albeit second-class. Katya had dropped off Polly at the car park and took the children to Kelly in the crèche before returning to her office. Trudy was sorting out the post on reception, and Katya spent a few minutes catching up with the gossip.

Katya could still not get used to her name on the door, and thought how proud her mother would be if she could see it. She realised how much she was missing her.

Trudy bought in a coffee and the post, then went through the appointments today. The office provided a range of services and assistance for local refugees, and most people tended to just drop in and speak to Trudy or one of the team. They could also use the phone to call the Pristina office to speak with their loved ones.

Sometimes, however, on more confidential matters, there would be requests to see the centre manager, and such was the case today. Eleven o'clock, Mr. & Mrs. Mujota, it said in the diary. The only other appointment today was an introductory meeting at two o'clock with the local council officials to meet with the housing and community liaison department. Katya would need to go to the council offices, but as Clara was the contact point, she had no concerns about the meeting.

At just before eleven, Trudy rang through to say that the couple had arrived with their four-year-old daughter. Katya went to the reception area and escorted them through to her office while Trudy took the daughter to the children's area.

There were a couple of chairs in front of Katya's desk and the pair sat down.

Katya viewed the couple and introduced herself in Albanian. They were delighted when they heard their native tongue being spoken.

"I am Gordana; this is my husband, Hashim" There was an anxiety in the introduction.

Hashim was lean and fit, but his face was drawn as if he needed sleep. He was wearing a SD Security jacket.

"How can I help?" said Katya.

Hashim looked at his wife, who nodded to him in encouragement. With gradual confidence, he related his story of his escape and patriation. It was as harrowing as many Katya had heard.

"Eventually, we were sent here, to U.K, at first in hostel, then here," continued Hashim.

"When was this?" asked Katya.

"It was in September. We were given a house in Newcastle, in the north, many houses there, but we are well looked after."

"Tell her the rest," said his wife, nudging his arm.

Hashim continued hesitantly. "I was given work at a nightclub here. I work many hours every day until three, sometimes four in the morning. I do not mind this, at least I have money."

"What do you do there?" asked Katya.

"I am with the security." He looked at his wife again.

"It's ok, go on," encouraged Katya.

He continued in Albanian; his wife was holding his hand, squeezing it in reassurance.

"Two months ago, things, they changed."

Gordana started to cry.

"Would you like a break, some water perhaps?" asked Katya, seeing their distress.

"No, it is ok," said Hashim. "But please, I beg you, do not say anything, they will kill me."

"Who will?"

"There is a man who comes to the club, they called him Sergei, from the Ukraine. very bad man."

Hashim stopped briefly to choose the right words.

"He strikes fear, terror into the staff. A very bad man," he repeated.

"He slaps the foreign girls if they do not give him…" Hashim paused again and looked at his wife. " *'Kënaqësi'*… pleasure."

He stopped again.

"It's ok, take your time," said Katya.

"A few weeks ago, this Sergei said that we would have to sell drugs to people. He tells only foreign workers because he knows he can threaten them with deportation, but many others, local people, do it too for the extra money. They were not threatened."

He paused again.

"So, what happens? How do you sell the drugs?"

Hassim looked at his wife; he was still extremely anxious. "Er, there is a… a room at the back of the club. It is through a, a secret door. Er, each night, those who had been told to sell the drugs, they pick up some drugs from there. They teach us how to, er." He struggled for the right words. "Give out the drugs for money. Then we give the money to Sergei before we leave."

"Which club is this?"

"Mr. Gees," replied Hashim.

Gordana interrupted. "My husband is a good man. He has no interest in drugs, but this Sergei, he does terrible things. They say that he has killed the girl from the other nightclub, the one was in the newspapers. Hashim, he cannot sleep or eat much, so much worry."

"Have you been to the police?"

"*Ne! Ne Polici!*" the woman exclaimed. "They have already threatened to kill anyone who goes to the police. They are watching them all the time."

"So, how can I help?" Katya asked.

"Please help us get back to Kosovo, please, as soon as possible," said Gordana.

"Yes, of course. I can get you on a repatriation flight; it will not be a problem, but it might take a few weeks," said Katya.

Gordana cried again and hugged Katya's hand. "**Thank you, thank you.**"

Katya took their details. "Please phone me or call here if you have problems. I will phone you as soon as I have any news about your departure date." She looked at Hashim. "Why don't you stay at home, say you are sick or something, and not go to work until you can leave?"

"No, no, they will come for me if I do not work," said Hashim. Gordana grasped his hand again.

The couple got up.

"Thank you, thank you," said Gordana again. "Please do not say anything, please, our lives depend on it."

"Of course, you have my word," said Katya.

Hashim and Gordana seemed relieved as they left Katya's office.

That evening Katya was at home making the dinner and Polly was entertaining the children. The morning's conversation with the Mujotas was bothering her, and she wanted to talk to Polly about it. She explained the background and wondered what she should do.

"Well, pet, the obvious answer is to go to the police, but I can see why you canna do that. Why don't you pop across and see Bigsy? He knows all about this kind of stuff. He may have an idea, and he certainly won't involve the bizzies."

"What is 'bizzies?'"

"Sorry, police," clarified Polly and laughed.

So, after dinner, Katya went down the corridor, leaving Polly looking after the children. She knocked on the door and Carole answered.

"Katya, pet, lovely to see you. Come in. Would you like a glass of red?"

Before Katya could answer she was ushered into the living room and faced a further barrage of Carole's questions.

"How's your new job going? What's your new car like?"

Katya answered Carole's enquiries, then got to the point.

"I just wanted to talk with Bigsy, if that's ok?"

Bigsy was sat on the sofa watching a football match.

"Of course, pet, I'll open a bottle."

Carole went to the kitchen as Bigsy got up to greet Katya.

"Katya, pet, good to see you. How are you doin'?" he said, and kissed Katya on the cheek.

"Fine, the new job is good, very good, very busy trying to understand everything, but I am enjoying it, yes."

Carole came back with two large glasses of red wine and handed one to Katya.

"And how are things going with our Polly?" said Carole.

"Very well, thank you. He has moved in now. He does not see Allison so much, which is a shame."

"Ah, don't you worry, pet, she'll soon come around. She was very fond of you, you know."

"I hope so," said Katya.

Katya joined Carole and Bigsy on the sofa and Bigsy turned down the commentary on the football, but he could keep one eye on the game.

Katya explained the reason for her call. "Polly said you may be able to help; I want to ask for your advice."

"Aye, I'll try," said Bigsy.

"Ok, thank you, but I need to tell you things I should not. I am breaking a promise, but I want to help some people I met at work today."

Katya then outlined what had happened in the meeting and the threats.

"Which club is it? If you can say, like," asked Bigsy.

"It was called..." and she paused while she recollected. "Yes, I remember Mr, something."

"Mr Gees?!" asked Bigsy, who had now turned the television off.

"Yes, I am sure that was it."

"Tell us, was there anything else they said?" asked Bigsy. "Did they mention any names?"

"Yes, Mr Mujota said there was a... Ukrainian, I think he said. His name was... wait..." Katya paused again.

"Not Sergei, by any chance?" said Bigsy before Katya could recollect.

"Sergei...? Yes, yes, that was it. How did you know?"

Bigsy nearly fell off his chair.

"Sergei, you say. Are you sure? A Ukrainian called Sergei?"

"Yes, that's what they said."

Bigsy looked down at the floor then raised his eyes to Katya. He spoke in a soft, but serious tone, leaning forward in his chair.

"I know about this man, pet, and from what I've heard, the stories are probably true. You must not get involved at all; he is very dangerous."

"How do you know all this, pet?" interjected Carole.

"From my work at the clubs. He has a really bad reputation. Look, the best thing, Katya, pet, is to say nottin' and get these people away as soon as you can."

After she had left, Bigsy got up from the sofa and phoned Chirpie.

"I need a quick chat, bonny lad. Aye, downstairs, five minutes."

"Just popping down to see Chirpie," said Bigsy, and left before Carole could return from glass washing duties in the kitchen.

His buddy was waiting for him at the entrance to the flats.

"I've just been speaking to our Katya," said Bigsy, and related the story of the refugees to Chirpie.

Chirpie listened intently. "Aye, that makes sense, and I've met the guy you mentioned at the club, seems a canny lad; fit as a butcher's dog, ex KLA. I reckon he can handle himself,"

"What d'you want us to do, Bigsy lad?"

"Be very careful, and if it starts getting heavy, get yourself out and go to ground, I'll take care of things. It's drugs, that's what it's all about; I knew it had to be. I just couldn't work out how it was being done," replied Bigsy. "When are you next working the club?"

"Don't know, Sonny wants me to do the courier job for the moment, but I'll know more on Saturday at the party I reckon."

Back at police HQ, the team had made a small breakthrough; they had managed to track down Daryl, the erstwhile Scalleys' D.J.

Superintendent Adams was giving his team an update that evening.

"Right, people, listen up... The latest news we have is that D.C. Harris visited Anderson's mother again and she eventually told us he was staying at his brother's flat in Bayswater. We've managed to catch up with him, but he couldn't give us a great deal of information. He has, though, corroborated what we already know. He thought there might be things going on at the Scalleys, but all the staff had been warned by the manager not to say anything to anyone making enquiries. Gemma Calder had been seen talking to our under-cover guys, and he thinks that is why she was killed. That's when he decided to get out."

"Do we know anything about the manager?" asked D. S. Tunney.

"Not much; his name's Asif, but whether he's any relation to Sonny's business partner we don't know. Since Gemma Calder's murder we've had to tread carefully. There are a lot of nervous people around."

"Couldn't we just bring him in and give him the once over?" asked Tunney.

"Well, we've got him under surveillance. There're three undercover officers in Scalleys and we're keeping an eye on Mr. Gees. As soon as we've got enough information we'll go in. There's a lot at stake here, and I want to get the main players. The danger is, if we bring the manager in now, he'll have a good lawyer, deny everything, and we'll just end up with egg on our faces. We need more evidence."

Adams was about to conclude the briefing when one of the incident room's phones rang. The Superintendent scowled his displeasure; they would be normally diverted to a central office during briefings. D.C. Harris was nearest and picked it up; the room went quiet.

"It's for you, guv, urgent," she said, and passed the phone to Adams.

"Incident room... When was this? Whereabouts? Can you call a forensic team and set up a crime scene? We'll be with you as soon as."

Adams put the phone down and the team looked on expectantly.

"Another body, male, found in woods outside Stannington, just off the A1. A dog walker found it."

There were quizzical looks around the team.

"Right, let's get on it. Tunney, get over there; you can be SOCO. Harris, Frasier, with me. Ok everyone, briefing here nine sharp tomorrow. What would we do without dog walkers?" added Adams, and he went back to his office to change into suitable clothing.

The team arrived at the scene in less than half an hour after leaving Police HQ. The rush-hour traffic had subsided; it was eight p.m. There was the usual frenzy of activity at the scene. The body had been found buried in a small copse about a quarter of a mile from Stannington, a quiet village just off the A1. The Superintendent's car made its way along a small road out of the village and turned left onto a farm track that skirted the copse where the body was found. He could see the wood bathed in arc lights; the area had been cordoned off with police tape. The forensic investigation had started their work.

Adams stopped next to several other cars and walked towards

the trees accompanied by officers Harris and Fraser. It was a bitterly cold night, with a cloudless sky; the stars shone brightly in the absence of street lighting. The hard frost had kept away any prospects of snow.

Tunney had assumed his role and was speaking to the police pathologist when the Superintendent approached the scene.

"Ok, bring me up to speed. What have we got... anything?" Adams put on an overcoat.

Tunny turned to his boss.

"Not yet, guv, it appears a dog walker needed to relieve himself and went into the copse for some privacy. His dog followed him in and wandered off. Owner went looking for the dog and noticed it scratching at the soil. Luckily the man was carrying a good torch and saw what seemed to be a human hand sticking out of the ground. Went back home and called 999. He led the team here after the call. He's being interviewed by D.C. Baxter."

"Thanks Inspector, let's have a look."

They approached the scene about fifty yards inside a small wood on the edge of open fields. Two officers were carefully digging with trowels around the body which was now clearly visible. It had decomposed, and no facial features remained. There was no sign of clothing. Flashes from cameras lit the scene like fireworks, as the Superintendent and following posse surrounded the shallow grave. The pathologist was taking skin tissue samples, placing them in labelled test tubes, then depositing them in a cool box.

"Anything yet?" asked Adams to one of the men in white coats.

"Too early, but I would say, judging by the decomposition, that he's been dead for six or seven months. I can give you more on that when I get him back to the lab."

"Anything to indicate cause of death?" asked Adams.

"Well, he's got a fractured skull, so that would do it, but there are other broken bones as well, so he could well have been beaten. Speculation at this stage I am afraid."

"What about age?"

"Forties probably, but again I'll have more information in the morning. It's going to be a long night," said the pathologist.

Chapter Sixteen

Thursday, 20th January, nine a.m.

At the Police Headquarters, Detective Superintendent was providing an update for the team. There was an expectant atmosphere in the room and a lot of chatter.

"Ok, settle down." He paused while the noise abated.

"I've had the preliminary pathologist report. It confirms the body is of a male, Afro-Caribbean, age range mid-forties. Cause of death, not confirmed, but the doc said he looks like he's been in a train crash judging by the number of broken bones. Most likely, the blow to the head killed him. Without wishing to presume, this could be the missing doorman, Lionel Johnson. We're doing a trace on the database to see if there's a DNA match. If it is Johnson, then that's another link to Sonny Daniels and his organisation. Tunney, if you're still in touch, can you see if the D.J. can give us any information on Johnson. He was working at Scalleys at the time. We can bring him back if necessary as a potential witness."

"Yes guv," replied Tunney.

D.C. Harris was adding Johnson's name to the incident board as the Superintendent called her over.

"Harris, how do you fancy going under cover?"

"Great," replied Harris. "What've you got in mind?"

The Superintendent outlined his idea to her.

Back at the Refugee Council offices, Jenny Wheatley had returned from her London trip and was debriefing Katya.

"Any problems yesterday?"

"No, it was fine," replied Katya.

"How did you get on with the Mujotas?"

"Yes, it was fine. They just want to get back to Kosovo as soon as possible. I have asked for an early repatriation flight. I hope to get them away in about two weeks."

"Oh, that's a shame; I had to twist a few arms to get him the security job. He seemed happy when I last spoke to him."

"I think things have changed; they just want to get back," replied Katya, not wanting to give anything away.

They continued the catch up.

"Have you spoken to Sonny Daniels yet?" asked Jenny.

"No, I am going to phone him today and try to arrange a meeting."

"That would be good. We don't want to lose his support."

Later that morning, Katya rang the number on file and got through to the house. A very polite gentleman answered the phone and took the details.

"I can fit you in at eleven o'clock next Tuesday."

The meeting with Sonny Daniels, great refugee benefactor, was confirmed in Katya's diary. Jenny promised to give her directions. "You can't miss it."

Bigsy was at home Friday night reading the evening paper while Carole was cooking the tea, when another headline jumped out at him.

Police identify body found in shallow grave

Police have confirmed that a body found by a dog walker near Stannington on Wednesday night was that of Lionel Johnson (46). Mr Johnson previously worked as a doorman at Scalleys Night Club and was a familiar figure on the local scene. He had been reported missing by his family and had not been seen since leaving work last June. Police refused to confirm any link with the recent discovery of the body of Scalleys' barmaid, Gemma Caldwell, at Willington Quay. Detective Superintendent James Adams who is heading the investigation said at a press conference today that it was one of several lines of enquiry. He was unable to confirm cause of death. He appealed for anyone who knew Lionel Johnson or could give any information regarding his disappearance to call the incident room on 0191 735 2232.

Bigsy rang Wazza and alerted him to the story.

"Have you seen the paper tonight, bonny lad? Aye, it seems our boy's turned up dead. The body count's increasing at an alarming rate."

"Aye, you're not wrong there, Bigsy lad," replied Wazza.

"Are you still ok for the meet with Denzel tonight...? Aye, seven-thirty at the club. Meet us downstairs at ten-past. Can you let Chirpie know? Ta, speak later," said Bigsy, and went back to his newspaper.

"Just popping out to the club in a while, pet, see Wazza and Chirpie, won't be late," he shouted to Carole who was in the kitchen.

An hour later, Bigsy took the lift and met up with his two buddies and headed for the club. They decided to walk the mile and a half. Some serious consumption of broons was on the cards.

Denzel arrived at precisely seven-thirty, and the three buddies were waiting in the car park. It was yet another van. Bigsy had booked the office again so they would not be disturbed; three broons and a mineral water were waiting for them on the table.

"Thanks, Bigsy, mon, you always look after us well," said Denzel, as they entered the room.

Bigsy brought Denzel up to speed and told him about the Kosovan refugee and the drug connection at Mr Gees.

"It seems this bloke Sergei has previous. His name keeps cropping up everywhere. There's a rumour he killed that barmaid, Gemma, and my guess, Lionel Johnson an' all. It's getting very dangerous."

Denzel nodded in agreement. "Yes, I can see dat."

"We have some other news as well. Chirpie here has landed a job as Sonny's courier."

"Really?" said Denzel.

Bigsy explained about the briefcase and gave him the address in London where Chirpie had made the drop.

"Tanks, dat's very helpful. I will pass dis on to Errol. He's in Brixton so he can check dis out. We may need to pay dem a visit sometime."

Bigsy looked at Chirpie. "Chirpie's got an invite, like, and I think it could be a great chance to find out what's really going on."

Denzel turned to Chirpie. "You will need to be very careful, Chirpie, mon; it is very dangerous. Errol is very concerned at de risk you are taking on his behalf, and he will not forget dis."

"No problem, bonny lad," said Chirpie modestly, who seemed to be warming to his new role as centre of attention.

Denzel got up to leave and produced his Friday envelope from his inside pocket.

"Dere is an extra bonus from Errol, to show his appreciation," said Denzel, and he passed the envelope to Bigsy.

"Ta Denzel, bonny lad, and pass on our best to your man. I'll be in touch with any news next week."

Bigsy escorted Denzel back to the car park, and, as they were walking to the van, Bigsy spoke to him. "D'you have any idea what Errol is going to do?"

"Not yet, Bigsy mon, but someting big is going down if you can find out it was definitely dis Sergei dat killed Everton and Layton."

"Aye well, we'll keep digging," replied Bigsy.

"Well, you take good care, mon," and Denzel got in the van and drove off.

Bigsy went back to Chirpie and Wazza and checked the envelope, counting out the twenty-pound notes on the table.

"A grand, I make it. That's very thoughtful of him," said Bigsy, and gave the additional money to Chirpie for his efforts. Wazza was happy with his usual cut.

Friday seven p.m., back at police HQ, Superintendent Adams was providing the team with the latest information. It had been another hectic day.

"As you know we've been able to identify Lionel Johnson from NDNAD records. We were lucky; he'd served eighteen months for GBH in 1996, and we got a positive hit. This gives us a definite lead into Scalleys. Unfortunately, the only people who worked at the club with Johnson were Gemma Calder and Daryl Anderson. Gemma is dead,. and our colleagues in the Met called at Anderson's brother's flat yesterday, and it appears that he's has done another runner. His brother thought he might have gone to Spain, but we can't confirm that. Asif the manager has been interviewed by Tunney and Frasier... Gentlemen?"

Tunney got up and referred to his notebook. "We interviewed Asif yesterday evening and he was as slippery as an eel. However, he did provide proof he did not work at Scalleys at the time of Johnson's disappearance. He didn't join until September. The previous manager, a..." He checked his notes again. "Gerry Shoesmith, according to Asif emigrated to Australia, would you believe. We are checking emigration records, but at the moment there's no trace of him. A blank I'm afraid."

"Did he say anything about Gemma Calder?" asked Adams.

"Again nothing, he says he was away the night she disappeared. Not able to confirm that," said Frasier.

Adams was wringing his hands in frustration. Before he dismissed his team, he had another piece of information for them.

"If you were wondering about Detective Constable Harris, she's going under cover. We're trying to get her into Mr Gee's on the bar staff. It's the only way we're going to get anywhere. Everything is shut tight as a drum."

"What about TV, a Crimewatch appeal perhaps?" asked Frasier.

"We're speaking to the producers next week for a possible inclusion on the next programme to try to get some more leads on

Gemma Calder's murder," replied Adams.

Superintendent Adams dismissed his team and headed home. It had been another testing week.

Saturday evening, Chirpie was getting ready for his big night. It hadn't started well; Newcastle United had lost two-nil, away to Wimbledon.

His phone rang.

"Bigsy, bonny lad."

"Just wanted to see if everything was ok for tonight."

"Aye, it's ok, bad result today, mind. Hope it's not an omen."

"Aye, you're not wrong there, a right bunch of cloggers. Anyroad, I just called to say keep your head down and your ears open. If you're in any bother, get yourself away and call me, ok? I've got a feeling this could be all over soon."

"Aye, will do. I hope you're right, bonny lad."

After more words of reassurance, Bigsy rang off. The call had given Chirpie some encouragement and brightened his melancholy. He was beginning to have regrets about accepting the invitation, anxious at what might lay ahead.

He was in his bedroom trying to decide what to wear. Sonny had said something about bringing his swimming stuff but, as Chirpie hadn't swum since he was at junior school and thought he would feel self-conscious in a pair of trunks, he decided to pass. If necessary, he could always play snooker.

He decided his courier gear would be appropriate for the occasion.

Just as he was about to leave, Joy looked up from the television. "You know, you're different since you poshed up. I hope you're not getting all fookin' snooty on us."

Chirpie ignored the remark and left the flat.

He reached the ground floor just after seven-thirty. Waiting in the precinct car park was the red Ferrari. Chirpie couldn't believe his eyes. A crowd had gathered to look at it, mainly young lads.

"Hey Chirpie, you won the lottery?" shouted Rikki Rankin, who was watching from outside the video shop.

"You make sure you keep your hands off it or I'll have your balls on toast," riposted Chirpie with a smile as he got in.

Unfortunately, Chirpie's boarding of the car was not completed with the grace and elegance that he had hoped. Given his size and the frugal space, Chirpie had to shoehorn himself into the car in an undignified manner. By the time he'd got in, he was almost lying down, much to the amusement of the watching crowd.

Roland greeted him warmly.

"I do hope you will enjoy yourself this evening; Sonny does try so hard, you know."

They sped off shooting a cloud of dust and gravel from the wheels, the force of the acceleration pinning Chirpie to his seat. The gang of lads looked on with a degree of wonderment. A Ferrari on Heathcote had never been heard of before.

Arriving at the gates of Sonny's mansion, Roland pressed the intercom, and they swung slowly open. He eased the Ferrari up the drive and stopped in its parking spot in front of the mansion. Roland went around to the passenger side and held the door open while Chirpie extracted himself from the seat.

"Ta very much, bonny lad, that was amazing," he said, as he straightened himself up and smoothed out the creases on his suit.

Chirpie looked around the car park and his jaw dropped as he looked at the up-market cars on the driveway.

"A fair bit of dosh here, Roland, bonny lad," said Chirpie, as they walked past the vehicles. Roland smiled.

Sonny was greeting guests dressed in a pink suit, yellow shirt and trademark glasses. He beamed as Chirpie emerged from the entrance lobby into the hallway.

"Chirpie, so glad you could make it," said Sonny, and proceeded to give Chirpie a man-hug. Chirpie found it difficult to respond.

"Help yourself to drinks, erm, and I'll introduce you to some of my friends."

A young lady dressed as a French Maid with a very short skirt and almost exposed breasts, approached with a tray of drinks. Chirpie tried not to stare.

"Champagne, Chirpie?" asked Sonny.

"Have you got any broons, bonny lad?" he replied.

"I don't know, I'll ask." Sonny spoke to the girl.

A few minutes later, the young lady returned with a large bottle of Newcastle Brown and a bottle opener on a tray.

"Ta, pet," said Chirpie, opening the bottle and ignoring the accompanying glass.

The waitress wandered off to fetch more drinks. Chirpie took a sip from his bottle and watched her walk away.

Sonny noticed Chirpie ogling the girl.

"Don't worry Chirpie, erm, there's plenty more where she came from."

Chirpie looked down in some embarrassment.

"Why don't you have a look around," said Sonny. "Did you bring any swimwear? You can use the pool if you like; although not many seem to bother with clothes at my parties," Sonny added with a smile.

"Aye, I'll do that," replied Chirpie.

Sonny wandered off to greet more guests.

For a minute he'd almost forgotten his mission, dazzled by everything going on around him. He checked the guests for any signs of the Ukrainian; he hadn't seen Sergei yet. He would be happy for that situation to continue.

He made his way along the corridor to the snooker room expecting to see a game in play. To his surprise, there was a very attractive young lady on the precious baize, totally naked, with lines of white powder laid out on her stomach and lower abdomen.

He stared, trying to process the sight.

A man in his thirties pushed past him and approach the table holding a straw. Chirpie watched in disbelief as he sniffed one of the lines. The man pinched his nose and shook his head when he had finished, and walked off back to the throng in the lobby area. Chirpie looked at the girl again.

"Help yourself, pet," she said, in a strong local accent.

"No, you're all right, thanks for the offer, like. I was just looking for a game of snooker." Chirpie was trying not to stare.

"There'll be more interesting games to play tonight, pet, if you catch my drift," said the girl.

"Aye, bonny lass, you're not wrong there."

Chirpie headed back along the corridor attempting to shake the image of the girl from his mind, and returned to the lobby area.

More guests had arrived, and Sonny was doing his hosting duties with his usual panache. Chirpie thought he recognised one or two people from pictures in the local paper. There were a couple of minor celebrities with glamourous-looking partners on their arm and a city counsellor who Chirpie was trying to place, but thought he might be on the Planning Committee. He wasn't that aux-fait with local politics, but there was something in the Evening Chronical recently regarding certain irregularities, and thought it was the same man.

Suddenly, Chirpie spotted his nemesis, Sergei, enter the lobby with the beautiful Rashmi. He ducked quickly behind some guests and headed down the passageway on the opposite side from the snooker room.

At the end of the corridor, he could hear laughter and splashing water. He opened the door and found himself in the pool area. Chirpie stood in amazement as he viewed the opulence.

The pool was probably half the size of the one at the local swimming baths that Chirpie remembered, but that is where any similarity ended. There were large picture windows which in the summer would provide spectacular views of the grounds and countryside beyond but tonight they were steamed up. The area was bathed in bright arc lights which created shadows on the walls. Potted-palms and sun-loungers were spaced around the poolside. There were about ten people either swimming or lounging, but his attention was drawn straight away to a couple in the pool at the end nearest him. The man was about waist deep in the water and the woman holding onto the rails with her arms outstretched, her legs wrapped around him. Her head was tilted back, resting on the pool side with her eyes closed. There was a look of concentration on her face. They were both naked and clearly not swimming. Chirpie was transfixed. He took another gulp from his bottle.

He was startled by a voice. "Hello, are you going for a swim?"

Chirpie turned. In front of him was a stunning dark-haired girl in her late twenties, wearing a tiny bikini top and thong.

"I... I... I haven't brought any gear," he managed to stutter.

"That's not a problem," she said, and peeled off her top, then tugged the knot that tied the thong around her waist, and it fell away. Chirpie was dumbstruck.

She turned. "Come on, don't be a sissy," she shouted with a giggle.

She turned and completed a perfect dive into the pool hardly causing a splash.

"It was never like this at Seaton Leisure Centre," he recalled, but was now facing a dilemma.

"I'll be back in a minute, pet, just going to fill my glass." He headed for the door.

"Don't be long," he heard her shout.

Chirpie found his way back to the large entrance lobby, now full of people gradually dispersing into various rooms. The early musak had been replaced by more upbeat dance music which had changed the atmosphere. It was louder now with people in animated discussions. Desperately trying to get the sight of the naked swimmer out of his head, Chirpie swapped the empty bottle of Newcastle Brown for a glass of champagne from another French maid and decided to do some further exploring. Back along the first corridor, loud music was emanating from one of the rooms to the left, immediately before the snooker room.

He opened the door and there was a disco in full swing with about twenty people gyrating to the accompanying sounds. Chirpie looked around. It was large, probably Sonny's living room. A space in the middle had been cleared and there was a parquet floor surrounded by beautiful Persian carpets. Three leather sofas surrounded the dance area, in the corner, the entertainment system. Chirpie's jaw dropped, a lad's paradise.

He looked around at the dancers, attired in their finery; the men in dinner jackets, but most having dispensed with their bow ties, the women in short, some of them very short, cocktail dresses. In the corner of the room a D.J. had set up his equipment and was asking for requests.

Chirpie left the disco, and noticed the door to the snooker room was open, and almost in darkness. The table was now covered by a protective cloth; there was no sign of the girl. The light over the table was off; the room illuminated by four small wall lights, each highlighting a framed print of one of Boris O'Klein's 'Dirty Dogs of Paris' cartoons.

Chirpie hovered in the doorway for a moment. He could see figures in conversation on the other side of the room. He was not visible from the entrance, which was in relative darkness and, with the noise from the disco next door, his presence had gone unnoticed.

Chirpie made a decision. He ducked down and crawled under the snooker table. He could see three sets of legs. They started walking towards an open door on the far side of the room that he hadn't noticed before. He recognised the voices; Sonny, Sergei, and another man, possibly the one from London, were in heated discussion.

The men disappeared down some steps out of Chirpie's line of sight; the door appeared to close automatically behind them.

Chirpie crawled out from under the table and approached the door. The opening had gone, vanished. He wondered if he had imagined it, but on closer inspection he could see that the heavy mahogany veneer had been cleverly camouflaged to cover the opening.

On the wall next to the entrance was, what looked like, a central heating control panel, but when he examined it in more detail, he could see it was a security pad numbered from zero to nine. He was examining the device closely, when suddenly a voice made him jump out of his skin. His glass dropped from his hand and shattered on the floor, wetting the carpet with what was left of his drink.

"Can I help you, sir?"

It was Roland.

Chirpie was trying to keep his composure and not betray his shock at being caught out.

"Roland... bonny lad... I... I was just looking for the lights. I was going to have a game of snooker, like," Chirpie managed to say in a quivering voice.

He anxiously bent down to attend to the broken glass.

"Don't worry about the glass, sir, I'll see to that. The light switch is over here," and the chauffeur led Chirpie to the other side of the table near the door where a row of switches was clearly visible.

"Didn't see them there," he said, desperately hoping he hadn't been discovered.

"Quite so," said Roland. "Do you have a partner, sir?"

"No, I can't find anyone. D'you fancy a frame, bonny lad?" asked Chirpie, thinking quickly.

"Regrettably, I can't sir, things to do; I am on duty this evening" Roland switched on the light over the table.

"You will need to take the cover off, before you set the balls, sir," said Roland, without a hint of sarcasm.

"Aye, I know that, bonnie lad."

Chirpie removed the cloth and started taking the balls from the pockets and rolling them onto the table.

Roland left the room as Chirpie was racking up. His hands were shaking so much he could not hold the cue properly as he tried a couple of practice shots down the table. It was only nine-thirty, and he was beginning to wish he was back home.

A couple of minutes later, Roland returned with a dustpan and brush and swept up the remains of the broken champagne flute. He padded the damp carpet with a cloth.

"Sorry about that, Roland, bonny lad."

"Couldn't be helped, sir," replied Roland.

Roland left the room again and shut the door leaving Chirpie on his own. The cacophony from the disco was down to a dull rhythmic thud. Chirpie started his game.

After clearing the reds, he was about to line up the yellow when he heard a slight creaking noise and the mystery door started to open slowly.

Chirpie dived under the table again before he had been spotted.

The three men exited the hidden stairway, and the door automatically closed behind them. Sonny stopped and looked at the table.

"I do wish they would put the cover back on the table after they have finished; some people have no manners." He proceeded to roll the remaining balls into the pockets.

The third man spoke, not in an English accent, continuing an unfinished conversation. Chirpie thought he recognised the voice; it was almost certainly Aziz. He could see the six legs moving around the table. He could hear his own heart beating.

"What are we going to do, Sonny? There is too much money at stake to shut down the operation. I don't think the suppliers will be that accommodating," said the third man.

"Well, we wouldn't have to if Sergei here wasn't so... how shall we say? Conscientious," replied Sonny's Liverpool-accented voice.

"I was doing my job. The girl, she had to die. She was talking to the police," said Sergei.

Chirpie was trying to hold his breath.

"But all it's done is bring attention to the business," said Sonny. "Police are crawling all over my clubs and now they have found Jonno."

"They should not have found him. We made very sure," said Sergei.

"Not sure enough," replied Sonny. "I told you to be more careful after that business with the Rastas. Outside my club for fuck's sake, what were you thinking about, eh?"

"But you said we had to, how you say? Deal with them. They were trying to take over, you said," said Sergei.

"Yes, but you should have been more discreet, Sergei, more discreet. Do you know what that means, eh?" replied Sonny.

Chirpie could hear everything but couldn't see Sergei's scowl. He was about to reply to Sonny, when the third man interrupted. "Come on Sonny, I need a drink, then we need to work out how we are going to take care of the loose ends."

Sonny picked up the table cover from the back of one of the chairs where Chirpie had left it and gave an end to Sergei.

Under the table Chirpie was trying not to breathe.

"Come on, Sergei, erm, make yourself useful. Give us a hand here," said Sonny.

The cover unfolded and between them they neatly placed it over the table and left the room, Sonny turned out the lights and shut the door.

Chirpie lay there in total darkness under the table almost frozen with fear. He wondered what to do. If Roland was to say anything about his presence in the snooker room, he could be next in line. He started to ease his way out from under the table when the door opened again and a shaft of light from the corridor illuminated the room for a moment. Loud disco music blasted from the passageway, then it went quiet again. Chirpie quickly went back under the table. He could hear whispering.

"Quick, here will do," a man's voice.

"What on the table?" replied a woman's voice.

"A good a place as any," replied the man and she giggled.

For the next couple of minutes, Chirpie lay under the snooker table listening to the grunts and groans of the couple copulating vigorously above him. There was a stifled scream and then quiet. Chirpie in his anxiety felt the need to visit the gents; the bottle of broon and the champagne were making their presence felt. He could hear sounds of zips, clothing fasteners and giggling. "Here, help me with this," whispered a woman's voice. Moments later the couple got off the table and made their way out of the room; more light and loud music, then silence as the door closed behind them.

Quickly, Chirpie got up and moved anxiously to the wall next to the entrance. He stood for a moment, trying to calm himself; he was visibly shaking. He cautiously reached for the handle and slowly pulled the door towards him, hoping no-one on the other side would notice. He had no idea who, or what was beyond the door. If it was Sergei or Sonny, he was dead.

A shaft of light illuminated the snooker room. A little further, then he leaned around and took a peek. His senses were on high alert, the need for the gents entering the desperation stage.

Coast clear.

As quickly as he could, he opened the door wide enough to pass through. He left the snooker room and pushed the door closed behind him. He blinked as his eyes for a moment as became accustomed to the light. He could hear the rhythmic bass lines of music coming from the disco to his right.

He could see people still milling about in the lobby at the far end.

Chirpie breathed a huge sigh of relief and hastily opened the door to the disco. He needed to be around people to cover his tracks. The dancing was just as raucous as before. Suddenly a hand grabbed his arm which made him jump.

"You're not getting away that easily again."

It was the girl from the swimming pool now dressed in a black low-cut top, bare midriff, and black mini skirt.

"Come on, I want to dance or are you queer?" said the girl.

"No, pet, nottin' like that," said Chirpie. "I've been talking to a few folks and having a bevvie or two."

She grabbed his hand and led him to the dance floor. His need for the toilet had disappeared.

Chirpie couldn't believe what was happening. Dancing, however, was something totally removed from his life's experience. Discos did not have any appeal. Part of the problem was his ungainly appearance which made him self-conscious, but here any inhibitions had been lost in a heady concoction of alcohol and adrenaline.

As he was dancing with the girl, he was trying to put what he had heard to the back of his mind. He needed to speak to Bigsy urgently, but knew there was no chance of leaving yet; it would arouse suspicions, and he was still unsure whether Roland had believed his story about the snooker room.

The girl was smiling at Chirpie; somehow he felt empowered. Chirpie smiled back, not knowing what to say.

"You're a shy one, aren't you?" said the girl. "What's your name?"

"Colin," he said, without a moment's hesitation.

"I'm Vanessa."

"How d'you do, Vanessa," said Chirpie.

"Do you like dancing, Colin?" asked the girl.

"I don't get much time for it, if I'm honest, like," said Chirpie.

"I bet you are, aren't you?" said the girl.

"Are what?" said Chirpie.

"Honest."

"Aye, most of the time," said Chirpie.

"Come on let's go somewhere else."

Vanessa grabbed Chirpie's hand and led him out of the room, along the corridor and into the entrance lobby which was almost empty now. Trays of drinks were strategically positioned on tables. Vanessa let go of Chirpie's hand and picked up two glasses of champagne.

"Here's to decadence," she said and handed Chirpie a glass.

"Aye, I'll drink to that," said Chirpie.

They both took a sip, or at least Vanessa did; Chirpie took a mouthful.

Vanessa laughed. "Come on," she said, and led Chirpie by the hand again, up the winding staircase to the gallery. They turned right along an oak-veneered corridor. There were several doors which Vanessa bypassed, and then they reached the end of the passageway.

"This one I think," she said, opening the final door.

Chirpie followed her inside and Vanessa closed the door and turned a key. "There… We won't be disturbed."

Chirpie looked around at the stunning room. High ceiling, chandeliers, tapestries and erotic paintings on the wall, and at one side, a huge four-poster bed. The curtains were heavy, ornately decorated, and drawn. There was an en-suite bathroom. Chirpie had worked out they were above the snooker room and, despite their relative proximity, the sound of the disco was barely audible, such was the quality of the building.

Vanessa looked up at Chirpie, draped her arms around his neck, and kissed him passionately. Chirpie couldn't remember the last time he'd been kissed, never mind with any passion. Chirpie responded and then watched as Vanessa took off his tie and unbuttoned his shirt. She started kissing his chest. Chirpie was beginning to think he might be dreaming. She unzipped his trousers, and he felt her hand exploring beneath, he gasped as her fingers curled around his manhood and start rub up and down.

"Wow you *are* a big boy," she whispered.

She stopped momentarily to remove her top, as Chirpie rather clumsily extricated himself from his trousers, leaving them in a pile on the floor. He stood there self-consciously as Vanessa removed her skirt and panties before resuming her work on Chirpie's penis. He moved his hands, gently fondling her breasts.

Chirpie was in uncharted waters, but let nature, and Vanessa, take him to places he had never been before. Whether she sensed his unease or not, he wouldn't know but she took control.

"Lay down," she whispered. Chirpie complied.

Then she lay on top of him rubbing her body against his in the tradition of a Thai masseuse. When he tried to touch her, she pushed his hands away and folded them above his head.

"Lay back and enjoy."

Chirpie did as he was told. When she sensed the time was right she sat astride him and gently eased him inside. She groaned as he filled her, and then she started a rhythmic movement that built into a crescendo. Chirpie followed his instincts and reached up and caressed her breasts. She moaned in pleasure. He couldn't hold back any longer and exploded inside her. She collapsed forward on to Chirpie's chest and kissed him again, panting from the exertions.

Chirpie lay there, his big arms almost engulfing the diminutive Vanessa, contemplating the situation. He had no feelings of guilt, certainly not about Joy. They hadn't had any sort of relationship for years; she was more like his mother. Here, things were different; he was somebody. He counted for something.

Vanessa leaned over and kissed him again and passed him a glass of champagne.

"Where did you learn to do that?" she said, and Chirpie just gazed at her, taking in her beauty.

"Just a gift," he replied and smiled.

"Well, I hope you aren't in any hurry, because I will need a re-run... soon, and she gently rubbed him."

"I've got as long as you like, pet."

It was one o'clock before Chirpie and Vanessa left the bedroom and made their way downstairs. Sonny was carrying out his host duties bidding farewell to the guests. He noticed them coming down the staircase.

"Chirpie, where have you been? I haven't seen you all evening."

He looked at Vanessa and back to Chirpie. "You naughty boy, I hope you haven't been doing anything I wouldn't do," he said and laughed.

"Would you like Roland to give you a lift home?"

"Aye, if it's no bother, like," replied Chirpie.

"I see you've met the delightful Vanessa; she's one of our most popular guests, aren't you, dear?" Sonny looked at her. "I expect you'll be staying a while-longer won't you, Vanessa?"

"Yes, Sonny." Vanessa went up to Chirpie and kissed him.

"See you Colin. It's been fun…. You were very good, you know," she whispered, before leaving in the direction of the disco.

"Don't worry about our Vanessa; she'll be well-looked after," said Sonny.

Chirpie suddenly felt empty, as he watched Vanessa disappear down the corridor.

"Thanks, Sonny for the invite, like," said Chirpie, refocussing.

"Pleased you could join us, Chirpie. You must come to the next one."

Roland was duly summoned, and he led Chirpie out of the house to the waiting Mercedes.

"The Ferrari is a little loud for this time of night," he said, as he opened the rear door.

"Can I sit in the front?" said Chirpie.

"As you wish, sir," said Roland and he opened the passenger door.

Chirpie got in and they set off. As they went down the drive, Roland spoke to Chirpie.

"If I can give you some advice, sir. Anything you may or may not have seen this evening must remain between you and Sonny. The consequences otherwise are too terrible to contemplate."

Chirpie took this as a warning.

"Aye, Roland, bonny lad, I've got that."

Chapter Seventeen

Sunday morning, the normal football match had been cancelled again; the pitches were rock hard from the frost.

"We'll be playing in August if they cancel many more games," Bigsy had commented the previous evening, when the coach had called to confirm the postponement.

Bigsy was fast asleep when his mobile rang; it was seven-thirty. His arms flailed around trying to find the source of the noise. Carole started complaining about being woken up.

"Hello," he managed to wheeze down the phone.

"Chirpie? What time d'you call this? It's Sunday morning, bonny lad."

Chirpie explained the urgency of the situation.

Bigsy was in the video shop by nine o'clock, listening to his buddy's revelation.

"He said what?!" exclaimed Bigsy.

"Aye, it's true," said Chirpie, as he recounted the dialogue in the snooker room word-for-word as he could remember it.

He'd been going over it in his head for hours; he'd had very little sleep. He was also thinking about his liaison with the beautiful Vanessa; it was the stuff of dreams. He decided not to say anything to Bigsy about it; he wouldn't have believed him anyway.

Bigsy was trying to take it all in. "So, let's get this straight, you heard Sonny say that Sergei killed, Lionel Johnson, Gemma Calder, as well as Everton and Layton."

"Aye, as sure as I'm standing here, man. I was hiding under the snooker table, and they were arguing. Said something about 'loose ends', but I've got no idea what that was all about. But Sonny definitely said Sergei had killed the lot of 'em. He was well-pissed off an' all, Sonny was, on account of all the bizzies around his clubs, ruining trade, like."

"I must speak to Denzel and let him know. Then the shite's gonna hit the fan big-time."

Bigsy made them both a coffee.

"So how was it… the place, like?" asked Bigsy as he sipped his tea.

"You have no idea, man," and Chirpie explained about the gadgets and the secret passageway. "Like something out of a film. You just don't know what's going on in other people's houses."

"When are you working for Sonny again?" asked Bigsy.

"I don't know. He said he would contact me. Guess I'll have to sit tight."

Chirpie left the video store and went back to the flat to get some more sleep while Bigsy called Denzel. He arranged to see him at the working men's club at twelve o'clock, just after it had opened.

Later, Chirpie, looking more refreshed, joined Wazza and Bigsy for the journey to the Working Men's club and the meet with Denzel. Chirpie continued to describe his experience of the previous evening, or most of it, as they walked.

They reached the club just before midday and waited a few minutes in the car park. Denzel arrived dead on twelve o'clock in yet another van.

They watched as he left the van and walked towards them, dressed in his leather overcoat, and sporting a beret to ward off the cold.

"Hiya, Denzel, bonny lad. Sorry I couldn't talk on the phone, but this was too important. You never know who could be listening. We'll go to the room again; it'll be more private," said Bigsy.

"Dat's ok, Bigsy, mon, no probalem."

The four men walked around to the front of the club and through into the office. They all sat down, and Wazza was sent to get the drinks.

"So, what's happening?" said Denzel, and listened as Chirpie apprised him of his evening and his eavesdropping under the snooker table.

"You actually heard them saying they did for Everton and Layton?" said Denzel.

"Aye, as sure as I'm sitting here. Sergei shot the three Rastas outside the club. That's what they said, and they killed the barmaid and the doorman. Sonny was going mental at Sergei. He said he should've been more discreet, kept saying it," said Chirpie.

Denzel opened the bottle of mineral water that was on the table and poured it into a glass; he pondered, taking in the information.

"Lionel as well? Dat's a shame. Everton spoke well of him; he was a good man. I was hoping he'd got away. I was sad when I heard he was dead."

"What're you going to do, bonny lad?" asked Bigsy.

"I will speak to Errol today and tell him we have de evidence. He'll be making plans to deal with de situation. We'll let you know. Errol will be very grateful I know dat."

"D'you want us to carry on with the investigation, like?" asked Bigsy, "I mean now you've got the evidence."

Chirpie heard this question with mixed emotions. What he was doing was dangerous; he knew that, but somehow, he had been invigorated by the experiences of the past week or so. He had enjoyed all the excitement and attention, and he certainly liked the money. So, before Denzel could answer, he interjected.

"Well, I think we should carry on, like; I mean now I'm on the payroll and in Sonny's good books. I could get more information, you know, where they're going to be, an' that. Maybe I can find out some more about the drop in the smoke."

Bigsy looked at him incredulously.

"Dat's very good of you, Chirpie, mon," said Denzel. "If you're sure you are not in trouble because you know what will happen if you get caught."

"Aye, I know that. I'll be careful, no bother," replied Chirpie.

"Ok den, we'll meet again on Friday as usual, and I may have more information."

After Denzel had left, Bigsy confronted Chirpie. "What did you say that for? It was your chance to get out and leave it up to the Rastas to sort out. You've done your bit."

Chirpie looked a little sheepish. "Aye, but I still think there's more I can do. Don't worry, I'll be careful."

Bigsy sipped at his broon, thinking.

Tuesday morning, at the offices of the Refugee Centre, Katya was preparing for her meeting with Sonny Daniels. She checked his file and noticed that, as well as giving at least twenty-thousand pounds to the Refugee Council in donations to support local Kosovan refugees, he had employed three of them, Hashim the security guard, and two women who worked as cleaners at the gym. She picked up the directions she had been given from Jenny and popped in quickly to see Kelly and the children to explain her absence. "I shouldn't be long."

Katya went around to the car park and put her briefcase on the back seat. It was just after ten-fifteen, the rush-hour was thankfully over, and traffic was running smoothly. She headed out on the Central Motorway and followed the signs to the airport. "It's the easiest way," Jenny had explained.

Katya took in the scenery as she left the city boundaries. Northumberland was beautiful, even on a cold January morning; at least it hadn't snowed again. She thought of the snow in Kosovo, it would be a metre deep this time of year.

She slowed as she saw a landmark that Jenny had told her to watch for and, sure enough, just around the next corner, the perimeter of Sonny's estate came into view. Then she realised it was the house she had seen on her journey from the airport with Carole. She pulled into the entrance area to the gates and, as she couldn't reach, she got out of the car and pressed the intercom button.

"Hello," came a voice.

"My name is Katya Gjikolli from the Refugee Council; I have an appointment with Mr. Daniels."

"Orange three to control, over."

"Control to orange three, come in."

"Metallic blue Ford Fiesta has just entered property, registration Sierra Five Six Three Hotel November Victor, over."

"Thank you, orange three... Will get back to you, control out."

The iron gates swung open slowly. Katya got back in the Fiesta and headed up the drive to the front of the house. She parked next to the Mercedes and noticed a Red Ferrari, the only other car on the gravel forecourt, being cleaned by a young lad. She also noticed a motorcycle parked at the front but away from the entrance, towards the side of the building.

Before she could announce her arrival, the front door opened and a man in a smart smoking-jacket appeared and shook her hand warmly as she reached him.

"You must be Miss Gjikolli," he said with perfect pronunciation, albeit with a Liverpudlian accent. "I am Sonny Daniels, very nice to meet you."

"Katya, please call me Katya. Nice to meet you, Mr. Daniels.'

"Please, please call me Sonny; everyone does... Katya, what a delightful name."

"Thank you, er, Sonny."

He led Katya into the entrance hall which had been completely transformed from Saturday night. It was restful, and Katya took in all the paintings on the wall and friezes. She looked at one with interest, a man and a woman in compromising positions.

"I see you like my Jack Vettriano."

"Yes, it is very good," said Katya.

"I have three of his, originals. He's very collectable at the moment; not everyone's taste, but I like him."

"No, it is beautiful."

"I can see you and I are going to get on very well. Would you like a coffee?" asked Sonny. "I have Columbian or Kenyan."

"Yes, please, either, I don't mind," said Katya, still engrossed in the paintings.

Sonny escorted Katya down the corridor to his lounge, where the disco had been situated on Saturday. Katya was amazed as she looked at the decor and more paintings.

"Your house is very beautiful."

Sonny started to give Katya a short history of the building, before Roland appeared with a steaming cafetière and two cups, a bowl of sugar, and a small jug of cream.

"How do you like your coffee, madam?" asked Roland.

"Just black will be fine, thank you."

Sonny continued his potted history, which Katya listened to with more than polite interest, before getting down to business.

"My visit is really for me to introduce myself so that you know who is taking over from Jenny."

"Ah yes, the lovely Miss Wheatley. How is she? I will miss her. I have invited her to my parties and use my pool, but erm, she has always been too busy, which is such a pity. You are invited too, of course, I insist. You will have a great time; I will make sure."

"Yes, I will try," said Katya politely.

Katya gave some background to her job and talked briefly about her escape from Kosovo.

"That must have been so awful, you poor thing," said Sonny.

"Yes, they were difficult times. I wanted to say, also, thank you, for all the good work you have done for the refugees."

"It's been my pleasure, my dear."

After half an hour, the formal business was done. Sonny got up from his seat.

"Would you like a little look around, Katya? I mean, what good is anything if you can't show it off?"

"Yes, thank you, yes, that would be nice."

Katya was greatly impressed with the house, the snooker room, the swimming pool, the kitchen, the paintings and furnishings.

"This is so beautiful, and you live here on your own?" said Katya, on completion of the tour.

"I do have a lot of friends. So, there are always people around," replied Sonny.

Sonny escorted Katya to the entrance lobby and was making his farewells when Sergei appeared from the swimming pool corridor. Katya recognised him.

"You were on the plane," said Katya as he approached.

"Yes, that is true," he replied.

"Katya, this is Sergei Hordiyenko, one of my associates."

She froze as she heard his name, then recovered.

"How do you do?" she said and shook hands formally.

"Such a beautiful lady. How are your children, two I think?"

Sergei's response seemed to have a certain menace about it. She tried to react normally.

"They are well, thank you."

She averted her eyes from his piercing gaze.

With promises of further visits, she returned to the car and headed back down the drive; the Ukrainian's stare was still firmly in her mind. She hadn't connected him with Sonny Daniels, and wondered about the term 'associate'. There were different interpretations in Albanian.

The exit gates opened as she approached, and she turned onto the Newcastle Road and headed back to the office.

"Orange three to control... Fiesta has now left the property, over,"

"Control to Orange three... Be advised that vehicle is registered to the Refugee Council, over."

"Roger that, out."

Later, that afternoon, Chirpie received two calls on his mobile. The first was from Rashmi with a message from Sonny. There would be no London trip this week, but there was a shift available at Mr. Gees on Friday night if he was interested. Chirpie was pleased to get the call; he was getting bored without the excitement of recent weeks, and agreed without hesitation.

"What time, pet? Seven till midnight? Aye I'll be there."

Then a few minutes later, he received another, unexpected, call.

"Is that Colin?"

"Aye,"

"It's Vanessa." Chirpie was momentarily stunned.

"Vanessa? I didn't think I'd be hearing from you again, pet. How d'you get my number?"

Chirpie's hands started to shake as he was speaking.

"Rashmi... I see. How d'you know her? Ah, right. No, there's nottin' to explain, pet. Aye, I'd like that very much. Tonight? Aye, champion; I'm not doing anything. What time? Eight o'clock, by the Monument. Aye, I know it, see you there."

Chirpie rang off and couldn't believe what was happening.

He started to feel strange, a nervousness that he'd never experienced before... and exhilaration. He felt like a kid again and wanted to jump in the air, but thought that might draw unnecessary attention to himself. He'd just bought some milk, and was stood outside Mr. Ali's. He wondered if he should call in to the video store and tell Bigsy, but then thought of the ribbing and third degree; he would keep this one to himself.

Suddenly, a thought entered his head. "Shite!" he said, louder than he intended. He looked around to ensure no-one had heard him.

He hadn't got anything to wear! He smiled at the thought; it had never remotely been an issue before. His shell-suit or tracksuit had done for almost every occasion, and he had his jeans for best. He couldn't wear his suit again and his shirt was in the wash.

He looked at his watch; it was three o'clock, and the kids would be coming out of school. The buses would be packed, but he had no choice. He went back to the flat and deposited the milk in the fridge and went into his bedroom and his jacket in the wardrobe.

He retrieved the envelope from Denzel, took out the money, and put it into the pocket of his tracksuit. With the weight of his door keys, the tracksuit bottoms started to sag, and he had to hitch them up over his waistline.

His wife was slobbed out on the sofa, eating a packet of crisps and watching a re-run of Colombo.

Chirpie called to her as he left the flat. "Just popping into town, pet. Got another job on tonight."

"Aye, ok, pet," she replied, without taking her eyes off the screen.

Chirpie waited a few minutes for the Hoppa, and, as he feared, it was full of children. Luckily, when it pulled up at the precinct stop, most of them got off, allowing Chirpie to find a seat.

He took the ride to the Interchange and wandered up the High Street looking for a suitable outfitter. Given his size, he would normally have difficulty in finding something off-the-peg, and some of the regular chain stores were not quite as stylish as his Saturday night attire. Then he spotted a man's boutique. Even better, the sales were still on. He went inside and explained to the manager what he wanted and negotiated an appropriate discount for cash. "I am sure we can come to an arrangement," said the proprietor.

He couldn't believe it had taken so long to shop for clothes; he didn't think it was possible, not for a bloke anyway. It had cost, mind. A jacket, top-coat, two shirts, a pair of smart casual trousers, and size thirteen brown loafers; over five-hundred pounds on the ticket, but three hundred for cash. He came out of the shop with two carrier bags and a suit holder, with a huge grin on his face.

By the time he'd returned to the flat, it was gone six o'clock. He went to his bedroom with his bags. Joy was in the kitchen wrestling with the packaging of a ready meal and didn't take much notice. Chirpie heard the ping of the microwave.

"Nottin' for me, pet; I'm going out. I'll get something later."

"Suit yourself," came the reply. "Where are you going?"

"Just a business meeting, pet."

There was another 'ping'.

Chirpie grabbed a shower, which again was unusual. Showers were normally reserved for Saturdays unless he was working, and that hadn't been very often until recent weeks. Chirpie took out his clothes from the carriers and laid them on the bed. The man at the outfitters had been particularly helpful in choosing the right apparel for the occasion.

It was just after seven.

"See you later, pet," said Chirpie, as he was about to leave. Joy looked up from the television.

"What are you all dolled up for, looking like the fookin' dog's dinner?" said Joy.

"Nottin' pet, just a meeting. Might be late," he replied, and left the flat before any further interrogation.

He was pleased with his purchases, although his shoes were starting to pinch. He caught the reflection of himself in Mr. Ali's window and felt an excitement in the pit of his stomach. Bigsy saw him waiting at the bus stop and went out to see his buddy. Chirpie had already phoned to tell him about the job on Friday night.

"Hiya, Chirpie, bonny lad, you got a hot date?" said Bigsy.

"Nah, just going into town, like," he said without elaborating.

Bigsy was curious, but just then the Hoppa turned up.

"You be careful, bonny lad. There's some strange people about," said Bigsy, and went back inside the video store.

Chirpie arrived at Grey's Monument, a landmark in the centre of Newcastle, at about ten-to-eight. It was another chilly night, but no threat of snow.

Chirpie's topcoat was keeping the cold at bay, but his hands were beginning to feel it. He had to blow his nose a couple of times to prevent a drop of mucus from embarrassing him. As he exhaled, his breath was visible in the night air. He shuffled from one foot to another; his shoes were still pinching his feet, but were beginning to bed in.

A distant clock chimed eight o'clock. A thought ran through his mind that he might be stood up, and the anxiety levels started to rise. He blew into his hands again.

Ten minutes went by, then he spotted her walking up from the Eldon Square direction. She looked as stunning as he remembered her, long boots just below the knee, short coat, min-skirt, and leggings.

"Hello Colin," she said as she approached, and leant up to kiss him. She was almost a foot shorter than him.

"Hiya, Vanessa, pet. I have to say I never thought I'd be seeing you again, but I'm really glad you called."

"Me too. Look, I feel conspicuous here, can we go somewhere?"

"Aye, anywhere you like, pet. What d'you have in mind?"

"Well, we could go back to mine if you like. Rashmi's out for the night with Sergei."

"Aye, if that's alright."

"Yes, of course. Do you have a car?"

"No, pet, came on the Metro."

"That's ok. I was going to suggest you follow me, but I'll drive you. I'm parked in the multi-story."

They made their way back to Vanessa's car, not saying very much. Chirpie had never been any good at small talk, and didn't know what to say.

They reached the car park and took the lift to the fourth floor. He wanted to kiss her again, but wasn't sure whether he should or not. The lift opened to an almost deserted floor, and, adjacent to the exit door, was a brand-new, orange-coloured Porsche Boxter. Chirpie's eyes lit up.

"Is this yours?" It was all he could manage to say.

"Yes, present from Daddy. He feels guilty because he doesn't visit since he divorced my mother, so he buys me things."

"Well, I admire his choice," said Chirpie.

Vanessa unlocked the door and Chirpie got in. She started up the car, and there was a throaty roar as it responded. They slowly descended the multi-story and stopped at the ticket-barrier to pay. Vanessa had change. Then they headed out towards Gosforth.

When she wasn't changing gear, her hand was resting on Chirpie's thigh. He couldn't believe it. After a couple of miles, Vanessa turned into a side road, an avenue of smart, pre-war, town houses. She pulled into a drive halfway down the road.

They both got out and Chirpie looked up at the house, a three-bedroomed detached property, very much sort after by the professional classes.

"Nice place," said Chirpie.

"Yes, Daddy bought it when I went up to Uni. I've had to let out a couple of rooms to pay the upkeep. Rashmi has been living here for about six months."

"You went to University in Newcastle?" said Chirpie, as they reached the front door. Not with any surprise, just making conversation.

"Yes, studied law. I work for Johnson and Taylors. They're one of the big solicitors in town."

The only lawyers Chirpie had met were across a court room. He was totally out of his depth; the anxiety returned.

Vanessa opened the door. "Go through into the lounge; I'll bring us some drinks," and indicated the way.

"Aye, ta," said Chirpie, and he went through into the nearest room while Vanessa went to the kitchen.

The house was tastefully decorated, yet seemed lived in,

certainly no pretensions, unlike Sonny's place. A functional, rather than ostentatious television, a sofa and two armchairs, a coffee table and a gas fire with fake coals giving a flame effect. The wall lights provided an intimate feel.

After a few minutes, Vanessa returned to the lounge with a bottle of red wine and two glasses. She had taken off her topcoat, boots and leggings and was wearing a blouse undone to her cleavage and the mini skirt. Chirpie looked at her and had trouble in making conversation. She poured out the drinks.

"I wanted to see you again for two reasons. The second one is, I wanted to explain about Saturday and some of the things Sonny said. I didn't want you to get the wrong idea."

"None of my business, pet," replied Chirpie.

"No, I know, but I thought you might be thinking I was being employed by Sonny in some sort of professional capacity, and that's definitely not the case. Rashmi is my housemate and friend, and she invites me to Sonny's parties to keep her company. Sergei is always busy."

"Aye, I bet he is," said Chirpie. He took a mouthful of red wine and looked at her. "As I said, it's none of my business."

She was sat opposite him on one of the armchairs. She took a large sip of her drink and then put her glass down.

"The other reason I wanted to see you again."

She stood up and took off her blouse and skirt then went to him on the settee in just her underwear. She took his glass from him; then they were kissing. He responded with more confidence than at the weekend.

She turned so Chirpie could undo the clip and remove her bra. He watched as her breasts bounced free and started to trace the outline of her nipples with his tongue. She tossed her head back and groaned as she took in the sensations. She beckoned him to stand up and began unbuttoning his shirt, then unzipped his trousers and slipped her hands down the front of his pants, feeling his hardness.

This time <u>he</u> groaned.

"God, I need you so bad," she said.

She bent over the sofa and removed her panties.

It was over in a couple of minutes, and they collapsed on the settee. Chirpie enveloped her in his arms. There was a silence for a moment before he needed to say something.

"You know something, I'm havin' to pinch meself here, pet; you're absolutely stunning, but, I honestly don't know what you see in me; I don't, really."

"I think that's exactly what I see in you. It's your total innocence and honesty."

She leaned towards him and kissed him again.

"Most of the men I meet are a bunch of tossers, to put it bluntly, all trying to impress. You don't. You are just... you. No airs or graces. What you see is what you get, and you're a bloody good shag," she said and kissed him again.

They lay there for several minutes, she, almost lost in his huge arms. Then she spoke.

"What do you know about Sergei?" she said, temporarily breaking the spell.

"What do you mean, pet?"

"I've heard he's a very dangerous man," said Vanessa.

"Aye, I've heard that," said Chirpie.

"No, I mean really dangerous. He kills people."

"Aye, I've heard that an' all."

"He beats her up you know, Rashmi. He gets off on it, a real sadist."

"Why does she put up with him?" asked Chirpie.

"He says he will kill her if she leaves him," replied Vanessa.

"All the more reason to get out of it," said Chirpie.

"Easier said than done. He said he would track her down, and he's certainly capable. Some of the stories she tells me are unbelievable, drugs, money laundering. You know the package you took to London?"

"How d'you know about that?" said Chirpie.

"Rashmi told me; she had to arrange all the transport. Sergei told her it was money out and diamonds back," said Vanessa.

"So that's it? I did wonder, like. But I thought she was in cahoots with 'em all."

"No way, no; if she could get away she would, but Sonny and Sergei are not people to mess with."

Chirpie thought about this revelation, another piece of the jigsaw.

"Do you think you could help her, Colin?" she said, rolling her fingers through his chest hairs.

"What can I do? As you say, they're not people to mess with," said Chirpie

He thought about saying something about the possibility of the pending action from Errol and his boys, but it was not the right time.

Vanessa pulled a pouting face. "I was hoping you might know some people, you know, someone who could help."

Chirpie was beginning to wonder if he was being set up or tested in some way, but for the time being, put that thought to the back of his mind.

"Aye, well, I do know Sonny's made some powerful enemies. My advice is, just tell Rashmi to sit tight and keep her head down. Wait and see what happens, eh."

Vanessa smiled. She reached down and started stroking Chirpie again; it had the desired effect. This time she led him to the bedroom. Afterwards, as they lay in each other's arms, Vanessa spoke first.

"Do you know something? I feel so safe with you. I want you to be here for ever, protecting me."

She looked into his eyes. "Do you want to stay?"

This gave Chirpie a real dilemma. Whatever their relationship, Joy would worry if Chirpie did not come home.

"I would love to, but better not, pet."

"I expect you have a wife or someone," said Vanessa, removing herself from Chirpie's arms and lying back on the pillow, staring at the ceiling. "I didn't like to ask."

"I'll tell you anything about me you want to know."

"I know you will, Colin. I just didn't want to hear the answers," and she moved back to his chest again. She waited before asking the question.

"So, what's she like. This wife of yours?"

"You really want to know?"

"Yes."

"She's nineteen stone, spends all day watching the tele and eating crisps. We have separate rooms, and we haven't had sex in three years, and that's the truth," blurted Chirpie.

Vanessa was shocked and raised herself on one elbow looking into his eyes.

"Why on earth don't you leave her?"

"And go where? It took us three years to get the council flat, and I don't have any money."

"But that's terrible," she said, which sounded patronising. There was a pause for several minutes as she digested this information.

"What time do you have to get back?"

"No specific time; it's just... well, she'll worry if I don't get in, that's all."

"It's ok, I can't be too late either; I'm due in court tomorrow morning at eleven. What time is it now?" Chirpie looked at his watch. "Ten-thirty."

"Oh, good that gives us plenty of time," and she started to work on him again.

"You're insatiable, pet."

"Are you complaining?" said Vanessa.

"God no," said Chirpie.

At just before midnight Vanessa made them both a coffee and

offered to drive him home.

"Ta very much, but I'll get a taxi. You don't want to go losing your licence."

"If you're sure," said Vanessa.

"Aye, it's fine." Chirpie made the call to the taxi office, but not one of Sonny's.

While they were waiting, Chirpie looked at her.

"So, what do we do now? Will I hear from you again?"

"Oh yes. I'll text you tomorrow if that's ok?" replied Vanessa.

"Aye, that'll be champion, pet."

A few minutes later his lift arrived, and they said their farewells. The taxi pulled away and made the journey back to Heathcote, the real world. Chirpie had that empty feeling again; he was desperate to escape.

His stomach growled, and then he remembered; he hadn't had any dinner.

The following day, around lunch time, Chirpie felt a vibration in his pocket. He extracted his phone from his tracksuit bottoms. It was his text from Vanessa. "*Hi big boy, miss you V xx*"

Chirpie nearly choked when he read it. He was not adept at texting, his thumbs were too big, but he managed to return the message. '*Same here*'.

That evening, he was in the precinct on the way to see Bigsy when his mobile ringtone sounded. He took out the phone from his pocket, and recognised the number straightaway.

"Colin, it's Vanessa. Are you ok to speak?" She sounded very worried.

"Aye," said Chirpie, trying to hear her against the noise of the wind echoing around the buildings.

"I'm really worried about Rashmi. When I got back from work, she was sat on the settee in a bad way. She's got a black eye and bruises on her face. When I asked her what had happened, she wouldn't tell me anything, but it has to be that animal, Sergei. There must be something we can do. He's going to kill her if we don't stop him."

Chirpie thought for a moment.

"Look, I know it's hard, pet, but tell her to get to her Ma's or somewhere, anything to get her out of the way. Things could change very soon."

"What do you mean?" asked Vanessa.

"I can't say; nottin' definite, like, just something I've heard. Look, just try to get her away, just for a few days."

"Yes, ok, I'll try."

Vanessa didn't press further and changed the subject.

"When can I see you again?"

"I don't know, pet, it's up to you. I'm working back at the club tomorrow night, but I don't finish till midnight."

"Mr Gees??"

"Aye," replied Chirpie.

"That's ok. I could pick you up. You could come back for a nightcap."

"Aye, that'll be champion. If that's ok, like."

"Yes, of course. See you tomorrow night. Can't wait."

"Aye me an'all," said Chirpie

The excitement of that conversation meant another sleepless night for Chirpie.

Chapter Eighteen

Friday 28th January would be another defining day in the chapter of unfolding events.

In Police H.Q., the mood was more upbeat. Detective Constable Harris had managed to get a barmaid job at Mr. Gees on a two weeks trial. Although early days, she had provided the team with some useful information about the nightclub's operation and its layout.

Nine o'clock, Detective Superintendent Adams was giving an update. There was the usual hubbub in the room. Adams lit up a cigarette and took a long drag.

"Right, everyone, settle down." He proceeded to give the team the latest news.

"As most of you know, D.C. Harris has been working at Mr. Gees for a couple of days. She's still finding her feet, but we now know more about the workings down there. She's discovered that there's a back room where no-one's allowed to go apart from certain people. I've asked her to find out what she can about what's going on there, but it's not easy and potentially dangerous. The internal security is very tight, and they are under constant supervision from CCTV. She says there's a lot of nervousness among the bar staff after what happened to Gemma Calder."

He continued from his notes. "The static obs are continuing on Sonny Daniel's house, and we think we've identified the man known as Sergei Hordiyenko." His name was now on the incident board. "He's riding around on a Honda 500 and spends a lot of time at Daniel's house. We're trying to keep tabs on his movements, but that has proved more problematical due to his mode of transport. We've not been able to identify an address for him as yet. Needless to say, he doesn't appear on the electoral role."

There were chuckles from the team.

"We do have people on that one," said Adams.

"Why can't we just hit Mr. Gees? We would seem to have a good case," asked Tunney.

"There's not enough yet. I want to make sure we get Daniels and his whole operation. Everything we have is circumstantial. No-one's talking and there's no concrete evidence that drugs are being traded there, or to connect any of them directly to the murders, but I think we are close. I've asked Harris to see if she can get more information so we can take them all down; otherwise, it will all resurface somewhere else."

Adams spent a few more minutes on procedural matters and then dismissed the team.

At two o'clock, Chirpie called at the video shop to see Bigsy. He had a sensitive subject to raise which he had been wrestling with during his waking moments the previous night. Bigsy and Wazza had already said they would go with him to the club that evening in case he got into trouble, but in the light of Chirpie's new arrangements, he needed to alter things. He hadn't really come up with any solution, but there was no way he was going to confess that he was meeting a woman; there would be too many questions. He decided he would confront Bigsy and take it from there.

The shop was empty, and Bigsy was fiddling with a cardboard advertising display for one of the new releases when Chirpie walked in. Rikki was behind the counter checking in some returns.

"Chirpie, bonny lad, how's it going? Still on for tonight?"

It was not what Chirpie wanted to hear. He was hoping to raise the subject gradually.

"Aye," said Chirpie. "I wanted a word with you about that if that's ok. I've been thinking, like."

"Come on through to the back. Nottin' wrong is there?"

Chirpie followed Bigsy into the kitchen.

"Nah, but as I said, I was thinking, there's no need for you and Wazza to hang about. It can't be much fun just waiting around. I mean, now I'm in Sonny's good books, like, I reckon I can handle things, and it'll save you a late night."

Chirpie was far from convincing, and Bigsy thought it strange but went along with his buddy's request.

"Aye, if you're sure, but we don't want to see yas in any trouble."

"Nah, I'll be fine, Bigsy, honest."

"Well, we've got another meet with Denzel tonight to pick up the readies, so, in that case, I'll go with Wazza, and we'll catch up tomorrow, as long as you're sure you're ok with that. I can let you have your cut when I see you." There was a pause. Bigsy looked at Chirpie. He seemed anxious. "We can come down to the club after, later on, like. It'll be no bother."

"Nah, I'll be fine, don't you worry. I'll catch up with yas in the morning."

"Only if you're sure, mind."

"Aye, you're alright, ta, Bigsy, lad, I'll see you tomorrow."

Chirpie left the shop with Bigsy ruminating over Chirpie's new, more confident demeanour. There had been a definite change in his buddy since he took on his new role.

Bigsy and Wazza were at the club at seven-thirty for the latest meeting with Denzel and, again, had the office to themselves to conduct their business.

Denzel opened the proceedings. "Errol is very pleased with de information you have given us, and he is planning to visit with some friends Monday or Tuesday next week. He will ring you and let you know. He is very keen to find out where dis Sergei mon lives or hangs out, if you can help, Bigsy."

"Aye, bonny lad, Chirpie's working on it. He's at the club tonight, which is why he's not here. He's trying to get more info, like."

"I hope he'll be ok. It is a brave ting what he is doing."

"Aye, that's for sure." Bigsy looked at Wazza with a concerned expression.

"Errol has sent this for you," and Denzel produced an envelope from inside his jacket and handed it to Bigsy. "Dere will be some more when we take dat bastard Sergei down."

"Ta Denzel, and thank Errol for us. It'll be good to see him again," said Bigsy. This time he meant it.

Denzel got up and said his goodbyes.

"I'll just see him off," said Bigsy. Wazza nodded, and took a slug of his broon.

"Where's Errol staying when he gets up here, like?" asked Bigsy, as they walked towards the car park.

"Not sure, in one of de hotels I expect. Errol will give you a ring when he gets here. You can ask him," replied Denzel.

Denzel left in yet another van. This time a rental.

Bigsy got back to the office and opened the envelope which seemed bigger than usual.

He looked inside. Instead of the usual twenty-pound notes, it was full of fifty's. Wazza's eyes nearly popped out of his head.

"Fookin' hell," said Wazza.

"You're not wrong there," said Bigsy, and began counting it.

"Fookin' hell, there's five grand here!" He looked at Wazza in amazement.

"What're you going to do with all that?" asked Wazza.

"We'll split it three ways," said Bigsy

"Aye, but Chirpie should get more than me. I've not done anything apart from driving about and there's not been much of that recently," said Wazza.

"That's a generous gesture, Wazza, lad. Look, you take a grand and I'll split the rest with Chirpie. How's that sound?"

"Aye, that's fair," said Wazza, who put his cut in the pockets of his jeans.

"Mind you don't get mugged," said Bigsy.

Half an hour later, Chirpie was at Mr. Gees in his SD Security jacket waiting to start the shift. An air of expectation hung around him. He couldn't wait for the midnight liaison with Vanessa and was finding it difficult to concentrate.

About ten minutes before the club was due to open, the security and bar staff, about twenty-five, Chirpie reckoned, were called to a meeting at the far end of the club to be addressed by the new manager. Chirpie recognised him straightaway; the same man they had seen in Scalley's, the night of their recce.

He spoke with a strong Middle eastern accent introducing himself as Asif. He mentioned that Rashmi would not be coming in as she was feeling unwell, which confirmed Chirpie's information. Asif continued and introduced some new staff including Marvin, who had also moved up from Scalley's to help on the security side. Chirpie looked at the shaved head and crooked features and certainly remembered him. It was the 'Monster', the guy who had caught Gemma and Bigsy together; he made a note to tell Bigsy.

"You," Asif said and looked at Chirpie. "What's your name?"

Chirpie jumped not expecting to be singled out.

"Colin," replied Chirpie.

"Yes, Colin, you will stay on floor duty in the club tonight, and Marvin will join Sol on the door," said Asif.

Chirpie was pleased with that arrangement, far better than taking grief from disgruntled punters, and it was warmer.

Asif then introduced a new barmaid. "Welcome to Diana, Diana Baines."

Chirpie didn't take much noticed; he was still thinking about the 'Monster'. He would need to steer well clear of him.

Asif continued with the barmaid's introduction. "Diana used to work at the Pig and Whistle on the Waterfront. She joined us earlier this week, but this will be her first Friday night."

"Best of luck, pet, you'll need it," said one of the lads.

Diana nodded her head in acknowledgement.

As they broke up, Chirpie noticed Hashim, the Kosovan, and

approached him.

"Hiya, bonny lad, how're you doing?" said Chirpie.

Hashim looked at Chirpie with some suspicion, but acknowledged his greeting. Chirpie wondered what that was all about.

As usual there was an immediate rush as the doors opened at seven-thirty, and within no time the bar was surrounded by thirsty drinkers. Chirpie stationed himself close to the bar in case of any abuse. There were ten bar-staff on duty including the latest arrival Diana, a.k.a. D.C. Wendy Harris, who looked very different in her off-duty clothing.

The early evening was uneventful, the usual drunken behaviour, girls trying to out-dare each other; lads engaging in mock courting rituals trying to impress the girls and so on.

At about ten o'clock, Chirpie noticed two men talking to Hashim. He seemed to be getting a little animated. Chirpie made his way to the group.

"Everything alright, lads?" said Chirpie. The two men looked at him and skulked back to their alcove.

"What was that all about?" said Chirpie, turning to the Kosovan.

"They want to buy drugs. I tell them we don't do drugs, and they didn't believe me. I tell them to go. I do not understand some things they said," replied Hashim.

Just then Chirpie spotted Sergei approaching them.

"Shite," said Chirpie

"What is going on?" said Sergei, as he reached the pair.

"You what?" said Chirpie, his hand cupped to his ear as if unable to hear over the sound of the blaring music.

"You two come with me," he shouted, and they followed Sergei to the other side of the club and through the security door. They went down the corridor, past the office and into the manager's room.

They stood in front of the desk like naughty schoolboys. Sergei went behind it, looking menacing

"What was going on back there? What were you doing talking

to those men?" Sergei asked again but before the Kosovan could speak, Chirpie interrupted.

"It was nothing Sergei, bonny lad. Just some punters getting ahead of themselves."

"What do you mean 'getting ahead of themselves'? What does that mean? You...you, Kosovan, what did they want?"

"They want to buy drugs," said Hashim nervously.

"And what did you tell them? Come on, I'm waiting. What did you tell them?"

"Nothing," replied Hashim.

"I don't believe you. They were police. Couldn't you tell, you idiot," snarled Sergei.

Chirpie tried to intervene. "Sergei, bonny lad, it was a misunderstanding. He didn't tell them anything. I was there."

"I don't believe you. You are an informer." Sergei was right in Hashim's face screaming at him.

"You, Chirpie, stupid man, get out, go back to your work. You Kosovan, stay here."

Chirpie was given little choice and, reluctantly, walked out of the room.

"Shut the door!" Sergei bellowed and Chirpie complied.

Back in the room Sergei approached Hashim again and started shouting.

"Now, one more time, what did you tell them?"

"I told you; I say nothing;" he said in his fractured English. "They want buy drugs and I told them I know nothing."

"You are a liar. You are an informer, and you know what we do with informers don't you?"

"I do not understand. I say nothing!" Hashim pleaded.

"I am going to feed you to the fishes."

Hashim was petrified and feared for his life. He bent down, almost half kneeling, his right hand lifted the leg of his trousers six inches or so and felt for the knife that was strapped around his ankle. In a single movement he pulled it from its sheath and charged at Sergei. Although taken by surprise, Sergei managed to fend off the blade, but took a glancing blow which ripped his jacket. Blood started running down his arm.

Sergei looked at the wound, then looked at the Kosovan, his eyes wild with anger.

"You are dead; you are dead," he shouted.

Hashim hadn't taken any notice of the cupboard to his right where normally the manager's coat was kept. He was just looking at Sergei, wide eyed ready to fight for his life. He had taken out a few Serbs in his time; this was no different. Hashim made another lunge, and, again, the Ukrainian deflected the blow like a toreador to a charging bull. He struck the Kosovan across the back of the neck with his fist sending him crashing to the floor on his face. Sergei, in one movement, opened the cupboard door and grabbed a full-size baseball bat. Before the Kosovan could get up Sergei had brought it crashing down on his head.

Hashim didn't move, his head had been caved in, such was the force of the blow. Blood and gore were seeping from the wound to his skull.

Sergei just stood there, arms by his side, breathing deeply, his nostrils flaring like a wild stallion, his shoulders rising and falling with every breath. It was as though he was on a high, in a totally different world. He dropped the baseball bat and stood there in his trance-like state. The door suddenly opened, and Asif walked in.

"What's all the noi...?" He couldn't finish the word and just stood there for a moment staring at the motionless Kosovan. "What have you done Sergei? What have you done?"

"He came at me with knife. I protect myself," said Sergei.

Asif kept staring at the prostate body, then at the Ukrainian, unable to take in the scene. The pool of blood from his head was extending further across the carpet.

"But you've killed him, and the place is probably swarming with police. Sonny will have to know about this; he will go mad. You're not going to be able to fight your way out of this."

Sergei gradually regained control.

"Asif, go to the store cupboard and get me, how you say...? Er, the black... er for the trash, yes... quickly, and close the door, don't let anyone in."

A couple of minutes later, Asif returned with some bin-liners. Sergei locked the door.

"Quickly, you help me," and they proceeded to open the sheets of plastic. Sergei took off the Kosovan's jacket and examined it, there didn't appear to be any blood that he could see. He put three bin liners over the top half of the body while Asif did the same with the bottom half. Then they fastened a couple more round the torso until there was nothing showing.

"Now, carpet, help me," said Sergei.

The place where Hashim had landed was in the middle of a rather old and drab ten feet by eight feet carpet which lay in front of the manager's desk. It was soaked with the blood from the Kosovan's head. They quickly wrapped the mat around the plastic-covered body of Hashim.

"Quick have you something to tie, er... something?" said Sergei, using hand gestures.

"Only Sellotape," replied Asif.

"OK, that will be fine, anything." Asif opened the desk drawer and pulled out a large roll of tape. Between them they managed to secure the carpet so it wouldn't open. They had used up the roll in the process.

"You won't get away with it. They'll be watching the club. They'll be everywhere. You know what Sonny said. 'Lie low for a while'. That's what he said," exclaimed Asif, who was starting to panic, big time, and irritate Sergei in the process. He continued to fire off invective in Arabic, which Sergei didn't understand.

"Shut up, you silly man. It is done now; we will see to it."

"How are you going to get it out of the club?" asked Asif, appearing to sneer at the Ukrainian.

"No problem, we buy new carpet. Get, er, boxes from storeroom, and close door," said Sergei.

Asif unlocked the door and left. After a few minutes he returned with some cardboard boxes. Sergei dragged the carpet containing Hashim's body to the space behind the manager's chair and arranged the boxes so no trace of the carpet could be seen from the doorway. There was a large damp stain of blood on the floor which they could do nothing about.

"Tonight, we keep door closed; tomorrow we buy new carpet, yes? I will deliver it and we will take the old one out and put it in the van. We will do it tomorrow, lunchtime; there will be lots of people around. No-one will notice anything."

"You are mad? You won't get away with it, you fool. Sonny will go crazy," cried Asif.

Sergei went up to Asif and put his right hand to his face and squeezed his cheeks together. He had picked up the baseball bat which was on the floor with his left hand. Sergei's eyes were starting to get wild again.

"Now listen, little man, if you don't want to end up the same way, you shut up your mouth and be quiet. We will see to this, we will. It will not be a problem. Do you hear?"

Asif was starting to go red and gradually Sergei loosened his grip. The manager nodded. His eyes were filled with terror.

Back in the club, Chirpie was getting concerned; he hadn't seen the Kosovan for at least an hour. He went to look for him. He went through the security door to the corridor which led to the manager's room, when Sergei appeared from the opposite direction, nearly knocking him over.

"What do you want?" asked the Ukrainian.

"Just wanted to see if Hashim was ok, like. Haven't seen him for a while," replied Chirpie.

"I have sent him home. He was not feeling well. Go back to your work."

Chirpie turned around and went to head back to the dance floor. He took this to mean he had probably taken a beating but would be ok. The thought of what really had happened hadn't entered his head.

"Aye, no problem, just concerned that's all," replied Chirpie.

"Get on with your job," repeated Sergei, and Chirpie headed back into the club.

The rest of the evening dragged. Chirpie had only one thing on his mind. He couldn't ever remember feeling this way before; the truth was, he hadn't.

At twelve o'clock, he went to the office and signed for his hours. A rather stout woman in her forties was doing the duties in Rashmi's absence.

"Name?" she said sternly.

"Colin... Longton."

She found it on the sheet and counted out fifty pounds from the cash box, then got him to sign the chit.

Chirpie went to the staff cloak room to collect his topcoat. It had started snowing again according to one of the bar staff returning from a cigarette break. As he removed his coat from its hanger, he noticed a security guard jacket hanging at the end of the rail on its own. He thought this unusual; Sonny liked to have his staff dressed in their jackets at all times while on duty. He parked the thought. He had other things on his mind, and it wasn't stray 'SD' jackets.

Chirpie left the club and took a huge deep breath as he walked down the steps. He passed Sol and said goodnight; there was no sign of Marvin, 'The Monster'.

He turned around the corner and could see the orange Porsche parked on the opposite side of the road, engine running. The headlights flashed twice. He walked over to the passenger door and got in.

"Hiya Vanessa, pet," he said and leaned over and kissed her. Vanessa responded immediately.

"Oh, am I glad to see you," she said, and she put the car into first gear and pulled away. The snow was still falling but the gritting trucks had been out early. The road surface was clear but wet.

They caught up on the news, as they drove, Vanessa's hand again resting on Chirpie's thigh.

"Rashmi is at home, she is feeling better, and her eye is not so swollen," said Vanessa.

Chirpie was trying to hide his disappointment, but it hadn't gone unnoticed.

"Don't worry, she'll be in her room by now," Vanessa said and smiled.

When they got to the house, Rashmi was sat on the sofa in the lounge with a glass of wine. Vanessa went into the room, followed by Chirpie.

"Hi," said Rashmi.

"Hi," said Vanessa. "You remember Colin, don't you?"

"Of course," said Rashmi and got up.

Chirpie went over and shook hands, rather formally.

"Hello Rashmi, nice to see you again."

Rashmi was wearing a dressing gown. Chirpie noticed she was wearing makeup, an obvious attempt to hide the bruising, but there was still some swelling. Chirpie tried not to stare.

They sat in silence while Vanessa went to the kitchen and opened another bottle of red wine before heading back with two glasses. Chirpie looked at Vanessa as she walked into the room. She had taken her coat off and was wearing a camisole top, matching mini-skirt and black fishnets. Chirpie caught his breath.

Rashmi smiled, looked at Vanessa then back at Chirpie. "How are things at the club?"

Chirpie told them about the incident with the Kosovan.

"Sergei, he is an animal, he really is," said Rashmi, and gazed into her empty glass. Vanessa poured her another.

Chirpie broke the silence. "Listen, if you want my advice, I would get yourself out of here pronto. He's going to come looking for you again; you know that. Can't you get away somewheres, just for a few days, like? I reckon by next week you'll not be bothered by him again."

"What are you saying, Colin? Do you know something?" asked Vanessa.

"Not definite, but, like I was saying, he's made a lot of enemies and, well, word is, things are hotting up. I think it would be in both your interests to disappear for a few days, a week, maybe."

He knew he was taking a significant risk but felt now he could trust them. The girls looked at each other with concern.

"Do you know where he lives?" asked Chirpie.

"Yes, he lives in Ouseburn. Rents a flat in a student block," replied Rashmi.

"I don't suppose you know his address, by any chance?" asked Chirpie.

"Yes, it's in Jesmond Terrace; he takes me there sometimes." She thought for a moment. "Number seventy-three, I think ... yes, seventy-three... Flat 1, the basement. Why do you want to know?" said Rashmi.

"Just curious," said Chirpie. "Might come in handy."

Chirpie re-ran the information in his mind to make sure he would remember it, then looked at Vanessa.

"What about your Da? Couldn't you stay with him for a few days?"

"That's a possibility, he's got plenty of room," said Vanessa, looking at Rashmi. "He's always inviting me to stay." Vanessa was in deep thought. "Well, I'm not due in court next week and I do have some leave owing. It'll mean rearranging some appointments on Monday, but my secretary can sort that out. What do you think,

Rashmi?"

"Yes, if that's alright. Are you sure your father won't mind?"

"No, of course not, he'll be pleased to see me."

"Well, if I were you, I would leave as soon as you can, tomorrow if possible. I think Sergei may come looking for you, as you weren't at work, like."

"He's right, Rashmi. We'll leave first thing," said Vanessa.

Vanessa finished her wine and grabbed the bottle.

"Let's take this upstairs," she said to Chirpie, and Vanessa took his hand and led him out of the lounge. To his surprise Rashmi turned out the lights and followed them up the stairs, but instead of going into her own room, she followed Chirpie and Vanessa into the bedroom.

"I can't be on my own tonight. Is it all right?"

"You don't mind do you, Colin?" said Vanessa, more a statement than question.

Chirpie was speechless.

Saturday morning six-thirty, Vanessa was in the kitchen making coffee. Chirpie was dressed and sat in the lounge still unable to take in this latest experience. Rashmi came in with a hold-all, and the three drank their coffees in virtual silence, Chirpie not knowing what to say. Vanessa went upstairs and came back with a small suitcase.

"I've phoned for a taxi for us, like. It'll be here in ten minutes. You need to get going," said Chirpie, as she came into the kitchen.

Vanessa went up to him and kissed him. "I don't think we will ever be able to thank you, Colin."

Chirpie looked at her. "Don't be daft, pet, I've not done much." He looked down. "Will I see you again?"

He wasn't sure what would be the answer; there was still the thought at the back of his mind that he was being used. None of this was real.

"Of course, silly, I'll text you when we get down to Daddy's, and you can let us know what's happening. You can always ring me, anytime."

"I'm going to miss you pet, I really am," said Chirpie.

"And I'll miss you, too, Colin."

The taxi arrived. Chirpie told the driver to wait while he helped the girls load up the Porsche.

Rashmi kissed him and got into the passenger side.

"Thank you for everything."

Vanessa came up to Chirpie and gave him something. "These are a set of my house keys, just in case. You take care of yourself. I want you in one piece when I get back."

She kissed him again.

"I love you, you know," she said, and got in the car and reversed out of the drive.

Chirpie was speechless and just waved frantically like a six-year-old bidding farewell to a favourite grandmother. He saw the Porsche turn left at the end of the street and disappear. He suddenly felt an incredible emptiness. The taxi was still waiting, and he opened the passenger door and climbed in.

"Heathcote Tower, bonny lad."

It was gone seven before Chirpie arrived at his flat, and the place was in a right state. He looked at the washing piled up on the chairs and the empty crisp packets on the floor. He shrugged his shoulders. Welcome to the real world.

He went into the bathroom. Joy's bedroom door was shut, and he could hear snoring. He washed himself down and went to bed.

It was gone midday before he resurfaced. He walked groggily through the lounge to the kitchen to made himself a coffee. Joy was on the settee in front of the television, watching a black and white film with a packet of biscuits in her hand.

"Didn't hear you come in," she said, without taking her eyes off the screen.

"Aye, it was late."

While the kettle was boiling, Chirpie phoned Bigsy to bring him up-to-date and give him Sergei's address.

"How did you manage to get that, bonny lad?"

"Just a contact," said Chirpie.

"Errol will be pleased, that's for sure. Talking of which, can you pop over to the shop this afternoon, I've got something for you?"

"Aye, I'll be across about two," replied Chirpie and dropped the call.

He couldn't face Joy, and stayed in the kitchen while he drank his coffee, deep in thought. Then walked back through the lounge to the bathroom. Chirpie washed and changed into his tracksuit, before returning to the kitchen to get something to eat.

He was eating a bowl of cornflakes at the table, reading the previous evening's newspaper. Joy was still watching her film.

Suddenly, he heard the beep on his phone indicating a text. He flicked open his phone and read the message. "*Arrived safely will speak later xx.*"

His mood changed and he finished his breakfast, then grabbed his jacket.

"Just going to see Bigsy."

Joy didn't reply or take her eyes from the television screen.

"Hiya, bonny lad, how did it go?" said Bigsy, as Chirpie entered the video shop. Bigsy was behind the counter cataloguing some new stock.

Bigsy left his work and led Chirpie into the kitchen.

"Fancy a brew?" He started filling a kettle with water.

As Bigsy was making the tea, Chirpie recounted the events at the club involving the Kosovan.

"Sergei was going ballistic. I don't know what happened, mind. He said the lad had gone home."

Bigsy gave Chirpie his envelope.

"There is a couple of grand in there from Errol, a token of his appreciation. Don't you go spending it all at once."

Chirpie didn't know what to say. "That's champion, man, ta very much."

"You'll be able to thank him yourself. He's visiting next week."

"So, it's definitely kicking off, you reckon?"

"Aye, seems like it, bonny lad."

Back in town, an anonymous white Transit van reversed up the narrow alleyway at the side of Mr. Gees. Early afternoon, the street was packed with shoppers. With no football matches being played this weekend, it was busier than normal. Menfolk were being dragged into town by their long-suffering wives. Sergei was dressed in a hooded top and wearing sunglasses and from a distance was not easily recognisable. He got out from the passenger seat, unlocked the side door of the club, and went inside to turn off the security system. Another man got out from the driver's side and opened the back of the van. The two men carried a carpet, wrapped in a clear plastic covering, into the club and shut the doors.

Twenty minutes later the side door opened. The second man opened the van again and went back inside. The two men carried the much heavier old carpet and slid it into the Transit. While man number two closed the van doors, Sergei reset the alarms and locked up. He got into the passenger's side. The driver started up the engine and gently threaded the van out of the alleyway in between the massed ranks of shoppers.

"Orange 4 to control, over."

"Control to Orange 4, come in,"

"White Ford Transit, license number tango, four, five, three, Sierra, November, bravo, has made a delivery, looked like a new carpet, and left. Two unidentified males, over."

"Thank you, Orange 4, call logged fourteen twenty-two. Wait further instructions, out."

Chapter Nineteen

Monday 31st January.

Katya was at her desk, her first day on her own and she was looking forward to being in charge. She had already thought of some new ideas and was keen to put them into operation. She wanted to streamline some of the roles and give some more responsibility to one or two she thought were not as busy as they should be.

At nine-thirty, Trudy the receptionist, brought Katya a coffee. "Mrs. Mujota's outside, says she wants to see you urgently. I told her she would need to make an appointment."

"No, that's ok. Can you show her in and make her a drink if she wants one?"

A couple of minutes later, Mrs Mujota was led in with her daughter, clearly distressed. As soon as she saw Katya she started to sob bitterly.

Katya spoke in Albanian. "What is the matter?"

"It is Hashim; he is gone."

"Gone?" What do you mean?" said Katya.

"He went to work on Friday, usual time, but he didn't come home."

Mrs Mujota started sobbing again which, of course, had upset her child.

"I went to the nightclub on Saturday night to try to find him, but nobody had seen him. They said he had gone home early on Friday night because he wasn't feeling well. I've tried to call him on his mobile phone, you know, the one he had from here, but it isn't working."

She continued sobbing uncontrollably; her daughter was trying to put her arm around her to comfort her.

"He hasn't come home; something is very wrong. Please help

me."

Katya remembered Bigsy's warning and immediately was very concerned.

"Have you spoken to the police?"

"Ne polici! Ne polici!" she exclaimed.

"But we must. Do not worry, you will not be deported, I promise; we will look after you."

Katya rang through to the office. "Trudy, can you get me the local police, please."

The call came through. "Hello, this is Katya Gjikolli from the Refugee Council. I have one of the refugees with me who says her husband has gone missing. No, no I don't want to speak to missing persons. No, I think he may have come to some, er, harm. He works at one of the nightclubs in town and his wife says he was being threatened."

"Which club?" asked the collator.

"Mr… er… Gees, I think it's called," said Katya. Mrs Mujota nodded.

"Just a minute." There was a pause on the line, and then a new voice came on.

"Hello, this is Detective Sergeant Tunney. Who am I speaking to?"

"I am Katya Gjikolli from the Refugee Council, in Blenheim Terrace."

Katya explained again the situation.

"Can we come round…? Ok, we will be there in five minutes. Keep Mrs Mujota there, we will want to speak to her," said Tunney.

"Of course," said Katya and the man hung up.

"Would you like some tea, or a glass of water?" said Katya.

"Just some water please," said Mrs Mujota. Katya asked Trudy to bring some.

A few minutes later, a call came through. It was Trudy again. "Two police officers are here to speak to you, Katya."

"Send them through. Can you see if they want coffee?"

The two officers came into Katya's office. Trudy brought in two more chairs. It was quite cramped in the room now.

The two officers introduced themselves as Detective Sergeant Dave Tunney and Detective Constable Hilary James. Mrs Mujota was still crying.

"It is ok; she is so frightened of the police. In Kosovo they put people in prison and not let them out. It has happened many, many times. Mrs Mujota doesn't speak a lot of English, but I can translate for you," said Katya.

"Will you reassure her that nothing will happen to her. We just want to help her find her husband," said James in a soothing tone.

Katya translated and Mr. Mujota gradually calmed down. Just then they were interrupted as Trudy brought in the coffees.

"So, what can you tell us?" asked Tunney, and Katya told him of the couple's previous visit and how Mr. Mujota was being forced to trade drugs at the nightclub.

"This was at Mr. Gees, right?" The sergeant wrote it in his notebook.

"Yes, I told them they should contact the police, but Mr Mujota was so scared. Her husband said they had threatened to kill him and have his family deported if he refused to co-operate," replied Katya.

"When did Mrs Mujota last see her husband?" Katya translated.

Katya translated Mrs Mujota's response. "He went to work on Friday about six-thirty and she hasn't seen him since."

The officers asked for some background on the refugees, and Katya explained their escape from Kosovo and resettlement in England from the earlier conversation. She also explained that Sonny Daniels had recruited him to the club. The two officers looked at each other.

"Did Mr Mujota mention any other names?" asked Tunney.

'Yes, there is a man called Sergei who everyone fears," said Katya.

"What did he say about him?" asked Tunney.

"He was the man who asked Hashim to trade the drugs," replied Katya.

"Are you sure?" said Tunney. Katya translated again.

"Yes, she is certain. I have seen him also at Mr Daniels' house. A very creepy man," said Katya.

"When was this?" asked Tunney.

"Last week. I had a meeting with Mr. Daniels. He is an important supporter for the Refugee Council," said Katya.

"So, you have been to his house, Katya?" said Tunney.

"Yes, I said, last week, Tuesday."

"Would you be able to tell us what it's like inside?" asked Tunney.

"Yes, I think so; he showed me around."

"Excellent. Can you spare some time at headquarters, later?"

"Yes, of course, when?"

"This afternoon, if you're free, say, about two?" said Tunney.

"Yes, I can do that, where is it?"

"We will send a car for you. It's not far."

They continued their questioning.

"Have you a photograph of you husband, by any chance?" asked Tunney.

She went to her handbag and produced a rather crumpled picture which showed the family in happier times. Mrs. Mujota started to cry again.

"Don't worry we will let you have it back," said the officer. Katya translated.

After about an hour, the officers left Katya's office to report back.

"Don't worry, Mrs Mujota, we will do everything we can to find your husband." James put a comforting hand on her shoulder.

He looked at Katya. "We will call for you at two," said Tunny.

Katya arranged for a taxi to take the two Kosovans home. Mrs. Mujota gave Katya her phone number; Katya promised to call her with any news.

At two o'clock, Katya was waiting in reception talking to Trudy when one of the officers called to take her to the headquarters. The drive took only a few minutes, and Katya was taken straight to the incident room and introduced to Detective Superintendent Adams.

Katya was amazed at all the activity, and was taken into a room where two more officers were waiting to speak to her. Adams introduced her to the men from the serious crime division. One of them produced a set of drawings which she recognised were plans of Sonny Daniels' house.

"Thank you for helping us, we're very grateful. We would like you to take us through your visit. Last week, wasn't it?" said Adams.

"Yes, Tuesday," replied Katya.

The first detective opened up the plans and produced the south elevation which showed the drive.

"What did you do when you reached the gates?" asked the detective.

"Pressed the... how do you say? The, er, button and someone asked who I was."

"The intercom?"

"Yes,"

"And then?"

"The gates, they opened, and I went to the house."

The detectives quizzed her on everything she could remember, decor, curtains, furnishings and so on. Then they asked a strange question.

"What about this room, the games room, we think it is. Did you go in there?" asked Adams.

"Yes, but only short time."

"Can you remember if there were any other doors?"

Katya thought. "I don't think so, I can't remember any others."

"Are you sure, because, as far as we can see, the plans don't seem to match the actual layout?" said Adams.

"No, er, I was only there for a few moments," replied Katya.

"Well, thank you so much, you have been very helpful." The officers got up and walked out. A couple of minutes later, the Superintendent appeared again.

"I would like to go over your statement again, if I may. I'm concerned for the safety of Mr. Mujota and there might be something we have missed that might help."

"Of course," said Katya, and Adams went through the statement again slowly, clarifying certain areas with more detail. It was helping the detectives put the pieces together.

After another hour, the superintendent was satisfied, and offered Katya a lift back to the office, but she declined. "It is ok, I will walk, it is not far." She needed to clear her head.

Back in the incident room, nobody noticed an outside call by one of the officers.

The phone rang at Sonny's mansion. Roland answered and passed the phone to his boss.

"Sonny Daniels speaking. I see... When was this? And you are sure. The girl from the Refugee Council. Thank you, I am, and will be, very grateful."

Sonny turned to the chauffeur. "Roland, is Sergei about? We might have a problem."

"He was going to the basement, the last I saw," said Roland.

Sonny headed down the corridor through the snooker room, punched four numbers in the security pad and the door in the wall panel slowly opened. He walked through and it immediately closed behind him, then down the stairs and through another door into the basement. The room was furnished like a smart, carpeted office about ten feet by fifteen. It had air conditioning which meant it was a pleasant temperature, but there were no windows; illumination was by florescent strip lights. There were three computer monitors, various printers, phones, faxes, modems on a long desk which went right around three sides. Against the far wall, various filing cabinets and a substantial upright safe completed the furnishings.

In between the filing cabinets was another door, and Sonny went through. He entered a larger, longer room, probably an outhouse in a past time. It was lined with concrete, and much colder; the heating hadn't permeated this area. There were benches around the outside with D.I.Y. equipment on the top - saws, hammers, a vice, pliers, etc. Chairs were scattered about, and a roll of electrical cabling hung on the one of the walls. There was another short staircase at the far end which led to an exit at the back of the property. That, too, was well-camouflaged with trees and bushes.

Sergei was at one of the benches, pottering about.

Sonny approached the Ukrainian; he was still angry.

"Sergei, have you managed to dispose of your latest aberration?"

Sergei had no idea what Sonny was saying and shrugged his shoulders.

"I don't know why you had to add to our problems?"

"I told you; he came at me with a knife. I was protecting myself. Don't worry, I have got rid of it. It is finished."

"Not quite, I'm afraid," said Sonny. Sergei looked at him inquisitively.

"Why you say that?" said Sergei.

"Well, it seems the delightful Katya, you remember, from the Refugee Council, she's told the police that the Kosovan you murdered was being forced to sell drugs at my club. You know what that means? They have evidence now."

"No, there is no evidence, the word of a refugee, who's going to believe her?"

"I don't think we can take that chance, do you? According to my source, this has got them all buzzing, saying arrests are imminent, and everything… We've got to make sure she can't stand up in court, or, better still, can't stand up at all." Sonny laughed at his attempted humour.

"What do you want me to do?" asked Sergei.

"At the moment, nothing; but I have an idea." Sonny walked away with a wry smile.

Tuesday morning, Detective Superintendent was briefing the team.

"Good morning, everyone." There was an acknowledgement from the team. "We've made some progress in the last twenty-four hours. At last, we have a viable witness. The information that the manager from the Refugee Council provided has given us a significant lead. It confirms that Sonny Daniels is employing refugees then intimidating them into selling drugs. We do have another missing person, however, Hashim Mujota." His name was now on the incident board. Adams continued.

"He was last seen on Friday night and reported missing by his wife yesterday. Given recent course of events, we have to assume that his life expectancy is probably negligible. It is imperative we pull out all the stops here."

"Why did it take so long to report, guv?" asked D.S. Frasier.

"Well, according to the Refugee Council manager, they've been threatened with beatings, deportation, even death. They are also scared of the police. We're actually fortunate to get this one reported, and we wouldn't have, if it wasn't for Miss Gjikolli's quick thinking, and bravery."

Adams looked around at the team; there was a tense atmosphere. He took a drink from a mug of cold coffee, winced and continued.

"Now, we're pretty sure that the missing security guard is the one approached by a couple of our undercover team on Friday night trying to get a lead on the drug connection. According to their notes, they thought they were getting somewhere with him, but he didn't speak good English and didn't appear to understand. Then another bouncer intervened and that was the end of that. Unfortunately, the pair were lost in the crowd, so we didn't see what happened after that. Detective Harris heard there had been a rumpus and that the Kosovan had been sent home. The club manager told her to mind her own business when she tried to press the subject."

"I bet that went down well," said Tunney, to much mirth. Adams smiled, then tugged on a cigarette billowing smoke out into the room.

"Right, settle down and listen up. I've spoken to the Chief Constable, and I can confirm we're going to hit Daniel's empire tomorrow night."

"Why the delay, sir?" asked one of the team.

"It'll take us twenty-four hours to get the team prepared and equipped. There's a lot of planning to do. We'll have armed units and dog-teams on hand. We're going in on the two nightclubs, Sonny's house, and the gym. Our colleagues in North Shields are looking after the casinos. Sonny Daniels and this Sergei Hordiyenko are the key players here and we must get them, but we will also need to bring in the Security Staff as well, the ones with the SD Jackets. They'll have vital information. I don't have to remind you about security; not a word to anyone. If this is going to work, we must have complete surprise."

"What time do we go, sir?"

"There'll be a final briefing at fifteen-thirty tomorrow, you'll be told then. In the meantime, keep following your existing lines of enquiries, but avoid the clubs and casinos for the time being. I'm pulling in all the undercover teams as well," said Adams.

"I thought Detective Harris made a good barmaid, sir," said Frasier to the amusement of the team. Adams smiled and dismissed them.

An outside call was made from the general office. "Hello, is Sonny there? When will he be back? Oh, ok, I'll call back later. No, there's no message."

Later that afternoon, Polly was waiting by the car in the car park at the Refugee Council office after Katya had finished work, and he helped her load the car with the children. On the journey back, she told him of the events of the day and the visit to the police station.

"You be careful, pet, these are dangerous people," said Polly.

"Of course, I will be careful. I just hope Mr Mujota is safe."

Late afternoon, Bigsy received a call.

"Errol, bonny lad, good to hear from you. You're in town? Aye, that's champion. Seven-thirty, at the club. Aye, you too, see you then."

Bigsy phoned Wazza and Chirpie to let them know of the recent arrival and the arranged meet. At just after seven, they walked to the working men's club ready to see Errol and Denzel.

They arrived just as the black BMW pulled into the car park. Errol and Denzel got out with two other men and Errol greeted Bigsy like a long-lost brother, complete with the now obligatory man-hug which Bigsy still found uncomfortable.

"Bigsy, mon, what's happening." It was a greeting, not a question, speaking in his strong West Indian drawl.

"Errol, bonny lad. Good to see you. I've laid on some scran for you and the lads in case you were feeling peckish, like."

"Dat's very good of you, Bigsy, mon," not really understanding what Bigsy was saying. "I was telling de lads we are always well looked after when we come to de North. Let me introduce my associates."

Denzel stood back as the two huge West Indian gentlemen wearing long overcoats came forward and shook hands. Bigsy avoided the knuckle touch.

"Dis is Eugene. He's from Jamaica and dis is another bruddah from Brixton, called Curtis."

They acknowledged each other, and Bigsy introduced Chirpie and Wazza.

As they walked across the car park, Erroll turned to Chirpie. "Chirpie, mon, I appreciate everyting you have been doing on my behalf. We will always be in your debt. If dere is anyting I can do for you, anytime, you just have to ask."

"Ta very much, Errol, bonny lad," said Chirpie.

Errol roared with laughter at the 'bonny lad' address.

They went into the club, and Bigsy led them into the committee room that he had reserved with Stan. A selection of snacks was laid out on the table in the middle of the room. The group made themselves comfortable as Wazza pealed the Clingfilm off the plates containing the food. Everyone tucked in, except Errol who had again excused himself for dietary reasons.

"So, what's the plan?" asked Bigsy, as he tackled a sandwich.

"We need to have a look round first; we don't know de area. Denzel has de address you gave him, and he knows whereabouts de house is. So tonight, we will go dere, stake out de place, and den we will put someting together. Tomorrow night we will be waiting."

"I'll be happy to join you if you need an extra hand, like," said Bigsy.

"I know dat, but dis is family business and we have to take care of it, but tanks for de offer Bigsy."

After about half an hour, Errol stood up and said his goodbyes; the food had been eaten. There was another man-hug for Bigsy and one also for Chirpie, who was now officially an honorary 'bruddah'.

Bigsy accompanied Errol and his team back to the car park.

"I'll be in touch," said Errol, and the black BMW pulled away.

Wednesday morning, nine o'clock, and a discussion was taking place in Sonny's mansion.

"What are you going to do about Miss Gjikolli?" asked Roland.

"I've already been discussing the delightful Katya with Sergei, and we've decided to get her here."

"But that's madness, the police will trace her straightaway if you do that," argued the chauffeur.

"That's fine, we have nothing to hide. If she comes here legitimately, to, say, pick up a donation; we will just say she left again. In fact, she <u>will</u> leave again."

"I don't understand, what do you mean?" asked Roland.

"I'll explain all," replied Sonny.

At ten o'clock, Katya was back at her desk when a call came through from reception. "It's a Mr Roland Carter from High Fields," said Trudy.

Katya wracked her brain, "High Fields? I don't know any High Fields," and then she twigged. "Ah, yes, 'High Fields', of course, it's Sonny Daniels' house." The call was put through.

"Katya Gjikolli, can I help you?"

"Ah, Miss Gjikolli, Mr Daniels is away on business, but he wondered if you would like to pick up a cheque; his half-yearly donation, five thousand pounds. He apologises for the lateness, he had promised it to Miss Wheatley, but he has been so busy of late. He asked me to remind him, but you know how it is, he can be so forgetful. He wanted to give it to you in person, with some publicity, but thought you would prefer it in your bank account. He won't be back until next week." Roland paused for effect. "It can wait of course."

"No, no it will be fine," said Katya, not wishing to turn down the opportunity of much needed funds. "What time?"

"Shall we say this afternoon, about three o'clock. If that's convenient."

"Yes, I think so."

She glanced at her diary in front of her.

"Yes, I can do that. I will see you at three," replied Katya.

"Excellent, the cheque will be ready."

Katya put the phone down, walked from her office into reception, and spoke to Trudy. "That was the man from Sonny Daniels' house;

he has a cheque for us. He wants me to pick it up this afternoon."

Trudy looked surprised.

"That's funny; he usually likes to make a big fuss, get his name in the papers."

"Yes, that's what the man said, but he said Mr Daniels is away till next week," replied Katya.

Despite everything, she was not unduly alarmed at the prospect of collecting a cheque from the house, especially as Sonny would be away. She did not consider herself in any danger for one minute, and the money was very important. She had no wish to miss opportunity of such a generous donation.

Katya completed her admin work during her lunch-hour, then called into the crèche to see Melos and Arjeta before leaving around two-thirty.

Katya went to see Trudy on reception as she was leaving. "I shouldn't be long. I need to be back before five o'clock to pick up the children."

It was a pleasant afternoon for early February, but there were still patches of snow in the fields. The bright sun was low in the sky, and Katya had to make use of the visor as she made her way to High Fields. She reached the gates just before three o'clock and pressed the intercom. She had remembered to park closer to it this time, so she didn't have to get out of the car. The gates swung open and she made her way up the long drive looking at the wonderful landscape around her.

"Orange three to control, over."

"Control to orange three, come in."

"Blue Ford Fiesta has just entered property, registration Sierra Five Six Three Hotel November Victor. It's the same one that visited a few days ago from the Refugee Council... over."

"Thank you, orange three... Will get back to you, control out."

Roland answered the door, took her coat, and led her through to the entrance hall.

Katya stood for a moment admiring the décor; she didn't hear the approach behind her.

A hand round the mouth.

She would have felt the slight scratch of the hypodermic as it emptied a phial of Propofol into her neck. She slumped to the floor within five seconds. Sergei picked up Katya's comatose body and carried her over his shoulder. He left the hall and went down the corridor, through the snooker room, through the open hidden door, and down the stairs. He continued through the office area into the outer maintenance room and placed her on a chair. She would remain unconscious for some time. He tied her hands together behind the chair with plastic plant-ties and bound her securely to the seat with a piece of electrical cabling. Her head was slumped forward on her chest.

Sonny followed and looked at her.

"She will be asleep for two, three hours, maybe," said Sergei.

"I want to know as soon as she starts waking up," said Sonny. "She has some explaining to do, then she's all yours."

"Yes, she is very pretty, more so than the barmaid. We can have a good time, I think," and the Ukrainian smiled at Sonny.

"And now part two of our little deception," said Sonny, and walked back to the hall where Roland was waiting in Katya's coat, a blonde wig, and a pair of sunglasses.

"You look almost attractive from a distance," joked Sonny. "You know what to do, just drive her car into town. Park it in one of the multi stories by the shops and, erm, get a taxi back. You can lose the disguise in a rubbish bin somewhere, and make sure you're wearing gloves. We don't want loose ends."

"Orange six to control over,"

"Control, over,"

"Blue Fiesta leaving the property, blonde female driver."

"Roger, orange six; call logged fifteen twenty-two, out."

Three-thirty p.m., Police HQ, and the briefing for the raid was taking place, Detective Superintendent Adams was centre stage.

"We go in at nineteen-hundred tonight. According to Detective Harris, all the staff should be in the clubs by that time preparing. There won't be any punters around. We'll close Mr. Gees and Scalleys for the night. Notices have been prepared. Right...code words - Sonny Daniels is 'Head Boy' and priority one, the Ukrainian is the 'Knave', the security team, that's anyone in the SD jacket are 'pawns'."

Adams paused to check understanding and took a couple of questions, then continued.

"D.S. O'Connor will lead Mr. Gees' team, you are code name 'club one'; D.S. Jones will lead Scalleys, that's 'club two'. You'll oversee the tactical support and armed officers as well as the dogs; that's about twenty officers. You know what you have to do. Seal everything off, bring in as many pawns as you can and interview the bar staff. We don't think Head Boy, or the Knave will be at the clubs. We're pretty sure Daniels will be at his house. Any news on that, sergeant?" He looked at Tunney.

"All quiet at the house, guv; he's still there, as far as we know," replied Tunney. "He had one visitor this afternoon who's since left, but that's the only activity."

Adams acknowledged, then continued. "Make sure you have enough female officers on hand when you hit the clubs. We don't want any cries of intimidation, sexual or otherwise. The same procedure for the Gym and Lucifer's." Adams paused and looked around. "Where's D.C. Pearson?"

"Jason left after yesterday morning's briefing, guv," said Tunney. "Said he was meeting an informant. Didn't come back; phoned in sick this morning."

"OK, in that case Smith, you lead the team on the gym. I'll lead the team on the house with Tunney, Frasier and Harris. Tunney you'll be crime-scene officer and liaise with forensics once the house is secure. We've got specialists who'll get us through the gates; then speed will be the key. It'll take a couple of minutes to get to the house from the perimeter. That's when we'll be vulnerable. We'll have roadblocks set up round the house, but we'll need some luck and the element of surprise if we're going to get our key players. Remember 'Head Boy' and the 'Knave' are priority targets but be careful, they are likely to be armed and dangerous. Good luck everyone."

Five-fifteen, Polly had been waiting in the car park for some time and couldn't understand why Katya's car wasn't in its normal place. The weather had turned much colder; there was already a sharp frost, and he was shuffling from one foot to another to keep warm. Katya was not usually late, and he was growing concerned. He walked around to the front entrance and rang the bell.

Trudy answered. "Hello Polly, come in, Katya's not back yet." Kelly was sitting in the reception area with Melos and Arjeta who ran to him when he entered the room.

"What do you mean, she's not come back yet? Where's she been? She'd not mentioned she would be going out," said Polly, lifting up Arjeta into his arms.

"She went to pick a cheque up from Sonny Daniels' place earlier."

"When was that?" asked Polly.

"It would be just after two-thirty. She said she would be back by five," replied Trudy. "And her phone's switched off. I've been trying for the last half-hour."

Polly's face drained. He thought for a moment, then took his mobile phone from his pocket and punched in the numbers. Bigsy answered.

"Bigsy, it's Polly, I'm worried about our Katya. I'm in town at her office. They say she went up to Sonny Daniels' house this afternoon and hasn't come back yet; I'm really worried. The thing is; you know that missing refugee she spoke to you about?"

"Aye," said Bigsy.

"Well, she told the police about it yesterday… You don't think it has anything to do with that do you?" said Polly. It went quiet. "Bigsy, Bigsy are you still there?" Bigsy had been thinking.

"Aye, get yourself back here, bonny lad. I'll make some calls."

Aye, will do."

Polly dropped the call and rang for a taxi.

Bigsy was in his video shop and called Chirpie; his phone was engaged. He kept trying, but it was twenty minutes before he heard the ringing tone.

"Chirpie, bonny lad, I've been trying to get through... That's ok, listen, I think we've got a problem," and Bigsy outlined the call from Polly. "No, it doesn't sound good. Aye, see you in five minutes."

Chirpie came into the shop and went straight through to the office. Bigsy turfed out another browsing punter.

"I reckon she may have been kidnapped," said Bigsy.

"Aye, that's what I'm thinkin' an' all, and we won't have long if what happened to young Gemma is anything to go by," said Chirpie.

"Have you any ideas Chirpie, lad? I mean you know these guys."

"Aye, I'm going to pay them a visit. Can you get a taxi for us; I just need to make a call?"

For some reason Chirpie wanted to speak to Vanessa again, although he had only just finished speaking to her.

"Vanessa, pet, look, things are happening up here, and I won't be able to phone you till later. Aye, can't say much now; tell you when I can. Aye, you too. Aye, I'll be careful."

The taxi arrived. Chirpie turned down Bigsy's offer to accompany him.

"No ta, they'll be suspicious if they see someone else. I can handle it," said Chirpie, although, in truth, he had no comprehension of what 'it' was.

"Ring us as soon as you can, bonny lad, and look after yourself," said Bigsy, and the taxi pulled away from the precinct.

Chapter twenty

Being the height of the rush-hour, it was quarter-to-seven before the taxi reached the gates of 'High Fields'. The entrance was illuminated by two powerful arc lights.

"Wait here a sec," said Chirpie to the driver and he went up to the intercom and pressed the button.

Roland had completed his deception mission, and returned to the house around five. His taxi was logged by the watching police car, but no further action was taken. They had not stopped the driver, unwilling to break cover at this stage.

Roland was preparing some food when the gate intercom sounded. He pressed the kitchen control button and the grainy picture of someone at the entrance appeared on the small screen just below. He couldn't make out the figure clearly; the lights were casting strange green shadows. He answered.

"Roland, it's Chirpie, Colin, can you let us in, bonny lad, I've got some really important information for Sonny. He really needs to hear this."

Roland thought for a moment, then complied; he knew Sonny trusted and liked Chirpie.

The gates slowly opened and Chirpie breathed a sigh of relief. One hurdle crossed. He got back into the taxi, and it continued up to the house. Chirpie handed the driver a tenner. "Keep the change, bonny lad."

The taxi pulled away back down the drive.

"Orange 6 to control, another taxi has just entered the property. One male passenger got out and entered house. Taxi returning, over.

"Roger that, wait... Message... intercept taxi and detain driver for questioning.

"Understood, will do..."

"Control out."

Roland opened the door and the two men went into the hallway.

"Mr. Daniels is a little busy at the moment if you wouldn't mind wai...."

His voice was cut off in mid-flow from a hand gripping his throat and squeezing tight. Chirpie was a good foot taller than Roland and walked him forward until he was pinned against the wall on the far side of the hall.

"Now listen Roland, bonny lad, I liked you, you know. I thought you were a decent man among all this scum, but it seems you're as bent as the rest of 'em. Now, I don't want to hurt you, but I will. There's a very good friend of mine and she's here somewhere, and I want to know where. Do I make myself clear?"

Roland was starting to go red in the face as he was trying to take a breath. Chirpie squeezed harder and Roland's eyes were starting to pop.

"I said, do I make myself clear?"

Roland nodded and indicated to the right with his eyes.

"Through the snooker room?" asked Chirpie and Roland nodded.

Chirpie continued walking Roland backwards with his hand gripped around his throat, down the corridor until they reached the snooker room. Chirpie was on the lookout for any sign of movement; his whole senses were on overdrive. The house seemed deserted. He stopped and took a snooker ball in his left hand, his right still holding Roland by the throat.

He went over to the panel where he had seen the secret door.

"Down here is it?" Roland nodded; his eyes wide with fear.

"You know the numbers?" Roland nodded again.

"Then do yourself a favour and tell us."

Chirpie had him held against the wall beside the door his right hand still around his throat. Because of Chirpie's reach Roland could not use his hands to mount any sort off retaliatory attack.

Chirpie loosened his grip to allow Roland to speak.

"Five – Four – Three – Two," he rasped.

"Right," said Chirpie, and struck Roland on the side of his head with his left fist which contained the snooker ball. It was a good connection, and Roland fell to the floor unconscious.

Chirpie shook his hand from the pain of the blow and flexed his fingers.

He checked around looking for any sign of movement, nothing. He put his ear to the wood panel for any noise, but couldn't hear anything. He took a deep breath and keyed in the numbers. There was a creaking noise, and the door panel slowly opened. It seemed to be loud, but that was just Chirpie's heightened senses. He had one more look at the unconscious Roland, and slowly went through the door. There was a set of stairs in front of him.

He made his descent as quietly as he could, taking one step, stopping, listening, and then to the next, twelve times, until he reached the door at the bottom.

He turned the ball-handle and slowly pushed it open. He found himself in the office. The lights were on, but it was empty, nothing, no sign of Katya. He stopped again and looked around, getting his bearings. He saw the door on the opposite side of the room and moved cautiously towards it. He listened again, and thought he could hear the familiar Liverpudlian accent.

"Come on Katya, I just want to know what you told the police and then you can go home," said the voice.

Chirpie waited, defying his natural instincts. If Sergei was also in there, he would be in trouble. It was less than a minute but hearing Sonny raising his voice to Katya was more than he could stand. He took a chance and went for the door handle. Slowly he turned it downwards and edged the door forward until he could see. He thought about trying to bluff it out, remembering that he was in Sonny's good books, but that was naive. Luckily, Sonny was facing Katya with his back to Chirpie; there was no sign of Sergei.

Sonny may have been aware of movement behind him for a split second, but the speed of Chirpie's right hand, which now contained the snooker ball, took him by surprise and the connection was sweet. In all his fights he would never have been hit harder, and Sonny crumpled in a heap on the floor, his trademark glasses flying through the air and smashing on the concrete floor.

Chirpie rushed to Katya and lifted her head; her eyes were glazed, but came into focus as he spoke.

"Katya, pet, it's Chirpie. Come on we're getting out of here."

He went to the bench and picked up a pair of pliers; then quickly cut the plastic garden-ties that had bound Katya's wrists. He did the same with the cabling that was securing her to the chair. In seconds the restraints were cut, and Chirpie helped Katya off the seat. She was wobbly on her legs, but managed to hold her own weight. Chirpie put one of her arms around his shoulder and, stepping over Sonny's motionless form, walked towards the office door. It was spring loaded and had shut behind him, which meant he had to pull it open and hold it for Katya to get through. She let go of Chirpie and managed to walk, albeit unsteadily, on her own steam. Chirpie was almost through when a voice from the far end of the room bellowed out.

"HEY, YOU! You stupid man, where do you think you are going?"

"Run, Katya, run," said Chirpie, and he closed the door behind her and leant against it blocking the way. It was just him and Sergei.

The Ukrainian ran from the far end of the room towards Chirpie, who just stood there, leaning against the door, defiantly. Sonny was still unconscious on the floor. Chirpie cupped the snooker ball in his right hand ready to defend his ground. He didn't see the gun in Sergei's hand as the Ukrainian approached.

Katya, meanwhile, was totally disorientated, but had managed to open the inner door and was struggling up the steep stairs towards the snooker room. One at a time, staggering, twice almost falling backwards, but held onto the wooden handrail. She reached the door at the top. There was no handle. She pushed and banged, frantically trying to get it open, but it wouldn't budge. Then she spotted a bellpush on the wall and pressed it. With a groan the door slowly opened, too slowly; hurry, hurry, hurry, she pleaded. The gap was three inches, four inches, six inches, ten inches; now! She squeezed through and then heard a shot ring out. It came from somewhere behind her. Quickly, quickly, her brain was saying, but her body was having difficulty responding

She stumbled into the snooker room, ignoring the prostrate form of Roland lying on the floor. Then staggered towards the door to the corridor, holding onto the snooker table for balance. Suddenly, all hell broke loose.

"Armed police! On the floor!"

She fell to the ground and was immediately surrounded by officers in black combat gear, carrying Heckler & Koch MP5s.

D.S. Tunney recognised Katya immediately.

"It's ok, it's the Refugee Council Manager…" He turned and shouted to his colleague. "Harris, look after her; it looks like she's been drugged."

Detective Harris went to Katya and helped her into a seating position. She spoke into her walkie-talkie. "Ambulance now!"

Two officers went to Roland who was starting to come round. They turned him on his front and handcuffed him.

The door to the passage was now starting to close again. Two other officers grabbed the panel and held it open while three more raced down the stairs, their rifles at the ready. Shouts of 'Armed Police' echoed down the stairway. They were well-drilled and, as in any exercise, one stayed behind the door as another cautiously pushed it open while the third went through. Into the office slowly, rifles scanning the area. "Clear," shouted the lead officer. Then into the outer room, same procedure. The squad poured into the room. The empty chair with the broken cabling littered around was in the middle of the room. One officer spoke into his mouthpiece.

"Two males down. One with gunshot wound, alive, the other... unconscious."

Tunney went to the men on the floor in turn as other officers started searching the room.

"This one is 'Head Boy'," he said, looking at Sonny. "This one, I don't know, but he looks in a bad way... Get the medics down here quick."

A quick search of the room revealed no-one else present.

Tunney spoke into his walkie-talkie. "Guv, area secure. Head Boy unconscious and in custody, unidentified male with gunshot wound to the chest, in a bad way. No sign of the Knave. Oh, and Harris is looking after Miss Gjikolli, the woman from the Refugee Centre. Seems to have been drugged but looks ok. Medics are on their way."

Tunney went to Chirpie who was bleeding and unconscious to check for ID. He found his mobile phone and turned it on. There were three missed calls from 'Vanessa'. The officer pressed 'call' on the latest one. It rang, and a female voice answered.

"Colin is that you? I've been so worried."

"Who is this please?" asked Tunney.

"Colin...?" asked Vanessa.

"This is Detective Sergeant Tunney, North Tyneside Police. I'm afraid there's been an incident. Do you know the owner of this phone?"

"Yes, what sort of incident? What's happened? Is Colin all right?"

"I'm afraid he's been injured. I can't say any more, the medics are on their way. What's his name please?"

There was a pause. "It's Colin, Colin Longton."

"Are you his next of kin?"

"No, no, just a friend."

"Do you know where he lives?"

"He lives in one of the tower blocks somewhere; Heathcote, I think," said Vanessa. "Is he alright?"

"Thank you, Miss..." The line went dead.

D.S. Tunney called one of the junior officers over. "A provisional ID on the second male... a Colin Longton. Check the electoral roll for Heathcote Tower and get an address. Then send someone over there. Any news of the medics? This guy's going to bleed out if we can't get him away soon."

Five minutes later, the paramedics came down the stairs and into the room where Chirpie was just about holding on.

"Right, what've we got?" said the first one.

"Male, a Colin Longton, we think. Gunshot wound to the chest, unconscious when we got here," said Tunney.

The paramedics made Chirpie comfortable and dressed the wound to stem the bleeding. An oxygen mask was placed over his face and a line was put in his arm for fluids. Getting him up the steep steps proved a problem, given his size and weight and it took six of them to gently manoeuvre Chirpie to the snooker room.

D.C. Harris, who was still looking after Katya in the hall, saw the stretcher being carried from the snooker room followed by D.C. Tunney.

"Who have we got, Dave?" she asked.

"This one is a Colin Longton, we think," said Tunney.

"Colin Longton?" He was on our board. "Wonder what he was doing here."

"I hope we'll be able to ask him," said Tunney.

The paramedics walked quickly to the waiting ambulance. It sped away into the night with sirens blaring and lights flashing.

Back in the hall, Katya was beginning to revive. She was on a stretcher and had been given oxygen and made comfortable by another paramedic team.

"Would you like to call someone?" said Harris.

"Polly, I must call Polly," said Katya, and gave the officer the number. The officer dialled a mobile.

"Hello, this is Detective Constable Harris from the North Tyneside police. I have someone who would like to speak to you." She passed the phone to Katya.

"Polly, Polly, yes I am ok, sleepy, but ok. I am at Sonny's house. They drugged me and tied me up, but Chirpie saved me... I don't know, but someone has been shot. I hope it is not Chirpie... I don't know, I will ask... Where will they take me?" Katya asked the sergeant.

"North Tyneside General, in a few minutes."

"Polly, are you there? North Tyneside General... I don't know, but soon I think... Yes, I will see you later. Don't worry, I'm ok... I love you too."

Katya thanked the officer and watched as Sonny and Roland, who were now on their feet, being escorted by armed police outside.

Back at the flat, Polly was frantic with worry. He had called his mother who had agreed to come up and baby-sit. Then he called Bigsy and told him about Katya.

"Any news of Chirpie?" asked Bigsy.

"No, but Katya said someone's been shot. I hope it's not him."

"I'll give Wazza a call and get him to run us to the hospital. Meet us downstairs in five minutes," said Bigsy.

By the time Polly got to the ground floor, Bigsy and Carole were already waiting.

"I'm going with you," said Carole, and wouldn't take 'no' for an answer.

"Has anyone spoke to Joy?" asked Polly.

Just then, a police car pulled up.

"Do you know a Colin Longton?" asked the driver.

"Aye, that'll be Chirpie, flat seven-o-five, seventh floor," said Bigsy. "We're his friends, like, can you tell us what's going on,"

"Sorry, haven't any information at the moment. Does he have

any relatives?"

"Yes, his wife, Joy."

"Thank you," said the officer and they got out of their car and made their way to the lifts.

"I don't like the sound of this," said Bigsy.

Wazza came around the corner from the lockups in the Escort. The three passengers got in and they sped off to the hospital.

Elsewhere, more events were unfolding.

Following the shooting, Sergei had heard the arrival of the police and, rather than chase after Katya, had made his escape through the far exit and the outhouse. His Honda 500 was parked outside. He put the gun down the back of his trousers and donned his crash-helmet. He kick-started the bike and headed out across the top field onto a farm track before reaching a minor road which skirted the estate. He knew the area well; this was a familiar point of entry to the house and away from prying eyes. He turned right, off the road, along another track and past a farmhouse. Using the farm's long access road, he was able to avoid any possible roadblocks, and he eased his way onto the main Newcastle Road towards the City without any problem.

The rush-hour was over, and traffic was light, but Sergei avoided the temptation to race, no point in bringing unnecessary attention to himself. So, adhering to all speed limits, he made his way back to his flat. He had debated whether to return home or not, but he had no option, he needed another passport and some money. He knew he had to get out of the country as quickly as possible, but he could no longer be 'Sergei Hordiyenko'; he was a wanted man. Sergei had an escape plan in mind. He would head for one of the ferries, the Hull to Rotterdam, which left at eleven-thirty, and then to Germany where he had connections. He would, however, need a new identity. Unfortunately, his alternative passport was back at his flat, together with a substantial amount of money. He would also need to pack a few things.

He arrived at Jesmond Terrace just after eight o'clock and parked the Honda outside number seventy-three. He went down into the basement flat without taking any notice of the white van parked thirty yards down the road.

Four shadowy figures got out of the vehicle and walked towards the house, a large Victorian residence which had been converted into flats. They descended the steps to the basement and approached the entrance; the light was on. The front door was wooden with four frosted-glass windows; not particularly robust, especially when confronted with a large West Indian with a long-handled sledgehammer. With one blow, the door flew open, and the four 'brothers' charged in. Sergei was rifling through a drawer, looking for his other passport as they burst through the door; he had no chance of reaching his gun.

Errol stood there in the doorway, and looked at the man; Denzel was beside him. He turned to Errol. "Dat's de dude, dat's him."

"So, you're de scum dat's caused all de probalems?"

Sergei was looking at them wide-eyed and angry, ready to fight for his life, but, before he could move, Errol had brought the sledgehammer down on his head like a watermelon, almost splitting his skull in two.

"Right lads, our work is done. Let's get out of here," said Errol to his associates, and they casually walked back to the van, Errol still carrying the hammer.

"Denzel can you take dis and drop it in de river somewheres and den torch de van. Den we can go home."

Wazza parked the Escort in the hospital car park, and the four made their way to the Accident and Emergency Department. Police were everywhere, and Polly approached one of them.

"Katya… Gjikolli? Where is Katya Gjikolli?"

The officer went to another in plain clothes who came over to see them.

"And you are?"

"James Polglaise, Katya's partner."

"Ah, you must be Polly. I'm Detective Sergeant Frasier; Katya's fine. She's been asking for you, but she's still a little groggy. The doctors are just going to take a look at her; she should be out shortly. We'll want to speak to her, but that can wait until the morning in view of her ordeal."

Bigsy approached, "What about Chirpie, Colin… Longton?"

"He's in theatre. The surgeons are operating on him as we speak. It'll be touch and go I'm afraid," said Frasier.

Bigsy was numb, and Carole held onto him. Wazza just stared ahead not knowing what to do.

It was about half an hour before Katya walked through from one of the cubicles. D.C. Harris was with her. Polly rushed to her and the couple embraced.

"Oh Katya, I thought I'd lost you again." Katya was crying.

"I'm ok Polly. I'm ok, really, just sleepy. The doctor said I will be fine in a day or two. What about the children?"

"They're fine, me Mam's looking after them," replied Polly.

Katya introduced Polly to D.C. Harris. "This is Wendy she has been so kind."

"So, you're Polly, I've heard a lot about you. She's a special lady, this one. You need to care of her," said the officer.

"Aye, I know that alright." He hugged Katya.

They decided to wait for a while to see if there was any news of Chirpie.

A few minutes later, another WPC came into the department followed by Joy Longton. No-one had seen her since New Year's Eve, and they couldn't believe what they were seeing. She was dressed in a large black tracksuit and was so fat she had trouble walking and was shuffling along. Her hair was matted together and looked as though it hadn't been washed for weeks. Carole was first to go across.

"Have you heard anything, pet?"

"No, they don't know fookin' nottin'," said Joy, totally in a daze. "He's being operated on, that's all I fookin' know. They said I can go up when they've finished."

They all sat down, except Polly.

"I need to get our Katya back; she needs to get some rest."

"Aye, bonny lad, you get going. I'll give you a call if there's any news."

Polly took out his mobile and called a taxi.

On the way back to the flat, Katya told Polly what had happened, the phone call in the morning, and the ordeal at Sonny's house.

"They wanted me to tell them what I had said to the police. They said they would kill Melos and Arjeta. I was so frightened, but I couldn't remember anything because of the drugs they had given me. I was trying to think. Then I saw Chirpie. He hit Sonny Daniels and untied me. He saved my life, I know that."

The vigil at the hospital lasted all night, but there was no news. Chirpie was in an induced coma to give his body a chance to heal. At six-thirty a.m. the doctor told the waiting friends that there was not much point in staying any longer. Chirpie would remain unconscious for some time until his body could function on its own.

They decided to call it a day and go home. Wazza offered to take Joy back in the Escort, but it was quite apparent she would not be able to get in, so she settled for a taxi.

Later, Carole phoned in sick and, after a couple of hours sleep, got up to make a brew. She took the tea into Bigsy in the bedroom.

"Bigsy, pet, I've been thinking about what went on last night, like, and it doesn't make any sense. I mean, what was Chirpie doing over at Ponteland in the first place, and how did he know Katya was there?"

Bigsy feigned ignorance. "I guess we'll never know until he wakes up."

Carole was sure Bigsy knew more than he was letting on; she knew the signs, but let it drop.

Bigsy went to the video shop at two o'clock, to keep himself busy more than anything; he couldn't settle knowing his best buddy was literally at death's door. Rikki had opened up and was waiting for Bigsy as he walked into the shop.

"Hiya Bigsy. You ok?"

"Not 'specially, no. You heard about Chirpie?"

"Aye, it's all 'round the estate; got shot, apparently. Is he ok?"

"Aye, no, we don't know. He's in the hospital, but it didn't sound too good. I'll give 'em a call later and see how he is. We're popping over to see him tonight, try and cheer him up. You ok to cover for us?"

"Aye Bigsy, course. Oh, a couple of Rastas came in last night, looking for you. Brought in a box; they said I was to give it to you when you came in. I haven't touched it, like."

"Where is it?"

"I put it in the kitchen."

Bigsy went in the kitchen and sure enough a cardboard box, sealed with sticky tape, was on the floor by the back door. He took a knife from the kitchen drawer and opened it. Inside was an old duffle bag that he recognised immediately. It was Everton's old money bag that Bigsy had kept hidden in his central heating vent for several weeks the previous June. Bigsy looked inside there was a note.

"*Problem sorted, favour repaid in full, this is now rightfully yours. Errol.*"

Inside was the money that Bigsy had kept safe for all that time, over twenty-thousand pounds. Bigsy just sat there and stared.

Thursday 3rd February. Earlier that morning in the briefing

room at police HQ there was a buzz about the place. Detective Superintendent couldn't hide his satisfaction at last night's events.

"Thank you, thank you, settle down," he repeated it again to try to get some order, such was the excitement. He took out a pack of cigarettes and lit one.

"Firstly, I just want to say thank you for last night's work, a job really well done. I've received a message from the Chief Constable congratulating us. Splendid work, people."

He paused while the hubbub died down to a respectful silence.

"Let me bring everyone up to date. We've got Sonny Daniels and his assistant, Roland Carter, in custody, together with Asif Iqbal, the club manager at Mr. Gees, plus several security guards and assorted hangers-on from the gym and casinos. Everyone is singing like canaries, and we've enough evidence on Daniels to put him away for a long, long time. A large quantity of drugs, mostly cocaine, was found by sniffer dogs hidden in a back room at Mr. Gees. We also found heroin, ecstasy and cannabis hidden at the house, together with a substantial amount of cash and diamonds which were in the safe. Nothing's been found at Scalleys night club as yet; we're still searching. It looks like they'd cleared that one. On a more sombre note, we have found a fragment of human bone in the manager's office at Mr. Gees and there were blood stains on the floor under the carpet, which is being analysed, but it could well be from the missing security guard. There was also an unclaimed jacket in the cloakroom which was bloodstained and is being examined." The listening officers looked at each other. Adams continued.

"We also have news of Sergei Hordiyenko; he's being implicated by just about everyone. He would appear to be linked to at least four murders. Unfortunately for us, he was found at his flat last night with his head caved in. A neighbour reported hearing a commotion and called us. SOCO are still in there, but it looks like a professional hit. They've recovered a firearm at the scene which is being examined by ballistics. Can't see us making any arrests, but we're making house-to-house enquiries just in case anyone saw anything."

Adams paused again and took a drink of water; there was an unusual quiet in the room as he continued to detail the events.

"Interestingly, once word had got out that Hordiyenko was dead, everybody wanted to cooperate which gives you an idea of the hold he had on the enterprise. Forensics are continuing their investigation, and the techies are examining the computers which may give us more information."

"What about the guy in hospital?" asked an officer.

"Colin Longton? Yes, he was on our board earlier. Still unconscious I'm afraid, not looking very good. He was working as a security guard at Mr. Gees, but we have no idea what he was doing at the house. It does seem he might have saved Miss Gjikolli's life. According to her statement, Daniels was interested in what she had told us regarding the disappearance of the Kosovan security guard. She'd been drugged, and it could have ended up like Gemma Calder, but for our timely intervention."

He dismissed the team and as they were dispersing D.S. Tunney approached him. "I think you ought to see this, guv."

"What am I looking at?" said Adams.

"It's a list of phone calls made from this office to Sonny Daniels' residence from one of the extensions."

Adams looked at the list. "Who's phone?"

"D.C. Pearson's, guv. No one's seen him since Tuesday, and he's not at his flat."

"Right, we better find him," said Adams.

Two o'clock; there was a visitor at the reception desk of the North Tyneside General hospital.

"Which way is the intensive care unit?"

Directions were given. There was a policeman sat in the waiting area and a doctor and two nurses were busying themselves. There were no other visitors.

"Is it possible I can see Colin Longton, please?"

The policeman looked at the visitor.

"Who are you?"

"A very close friend, please, please. I won't be long."

"I'll need to come in with you."

"I don't mind. I just want to see him."

They went into the room where Chirpie was laid out, wires connected him to various monitors and there was a drip, feeding fluids into his arm.

The visitor held his hand.

"Colin, please be strong, I'm here for you. I really love you. Please come back to me."

For a second his eyelids flickered, and the visitor looked at the policeman. She squeezed Chirpie's hand.

"Hold on, Colin, please hold on."

The monitor beside the bed momentarily stopped beeping, then there was a long steady note.

"Oh, no," said the visitor and put her hands to her mouth.

The doctor and the two nurses ran into the room and immediately tried to revive him.

Bleeeeeeeeeep was the only sound.

A nurse was administering CPR; one, and two, and three, and four....

Bleeeeeeeeeep.

After a few minutes, the doctor stopped the nurse and, holding two defibrillator paddles, shouted to the surrounding medics. "Clear...? Shocking!"

Chirpie's motionless body bounced up and down unceremoniously on the bed.

Bleeeeeeeeeep.

The doctor checked Chirpie's heart with a stethoscope and then his pulse.

He looked at the nurses. "Everyone agreed?" They nodded.

"Time of death..." He looked at the clock. "Fourteen twenty-three."

A nurse started to remove the tubes and wires. The visitor left the room and sat on a chair in the waiting area, then cried. She composed herself and made her way back down the corridor.

At three o'clock, Bigsy was still at the video store and noticed a police car pull up at the tower block. Two officers got out and made their way into the flats. Fifteen minutes later Carole called.

"Bigsy...? Chirpie's dead."

Bigsy went to the office and sat down and buried his head in his hands and cried.

Chapter Twenty-One

The newspapers were having a field day. Headlines, not just local but many national tabloids, went into details about the arrests and course of events. Sonny Daniels had been one of the first celebrity boxers, and there was a general disbelief that someone who, on the surface, was so generous, could be embroiled in murder, drug dealing and money laundering.

Details of his infamous parties emerged with salacious stories, some wildly exaggerated for the benefit of the ever-hungry red-top readership. There were many prominent citizens who were trying to distance themselves from any association, but the press, as is their wont, managed to dig an enormous amount of dirt which led directly to a number of resignations and several more arrests.

The body of Hashim Mujota was eventually found on the riverbank in a bin bag at low tide three days after the arrests, and DNA tests confirmed that the bone fragment and bloodstains found at Mr. Gees were his, linking his murder directly to the nightclub. Asif was charged with being an accessory, together with Marvin, the bouncer who, Asif told police, had helped Sergei move the body from the club. The firearm found at Sergei's flat was confirmed as the one that fatally injured Chirpie, and also the gun that killed Everton Sheedie and Layton Gibbons.

The funeral of Colin, Chirpie, Longton took place the following Monday, 7th February. The cortege moved slowly through Heathcote estate; the coffin being drawn by two horses adorned in typical funereal tack. Inside the glass-windowed carriage containing the coffin there was a wreath that just said 'Chirpie'. A Newcastle United shirt was draped over the coffin. Bigsy and Wazza were pall bearers and, with four other members of the Seaton Working Men's Club, slowly carried the coffin into St Thomas's Methodist church.

The place was packed with well-wishers. Joy was on the front pew just staring blankly seemingly oblivious to the proceedings. She was being looked after by another large woman who looked very similar, probably a sister that Bigsy had never met. There were many members of the Working Men's Club, the whole of the football team and even Sol Miller from Mr. Gees, not wearing the 'jacket'.

Bigsy noticed two very attractive ladies sat at the back of the church; one of them seemed particularly upset and was being comforted by the other who looked Asian. Also on the back row, Bigsy was pleased to see Denzel and Errol, which was totally unexpected.

Bigsy and Carole sat in the front row but on the opposite side to Joy. Next to them were Polly and Katya, Polly's mum again having taken on babysitting duties, and then Wazza and his mum Hazel. The service was nice, everyone agreed, with the appropriate eulogies from the vicar, but Bigsy just felt empty; he just wanted to go home and mope.

The guilt weighed heavily on his shoulders. If it hadn't been for him, Chirpie would still be alive, and he knew that. Whilst he was stood in the congregation with his open hymn book mouthing tunes he didn't know, he thought how Chirpie had changed over the previous few weeks. How he had seemed somehow more content with himself, more confident, as if the job had given his life more meaning. Bigsy wished he could talk to him about it and wondered what the future might have been for his buddy had he survived.

After the service, Bigsy managed to speak to Errol

"Errol, bonny lad, it's good to see you, thanks for coming. Oh, and for the bag, like."

Errol started shaking Bigsy's hand.

"It was de least I could do. It was sad Chirpie had to die; he was a very brave mon. Bigsy, my friend, I meant what I said; if you ever get into trouble or need anyting at all, you phone me, ok? It is me who owes you de favour now."

Bigsy thanked Errol again, and the man-hug which followed this time, did not feel strange to Bigsy. It was an appropriate gesture of genuine affection. Carole looked on in curiosity.

Errol turned and walked back towards his Mercedes, while Bigsy re-joined Carole.

"Who was that Rasta you were hugging, pet?"

"Just a business acquaintance," replied Bigsy, and started mingling with other friends.

After the cremation, Stan Hardacre put on a buffet for fifty at the club and many returned to remember Chirpie in the traditional manner.

Katya returned to the Refugee Centre two days after Chirpie's funeral, preferring to bury herself in work rather than dwell on past events. One of the first things she had to do was to arrange for the repatriation of Hashim Mujota's body to Kosovo, another harrowing ordeal.

Two months later, Saturday 29th April 2000, an altogether more joyous occasion took place; the marriage of Katya Gjikolli to James Polglaise. Polly had proposed just days after Chirpie's funeral and Katya gladly accepted. On the morning of the service there was a surprise for Katya. She was in her flat with Carole getting ready; Polly was with Bigsy doing the same. Bigsy was best man. Carole, as maid of honour, was seeing to Arjeta who was bridesmaid and very excited at everything that was happening. Her English had improved considerably, and Carole had her dressed up 'looking like a princess.' Melos, who was toddling quite well, was pageboy, totally bemused by the occasion. Katya had chosen a beautiful ivory wedding dress, a present from Bigsy and Carole, who had also paid for the reception. She looked stunning.

Around eleven-thirty there was a knock on the door. Katya answered it and stood there for a few moments in a state of shock. It was Jenny Wheatley with Katya's mother and Afrim.

"How!? When!?"

It was all she could say. Then, she just hugged them both. Jenny explained that she had managed to get them visas through the Refugee Council and had arranged for them to fly to the UK. They had booked into a hotel.

Jenny, who was also a guest, had picked them up from the B & B. They would be staying for a fortnight, so they would have plenty of time to catch up. Katya and Polly had delayed their honeymoon until later in the year.

Although it was short notice, Katya asked Afrim if he would give her away. She had to explain to him in Albanian, Afrim's English was not very good. Bigsy had originally agreed to do it, but was very happy to relinquish the duties when Carole rang him to explain the circumstances.

So, at three o'clock on a warm spring afternoon, a year to the day that Katy Gjikolli had first arrived in the UK, she stood for the cameras with her mother and Afrim on one side and her new husband Polly on the other and Arjeta and Melos stealing the show in front, surrounded by her friends and a lot of love.

She had never been happier.

Epilogue

Two days after the raid on Sonny's house, reports in the London Evening Standard carried a story on page four, with the headline; *'Police search for brutal killers...'*

'The body of a forty-eight-year-old man, named locally as Abdul Aziz, was found in a house in Southwick yesterday afternoon. Emergency services were called to the house after a neighbour had notice the front door open. The body of Mr Aziz was found at the scene with what has been called significant injuries. Officers have confirmed that the victim was being linked to serious crime investigations in the Northeast. Police are seeking any witnesses to contact the incident room.'

On the same day, Detective Constable Jason Pearson was stopped at Felixstowe, trying to board a ferry to the Continent. He was later tried on several charges, including attempting to pervert the course of justice, and sent to gaol for ten years. Due to his status as a former police officer, it was likely that much of his sentence would be served in solitary confinement for his own safety.

The trial of Sonny Daniels was moved to the Old Bailey and lasted for three weeks. At the end of it, the jury found him guilty on all charges which included murder, extortion, and money laundering. He was sentenced to life imprisonment, minimum thirty years.

Katya did not have to attend the trial as a witness; there were numerous people only too willing to testify against him. There was a huge media interest, particularly in Newcastle, and Bigsy followed the trial closely. In the event, Sonny wouldn't serve his full term. Three months into his sentence, he was found in the shower room with a make-shift knife embedded in his throat. The police believed it was a contract killing, but nothing was ever proven, and no one was charged.

In the dock with Sonny was his associate, Roland Carter, who, in a plea-bargaining deal, turned Queen's evidence and pleaded guilty to the lesser charges of aiding and abetting. He served four of a nine-year sentence. He survived several attempts on his life while in gaol and was released in 2005. He has since disappeared.

February 4th, 2010 marked the tenth anniversary of Chirpie's death and Bigsy arranged a memorial service at St Thomas's to remember his friend.

Things had changed for Bigsy in the ensuing years. His video store empire has expanded, and he now owns four sites across the city. Having diversified into the computer games phenomena, business is booming.

Rikki Rankin was appointed manager of the Heathcote store, and, at twenty-five, is now a director of the company that Bigsy set up to manage the business. Rikki put a deposit on a two-bedroomed flat and moved in with his girlfriend on a new development on what used to be the old recreation ground where for years Polly used to fly his kites and Bigsy had scored many a goal. The council sold the land to developers in 2007.

Bigsy and Carole moved from Heathcote in 2001 and bought a house in Morpeth, which had once been beyond their wildest dreams. Errol's money had covered the deposit.

Bigsy has also moved up in the world, socially, having joined the local Chamber of Commerce. "You'll be playing golf, next," said Wazza when Bigsy told him.

Wazza is still living with his mother, and seems content with his lot. Bigsy had offered him the management of one of his video stores, but said he preferred to 'keep his options open'.

The highlight for Bigsy however was the delivery of a son in 2006. Bigsy wanted to call him 'Colin', but Carole wasn't keen, despite understanding the context. They compromised on 'Calum'. Polly and Katya were godparents. The joy was however balanced by the death of Mar Worrell in 2007 which left Bigsy devastated at the time. In the end, though, it had been a welcome relief, she had been ill for several years.

For Katya and Polly too, things have changed significantly. Polly, who is known by all but his closest friend as 'James', set up his own graphic design company after leaving University. The company has grown over the years and now employs ten staff. It is one of the most successful of its kind in the North.

Katya is now Doctor Katya Gjikolli. Although a British Citizen by marriage she retained her Kosovan surname which she felt was more in keeping with her work. She left the Refugee Council at the end of her contract in 2001 and went back to University in Newcastle to study for her PHD in Sociology, specialising in the treatment of Refugees.

She later took up a lecturing post at the University of North Tyneside, where she remains now, regularly giving lectures and attending conferences in the U.K. and internationally. She travels to Kosovo frequently to visit her mother and Afrim, who have also since married. Polly and the children joined her in Lapugovac for the wedding in 2004. Katya was able to give Polly a guided tour of her home country.

The children too have flourished in a stable environment. Arjeta is a typical teenager, doing well at school, and has inherited her birth-mother's skill with fabric and design. She only speaks English now. Melos, known by all his friends as 'Mel' is also doing well academically, and attends a local Grammar School. Like Bigsy and Carole, Polly and Katya also live in Morpeth and are near neighbours. Katya and Carole remain best of friends and still enjoy the occasional visit to the 'Meh'ro Cenna'.

The memorial service for Chirpie was advertised in the obituary column in the local paper, and there was a good turnout which included Bigsy and Carole of course, together with young Calum, Polly and Katya and the children, Wazza, Hazel and Alison, Davie

Slater and Danny Milburn from the football club, now disbanded, Stan Hardacre, and even Mr. Ali and Jamal from the general store.

There was someone who Bigsy didn't recognise, an attractive lady on the back pew of the church who was clearly moved by the service. She had a young boy with her about the same age as Melos, maybe a little younger, but taller with dark hair.

Unfortunately, there were some absent friends including the former Mrs Longton. Joy went into a diabetic coma in 2002 and subsequently died. The post-mortem said that she had been dead for over three days before she was found. The few friends that knew her said that she just gave up after Chirpie's death.

There would be no get-together back at the Working Men's Club. It closed in 2007. With the increase in popularity of computer games, and the state of the local economy, attendances dropped to single figures some nights and it became unviable. The site has since been cleared pending a road widening scheme. Stan Hardacre retired to a cottage in Whitley Bay.

That night in the local paper, Bigsy noticed a familiar entry in the obituary column. It just said, 'Colin Longton: *'Colin, rest in peace, my thoughts with you always. V'*. It had appeared on the anniversary of Chirpie's death every year. It was a mystery.

The End

Alan Reynolds

Following a successful career in Banking, award winning author Alan Reynolds established his own training company in 2002 and has successfully managed projects across a wide range of businesses. This experience has led to an interest in psychology and human behaviour through watching interactions, studying responses and research. Leadership has also featured strongly in his training portfolios and the knowledge gained has helped build the strong characters in his books.

Alan's interest in writing started as a hobby but after completing his first novel in just three weeks, the favourable reviews he received encouraged him to take up a new career. The inspiration for this award-winning author come from real life facts which he weaves seamlessly into fast-paced, page-turning works of fiction.